*The dark star of the North brings
retribution, silence and death*

DARK STAR

by

Nina Green

Pendragon Press Limited

Dark Star

Published in the UK by:
Pendragon Press Limited
Testa Teres House, Copse Road
Fleetwood, Lancs., FY7 7NY
Tel: (01253) 772788. Fax: (01253) 773359

ISBN 0 9530538 0 6

Printed in the UK by:
Dinefwr Press
Rawlings Road, Llandybie
Carmarthenshire, SA18 3YD

For Jim
who honours the Spirit of the Land

also for Jake, Adam and all the Alisdairs out there
who maybe one day will . . .

PRELUDE

~

England: Late Summer

One blooming desert and one parched wetland in the space of a week were too much for coincidence. Frank Kelly manoeuvred his cigar from one corner of his mouth to the other without using his hands, then leaned back in his editorial chair and shook his head. Had Darcy, goddam her, been right all along? Was it possible? It was asking a lot; stretched credibility to the limit. She may be his favourite – her column certainly was with the punters – but by Christ, was he really to believe all those crazy warnings? All that crap about the old geyser she lived with at that place – what was it called now, ah yes, Westwalls – or 'the last outpost of civilisation' as he was fond of calling it. That had got right up Darcy's nose, that one; but then it didn't take much these days, did it? Bolshy young bugger when crossed, but the most promising filly in the Manchester News stables to date, for all that.

Then the crunch: that stuff about finding a meteor from Mercury that had remarkable powers to regenerate, stunt or destroy the environment. Or people. He sighed and ran one of his large capable-looking hands through the dark mane that despite a liberal application of the latest in guaranteed-to-stick-down-gels, never managed to survive the first of the day's crises without reverting to its former unruly state. Leaning forward he picked up the fax message that had come through minutes before and skip read it through again: *rumours substantiated; site conditions confirmed.* Following this rather prosaic beginning came a gush of enthusiasm so that reading it, Frank could almost hear his star correspondent burbling: *site location – approx 1 mile Bedouin camp. Natives swear nothing but sand and flies last week. Now area of lush vegetation. Trees getting up at alarming rate. Fauna as well as flora*

1

appearing: lizards, rodents, and fantastically coloured birds (ornithology not my strong point Frank – prefer non-feathered variety) settling in shrubs and trees. But most fantastic bit – weather changes – seemingly to ensure sustained growth. Past record this area: no rain in forty years. Arrived yesterday in brief downpour. Slight rain again approx 8am. this morning. All for now – will be leaving later today after another photo/ sample session. Hit it Frank – this is the Big One! Over and out for now – Carl Bayliss.

Frank switched on the computer and once into the Press Network scanned through the columns of privileged information. A grin of excitement and triumph split his craggy good-natured face. Carl had done a good job, got there before even the top Nationals. One in the eye for the *Independent* and *Guardian!* Thank God for modems and lap-top computers, the technology that allowed Carl to fax him without even leaving the desert. Well, desert that was. Seems things had changed around the sand hills. But he had to get things moving this end. Switching off the computer he flicked a switch on the desk consul. "Jay? Get Cameron in here – like yesterday. Good girl." He grimaced as he switched off the intercom. Jay – I ask you. What the hell sort of name was that for a girl? Mind, she could chatter like one at times, but she was a damned fine secretary. Pretty too. He pictured her long legs encased in their shiny sexy stockings and smiled to himself. If thoughts were public knowledge, he would have screams of 'sexist pig' ringing in his ears by now, but this old hound was a bit too long in the tooth for the newfangled bullshit.

Moving behind the desk he scanned the world map that partly covered the rear wall. Frowning he turned and selected a pin with a green flag attached from the box of multicoloured ones on the desk and stuck it in the Arabian Desert close by the Nubian border of the Sudan. Incredible. *Bloody incredible.* But dare he trust Darcy's intuition? Could he hint at a reason behind this latest phenomenon?

What if she was wrong? Her 'mad scientist' villain of the piece was one of the country's top physicists and pride of Hilldean University. Christ, just the thought of it was making him sweat. Taking a handkerchief from his pocket he dabbed at forehead and lips. Crossing to the window he stood looking out at the sunlight dancing on city rooftops, gilding their grime with hope. Over a hundred feet below, matchbox miniatures ferried ant-sized humans to and fro in the daily rat-race. *What if she was right?* If she was, someone out there was experimenting, messing about with the natural environment. And given the first blight area was off the U.S. mainland and the latest one in the Sargasso, whilst the two areas of lush new growth were in the Middle East, there were no prizes on offer for naming the culprit as Iraq, he thought grimly. *If* she was right, how long before something a thousand times worse than Hiroshima happened on Earth?

Taking his cigar from his mouth he stubbed it viciously in the ash tray and plucked his jacket from the back of the chair. There was no question, no decision. "Come in," he barked, shrugging into the jacket as a knock sounded at the door. "Ah, Cameron. What kept you?" he demanded irritably, then went on without waiting for the younger man to speak, "This evening's edition – I want you to hold the front page. Got me?"

Cameron pushed his gold rimmed glasses further up his nose and frowned at his editor. "But the quarterly inflation figures are out today – and there's already a buzz from the City re interest rates."

"Peanuts compared with this," Frank snorted, brandishing Carl's fax message. "Demote it to page two. Hear me, Cameron," he said, leaning forward with a gleam in his eyes, "the old *Manchester News* is running the scoop of a lifetime as lead story. One to make even the Big Boys drool into their scotch with envy. Now sit down lad, and lick your pencil." And get those photos to me like yesterday baby, he silently begged the absent Carl.

But by Christ, Darcy, if you're wrong I'll have your guts for book binders, he promised himself as he sat down at his desk.

THE ARABIAN DESERT: THE SUDAN

~

Hell but it's hot. Carl Bayliss dropped another sample pot into his rucksack and taking a handkerchief from the pocket of his shorts, wiped the perspiration from his lean face. Screwing up his eyes he looked up at the white-hot sky. The web of lines around them deepened as he squinted into the sun and his eyes had the look of one used to searching far horizons. Believe it or not, those were rain clouds gathering up there. Tiny for sure; no more than oversized bathroom sponges, the natural ones with the holes, but clouds just the same. He paused to watch the flash of blue and purple plumage as a roller bird rose from the new undergrowth and flew above the squat baobab tree with a clatter of gaudy wings. Fantastic. Bloody fantastic. To think that last week there was nothing here but sand and desolation. He'd seen nothing like it in all his thirty-eight years.

Shaking his head in disbelief he stooped to push back the fleshy spikes of a giant aloe and paused to finger the exotic crimson blooms. Then his blue eyes sharpened and focused. *There you are my beauty. Come to daddy.*

Gingerly he dropped the hairy baboon spider into his specimen jar, and was unable to suppress a shudder of distaste as he clapped on the lid. *You'll owe me a drink or two for this one Frank,* he thought, passing his tongue over his lips as he pictured a frosted glass filled with amber ale and sporting a head the colour and texture of whipped cream.

As the afternoon wore on he cast frequent glances over his shoulder as he worked. A weird place this. It was nothing he could put his finger on, but there was something – the vague feeling he was being watched. Crazy of course. There was no other human being closer than the Bedouin camp, and they were superstitious about all this, wouldn't come near the place. He stopped and listened, thinking he heard a sound. Nothing. Only the raucous cries of birds and the whirring of insect wings disturbed the heat-hazed silence. He must have imagined it. A sound resembling wind chimes but even more delicate. He wiped his face again with his handkerchief and slapped at the flies that preyed on his legs and arms.

Well get that. He grinned and watched in amusement as the carmine bee-eater hitched a ride on the back of a bustard and feasted on the clouds of insects stirred up by the bigger bird's feet. Enterprising little devil – employing its own beater – and for *gratis* too! Frank would approve it; he was a great one for private enterprise. The thought of Frank made him resume work. He ought to be moving out and making his way back to civilisation – and the *Manchester News*. He pointed his camera and clicked at a monitor lizard that had obligingly paused as it climbed a kokerboom tree. They were also called quiver trees, Carl recalled, because their branches provided quivers for the bushmen's poison arrows. He moved on *click, click, clicking* his camera at the display of scarlet, orange and citrus blooms of various species of aloe, and the cactus-like giant euphorbias.

Here it comes – the first drop of rain. He lifted his face to a sky now overcast, and marvelled at it. Rain for the third day on the trot. And what a lightning transformation. It seemed the changes in plant life were echoed by the elements and the environment as a whole. Instead of a piece of arid desert, the area now resembled a steamy miniature jungle. Wraith-like vapour draped the baobab trees, making them appear more bizarre than ever. Even as he watched, steam rose from the undergrowth in lazy tendrils. He clicked off a reel of film and stuffed the camera in his backpack. Time to be getting out of here. The steam, the humidity – something – was making it difficult to breathe.

He snatched at air, gulping it greedily. What the hell was going on here? The heat was choking and the 'jungle' seemed to be crowding in on him. He staggered a few paces forward then stumbled and almost fell. A bloody tree root. It had almost seemed to reach out and trip him on purpose. And again that feeling of being watched. Not by a person, no. It was more basic than that. He shivered and looked over his shoulder. *As though Nature itself were watching.* And it wasn't a friendly sensation. Almost as though along with this unnatural spurt of lush growth, a malign power had also been liberated. Paying us back for all the crap, he thought wryly; for all the spraying, the leaking, the blasting, the dumping, the raping and the polluting.

He threw another nervous glance over his shoulder then squinted ahead. The vapour had thickened so much he could scarce see a yard in front.

His lungs were hurting. And the more he gasped, the more he needed to, like a fish beached by the ebbing tide. Something was wrong here, horribly wrong. He blanched beneath his tan. CO^2 – was that it? Was this topsy-turvy oasis with its deviant wildlife turning the very laws of nature upside down? With the advent of rain and resultant dimming of fierce sunlight, was it possible these plants had reverted to night-time activity and were no longer giving off oxygen but massive amounts of carbon dioxide? It was possible. The dramatic growth-rate could account for the phenomenal rise in levels. Whatever – no problem. Just get out of here, like yesterday. So long as he could find the way. He tried not to panic, to banish the thought that he could be staggering round in here until he dropped dead for lack of oxygen.

With an effort he pushed aside the tendrils of a strangler fig with aerial roots, a species normally found in rain forests. As he pitched forward he realised that he was not only gasping for air, but feeling suddenly ill. His vision was dimming. This swimmy green Turkish bath of a place was growing darker. It felt like he was pushing his way through a murky underwater world starved of oxygen and light. His hands went to his head. It threatened to burst with the pressure inside. Christ in heaven, it felt like his eyeballs were filling with blood. His face was wet. Wet and sticky. Clumsily, co-ordination now gone, he paused on his erratic flight to wipe it with the palms of his hands. He stared at them, faintly visible and covered with blood. He screamed and the lights went out. Must get back to Frank and warn him. Warn everyone. Because this wasn't just carbon dioxide poisoning.

It was then that he heard it again. This time there was no mistaking the strange poignant sound like unearthly music. The closest thing to it was the ethereal tinkling of wind chimes, but with a purity of pitch and tone he had never heard before. It grew then faded; rose and wrapped itself round the tropical tree-tops, now enveloped him with a haunting beauty as light and bright as star dust. The first music must have sounded like this.

He turned his blinded head first this way then that, like a wounded bull in the ring. Blood dripped from his eyes, ears and nostrils. He was going to die. He knew that now; there was to be no escape. But what had attacked him? Some unknown and deadly virus? But so fast? Impossible. He tried to scream as his body exploded in pain, but gurgled as blood bubbled in his throat. He crashed forward and sprawled full-length on the ground. The tinkling, drifting music now filled his perception, his whole existence. Its soothing notes suffused him with an unnatural calm as he faced inevitable death. A last thought struck him as his limbs crumpled and blood oozed from his pores. He was going to die, with the music of the Spheres playing a requiem for his immortal soul.

THE SARGASSO

~

Death, aching loneliness and the stench of decay. The chugging of the boat's engine died and nothing disturbed the silence but the slapping of water against its hull. Oliver Bryce felt an unexpected stirring of compassion. He didn't normally feel sentimental about fish. Despite his six-feet two and hunky shoulders, he was reckoned a sucker for puppies and kittens, but fish after all were cold-blooded creatures and a little more difficult to relate to. But this, this was something else.

Adjusting his shades which he had pushed up onto his forehead, he surveyed the scene of devastation. Poor little devils. The mass of dead eels moved as one with the floating island of seaweed that stretched for hundreds of miles. Half seaweed and half dead meat that is. Here and there a splash of brightly-coloured plumage or scales bobbed on the swell, a grisly reminder of tropical birds and fishes that had also perished and not yet fully rotted. He remembered Frank telling him that in 1492 it had taken Columbus two weeks to sail through the seaweed beds. A mine of useless information was Frank, he thought with a grin of affection.

Leaning over the side of the boat he hooked an elver clear of the water and his grin died. What in hell's name had caused this? Surprisingly the rotting flesh felt dry and shrivelled to the touch, rather than slimy as expected. With a gesture of distaste he dropped it into a specimen jar. Amazing really. If they had survived, the young eels would have made their way thousands of miles, over land if necessary, to their parents' birthplace – be it the U.S.A., Britain or even Europe. Shame, he thought replacing the lid on the jar; there would be no new generation of British eels visiting their ancestral homeland this year. He knew that the parent eels normally died after spawning, but for all the young to perish too? That was an ecological tragedy of no mean proportions.

The *slap, slap, slapping* of water against the bows was getting on his nerves. This place was spooking him out. *Get a grip on yourself Bryce* he admonished himself. He cocked his head and listened. The sound was joined now by the distant whine of engines and winches aboard U.S.A. federal vessels. He had seen them on the horizon as his boat approached the Sargasso death-fields, but they had pushed on further into the quagmire of bodies. What did they hope to find? Had top brass got any sort of an inkling into the cause? The seaweed island, carried along by currents from the Gulf of Mexico and the Caribbean Sea, normally provided, he knew, a haven for sea-going wildlife, so what had turned it into this surging graveyard? He looked up at the vast sweep of clear sky and shook his head. No freak storms had been reported, no oil-slick or other form of pollution so far as he knew. So what in hell's name had gone wrong? The sooner he was out of here the better, that's all he knew. He didn't like the spot. Couldn't quite dispel the *frisson* of unease that lurked beneath his shirt collar and which from time to time buzzed into life.

Perhaps it was the legends. The place was rife with them. For starters, it had long been rumoured to be the site of the Lost Land of Atlantis. More recent, and therefore more disturbing, were the reports of boats, ships and even aeroplanes disappearing without trace. Spooky. And well-documented too; and taken seriously enough by the U.S. Government to warrant investigation by specialist federal agents. Not that they had come up with anything; or if they had, nobody had been told, he thought wryly. Odd that this phenomenon should have taken place here too.

Shrugging off such thoughts he throttled the engine into life and the hired boat pushed its nose sluggishly through the marine weed and dead fauna, including disgusting masses of rotting flesh and crumpled feathers, the remains of a flock of aerobatic and quarrelsome gulls. That's it; he'd had enough. There was a creepy feel out here that he couldn't define. Besides, he had all the data and pictures he needed and if he wasn't back in England by Thursday night, Frank Kelly would use his innards for elastic bands, he thought with a smile, recalling one of his editor's colourful phrases. Setting course for Bermuda, he pulled down the peak of his yachting cap and eased the boat round in a wide arc.

At first he put it down to imagination, but then the pull of the current became too insistent to ignore. It was becoming impossible to navigate and hold course. The boat skewed round, and even as he fought the wheel and put all his weight behind it, it still spun through his hands as though with a mind of its own. He stared at the instrument panel as the needles swung madly out of control. What in God's name was happening here? This was crazy. A wind was getting up from nowhere. A tornado? Had he wandered into a freak whirlwind? Desperately he struggled to pull the boat out of the slow spin that was getting faster and faster. For some time now, the greenhouse effect had been worrying the authorities on both sides of the Atlantic, but whilst reports of climatic disturbances had been coming in, there had been nothing like this.

The wind was screaming now in his ears and shrieking around the deck. It tore at his clothing and plucked him off balance. Faster and faster the boat spun, like a cotton wool bud caught in the miniature whirlpool as the bath water drained away. His stomach lurched. He'd heard something like that said before. That something of the sort lurked at the bottom of the Sargasso: a giant plug hole that sucked everything from the surface with insatiable greed. Sucked them into nothingness, into a no-return, sub-marine and subterranean black hole, the equivalent to those in space that sucked whole universes into annihilation. Something awful like that was happening here, he felt sure.

There was a tremendous whining in his ears as the rate of spin increased and he was flung to the deck. He yelped with pain as his ankle struck a metal safety rail, and his head collided with a timber spar. At first he took it to be an effect of being temporarily stunned. Struggling upright, he clutched the deck rail and hung there listening. The screeching of the wind and the whining inside his head had softened and mellowed, taken on an incredible sweetness. The sound had the purity and simplicity of wind chimes he had once heard in a Japanese garden. He listened, mesmerised, then the deck pitched and he was flung down once more, tossing and rolling like a landed fish with no control whatsoever over his body.

The boat lurched, the deck spun beneath him and he was catapulted into the water. He gasped and threshed, fighting to stay afloat, but the seaweed had him in its grip. Wrapping him in slippery sinuous tendrils, it tugged him inexorably below the surface. What light had remained during the freak storm was extinguished as the mat of weed and organic debris closed over his head and he sank into a green world of silence. He gagged and choked as he swallowed rotting flesh and water rushed into his lungs. *Christ!* He was going to die. He was spinning now like the boat, dizzily plummeting down to the sea bed thousands of feet below.

Plunging down to the giant plug on the ocean floor from which there was no return. Lights exploded behind his eyes. It was then that he heard it again. Waves of music drifting towards him through the green gloom. Music of such beauty and delicacy that he forgot to fight, forgot he was going to die. His limbs grew limp and no longer threshed wildly as he allowed himself to sink. The music ran through his veins and cascaded in sparks and golden lights. A vice tightened around his chest. The tinkling spaced-out sound, strange and unreal, eased the pain. But it *was* real. He could hear it, couldn't he? Like the fabled unworldly sound of the celestial spheres. That's what it is, he thought as water rushed into his lungs and life drained away. He was hearing the Song of the Planets.

SEPTEMBER

~

Somewhere between Manchester and London

On a one way ticket to save the World! Darcy grimaced mirthlessly as she watched autumnal trees slide past the train window, the gold and red of their finery fused by speed into spurts of orange flame. At least, one small part of it for starters; Britain to be exact. Not that anyone would believe it. Events had turned her into a lone campaigner, shunned by the authorities and labelled 'nut-case' or worse. Frank's range of epithets had decidedly fallen into the latter category.

She grinned despite her desperation, then her expression swiftly sobered as she recalled the passenger on the opposite seat. His sharp suit, trendy hairstyle, and the filo-fax resting on his knee proclaimed him a Yuppy on his way to the City. He swayed slightly with each movement of the carriage as though lightly mesmerised, looking through rather than at her, and probably thinking about his latest database. Still, you never could tell; mustn't draw attention to herself. She glanced at the man's face then looked away again as she caught his eye and returned to her worries like a dog to an old and well-chewed bone.

If only you had believed me, Frank. Then Carl Bayliss needn't have died that terrible death, and Oliver Bryce may not have disappeared without trace somewhere out in the Bermuda Triangle. Her features flinched with the pain of memory. Good correspondents – the best – and good guys too. But Frank hadn't believed her, and they were dead.

Not that it mattered, because if she failed in her present mission the disease that now threatened Britain would sooner or later infect the whole planet. And the burden lay on her shoulders. No problem to the girls; Britain today, the World tomorrow, she silently mocked herself. Providing she arrived on cue, and once inside the building had time to locate the device. The finger of her wrist-watch had moved forward by one minute since the last time she had looked.

It was still hard to believe. That Mr. Ambrose really had given her a clue all those weeks ago; that he was the mystic Alisdair believed him to be, one of many around the globe willing to sacrifice themselves to save the planet. Perhaps after all he was just an eccentric old man with a crazy obsession. The answer would present itself soon enough, she thought with a shudder. If the latter was true, then there would be one hell of a bloody bang. Because one thing was sure: Jules Cain was real enough, and so were those particles and the evil they could produce.

*

The wheels of the train *click-clacked* over the points with hypnotic regularity, marking the seconds and minutes with frightening inevitability. Giving up her attempt to watch the passing landscape with any interest, she glanced once more at her watch. In approximately two hours time, the doors to the Royal Opera House would open and they would begin filing in: the diplomats, the prime minister and selected members of the cabinet, the president of the United States, the Russian and French premiers and of course, the World's leading physicists from the Einstein and C.A.D.E. Institutes. A 'by invitation only' audience, each member selected for his or her talent, power or prestige. A glittering occasion *par excellence* to mark the opening of the Mercury Space Convention – and the great Paluccini would sing for them. I hope to God it won't be their requiem, Darcy thought fervently. And not only theirs, but all within God knows how many miles radius. But she mustn't allow herself to even contemplate failure, despite the seeming impossibility of her task.

Something impelled her to look up. With a thrill of shock, she saw the man opposite had been watching her. He looked away quickly once detected, but not swiftly enough to hide the flash of intensity in his pale blue eyes. Immediately every nerve in her body tensed and screamed. One of them? Or merely a man caught eyeing a young woman? That was the trouble with this thing: it had made her so paranoid, scared and suspicious of everyone she met. The muscles around her eyes and mouth relaxed slightly as she told herself he was harmless enough, and that thugs – however educated or refined – didn't usually blush when caught spying. And to think it had all started out so innocently, with Alisdair finding that thing on the fell ...

BEGINNINGS

One

~

Hell Alisdair, I wish you weren't coming tonight. Darcy's knuckles were white as her hands gripped the steering wheel. Or any time, come to think of it, she thought, swinging the car off Corporation Street, down Fennel Street and up the approach of Manchester's Victoria Station. The muscles around her mouth tightened, giving her jaw an even more determined look than usual, and the grey of her eyes darkened in the way it did when she felt hassled.

Even the weather is in sympathy, she thought, flicking the switch of the wipers to the 'off' position as they squeaked and dragged against the windscreen now that the drizzle was easing off. She shivered. Cold with it too. No-one would think it was almost April. A man and woman, muffled in raincoats and hats against the chill and damp, struggled towards the taxi rank with their luggage. Darcy parked on the forecourt and glanced at the clock in the dashboard. The train from London, diverted from Piccadilly due to a bomb scare at the station, would be pulling in soon. No more reprieves. Alisdair would be on it, and that meant the end of her easy, independent way of life.

Trained by habit her reporter's mind registered the knot of youths crowding the station entrance as she got out of the car. Booze or dope, she decided, watching them pushing and shoving one another drunkenly from the corner of her eye. One youth stumbled into another and swore incoherently and spat on the ground. The girls who were with them laughed shrilly and hurled taunts. The place itself was depressing enough: a Victorian edifice of rusted iron, peeling paint and grimy glass, a place where litter floated on puddles and young people – without hope or support – drifted as aimlessly as the Big Mac carton being bowled along on the night breeze.

Come to think of it, her own life was pretty messy. Instinctively, as she locked the car door, her eyes went to the narrow gold band on her left hand. Okay, she had gone into the marriage knowing that Brant's work as a physicist attached to MI5 was demanding and at times dangerous – but in the priority stakes, he had made her feel a pretty poor second. Brant had gone but his ring stayed; she wasn't sure why. Squaring her shoulders Darcy began walking towards the entrance.

Her sense of unease heightened as the distance between herself and the rowdy youngsters decreased. The sound of breaking glass made her start. A youth wearing a fringed and worn-looking leather jacket had hurled a bottle against the wall. The reek of alcohol combined unpleasantly with the inner-city atmosphere. A beer can rolled to her feet. Raucous cries and laughter grated on her ears.

"Fancy a drink, luv?"

More nightmarish squeals and egging-on from the girls. Resolutely Darcy kept her mouth shut and her gaze on the entrance ahead.

"Not off you she don't Bazza, that's for sure," taunted a girl with black eye shadow and green streaks in her cropped hair. They had fallen ominously quiet now, like a pack of wolves before the kill. The youth moved towards her. "No, but I bet you fancy a feel, don't you darlin'."

A grinning face with a ring through the nose was stuck in front of her own.

Stay cool and don't panic, Darcy told herself. "Excuse me," she said icily as he blocked her path.

He grinned, revealing teeth stained with nicotine. "C'mon luv, be a bit sociable like, what d'you say?"

She almost gagged at the animal warmth and smell of him; that and the odour of stale tobacco, alcohol and sweat. Scared, she made herself speak with slowness and confidence. "Get out of my way please."

"Now don't be unfriendly. That might just upset me, mightn't it lads?" He turned and grinned over his shoulder.

"Yeah, and you don't want to do that luv," one of the other youths taunted with obvious threat.

"Nice tits," her tormentor commented. "Gizza feel, eh?" he reached out to a chorus of cat-calls from his mates. Darcy had been unknowingly holding her breath, now it exploded in outrage and she knocked away his hand.

"Go on, give her one Bazza," a grinning black youth shouted, whilst his white companion whistled and hooted.

Darcy recoiled and turned to run back to the car, but he grabbed her arm and spun her round. Frantically she looked about for help, but the London train was running late and the day's business was mostly done. A woman was just being driven off in a taxi; a man turned and stared over his shoulder, but then swiftly disappeared through one of the entrances to the station. Bystander-bloody-apathy, she thought angrily, twisting to free herself from the youth's grip. "Relax girl, ain't nobody comin' to help," he provoked with a grin, then his face and manner changed to one of resentment and hostility. "What's up, miss high and bloody mighty? Think you're too bleedin' good for me?" he snarled. "I said be nice," he added, pulling her against him. Darcy opened her mouth to scream but a hand was clamped over it. The skull-ring he wore was bruising her lip. He groped her breast with hard greedy fingers. His concentration lapsed and she jerked her head to the left, freeing her mouth. "Look," she panted, by now scared for real and falling back on cunning. "I'm sure a good-looking lad like you doesn't have to force it," she gambled, forcing herself to be calm. Because didn't guys like him get a buzz when their victims exhibited fear and shock?

He glared at her, suspicious. "You reckon?" He smirked then, succumbing to the temptation to believe that her sort of woman could find him attractive. That was as far as he got.

"What's with you Bazza? Fancy the bitch do you?"

One of the girls had stepped forward and now stood with arms akimbo, her skinny legs in their stretch pants and boots straddled like a man's.

"Give it a rest, Shiel," Darcy's attacker snarled, releasing her to give the girl a shove.

"Get your stinkin' hands off her," the girl yelled. "You ain't touching me up after messing with her, I'll tell you that."

"Don't get mouthy with me, slag." The youth pushed her harder so that she fell.

"There's no call for that," the black lad cried, and the girl with the green streaks added her voice to the protests.

The flash of a knife caught Darcy's eye. She backed off. Two taxis, one behind the other, drove past, the white faces behind the wheel impassive. They're not going to help, she thought stricken. Dog eats dog in this jungle. Just one more mugging, rape or gang fight. The youth who had grabbed her shouted out and clutched at his forearm. Darcy stared in horror as blood welled up through his fingers. Her legs turned to water. The girl had got up from the ground and now confronted Darcy. "You're the reason Bazza copped it," she cried, brandishing a shard of broken glass. Darcy felt the colour drain from her face.

Weak with relief, she heard the sirens seconds before the police car and van came swirling onto the forecourt in a flurry of wailing sirens and flashing lights. The girl swore and backed off. The doors were flung open before the vehicles screeched to a standstill and half a dozen or so officers spilled out.

"Pigs – split!"

In-fighting forgotten in the face of mutual danger, the gang broke and ran.

*

It was all over in no time. One lad escaped by shinning a drainpipe over a toilet block, the rest of the youngsters were rounded up and bundled into the van. Darcy thanked the officer who approached her, notebook open, but declined to press charges, and claiming that she had to catch the London train, hurried away before he could ask her name. The officer's disapproval stabbed her back as she ran to the station entrance. Public reluctance must be a frustration of the job, she thought crashing through the doorway. But there must have been something desperately wrong with those youngster's lives to make them act that way, and she wasn't about to make their lot worse. They were in enough bother as it was. Whatever, they could have the benefit of the doubt.

Someone must have telephoned the police after all, she reflected, her faith in human nature partially restored. But it wasn't enough; there would be no change of plan. Tonight's trauma had justified her planned move to the country. City life was out from now on, even though it would mean less contact with the Paper. Sending in weekly copy just couldn't compare with the buzz of being at the heart of the action, but it was better than nothing. It was good of Frank to square it with Max Dearden, the Manchester News' proprietor, so that she kept her column. She would make it work – somehow. *I only hope Alisdair will go along with the new arrangement*, she worried, breaking into a run as the Tannoy system crackled into life and a garbled male voice announced the imminent arrival of the London Euston train. What on earth would Alisdair think if she wasn't there to meet him?

She rushed through the subway, noting with distaste the daubed posters and graffiti covered walls. A tide mark of rubbish, the flotsam and jetsam of city living, lined their base. She moved nervously with constant glances over her shoulder. Ever since her last big story, and being pursued by a killer through the maze of the London Underground, she had hated subways. A man in a raincoat and brown felt hat pulled low over his forehead approached from the opposite direction. Heart pounding unpleasantly, Darcy kept her head down and her pace fast, and heaved a sigh of relief as he passed without a glance. Christ, she'd be glad when tonight was over. Then she was bursting out of the subway and onto the platform.

"Is that the London train?" she asked a man wearing a dusty, tired-looking uniform who was halfheartedly brushing out the waiting room. Darcy pointed down the track to the headlamps drawing steadily closer.

"Aye. Usually comes in at Piccadilly."

"Is this Platform eleven?"

"It is that – and the longest in Britain." He leaned on his brush as though glad of an excuse to do so. "Here, what was all that ruckus out front?" he asked, preparing for a gossip.

"Just some youths," Darcy threw over her shoulder as she moved away. The *clackety-clack* of wheels over points grew louder and the headlamps loomed larger, twin halos of light diffused by drizzle. Then the train was *swooshing* and clattering into the station, a giant metallic glow-worm shedding yellowed light at every window.

Anxiously she walked alongside, peering into compartments and scanning alighting figures as doors were pushed open and travel-weary men and women spilled out. There he was at last. Hair mussed, a bag in each hand and looking rather lost. It had been almost a year. He looked much the same, only paler and thinner. Darcy stood still, a lump in her throat, surprised by the sudden rush of emotion. Calling his name, she walked swiftly towards him. Alisdair, national health glasses askew and with one shoelace trailing along the ground, looked dazed by exhaustion. But then, Darcy thought on a wave of compassion, it had been a long day for an eleven-year-old orphan.

Two

~

Why, oh why, did you have to die Timothy? Darcy asked herself, opening the door of her flat. She had asked that question a thousand times since the car crash almost a year ago in which Timothy and his wife Gloria had instantly died. "Come on, Alisdair," she chivvied as he hovered on the threshold. "Give me a hand with these," she said exasperated, tugging at the largest of the three suitcases she had dumped in the hall. How the hell am I going to bear this? she thought, suddenly struck by panic. He had scarcely spoken during the drive back through the city's oily wet streets, and the atmosphere in the car had been funereal to say the least. Not for the first time, she felt anger at a Fate that had landed her with the job of looking after this odd child with whom she seemed to have nothing in common.

It wasn't even as though she'd been close to Timothy, she fumed, panting as she lugged another suitcase inside. He had been a glamorous stranger with a high-powered job and lifestyle which, she thought closing the door to her flat, came from him being five years older than herself. He had gone first to university then to Kuwait as a computer whizz-kid with a conglomerate. So although the loss of a brother must always leave an ache, she had accepted his death; her grief now was for the loss of her freedom and for the gloom that stretched ahead.

At last the luggage was all in the flat and guilt engulfed her as she looked at her nephew. "You must be done in. Look, go and wash and change ready for bed, then we'll have supper together," she said, handing him his overnight bag and pushing him gently towards the bathroom door. "That's your bedroom there," she added, pointing to an adjacent door before leaving him to go into the kitchen. His voice however followed her.

"Aunt Darcy."

"For Christ's sake, just call me 'Darcy'," she exclaimed in horror, then realised it wasn't the best way to speak to a child. "What is it?" she asked in a milder tone.

"My dressing gown's in the trunk."

"No problem. I won't wear mine either, then you won't feel left out," she said laughing to herself as she imagined the expression on his pale, too-grown-up-for-his-years face. "We'll have a pyjama party," she joked in an attempt to put him at ease.

Poor kid, she thought pouring milk into the pan. His life's been shattered and it's no great shakes being shunted onto me. But his boarding school, the second since the accident, had 'declined' to take him back this term. They had expressed the opinion that as Alisdair wasn't coping with school life at present, he would be happier in a more intimate family situation for the time being. Which, she thought sloshing the hot milk into two mugs, was a polite way of saying they were not in the business of dealing with disturbed boys, however bright, and Alisdair was certainly that; too much so for his own good. Which was all fair enough, she supposed, placing the mugs on a tray with a plate of biscuits. But it did seem unfair that she should be the one to pick up the tab. She had seen Timothy once during the past five years, and that at a family funeral. She should gripe. His wife hadn't seen much more of him. Not that it had seemed to bother her. The glamorous Gloria had been content with her modelling job and possessions – and Timothy had kept her well supplied with the latter. They had everything: detached house in London, country home in Berkshire, flash cars, a boat, and a farmhouse in Brittany for holidays. And now it was all gone. Only poor Alisdair remained. What in God's name was she going to do with him? To be perfectly honest, something about him gave her the creeps. He gave off an atmosphere, filled the car or room with suppressed hate and resentment. But she was being over fanciful, she told herself, carrying the tray into the sitting room.

"Watch the film with me?" she invited, as he finished his cocoa and stood by the sofa looking uncertain. "It starts in five minutes," she prompted when he failed to answer.

He glanced at the flickering screen with little interest. "No thanks," he said in that dull voice that held no expression and which made her want to scream. She reminded herself that he was doubly bereaved and still grieving.

"Harrison Ford's in it," she tempted. "You know, the 'Lost Ark' guy. This one's a murder story – supposed to be good."

"Not interested."

"Okay." Darcy sighed and held onto her patience. "What sort of films do you like then?"

"*Excalibur* was okay."

From the animation that blazed briefly behind those awful spectacles, she guessed it was rather more than 'okay'. "A bit bloody though," she ventured, taking care not to come over the stuffy aunt. He probably thought of her as 'ancient' as it was.

"That's how it was."

"I suppose so. But didn't it disturb you?"

He shook his head scornfully.

"It did me," she admitted, grinning.

"Merlin was great."

At least he was talking. "You like stories about King Arthur then?" she prodded, thinking she would get him a couple of videos.

"No, about Merlin."

He turned away from her and stared blankly at the television screen.

"We're going to Cumbria to live next week," she announced in a bid to regain his attention. Her parents had played it down when they pressurised her to take him on, but really shock and grief had turned him semi-autistic, she thought, feeling anger at her parents for concealing the extent of the problem.

"Will Brant be there too?"

Darcy almost dropped her mug upon hearing his name spoken out of the blue. "Er, no."

"Why not?"

"Pardon?" she stammered, thrown by his directness. How did he know about Brant? Then she remembered: they had met at Uncle Matty's funeral, and Alisdair had instantly taken to Brant.

"Why won't he be there?" Alisdair repeated.

"I'm afraid he's gone away."

His expression turned sulky and anger lurked just beneath the surface. "They all do."

"How do you mean?" Darcy asked, disturbed by the flatness and resignation in his voice.

He shrugged and regarded her myopically, his eyes huge behind the pebble lenses of his glasses. "Men, grown-ups – they never stay around."

Oh God, how absolutely awful she thought struggling for the right words to swab his internal bleeding. There were none. "I'm sorry Alisdair. Look," she continued, obliterating Harrison Ford with the tap of a lacquered fingernail on the remote control button. "Your Dad, your parents, they didn't leave you on purpose; they had no choice. They still love you, you know; love doesn't die."

He's heard it all before, she thought, seeing his glazed expression and closed look, and guessing he recognised the start of yet another lengthy and useless monologue of grown-up platitudes. She abandoned the cause. "As for Brant and I, it just didn't work out for us," she said instead, judging honesty to be the best policy.

He shrugged and moved to the doorway. "I'm not bothered," he said sulkily. "I never really thought I'd get to see his observatory."

"He was going to take you there?" Darcy cringed at the unworthy stab of envy. She had seen her visits there as an enjoyable privilege, now she would probably never go there again. She recalled the day she and Brant had sat on the sandstone cliffs of St. Gildas Bay. The observatory lay at the foot of a massive outcrop nearby and the enormous folding dome and radio telescope were clear in her mind. Even clearer was the memory of his hands and lips on her body as they made love in a sandy hollow whilst gulls and curlews keened overhead and the wind caressed her hair. She shook her head as though to physically remove the pain. "I'm sure he meant it at the time," she said lamely, turning her attention back to Alisdair. She was being bloody selfish; he was, after all, casualty of the month.

"They all do, don't they? They all mean it at the time, but they don't come up with the goods!" he cried.

Darcy stared, taken aback by his sudden loss of control. "Now come on, Alisdair," she began, alarmed by his expression.

"My mother said she'd always be there when I needed her – but she didn't really mean it, did she? And Dad said he would take me with him to Kuwait, but that's pie in the sky now too," he stormed, his face purpling with anger.

"Alisdair stop upsetting yourself," she commanded, feeling powerless to deal with this bizarre and unfamiliar situation.

"And Brant, I guess he only said he'd take me to his observatory to shut me up," he accused.

"Why? Why should he do that?" she demanded.

"Because grown-ups do that to kids," he yelled. There was scorn in his voice and a fury in his expression that scared Darcy. It seemed to build up all around him, all the pain, frustration and anger an eleven-year-old was capable of feeling, until it became a palpable force.

She spun round at the crash of breaking glass and stared in superstitious horror.

A photograph of Brant had fallen from the wall and smashed onto the carpet.

Three

~

Darcy stared at the shards of glass littering the floor and told herself to be sensible. It was crazy to suppose that Alisdair had anything to do with it. Or was it? Could his anger, bitterness and frustration have caused the photograph to fall from the wall? If so, what irony. Here she was preparing to whisk him away from the drugs, booze and crime of inner city life, when really the problem was coming from within himself. Great: to be buried in the back of beyond with a potential poltergeist host. Par for the course, she supposed, given the turns her life had taken of late. "Leave that," she said sharply as Alisdair stooped to pick up the mess. "I'll see to it in a moment – when you're in bed," she said pointedly; then tempered it with, "we can do without cut fingers I think," because he looked so hang-dog.

"Good night then," she said as he would have left the room without another word.

He mumbled something that passed for a reply and made for his bed-room.

"We'll be in Cumbria this time next week," she said attempting to cheer him up. "That's something to look forward to, isn't it?"

"Is it?" He stared at her rudely.

"Come on, lighten up Alisdair," she chided, trying to hide her exasperation.

"I don't want to go," he said sullenly, and noisily closed his bedroom door.

*

But go he did, albeit unwillingly and in virtual silence. The day was fine if a little cold, and as they left Manchester and eventually the motorway behind, the wild crocus, violets and daffodils lent splashes of purple and gold to the russet hedgerows. Then the rolling hills gave way to the barren grandeur of the west, where grey peaks loftily scraped an empty sky. Looking at them, Darcy had her first misgivings. It made sense not to look at Alisdair; his concern was palpable and filled the car. Which wasn't suprprising: she might just as well have been taking him to live on the moon. I must be mad, she thought, as they dropped down from a high desolate moor to the glacial valley below.

"Well, here we are," she announced too cheerfully, drawing to a halt before the wrought iron gates that blocked their way. They were slung between crumbling sandstone pillars with spherical tops, and were eight foot high if they were an inch. A mythical beast on the lines of a dragon emblazoned the central panel of each gate.

"Our house is in *there*?" Alisdair exclaimed.

"Sure is. Alcatraz has nothing on Westwalls," Darcy said with a grin.

"Is that why you chose it – because your name is Darcy West?" Alisdair asked curiously, in his longest sentence since leaving the flat.

"No," she said slowly, pulling on the hand brake as the car began to roll. "It was just coincidence." There came again the feeling that she had been brought here for some reason, stupid, but a strong one at the time of her first visit. It was such an odd place that she had almost expected the estate agents who had sent her the details to deny all knowledge of it on her return. Come to think of it, they had given her an odd look. "Anyway, out you get," she said brusquely.

"Here? Why?" he asked with a look of consternation.

"First rule of the countryside – passengers open gates," she said laughing.

"Okay."

The tone of resignation was belied by the ghost of a smile. Are we winning here? she asked herself, driving through the gates to their new home.

I'd forgotten what it was like, the lushness and abundance, she thought, navigating the drive with its weed-infested cracks. Despite the earliness of the season, foliage had burst its buds, and magnolia and camellia abounded with waxy blooms; even the lilacs dripped white and purple blossom. It must be a sheltered spot with its own micro-climate, Darcy told herself. The car rounded a bend in the drive and an elderly man tending a bonfire came into view. "Who's that?" Alisdair asked.

"That's Mr. Ambrose," Darcy replied, waving as the man turned his head. "I bought the house off him. He lives alone, and it was too big."

Alisdair looked puzzled.

"So why is he still here?"

"He lives in the lodge now," Darcy said casually, having previously left out the minor detail that they had an elderly man living in their garden.

"Where's the lodge?" Alisdair demanded, peering shortsightedly through the windscreen.

"The half-timbered building over there – you can just see it through the trees."

"And where is our house?"

"Oh, way over there." Darcy made an airy gesture with her hand as she climbed out of the car. "I have to collect the keys. Come and say hello," she added to forestal further questions.

Darcy shook hands with Mr. Ambrose and was struck anew by the startling blue of his eyes. The vibrant eyes of a young man looking out from an old and parchment-lined face, came the uneasy thought; especially as they now held a gleam of amusement that suggested he had somehow read her mind. "This is my nephew, Alisdair," she said, drawing him forward. Mr. Ambrose pushed the battered panama he was wearing to the back of his head, and ran slim fingers – as brown and gnarled as the ancient apple trees he had been pruning – through his white hair and pulled the hat down again.

"Welcome to Westwalls, Alisdair."

Solemnly man and boy shook hands. As their eyes and hands met, Darcy felt something pass between them, a sort of empathy. Amazing. Alisdair had resisted all her overtures, yet now she felt his reluctance evaporate like alcohol over a Bunsen burner.

"Have you lived here long sir?" Alisdair asked shyly.

"Ages."

Mr. Ambrose gave him a huge wink.

He took a grubby handkerchief from the pocket of his khaki-coloured trousers and wiped the dewdrop from the end of his nose. "Know how to tend a bonfire, boy?"

"I'm not sure; I've never-"

"Yes of course you do. Here take this. Look after it whilst I get the keys for your aunt."

Darcy waited for the protests; none came.

"Damp it down with those leaves when I give you a call for tea," he instructed. Holding out the rake upon which he had been leaning, he thrust it at Alisdair. "Come along then."

Obediently, Darcy walked behind the ramrod-straight back of Mr. Ambrose.

The lodge, not unlike its owner, exuded an old-world charm and a sort of shabby gentility that had a certain appeal. Run-down country houses, over-grown gardens and afternoon tea on the croquet lawn, Darcy couldn't help thinking. A closed world of dusty nostalgia and faded roses. In keeping with the rest of the garden, the clematis that sprawled over the porch was already covered with flower buds, and new growth spurted impatiently from the rambling rose.

"Albertines. Vigorous you know. Grow like the very devil," Mr. Ambrose commented, leading her inside.

Immediately, Darcy was aware of a delicious woody scent reminiscent of violets spiced with musk.

"Cedar," he supplied, evidently noting her appreciation. "Walls are clad in it. Here's the key," he added, taking it down from a hook on the wall. "So now, make yourself at home whilst I brew some tea."

Darcy settled down to wait and felt herself begin to relax. She loved the way the sunlight filtered through rose and clematis, so that the worn rugs and pine floorboards were dappled with patterns of light and shade. Natural wood, no paint or varnish in sight, and pieces of ancient furniture. Mr. Ambrose may be a queer old stick, but he sure had a lovely place.

The tea was poured from a tarnished silver pot, and Alisdair duly called. As he entered, Darcy caught his eye then looked pointedly at a huge painting on the far wall. Alisdair's gasp was audible. Shyness forgotten, he advanced into the room and peered through his glasses at the picture. Merlin, his eyes glazed with enchantment, stared out at them from amongst the foliage and blossoms of a forest bower. The enchantress Nimue, flesh glowing and gown clinging to her voluptuous curves, looked on as she weaved her spell. The tones, like the theme, were dark yet luminous with the quality of shot-silk. Given Alisdair's confessed interest in Merlin, Darcy mused, it couldn't be more appropriate. Sure enough, Alisdair was transfixed. If only he was always so well, 'normal'.

"Stop fretting about your nephew," Mr. Ambrose said in an undervoice.

Darcy turned from watching Alisdair, a startled look on her face.

"He will come to at Westwalls." The vibrant blue of his eyes held a smile as he handed her a fragrant cup of 'Earl Grey'. "Come and get some tea and cake, young man," he barked.

Alisdair reluctantly left the painting and did as he was told.

*

"I can see you are going to thrive at Westwalls," Mr. Ambrose observed a quarter of an hour or so later, as Alisdair accepted his third piece of cake.

And he's picked at his food like a bird since he came to me, Darcy marvelled. Still, don't knock it. Maybe this elderly friend would make Alisdair less of a nightmare to live with.

"Where does the name come from?" Alisdair was asking.

Mr. Ambrose brushed the crumbs from the front of his cardigan. "The 'West' bit speaks for itself, does it not?" he queried, and Darcy wondered at the look he threw her way, but then he went on to say, "Given this is west Cumbria. And 'Walls' – because that is an alternative name for 'fortification', and the property stands on the site of a fortified Roman villa."

Alisdair's hand paused on the way to his mouth and his eyes were huge behind his glasses. "Have you ever found anything? You know, swords and things."

Mr. Ambrose's crusty face split in a smile and rising, he opened the drawer of a side table and brought out a leather-bound box. "Nothing so exciting, I fear, just these." He handed Alisdair the box.

"Wow, is this a *denarius* do you think?" he asked, holding up the battered coin.

He's actually got some colour in his cheeks, Darcy thought watching him and noting the flush of excitement.

"Possibly," Mr. Ambrose was saying. "I'm impressed, Alisdair!"

Alisdair flushed pink. "Do you think I could search for treasure?" he asked shyly.

"Can't have you going around digging up the garden, boy," Mr. Ambrose growled, "but I was given a metal detector some years back and it's gathering cobwebs. Would you like to borrow it?"

"Oh, yes please."

"Tomorrow then. I'll show you a section of exposed wall. That is where you must search."

Darcy inwardly groaned. So much for harmony; Alisdair would now throw a wobbler for sure. But it couldn't be helped. At least, not until he started at the local school next week. "Sorry, Alisdair; I have to go to Manchester tomorrow to see my boss – you'll have to come with me and wait in the car."

Sure enough Alisdair's face fell. "Do I have to?"

"Afraid so. I can't leave you here on your own."

Mr. Ambrose rose and taking both their cups, placed them back on the tray. "Alisdair can stay here with me," he said without turning round.

There was no decision. Alisdair's face was one silent plea. She was doubtful about the arrangement – after all, what did she know about this old man? – but hadn't the heart to refuse.

"It's very kind of you," she said hesitantly.

"Not at all. Glad of the company. That's settled then."

Wondering how he had so easily managed to take control, Darcy followed Mr. Ambrose into the porch.

*

Darcy turned and frowning, looked over her shoulder as she walked with Alisdair to the car.

"What's the matter?" he asked, peering up at her through his hideous glasses.

She shrugged and carried on walking. "I don't know."

There was no earthly reason why the sight of Mr. Ambrose standing in the doorway framed by foliage, should fill her with foreboding.

Four

~

Back inside the lodge, Mr. Ambrose's thoughts were as the dusk outside: neither dark nor light but somewhere in between. It would have to be soon. He was growing weaker; his time was limited. Any day now the boy must make his discovery, and things would be pitched forward. A move that once made, could never be undone.

He lit the candles and peered deep into the silver web. It stretched tautly from the candelabra hanging from a hook in the ceiling, to the table beneath the window. So delicate was it that his exhaled breath caused tiny ripples of movement along its surface. So who have we here? He touched the crystal with a fingernail that resembled a talon, so that it bounced in the web. (Or was it just a raindrop from that leak in the roof he was ever-meaning to fix?) And there he was doubting himself again. But what if he was just a deranged old fool? No. He shook his head. They had been with him too long, the visions and strange dreams, the hint of other dimensions: like 'seeing' the boy Alisdair making his discovery on the fell. So had the *knowing*, the awareness of the living Earth, a giant heart and Will of which he and everyone else was a part. A huge organism, under threat from its own cancerous cells.

He picked at a pearl of solid wax on the table top. But he was rambling. Where were we? Ah, yes, the Sahara man. He had called him that as he had no way of knowing his name. He had seen it in the fire, the pictures forming life-like out of the charred wood and flames; a most distressing vision. But it was bound to happen; Gaia would fight back. Something had to make them sit up, these vandals who called themselves scientists and politicians, and who treated Earth like a giant ashtray. Now perhaps the rest of the world would take notice. Unwittingly, the man had sacrificed his life to Gaia. No doubt he would reap just reward in whichever part of the web he now inhabited.

Of course, the other situation was also regrettable, he mused, touching an adjacent crystal – (or raindrop). He had seen that vision in the fire too. But many had gone that way before, and many would go again. That plug hole in the ocean bed was simply an easy way out of the web – and back in again to a different quadrant. A sort of, 'out of the back door and in again by the front' situation. Or to put it another way, he would find himself in the sitting room instead of the kitchen, but still the same 'house', the same Universe. From matter to anti-matter, *then matter reformed*. Much in the way that black holes are doors to new universes and dimensions. So on balance, not much to regret there.

As he withdrew his finger, the movement reverberated throughout the web, bringing forth its creator from behind a candle stub.

"But all life is like that, isn't it, Spider?" he commented, watching the strands bounce and stretch. And so it was: every movement along each thread travelled through the network, the vibrations affecting the whole. "So it is with our lives; such is the Way of Wyrde," he said aloud. A system of influence rather than cause and effect, "but these days few seem to grasp it," he added, shaking his head. The spider crossed its silken trampoline, dipping and clinging with sure tread. It paused, front legs raised above its fat body as though listening to what the man said.

"And who have we here?" The bony finger moved on to the next crystal, and one that seemed to shine more brightly than the rest. *Ah yes, the boy*. It was with the likes of young Alisdair that the hope of this planet lay. "Very well, Alisdair," he said speaking aloud though the spider was no longer listening: it was busy dissecting and devouring, segment by segment, a juicy fly. "We shall see what we can do. All it takes is a pure channel like yourself, and a just cause – though there are limits on what I can do. Isn't that so, Spider?"

But the spider was preoccupied. With rhythmic flicks of its tongue, it was ridding its forelegs of sticky fly-debris. Mr. Ambrose sighed. "Ah well, never mind. Perhaps you, Alisdair, will help me redress the balance." He stroked his nose reflectively. "Though when it comes to it, the Darcy-girl must undertake the main task. Despite her youth and arrogance, she is basically good and has courage enough to succeed."

His eyes now held a faraway look. "Then Spider, I may return Home," he whispered, gazing out of the window into the twilight, above the trees to the distant fells. He blew gently on the web so that the crystals shivered and gave off tiny rainbows.

Five

~

Darcy shivered as though a cold wind had blown over her, yet it was quite warm here in the kitchen now that a fire had been kindled in the old Aga. She shrugged and put it down to tiredness and hunger. She emptied the thermos flask of stewed tea down the ancient Bristol sink and gave an exclamation of disgust.

"What?" Alisdair said, closing the cupboard door beneath the old dresser where he had been rummaging about.

"I didn't say anything." She stared at the tea leaves that had splattered against the sides. A dark stain on white enamel. She'd always hated it, even as a kid. "That's what happens when you act unkindly, Darcy," her mother had told her once after smacking her for refusing to lend her toys to the snotty Deirdre who's parents were the only ones to own their house in a row of rented terraces. "Each selfish act is a black mark on your conscience," she'd admonished, and Darcy had never forgotten. Mother wouldn't remember it now of course; she had buried that no-nonsense religious-style parenting at the bottom of the bedding chest along with her Union blankets and working-class origins. Darcy felt a pang of discomfort. Brant had called her 'selfish' that awful last night at the farmhouse on the cliffs of St. Gildas Bay. An ache that was almost physical caught at her chest. Nonsense, he was the selfish one, she retracted, sluicing the tea leaves down the plug hole so that the sink was restored to its former purity.

"We'll be able to have a cuppa soon, Alisdair," she said brightly, squinting at the worn thermometer on the Aga. Her heart sank at the sight of his down-in-the-mouth expression. Even the prospect of a day spent searching for "Caesar's treasure" hadn't dispelled his gloom on entering the house.

"But it's so *old-fashioned*," he complained.

"So's Mr. Ambrose's place," she reasoned.

"But so is *he*." Alisdair had pulled a face. "I like it for *him*, but not for *me*."

A line of reasoning she had not felt equal to pursuing.

"Plug the kettle in," he said now.

"Where?" she asked with a grin.

He looked around the low-ceilinged room with its oak beams and she saw the truth dawning. "You mean we have *no electric?*"

Darcy laughed. "Don't be a wimp! Wait until I see Mr. Ambrose. I bet he won't be impressed with you for long!"

"But what do we do when it goes dark?"

Wordlessly she pointed to the large oil lamp that hung suspended by a chain from a hook in the ceiling. "And there's plenty of candles," she added, filling the kettle and placing it on the hot plate.

"Oh, but what about my computer?" he wailed.

"You won't need computer games here." She was determined to wean him off packaged violence.

"It's to work on my physics formulae," he said looking aggrieved.

Darcy whipped round to face him. "You're doing physics already?"

"I skipped a couple of classes at school."

"Clever-clogs!" *So what have we here?* Darcy wondered. A budding Einstein – or another Brant? That pang again. Ridiculous, when she had left of her own choice. Odd too, that his name should come to mind for the second time in the space of minutes. "I'll see about a small generator – maybe," she conceded.

"Ace! When?"

"When I get time, have the money, and am convinced you and I can hit it off," she stated. "Say in about a month?" she added, relenting as he appeared to accept without fuss.

"Okay, that's fair, I guess," he sighed.

"It's a deal then," Darcy agreed, secretly of the opinion that by then he would have outgrown his computer-dependency and be into more healthy outdoor pursuits. "Right then, stop hanging about like a day-time bat, Alisdair, and go and make up your bed," she concluded, in a voice that brooked no argument.

"Which is my room then?"

"Come on, I'll show you." She grabbed his overnight bag from the seat in the huge inglenook fireplace and tossed it his way.

*

One game of snap and six of poker later, which said a lot about Alisdair's prep school, especially as she lost five of the hands, Darcy sat alone at the window gazing out at the rural night. Somewhere in the trees an owl hooted, and beyond the Georgian pane window the garden brooded and folded in on itself. On impulse she rose and stepped outside. Instantly it wrapped her in mystery and moonshine, and the premature lilac released its fragrance to the night. A magical place. A place in which she could have been happy, had things been different.

Holding out her left hand she stared reflectively at the luminous band of Welsh gold. Despite his arrogance and fiery temper, Brant was an incurable romantic. He had insisted on Welsh gold because of his Celtic soul, he had told her as they left the tiny stone church at St. Gildas Bay. Because, he had also said, that was the part of him to which she was now wed. She shivered suddenly, and realising there was a chill in the air, went back inside to her solitary bed.

Six

~

Darcy watched in amusement as Alisdair bolted his breakfast. "Don't keep Mr. Ambrose waiting," she said ironically.

Alisdair stuffed the last of his toast in his mouth. "I'm going as fast as I can."

She hid a smile. "Precisely."

He looked up from his plate like a baleful owl.

"We are not amused?" Darcy pursued, determined to break down the barriers of his dark world.

He sniffed. "Not really." But gave her one of his *Wow, you're a crazy woman* looks and shrugged his pathetically thin shoulders. He did seem to find her amusing at times, which was a start. We'll get some flesh on him out here in the country, she resolved, but first off, we'll get shot of those awful specs and get him some trendier clothes.

On impulse she suddenly asked, "Did you get on with your mother?"

Alisdair stared at her dumbly. "Well did you? I mean, were you friends? Do you miss her?" she insisted.

"We got on okay," he said with reluctance when she pressed for an answer. "But she was busy a lot of the time."

"Because of her work?"

"She had her picture in glossy mags," he offered defensively.

Some substitute. But all Darcy said was, "One up on the kids at school huh?" and saw mingled pride and embarrassment flit across his face.

"The kids thought she was brill – real sharp."

"From her pictures?"

"She came to speech day and things."

"Oh, sure. Hey, you'll be starting your new school next week," she said cheerfully. Enough was enough for the first time; no point in pressing him too hard.

"Is it far?" he asked looking anxious.

"Only a couple of miles. There's a school bus stops in the lane each morning at eight. But we might just get you a bike."

"A *mountain* bike?" he breathed.

"Maybe," Darcy teased. "More soldiers with your egg?" she said getting up from the table.

He shook his head. "*Soldiers?*" he repeated with scorn.

"You're never too old," she reproved him, camping it up. "Even I'm not too old for soldiers. Mind you," she said giving him a wink, "I prefer mine in uniform," and was rewarded with a grin.

"I've got to go now," he said scraping back his chair and snatching his jacket from the peg on the door.

"Okay, but don't dare come back without at least some of Caesar's treasure!"

"I don't think he got this far north," he said straight-faced.

If only he wasn't so serious about everything, she thought, then caught the gleam of mischief in his eye. "Out!" she ordered, realising with pleasure that he was having her on.

Did we make a small breakthrough here? she wondered, watching from the doorway as he ran down the path on his way to the lodge.

*

The traffic was light, the weather good and she made the *Manchester News'* office in record time. Frank Kelly scowled at her over the top of his reading glasses. "Hell, Darcy, you must be mad, going into exile in the frozen north!"

"It's not exactly Siberia, Frank," she said with a grin. He's looking better these days: now that his wife's stopped cheating on him, and he's cooled his affair with the whisky bottle. Good old Frank.

"Might as well be," he grumbled in his rich north country voice. Picking up the cigar that smouldered in the ashtray, he leaned forward and looked pugnacious. "Change your mind, girl; it's not too late." He rammed the fat cigar into his mouth.

"It is," she replied calmly. "It's my brother's kid, for God's sake, and after the other night, I'm not even going to try and bring him up here." Her first piece for Frank since Alisdair's arrival had been based on her experience at the station.

"But why you?"

"There's nobody else."

"End of argument." He removed the cigar from his mouth and leaned back on his chair. "Okay – just keep the goodies coming. Meet your deadlines – and whatever you send we'll print. Within reason, of course," he added scowling.

"I appreciate it Frank – letting me keep the column."

"We owe you one, kid," he said gruffly.

Darcy forbore to say more, knowing he referred to her last investigation and wrongful dismissal. "That's all history now," she ventured.

"I hope so. Don't go getting into mischief up there in the sticks."

"I won't." Darcy laughed and walked to the door. "Anyway, I intend coming here on a fortnightly basis; just to keep my hand in, if that's okay?"

"You bet! That way I can keep an eye on you. Besides, you'd best keep in touch with life in the fast lane. We don't want a column on W.I. meetings and the latest thing in sheep dip!"

"Very droll Frank. Can you really see it?"

"Not really. But that's the rub as they say. If there's trouble about – you'll find it. You take care now, d'you hear?"

"I will." She opened the door to leave.

"Oh, er, Darcy-"

"Yes?" She turned and looked at him inquiringly. Why the hell was he looking so fidgety?

"I saw that husband of yours the other day."

"Brant!" she exclaimed spontaneously, then strived to sound cool. "Oh, where?" as though they were talking about a mutual and minor acquaintance.

"The club."

She picked an imaginary hair from the lapel of her jacket. "What did he have to say?"

"Not a lot. We debated the state of the country and the lunch menu."

Darcy refused to meet Frank's eyes, but couldn't resist asking, "So how did he seem?"

"Like a man who's angry on the inside. You sure must have hurt the guy."

"Bullshit! I don't matter that much to him," she said bitterly.

"So why did he want to know if you were still at the flat?"

So that was it, the thing Frank was nervous of telling her. "Christ Frank, you didn't give him my new address?" she said, making a theatrical gesture. It wasn't easy to play indignant when her heart was racing.

"You ain't fooling anyone, Darcy. 'Specially not me. I like you too much and have known you too long."

"I don't know what you're talking about."

"The only person you're fooling is yourself. Wake up my girl! You thought he'd come running after you but he's too much of a man. And if you ask me," he yelled as she yanked open the door, "You've gone and cocked it up further by taking on the boy."

"See you Frank."

Darcy left his office and let the door bang shut.

*

She had known he would come, but had not expected him to be waiting as she got out of the car at Westwalls. She had not exactly forgotten how good-looking he was with his dark hair, lightly-tanned 'outdoor' skin, his lithe limbs and easy way of moving, and that irritating but also attractive air of authority, but the impact of his physical presence still came as a shock. A man's man her father had called him, whatever that may mean.

"Hello, Darcy."

She stared at him without answering. Did he still walk the fells with Brock and Mab, she thought irrelevantly, picturing him striding over the cliff top with his two springer spaniels.

"Are you going to ask me in, Darcy, or keep me standing here all night?"

Nobody ever said her name quite like Brant. Stupid, the way it used to reduce her to putty, she told herself. Well not any longer. "I suppose so." She took out her key and opening the door, went inside.

"Gracious as ever, I see."

There was no gleam of affectionate amusement in the smoky eyes, not like there would have been in the early days. Frank had been right about one thing: this was one angry man.

Not that I couldn't get him back if I wanted, she soothed herself, dumping her bag on the kitchen table and turning to face him with defiance. "Why have you followed me here?" she demanded.

"I arrived before you actually."

"You know what I mean," she said irritably. "What do you want?"

"To offer my assistance. I heard about Alisdair."

"*How* did you find out?"

He gave her a look as though to say 'come on now, do you really need to ask,' and she exploded. "Oh of course, the Department. How silly of me. I forgot they know every detail of our private lives."

"Don't be childish Darcy. There has to be security."

"Privacy is a dirty word to them." She turned her back. "I suppose you want coffee?" She filled the kettle at the sink and banged it down on the Aga hot plate.

"Why have you moved in here?" he asked, watching her as she took the lid off the jar and spooned coffee into two cups.

"That's not your concern."

He was round the table and by her side in a flash. Taking her by the arm, he swung her round to face him. "Let's get one thing clear – you are not my ex-wife yet – so for the time being, you *are* still my concern."

Darcy stared at him, her heart racing. *He still loves me and wants me back.* The rush of power was heady but short-lived as the maggot of doubt began to gnaw at her triumph. Don't be gullible, she told herself. "Don't you mean the business of the Department?"

"That's nonsense, and you know it," he snapped.

But wasn't that why he had come here? Because National Security now counted her a risk? The Department liked tidiness in the lives of its senior officers, not runaway wives and separate homes. That meant difficulties with surveillance and control. The bastards. And Brant Kennedy was the worst of the lot. He didn't still love her at all; he was annoyed she had caused him aggravation with the Authorities.

"You're hurting me," she complained, trying to free her arm from his grasp.

"Don't tempt me, Darcy. I've never slapped a female, but you're the one woman who could change all that," he said grimly.

"Is that what you've stooped to now – threatening a defenceless female?" It sounded phony and clichéd even to her own ears.

He laughed unpleasantly. "Cut the theatricals. You're about as defenceless as a black widow spider. Now, where's Alisdair? It didn't take you long to palm him off to get back to your work."

"How dare you! It has nothing to do with you, but I'll tell you anyway: Alisdair is with Mr. Ambrose who sold me this house. Alisdair relates well to him, and he is a gentleman – which is more than I can say for you. Now take your hands off me." She tried to prise open the fingers of his left hand, then with a pang recalled how the sun-bleached hairs and the chrome of the Rolex watch against the sunburned skin had once made her pulse quicken. The memory, and her own vulnerability, made her struggle harder.

"Now listen to me." He forced her to look him in the face. "That poor kid had his life wrecked along with his parents' car on the motorway. I happen to care what becomes of him – and that's why I'm here."

She recalled that Brant's mother had died when he was a child. No wonder he felt for Alisdair and was willing to get involved. "I do know all that; I'm the one who's giving him a home, remember?"

"Is that what you call it? With a rackety female who traipses across the country sniffing out 'scoops' instead of sorting out herself and her marriage?" he said scornfully, releasing her arms.

"What marriage?" she cried, whipping away from him to put the table between them. "Half the time, I didn't even know where you were."

"At least you knew I would come home; I have no such consolation."

"Is that so?" Unexpected tears sprung to her eyes at the memory of the awful nights of waiting, not knowing if he was dead or alive. Or who he was with, though she would never let him know of her insecurity. She recalled that his first wife had run off with another man. At least she could put him straight on that one. "I want you to know there's nobody else."

"And I'm supposed to be grateful for that, I suppose."

"Maybe," she was stung into replying. "After all, there has to be something wrong, when two wives up and leave you," she added cruelly.

They glared angrily at one another across the table. "It would have been less disruptive for Alisdair had you taken him to the farmhouse," Brant criticised.

"In *your* house? That's a ridiculous idea. You and I are separated."

"Are we? Thank you for clarifying the situation," he said caustically, "I was never quite sure."

Darcy flushed, knowing he referred to her failure to contact him since the night she left. She hadn't dared; the sound of his voice, or worse still, sight of his face would have undone her resolve.

"It's your house too. I wouldn't have bothered you there, had you consulted me." Refusing the coffee she banged down before him on the table, he moved to the door. "When I heard you'd taken on Alisdair, I dared hope that for once you'd learned to care for someone other than yourself. I also thought you might be ready to give a reason for your desertion."

"*Desertion?*" Darcy echoed, outraged.

"Correct."

"Of all the pompous –" she fought for control over her emotions. "I owe you no explanation Brant Kennedy," she retorted, her cheeks and even her lips white with anger.

"Fine. Then we'll leave it to the solicitors to thrash out, shall we?"

Darcy's eyes widened with shock but she answered smoothly. "Just as you like."

"I shall be back to see Alisdair," he said coldly before leaving the house.

As she heard his car revving up outside, Darcy wondered why she should feel like weeping on account of a man she no longer loved.

*

When Alisdair came running down the path, she had to work hard at putting her troubles aside and showing enthusiasm for his finds: a couple of encrusted objects that he assured her were Roman nails, and a scrap of almost unrecognisable leather, complete with corroded metal stud. By contrast Alisdair's countenance radiated pride and excitement.

"Excellent, but will you be allowed to keep them?" she asked doubtfully.

"Mr Ambrose reckons so."

"Then I suppose it's alright."

He replaced his 'treasure' in a black lacquered box given to him, it seemed, by Mr. Ambrose.

Darcy peered over his shoulder and frowned. "What's that carved on the lid?"

He looked up at her. "A pentacle – for protection. Mr. Ambrose says it will keep my treasure safe."

"Looks sinister to me," Darcy said, not bothering to hide her disapproval.

Alisdair turned to confront her. "You're thinking *Hammer House of Horrors*, aren't you?" he accused. "That stuff's just fairy-tales-for-grown-ups!"

Darcy pushed her hair back with a gesture of annoyance. "Okay, so put me right."

"The pentacle is an ancient sacred symbol," he stated with an assurance beyond his years. "In itself it's not good or evil. It's the same with nuclear energy: it can be used to wipe out disease – or the world! It depends on who's using the power."

"Has Mr. Ambrose been filling your head with all this?" she demanded.

Immediately there was a wariness in Alisdair's expression, and his mouth reverted to its familiar sulky line. "But it's true."

"Look, don't take it all too seriously, Alisdair. Mr. Ambrose is an elderly man living alone in the country. He's a bit well, eccentric – and out of touch with life out there."

Far from being cast down by this as she had feared, he answered cheerfully and with a new confidence. "No he's not; he knows all about dead stars, quasers and black holes, and stuff like that."

Defeated, Darcy retired to the pantry to fetch eggs and mushrooms for tea.

*

Alisdair sauntered over to inspect the contents of the pan. "I heard a car when I was coming down from the fell." He dipped a finger in the bowl of pancake batter and licked it. "Who was it?"

Darcy suppressed a sigh then said shortly, "Brant." Turning, she saw that he had a stricken look on his face. "Don't panic – he says he'll come back to see you," she admitted reluctantly. They could do without this emotional upheaval now that Alisdair was showing signs of responding.

"Great! When?"

"He didn't say, so I wouldn't count on it."

Alisdair's face fell a little, but then he nodded with confidence. "He'll come, you'll see."

"Okay, wash your hands ready for tea," she said throwing him a towel off the Aga rail.

"So you had a good day with Mr. Ambrose?" she said to change the subject.

He wiped hands covered in dirty lather on the clean towel. "Ace!"

His face had lit up again. He even had colour in his cheeks, Darcy noted.

"I told him your 'soldiers' joke and he laughed."

"I bet he did," Darcy said dryly.

"I said I wished I could always be happy and cracking jokes, and guess what he said?"

Darcy held out the pan to toss a pancake. "I've no idea; tell me."

"He said you were just as unhappy as me."

Darcy cursed as the pancake splattered the stone floor.

*

That night in her bed under the eaves, Darcy had to admit that Frank had been right about two things: Brant's anger, and the fact that she had expected him to come running after her long before now. It was a bit of a body-blow, she reflected, to learn that when he finally came, it had been to see Alisdair and not herself. A good job it was only her pride that was hurt. That, after all, was the only thing disturbing her sleep.

Seven

~

In the privacy of the lodge, Mr. Ambrose smiled to himself and peered into the web. Ah, so he has come. Here he is, next to the Darcy-girl. He touched the crystal lightly with the tip of a yellowed nail. Will they help or hinder each other in this quest? Whatever, the time had come now to set the thing in motion; jiggle the web so that each strand vibrates and the lives they support, for good or ill, interact.

He moved to the window embrasure. On a tripod stood a green leather-bound telescope with brass bands and screws along its length. A handsome object; an old friend. Swivelling the barrel he put the glass to his eye. Mercury leapt from the backdrop of night, blazing blue and green fire. It hung in the firmament: a huge crystal emitting points of light. One of the oldest stars, a witness to the beginnings of the Universe. He began to hum, softly and off-key, then sang in a voice that though cracked with age, was strangely potent:

> *The bright star of the East brings dawn's first breath*
> *The watery star of the West brings Life's emotional quest*
> *The summer-star of the South fires poet and bard*
> *But the dark star of the North brings to Earth*
> *Retribution, Silence and Death.*

As he moved away from the embrasure, the light from the planet appeared to magnify. It focused with the intensity of a laser beam as it streamed through the diamond pane window. He watched it form a blue crystal hologram at the centre of the room, where it trembled and pulsated with life. All forms were present within the complexities of its pattern. The blue-print for Life. Or was it merely his imaginings? How much was dream and how much reality? He ground his knuckles into his eyes. When he opened them again, he half expected to find that the image had gone, but it shimmered a moment longer, then disappeared.

He made his way back to the web. In spite of his wasted flesh and fragile bones, he moved with the agility of a younger man. Illusion or not, the game is all, so let's set it in motion. He plucked at the nearest thread and watched the movement ripple through the web.

Eight

~

Darcy was frowning slightly as she poured herself a second cup of coffee. Alisdair had just left the house and she had time now to sit and think. Progress, she told herself, was definitely being made. He had chosen his new glasses from the optician's at the nearest town, which was twenty-six miles away, and they would be ready for collection in ten day's time. She had also taken him to the school outfitters where he was kitted out with the appropriate uniform and sports strip, along with some trendy leisure clothes that transformed his old-fashioned image and gave his self-confidence an instant boost. Best of all in Alisdair's eyes, she had bought him the coveted mountain bike which he was now pedalling each day to and from the local day school. Apart from some teasing by his new classmates, he seemed to be settling down there. So why the feeling of unease?

Well for one thing, he was forever round at the lodge. Each evening he would gobble his tea and rush round to borrow the metal detector, then instead of just returning it, would stay there talking until bed-time. Whilst growing in assurance as a result of his friendship with Mr. Ambrose, he was becoming increasingly secretive and odd. On several occasions, when he had thought himself alone, she had caught him humming a strange and haunting tune. This in itself was nothing, she supposed, but the minute he saw or heard her approach, he would look guilty and stop. Finishing her coffee, she decided to stroll across to the lodge herself and sound Mr. Ambrose out.

She called on the pretext of borrowing some milk, provided by Jemima, Mr. Ambrose's nanny goat.

"But do you think it's a good thing for a young boy to spend so much time here?" she asked, sitting down but declining his offer of tea.

"Are you about to deprive a lonely old man of company?" he said craftily.

"Why have you chosen loneliness?" she challenged.

"Does one choose it?"

"Come Mr. Ambrose, you are fit, have all your faculties and are very articulate – yet nobody ever visits you, and you to my knowledge, never leave the place. It seems well, unnatural to me."

"I have no inclination to leave. And those who have need of me – and from whom I too have something to learn – *do* come to Westwalls, do they not?" he asked, raising dark bushy eyebrows that contrasted sharply with the white of his hair. He rested his elbows on the arms of his chair and interlaced his bony fingers with the forefingers forming a steeple-like point. "As for it being unnatural, I find the constant pursuit of pleasure more so."

"Is it wrong to be happy, to seek pleasure?"

He gave her a penetrating look. "Can one who constantly *seeks* pleasure, be said to be truly happy?"

She shrugged and conceded the point by her silence.

"I refer not to wholesome joy in life," he continued, "but to the constant round of parties, holidays, spending sprees and possessions – *anything* as long as we don't have to be quiet and still! Pleasure as anaesthesia is what I am talking about. People use these things to dull the pain of awareness. The greatest fear of this age is the fear of confronting oneself."

"You could be right at that," Darcy admitted, feeling strangely uncomfortable.

"Oh, I am. People are like little boxes, separated from their beginnings and only happy if they are wearing the correct label: like 'boss', 'employee', 'householder', 'shareholder', and so on. The miracle of the seasons, of sunrise, of a rainbow, or the voice of a mountain beck is lost beneath a welter of domestic detail: the clamour for the 'newest, biggest and best'."

"How do we get off the merry-go-round?" she asked, knowing he spoke the truth.

"We must look to the Alisdair's of this world, the next generation."

"That's why you encourage him isn't it? He's beginning to see the world your way," she said with sudden insight, and not a little fear.

"Not quite – yet. But the seeds are there and always were. He is a rather special young man. He has an eye for the elegance of Science, and for the infinite beauty of Space and stars. He shall form the bridge."

"Bridge?" Darcy asked, bemused.

He nodded sagely. "Between the Old and the New, between Science and Myth."

Darcy put a hand to her forehead in a distracted manner. What was going on here? It felt safe and intimate to be sitting in this room talking with Mr. Ambrose. As though she had done it before. A long-lost memory of safety in childhood, of familiar things in the dark. If she closed her eyes, the outside world might easily disappear; cease to exist, along with her pain about Brant. Because seeing him again had caused her pain, and no sense in denying it. But he was speaking again. "To me it is sad beyond anything to lose magic in mediocrity. Take care, my dear, that you are not about to trade your little portion of magic for predictability and routine."

She stared at him speechless. Of course, he couldn't have known she was thinking of Brant. But could he be right? Had she lost that which was precious by demanding safety and time-tabled togetherness from Brant?

The blue of his eyes had deepened, and the steeple formed by his fingers was pointing uncomfortably in her direction. "Playing games is fun. Playing games but pretending to others that you are not is even more fun! But playing games and pretending to *yourself* that you are not, is merely sad."

There was something about him, something that made her suddenly afraid. "I have to go," she said abruptly, getting up and moving to the door.

*

Determined to throw off the sense of unease, she walked briskly through the garden, taking pleasure in its show of abundance. But somehow the early spring sunlight was dimmed, the bird song less resonant and the scent of blossom less noticeable than before. She could not shake off the feeling that something had been set in motion, and that a dark cloud hovered on the horizon. Back inside the house, she threw herself into working on a piece of copy for Frank.

*

That evening Alisdair rushed out as usual after bolting his tea and dashing off his homework, saying he was going to search for Roman remains on the fell. An hour or so later he rushed into the kitchen where Darcy was sitting, excitedly shouting her name, and holding what appeared to be a skull in his hands.

Nine

~

Darcy rose from her seat by the window. "What on earth have you got there?" she asked, moving forward to inspect the peat and soil-encrusted object.

"It's a skull, it's a skull," Alisdair babbled in his excitement. His eyes behind the spectacles looked more owlish than ever, and his hands trembled slightly as he held out his precious burden.

"It could be I suppose; but it's a bit big," she said doubtfully. "Sorry Alisdair, but I can't see that beneath a Roman parade helmet!"

"It's not *Roman*, silly!" he said with obvious disdain. "Prehistoric more like."

Darcy's 'reporter's nose' began to metaphorically twitch, as it so often did before a story broke. The family jokingly said she was 'psychic', an idea she had always rejected, but since coming here it somehow seemed less idiotic. If this really was evidence of humanity's earliest ancestors, the story could be worth a fortune. Alisdair was burbling about having found it on the fell near the section of exposed wall; there could be more remains buried there. Her mind sped into action. How to get it identified without risking a leak? *Caro.* She would take it to her friend at Hilldean University for identification. Caro had put leads her way before and would be discreet.

"You're not listening," he complained.

"Yes, yes I am, Alisdair," she said, rummaging in the drawer by the sink for a plastic bag, "put it in here, and I'll get it looked at for you."

He hung back however as she held open the bag. "But what about Mr. Ambrose?"

She looked down and stretched the plastic wider. "I think we'd be better saying nothing, Alisdair," she said quickly.

He was looking mulish. "But why?"

"Think about it!" she said impatiently, "this might be something big. He won't want the media tramping all over this place, and might forbid us to do anything with it. He may even take it off you," she added, seeing him waver.

Conflict was written all over his face. "I'll have to risk it," he said at last, lowering his find into the bag. "It wouldn't be right if I said nothing. Come on, let's go!" he cried, his excitement returning as he raced for the door.

Darcy followed, torn between exasperation at his naivity and pride in his honesty.

*

A moment of silence and stillness ensued. There was a strange expression on Mr. Ambrose's face as he stared at the object now lying on his table.

"Is it a skull?" Darcy asked from across the table, whilst Alisdair shifted from one foot to the other in his impatience.

Mr. Ambrose peered at her over his gold *pince-nez*. "I think not." He returned to his examination, using a small brush to gently remove the encrusted reddish earth: a result of the iron ore it contained. "Though I admit I thought so at first," he added, pointing to the cavities that resembled eye-sockets beneath a jutting brow bone. And the smaller ones below could easily have been nostrils, Darcy concluded. "Are you sure?" she insisted, but he carried on working without making a reply.

Minutes later, she frowned and studied the thing more closely. Mr. Ambrose's brush had revealed a sort of marbled surface of black and ochre which looked incredibly hard. But the reason for her concern lay in the faint glow that emanated from the whole sphere, but in particular from the yellowish areas, now that the dirt had been brushed away. She touched Mr. Ambrose on the sleeve. "Is it my imagination, or –"

"No, there is a phosphorescence," he interrupted without looking up.

"What's causing it?" Alisdair demanded, pushing between them to get a closer look.

"Some sort of energy," Mr. Ambrose replied. "Move back: better be safe than sorry. Some of these fossils collect above-average levels of radioactivity – especially when, like this specimen, they have lain in granite."

Instinctively Darcy took a couple of steps backward and pulled Alisdair with her. "I think we should get this thing looked at," she said as Alisdair wriggled from her grasp and returned to his station at the table.

Mr. Ambrose turned his head and his eyes held a gleam of irony. "I rather thought you might."

"Well, you can never be sure with these things," she protested.

"Of course not."

It was said with old-fashioned courtesy, but she felt a prickle of annoyance at the smile which hovered at the corners of his mouth.

"I'm off to see my boss tomorrow in Manchester," she went on, determined not to be put off. "On the way back, I'll call in at Hilldean University, if you like. I have a friend – Mrs. Caroline Stevens – who is Senior Lecturer in the Department of Archaeology," she explained swiftly, then shifted uncomfortably in the ensuing silence.

"Can I come? Can I come?" Alisdair chanted, dancing up and down on the spot.

She detached his fingers from her sleeve. "You'll be in school, Alisdair," she said firmly, then added as she sensed a storm brewing, "I won't take it at all if would prefer?" which had the effect of reducing him to immediate compliance.

But Mr. Ambrose's permission was still not forthcoming.

"Oh, *please*, Mr. Ambrose," Alisdair pleaded.

Mr. Ambrose looked long and hard at Alisdair, then at the skull-shaped object on the table. He gave a strong impression of a man making a weighty and momentous decision. Finally he turned to Darcy and scrutinised her face. "Very well," he sighed at last, "I suppose you must."

"Thank you. But if you really feel I shouldn't-" It was a token gesture, and she saw that he knew it.

He suddenly looked old and tired. "Take it. Take it now," he said, dismissing them with a wave of his hand.

Scooping up her prize, Darcy glared at Alisdair and jerked her head in the direction of the door. Once there, she hustled him out of the lodge before Mr. Ambrose could change his mind.

⁂

The following morning she got Alisdair off to school by ignoring his pleas and protests, and with a promise to report everything to him the minute he came home. True, he had demanded a last look at the skull-thing as he called it, and so she had opened the boot of the car where she had stored it overnight in a cardboard box, given its mysterious glow, and allowed him an arms-length-only inspection.

Satisfied, he had pedalled off philosophically, if not with willingness, to school.

*

Whilst appreciating the beauty of sun and mist on the fells, and the purity of the mountain air, she was looking forward to seeing Caro again. The trees as she drove past the lodge already formed a canopy, despite the earliness of the season, yet this morning there was an odd feel to the garden; a sort of super-stillness that far from evoking tranquillity, brought to mind the proverbial lull before the storm. Shrugging it off as imagination, she turned on the car radio and left Westwalls behind.

*

"God, this feels good." Darcy had to speak up to be heard over the laughter, chatter and clinking of glasses in the Langdale Bar at Hilldean University. She smiled across the table at her friend. "You look good, Caro. Love the ethnic outfit. You're looking so trim too."

Caro laughed and looked askance. "No way – but just keep it coming!" she commented dryly. "Crash diets are out from now on. I've accepted the fact that I'm more Earth Mother than waif."

"Thank God for that," Darcy grinned. "You're great as you are. And I wish I had your eye for colour and texture."

"You don't need it – you've got a waist instead."

"Oh, it's lovely to laugh with you again," Darcy said, reaching across to briefly touch Caro's hand.

"Well yes, but you shouldn't have left it so long," Caro reproved her, replacing her drink on the coaster after taking a sip.

Darcy held up both hands. "I know, I know. But with all the trouble – well, you know how it is." She also drank from her glass and wiped the froth from her mouth with the back of one hand. "Good beer. Makes a change from wine."

"Campus wine is only for masochists; 'Jennings' is the safe option. It comes from a brewery up your way – Cockermouth. But stop changing the subject: Brian's always asking how you are. Why didn't you let us help? That's what friends are supposed to be for."

"Sorry, Caro, but I just had to shut myself off and throw myself into work for a time."

How can I tell her, Darcy thought hiding her face behind her glass, that to see her and Brian together, and so obviously happy, would only make matters worse.

"It's good to be back in good old Langdale," she said, looking around her. "It hasn't changed much, has it?"

Caro regarded her quizzically. "No but you have."

Darcy shrugged. "Maybe."

"You've lost your sparkle."

"I'm just tired. Alisdair is rather trying."

"Poor kid." Caro looked sympathetic.

"Poor me."

"Oh, you are having trouble with the men in your life," Caro said with a solemn expression.

Darcy grimaced good-humouredly, and studied the Toulouse Lautrec posters on the walls, and beneath them the groups of earnest-looking students leaning over their beer and putting the world to rights. So naive of them, to expect it to listen. But that was her problem wasn't it? That was how she had changed. Since leaving Hilldean for the sometimes glitzy but often seedy world of journalism, she had somehow lost her innocence. Or had she only become blasé and cynical since walking out on Brant? She brushed the thought aside. Today was an 'away day', a reunion to be enjoyed. However, Caro, it seemed, was thinking along the same lines.

"How are things in the real world then? Between you and Brant, for instance?"

"The pits."

"That bad?"

"Couldn't be worse," Darcy confirmed, brushing the crumbs from her cheese and french bread off the table and pushing aside her empty plate. "Frank told him about Westwalls, and Brant turned up there the other day. We weren't getting on of course, but I had no idea he could be such a bastard."

Caro finished her last mouthful of soup and put the dish aside. "Why, what happened?"

"He was so aggressive. And actually accused me of desertion!"

"I see."

Darcy waited for Caro's outrage, but it wasn't forthcoming. Instead her friend appeared to be studying the Tiffany-style ceiling lights.

"You don't agree with him?" she demanded, frowning.

"I didn't say so. But you did leave without explanation, and you've made no move to get in touch," Caro ventured.

"I had my reasons," Darcy began heatedly.

"Hey, I'm on your side, remember?" Caro said with a smile. "But I'm trying to understand how he feels too. It's my guess he's been through hell since you left, and now he's scared."

"Brant Kennedy? Don't make me laugh, Caro. He's afraid of nothing."

"Except love – and the hurt it brings. His first wife, and now you. I suspect he still loves you, but daren't show it."

*

Darcy accepted the apology of a youth with a ponytail who jogged her elbow in passing. "He's not hurt, he's *angry*," she asserted.

"But anger is only hurt turned outwards," Caro insisted, pushing back her thick auburn hair.

"Well if you're right, tough. He's blown it."

Caro gave her a sceptical look. "I don't believe you."

"You'd better. I wouldn't have him back now if he begged."

"Haven't you got that the wrong way round?"

Silence fell as Darcy stared at Caro. "What do you mean?"

"Just what I said: that it was you who walked out without a word. It would be Brant, surely, who would be taking *you* back?" Caro said gently. "And now," she said before Darcy could erupt, "Let's take a look at what Alisdair found on the fell."

*

Darcy removed the cardboard box from the boot of the car and carried it up to Caro's study in the Department of Archaeology.

"It's not a skull," Caro declared almost immediately. Then as Darcy's face fell, went on to say, "But whatever it is, it is very old." Rising, she closed the venetian blinds at the window and switched off the light. In

57

the darkened room, the phosphorescent effect was pronounced. For a second or two, Darcy could have imagined herself on the set of a sci-fi movie. The eerie yellowish glow from this thing that dated back to God knows when, was unnerving. "What is it?"

Caro, who had opened the blinds again and was busy examining the object, shook her head. "I'm not sure. But I have an idea, and would like to check it out. Can you leave it with me for a few days?" she asked, straightening up.

"Okay." Hesitantly Darcy agreed, though privately found herself worrying about Mr. Ambrose's probable reaction.

Walking back to the car, her attention was caught by the avenue of aspen trees that bent and thrashed like flails in the rising wind. She shivered and increased her pace. The wind was turning cold.

Ten

~

Mr. Ambrose was sitting on a rustic seat in the enclosed garden behind the lodge. He tilted his face to the morning sunlight which warmed his chilled flesh. It was early yet. The sun was still low in the east and a heavy dew spangled the herbs and shrubs. Reaching up he tugged at the brim of his panama so that it shielded his eyes. He may as well enjoy the garden whilst he could, for the changes were already evident. How sad; how inevitable it all seemed.

As he listened to the blackbird whose song today seemed increasingly poignant, he contemplated two moss-covered stone figurines – one a maiden, the other a young man – on the low wall at his feet. Leaning forward, he picked up the man and placed him next to the girl. "There my children. I wish I could help you, but the play is with yourselves," he murmured. He watched, sorrowful, as a dew-drop slid down the worn cheek of the maid and dripped onto the lichen-encrusted wall.

Eleven

~

A couple of days after her visit to Hilldean, Darcy was putting the finishing touches to her copy when she heard the low growl of an engine followed by a knocking at the front door. Odd: she wasn't expecting anyone and Mr. Ambrose used the back door. Cursing beneath her breath she left her typewriter and padded down the hall. "Brant!" She was acutely aware of the shabby ankle-length skirt, faded shirt and flat sandals that constituted her working gear.

"You look fine, Darcy," he said with a gleam of amusement in his eyes.

She coloured faintly and sucked in her breath with annoyance. He knows me too well, she thought.

He was standing with one hand in his trouser pocket, the other arm raised and leaning against the door jamb. His laid-back air made her hackles rise.

"Alisdair is at school," she said laconically.

"No problem. It's you I want a word with."

Her heart lurched. *What about? Legalities? A divorce?* The post – left in a rusty box at the gate – was a daily gauntlet to be run. So far, none of the envelopes she so nervously scanned on removing them had borne the obligatory three-barrelled name of a firm of city solicitors. Not that she feared divorce, she told herself; she would welcome it – when it suited. She, not Brant, would be the instigator. "You had better step inside then." She opened the door wide and smothered a strong desire to slap his face, given the look of amusement that told her he had caught the drift of her thoughts. But one didn't slap Brant.

She preceded him down the hall to the sitting room, but he stalked past the door and entered the kitchen. "I normally show *guests* into the sitting room," she said pointedly. After all, he could scarcely threaten her with lawyers as he had done on his last visit, and still expect to be treated as family. To her annoyance he simply smiled and sat down at a table slatted with sunlight and dappled with leaf-shadow. Outside the window a wood pigeon crooned, a peaceful sound at odds with the tumult of her emotions.

"So what do you have to say?" she demanded, pouring coffee from the pot standing on the Aga and placing the cup before him. Refusing to sit down and join him, she stood at the opposite side of the table.

"Now that I know your whereabouts, I've arranged for what I judge to be an adequate sum to be transferred from my bank to yours on the first of each month," he said crisply.

"I don't want your money; I have my job."

"And I have my principles."

"You mean your *pride*," Darcy retorted. "I suppose paying for your freedom makes everything alright?"

He gave her a long look, and she couldn't help noticing that the blue of his shirt deepened his eyes to the shade of a winter tarn, but one that reflected clouds instead of sunlight.

"No Darcy, it doesn't. But life on your own is hard enough; I don't want you also struggling for money."

So *he really does want his freedom*. Pain made her brittle. "Oh, but I don't find it at all hard. In fact I'm enjoying my independence."

"I see," he said slowly

She had to turn away from his scrutiny lest he see the truth in her eyes.

"I've also set up a trust for Alisdair, and a small monthly allowance," he went on, stirring his coffee before raising the cup to his lips.

"That's a trifle high-handed. Alisdair has no claim on you – or you on him," she added, pain driving her to cruelty.

"I've not done it because he's your nephew," Brant said coldly. "He is a bright boy who wants to be a physicist. Youngsters with both the vision and capability are thin on the ground. If he's still of the same mind on leaving school, then the money will pay for his education and training. I owe it to my profession," he said austerely.

"And of course, we have to do what's right by the Department."

She hadn't meant to let the bitterness show.

Brant rose and walked round the table to stand beside her. "That was uncalled for. And what about *your* career? There's not much you wouldn't sacrifice for a scoop, Darcy – including marriage to me, I suspect."

"That's a lie," she accused, flushing with anger.

"Oh? What about the time I got tickets for Paluccini at the Covent Garden Premiere? And what did you do? Pass it up for a lousy story about petty council corruption."

"I'd been working on that for months." Feeling to be at a disadvantage, she stood up to face him. "I couldn't help that it blew just then, as you very well knew. And it wasn't petty. It made the nationals – but I got there first," she added defiantly. Brant was being so unfair: the great tenor was one of her life's passions; she would have given almost anything to be there. He must know what a sacrifice it had been.

"Big deal. I hope the knowledge keeps you warm at night, dear."

"I don't need to rely on that if I'm cold, Brant Kennedy," she was stung into replying.

"What do you mean, Darcy?"

He had taken a step nearer so that she felt his breath on her face.

That, and the quietness of his voice should have been warning enough. Hurt pride made her plunge recklessly on. "That I could soon find somebody else to keep me warm."

His hand flashed out and he caught her by the arm. "Say that again and I'll kill you."

She stared, wanting to defy him, but too afraid. She had never seen such an expression on his face.

"You are still my wife – and don't forget it," he said, relaxing his grip on her arm.

Darcy remained silent but triumphant. "In name only," she taunted.

"We can soon remedy that." He pulled her roughly to him and kissed her hard on the mouth. She went rigid in token resistance, whilst inwardly exulting that he had claimed her again. Inch by inch she melted, letting the heat of his kiss melt the ice of her pride and resentment. She kissed him back, tentatively at first, then with all the passion of their first coupling. His arms were around her, his hand stroking her hair as in the early days, and once more she felt loved and cherished, and marvelled at the sensation. Oh, how she had missed this. The tip of his tongue glided over her lips and her breath came quick and hard. Instinctively she moulded herself to his body and felt the hardness of his passion. His fingers fumbled with the buttons of her blouse until the gap was wide enough for his hand to slip through. She made a moaning sound as his fingers made contact with her breast. Overpowered by the force of her feelings, she leaned with all her weight against him, and he half carried her to the door.

"Where?" he whispered in her ear.

Darcy took his hand and led him into her bedroom.

*

He does want me; I knew he did. Now they could go home to the house on the cliff. Afterwards, Darcy lay naked in bed, a smile on her lips, making plans for the future. Alisdair could go with them. Brant would be good for him. The sound of running water from the bathroom and the gurgle and bang of antiquated pipes made her smile. She stretched luxuriously, her hands grasping the brass rail of the bed above her head, then slowly released it as she relaxed again. How awful life could be one minute, and marvellous the next. They would enjoy long walks again along the cliffs. She would tease him as she used to, run away along the shoreline splashing in and out of the incoming waves, and he would chase her, catch her and then make love to her in the cave at the hidden bay beneath the cliff overhang. Aroused by the delightful fantasy, she became impatient for his return. She was about to call him when the bathroom door opened and Brant walked into the bedroom.

She knew immediately by his stiff posture and air of reticence as he entered, a towel wrapped around his slim hips, but refused to believe it. "Brant?" She rolled to the edge of the bed and opened her arms in invitation, but he turned his back, began putting on his clothes. "What are you doing?"

She stared in dismay as he pulled on his trousers and buckled the belt. He couldn't be doing this. He couldn't make love like that, then just leave.

"Brant?" Still he said nothing. "What are you doing for God's sake?" she cried, clambering out of bed and running to him. "Why are you acting this way, what's wrong?" She tried to move close but he grasped her forearms and held her at arm's length.

"I'm sorry Darcy, I shouldn't have done it. It won't happen again."

"But it's alright! I'll come home, and then we –" she faltered to a stop beneath the chill of his gaze.

"This hasn't changed anything Darcy. I never promised it would."

"But we've just – you can't do this."

"It was good. We enjoyed each other's bodies, but that's all."

She shook her head vehemently. "No! No! It wasn't like that – and you know it."

He had soared with her, she was sure of that. They had floated together connected by more than their physical bodies. But then she heard Caro's words again: *he's afraid of love.* "Brant, don't do this."

He picked up the towel from the bed and wrapped it around her nakedness, as though seeing her vulnerability caused him pain and embarrassment. "Don't upset yourself, please. Forget it happened."

Darcy stared into his face, her eyes huge, her cheeks bloodless, then raised her hand to hit him.

He caught her wrist. "Don't do that, Darcy," he said quietly, releasing her hand. "Now I'm going. It wouldn't work out, and we'd have to go through all this again. I'm sorry I've caused you more pain."

"No, it won't be like that," she cried desperately as he walked to the door.

He paused on the threshold. "I promised to take Alisdair to the observatory some time ago. I'll pick him up on Saturday if you'll have him ready. It's better that way."

Something inside Darcy snapped. "You bastard, Brant Kennedy. You absolute bastard!" She hurled the words at him like missiles. He flinched as though they had found their target, then left without another word.

*

When the first storm of weeping had passed, she showered, dressed – and feeling oppressed by the house and the memory of what had just taken place there – turned to the garden for refuge. She walked first in the cultivated area closest to the house, then left behind the flowering shrubs and cottage borders to follow a path which led to an iron gate that squealed on its hinges. On into a walled garden with box hedging and a crumbling sandstone sundial; a secret place when even this early in the season flies buzzed and bees droned as they collected nectar. In summer there would be drifts of alchemilla, vervain and lavender, and all manner of sweet-scented herbs she supposed, but its present sparseness and air of neglect was more in keeping with her mood.

How could he do this to her? Fresh tears of hurt and humiliation rolled down her cheeks, then brushing them away with her hand, she allowed anger to take over. She had been getting by alright before he had reappeared, and she would do so again. Rising from the chamomile seat where she had been sitting, she paused, her attention caught by the two worn stone figures on the low wall before her. "He'll only break your heart," she said aloud, and stooping took the male figurine from beside the maiden and placed it on the far side of the wall. The absurdity of her action made her smile despite her pain.

Picking up the path again she followed it over a rustic bridge, pausing to lean on the rail to watch the beck tumbling beneath. Then on through a water garden with a tranquil pool covered in lily pads, weeping willows and brown velvet bulrushes, and then the wild garden with its meadow of nodding windflowers, and beyond that still to the woodland that eventually merged with the open heather-clad fell where Alisdair had found his fossil.

Wandering through a copse of native birch, oak and rowan, she felt her stomach lurch on glimpsing a figure crouched in a clearing ahead. Indistinct in the waving grasses and sun-dapple, it had about it an air of unreality. She stopped in her tracks and blinked several times, no, it really was there. She crept closer, keeping to the tree-cover. On the edge of the clearing she stopped, and laughed nervously. It was a *statue* for God's sake. Of worn and weathered stone, it was carved as much by the elements as by human hand. The surface was a patchwork of green moss and grey and yellow ochre lichens. But derision faded as the figure exerted its presence. Squat and female with huge rounded breasts that exuded sensuality and power, despite one eroded nipple, it dominated both clearing and wood. The belly was full and round, suggesting pregnancy and fecundity, and was achingly beautiful in its primitive way. The curves of her arms sang with a strange symmetry, and her hands were folded serenely on her naked and potent thighs. The features had been eroded by time and weather, giving her a timeless and universal appeal. This, Darcy decided approaching, was Everywoman, the epitome of the female.

"Do you like her?"

Darcy spun round, her heart thumping. "You gave me a fright," she accused, her hands pressed to her chest. Mr. Ambrose was behind her, standing quite still. There had been no sounds of approach: no rustle of dried leaves underfoot, no swishing of grasses and no snapping of twigs.

He bent to sniff the windflower stuck in the buttonhole of his cream linen jacket. "But do you like her?" he repeated, raising his head to give her a quizzical look.

"Yes." She paused, head to one side, and considered the statue. "She *is* very old; and yet she speaks to me. She is me, in some strange way." She spoke naturally, despite his frostiness since learning the fossil was now at the University.

The blue eyes pierced Darcy to the soul. "Then listen to her – and heed what she says."

"Who is she?" she whispered.

"*Gaia, Dea Mater, Cybele, Isis* – the choice is yours; she answers to them all."

"How old is she? Where did she come from?"

"She just *is*."

With a jaunty tilt of his cane, Mr. Ambrose turned and walked away into the sun-haze. So swiftly did he disappear, that for one ludicrous moment Darcy found herself doubting that he had ever been there.

She remained for a while, allowing the peace and tranquillity of the glade to seep into her and soothe her wounds. Eventually, she left the Mother-statue as she now thought of her, to her solitary and leafy bower.

*

On returning to the garden, she noticed that the drifts of naturalised daffodils and narcissi were looking faded and old. She had been so pre-occupied with her own distress that she hadn't noticed earlier. Dropping onto one knee, she saw that the petals were brown and beginning to curl at the edges. She looked about her and felt a sudden chill. The lilac blossom had a dry and singed appearance, and reaching up to pull down a branch, she realised that the scent, so powerful a short time before, was now completely gone. The blossom on the spirea was also fading, and the new growth on the clematis was tinged with brown as though nipped by a late frost. Was that possible?

Feverishly she cast her mind back. No, it had been unseasonably mild. However much she would like to believe it, a freak frost was not the answer. So *what is?* The only anomaly she could bring to mind was the thing Alisdair found on the fell. Ridiculous to suppose that its removal from Westwalls could have such an effect. Was that what the Mother-statue was telling her? Warning herself that Brant had affected her sanity as well as her nerves, she went back into the house.

Somehow she had got through the day. Alisdair would be in shortly for his tea. Pouring herself a hefty gin and tonic she settled down on the sofa, then recalling that she had bought some batteries when in town with Alisdair, rose and selected a tape from her collection. The extraordinary power and tenderness of Paluccini's voice rose to the beamed ceiling and filled the room. The poignancy of *Che gelida manina* swept over her, transporting her from her own little sadness to a bitter-sweet world of star-crossed lovers and high tragedy. The barriers came down; she wept unrestrainedly as she listened. But there was comfort too in joining the legions of heartbroken lovers, and identifying with the exquisite pain of their loss. As the last note died away she dried her cheeks and felt able to face the world again.

Twelve

~

Darcy received a letter from Caro asking if she could meet her at Hilldean that afternoon. If not she was to telephone Caro from the village
and let her know. However, as Alisdair was now attending school, there
was no problem, and Darcy set off for the University in a state of plea-
surable anticipation. Caro, she figured, must have some information
about the fossil.

*

Caro was in her study waiting when Darcy arrived. "So what news?"
Darcy asked impatiently once the social preliminaries were out of the
way.

"Well, it's as I thought: the thing Alisdair found is not a skull," Caro
said, taking her jacket from the hook on the door.

"So what is it?"

"I'd rather not say anything just yet," Caro said guardedly. "There's
somebody I would like you to meet. A sort of 'distant colleague once removed' if you know what I mean."

"Okay, I'm game."

"Good. Let's go."

"Where?" said Darcy looking bemused.

"To meet Julian Cain, the colleague I've just mentioned."

"Is he in your department?"

Caro put on her jacket and held open the door. "Archaeology? Oh, no."

"So what does he do?" Darcy asked, passing through the door.

"He's in physics. Quantum physics to be exact."

Darcy, her mind reeling, fell into step with Caro who was walking
briskly towards the Physics Department.

*

Into the building, up the stairs and then along the first floor corridor. Cold tiles, white paint and the smell of disinfectant. Not a building to warm to, like Sociology or Philosophy, both of which had been temporary 'homes' to Darcy during her student days at Hilldean. Here was an atmosphere redolent with hard theory, empirical method and state of the art technology.

"Here we are."

Caro had stopped outside a door marked: *Prof. J. Cain* and she tapped lightly upon it. "He's quite famous in the world of physics: we're proud to have him at Hilldean," Caro whispered as she opened the door in response to a summons from within.

*

Darcy found herself in a room flanked with benches containing microscopes, banks of computers and a host of complex-looking equipment. The centre of the room was set out as a mini-conference or seminar area, with carpeted floor, easy chairs and a rolled-up slide screen. The man seated behind the desk was a million miles from the grey-haired scientist with precise manners and grave expression that she had been expecting. The man now rising to his feet had black wavy hair, intense brown eyes and swarthy good looks. He was smiling broadly and exuding a suave charm. He also had a devastating dimple dead-centre chin.

"Caro! Hi, come and sit down." He surged forward to greet them, and as he came from behind the desk Darcy realised he was all of six foot two and that his teeth were T.V. commercial whiter-than-white. "And this must be Darcy," he said, once Caro had been greeted and ensconced in a suitable chair.

He turned the full power of his smile onto Darcy who felt herself responding. "Hi, Darcy; I'm Julian Cain, glad you could make it."

"Pleased to meet you, Professor Cain."

"'Jules' will do just fine."

As she sat down, Darcy glanced at Caro and raised an eyebrow at Cain's familiarity.

"Coffee everyone?" He picked up the hand set of the internal telephone on his desk as Caro and Darcy both accepted. "Moira? Rustle up coffee for three, please. And now," he said replacing it, "I'm sure Darcy is wondering what the hell all this is about."

Why so gushing? He was, Darcy thought with sudden suspicion, acting like someone who had something to hide. And he had in his possession that thing from the fell. "Where is it?" she asked, looking around her pointedly. "I don't know if Caro told you, *Professor Cain*," she continued as an embarrassed silence fell, "but the object that was found does not belong to me. I promised Mr. Ambrose, the owner of the property, that it would be returned within the next couple of days."

"I'm afraid that won't be possible, Darcy," he said smoothly, ignoring her question and fastening upon the second part of her speech.

His proprietary tone caused Darcy's hackles to rise. "What do you mean?" She threw a questioning glance first at him, then Caro who shifted uncomfortably on her seat. Before either could answer a knock sounded at the door and a secretary walked in with the tray of coffee.

"Good girl. Just put it down there please, Moira. Mrs. Steven's will pour."

He indicated a low table and the girl put down the tray, gave him a sugary smile and departed.

"I'll let you explain whilst I see to the coffee," Caro said, setting out the cups on the table.

"Yes, do," Darcy said sharply. If he thought he could pull status over her, he had better think again. Neither was she going to fall for his charm like that stupid girl who had just gone out.

"I take it you know from Caro that it's not a skull?" he asked, suddenly the professional. His eyes, Darcy noted, had lost their look of lazy charm and were focused upon her like twin lasers.

"Yes. Other than that, I only know that she wanted me to meet you," Darcy said with a darkening look at Caro, who merely smiled and handed her a cup of coffee before pouring out two more.

"Yes, it's an odd coincidence that the elements and natural faults in the mineral should have resulted in that particular shape. The hollows channelled by underground water resemble the orbits and nasal openings characteristic of *homo sapiens Neanderthalensis*, but coincidence it is," he concluded, accepting a cup from Caro.

"I accept that," Darcy said with an impatient gesture. "So *what is it?*"

Jules Cain crossed one leg over the other and pushed back the waves of his hair with one sun-tanned hand. Darcy noted the attractiveness of the gold signet ring against the dark skin, then abruptly brought her mind back to what he was saying.

"I think it could be a meteorite."

"Oh." Darcy's face and voice must have conveyed her disappointment for he hastily added, "But maybe a rather special one. As it is —" he paused, interrupted by Caro's bleeper.

"Excuse me, Jules, may I use your 'phone?" Caro said, putting down her coffee before getting up from her seat.

"Sure; go ahead."

Caro crossed to his desk and spoke quickly and quietly into the internal telephone.

"Sorry, I have to leave," she apologised, replacing the handset. "Meet you back at my office, Darcy, when you are through, okay?"

Picking up her briefcase, Caro hurried out.

"Now where were we?" Jules Cain continued, his tone deepening to greater intimacy now they were alone. "Ah, yes. You see there are only around 2,500 known meteorites in the whole world, so they are quite a rare phenomenon."

"Oh, I had the idea they were always whizzing around up there in space – you know, meteorite showers and all that," Darcy contributed, relaxing despite herself.

"True, but not many survive their passage through the atmosphere. They become incandescent due to friction with atmospheric atoms and molecules, and unlike micro meteorites which are less than 1mm in diameter, they vaporise before they can radiate away the heat generated by this friction."

"And Alisdair's meteorite?" Darcy pressed.

"Contains a good deal of iron, which is unremarkable; but also some complex particles that do not behave in orthodox ways."

"And what does that suggest?" Darcy pressed, placing her empty cup on the table.

"Its possible origin, amongst other things."

"Which is?"

"I prefer not to commit myself to an opinion at this stage," he said smoothly.

"Why did you say I couldn't take it back to Cumbria with me?" Darcy demanded, aware that he was determined to divulge nothing and that there was little she could do about it. If only Brant hadn't rejected her so cruelly yesterday, she could have gone to him.

"You will have noticed it emits a glow; we know too little about it yet in terms of safety."

Darcy sighed with frustration; there seemed little argument against that.

"I've already found evidence for the existence of a mutant charm quark with its anti quark," he said, uncrossing his legs and leaning forward on his seat. Darcy sensed his repressed excitement and her 'reporter's' nose was twitching; there was a story in here somewhere. As though realising he was giving too much away, he inclined his body at a more relaxed angle and rested his hand on the arm of the chair. "But I must seem to be talking gobbledygook," he said with a rueful grin.

Darcy, who had been reflecting on the fact that he probably didn't know she was a reporter, answered automatically. "Not entirely," she said whilst making a mental note to warn Caro to say nothing about her profession, "my husband's an astrophysicist so I'm familiar with some of the terms." Immediately she sensed his ears pricking like a hound on the scent, and cursed her carelessness.

The lazy brown eyes sharpened and focused. "Would I know him?"

"I doubt it."

"Try me."

The hound had a bone and wouldn't let go. "Brant Kennedy."

She had expected he would know of Brant who was respected and widely-known as an astrophysicist, though not of course, in his capacity as advisor to MI5 on top-secret space programmes; what she had not been prepared for was the expression of coldness and malice with which Cain greeted this news.

"Ah yes, of course I've heard of Dr. Kennedy," he said smoothly, so that she found herself wondering if his animosity had only existed in her imagination.

The previously persuasive voice was brittle as he added, "And has he not advised you on the meteor?"

Darcy's hopes of not having to divulge her marital status were shattered. "My husband and I are separated," she said shortly.

She saw him visibly relax, obviously in the hope that they were not *in communicatio*, and that Brant therefore knew nothing about the meteorite.

"So sorry to hear it," he purred.

Like hell you are! And the meteorite is the main but not the only reason, she thought wryly, noting the increased interest in his eyes as he watched her. He unfolded his arms; a moment ago they had formed a barrier across his chest.

"Despite the fact," he added, "that Dr. Kennedy and myself enjoy – how shall I put it – a stimulating professional rivalry," he said, bordering on archness.

"Which means you dislike one another intensely and hold opposing views," she said dryly.

"Your directness is refreshing, Darcy," he said good-humouredly, so that Darcy had to smile.

"So where is the meteorite now?" she demanded.

"The research laboratory, under lock and key." He indicated a door at the far end of the room.

"So am I right in thinking you can take a sample for your research, and return the meteorite to me?" she pursued.

"I'm afraid it isn't that easy." He smiled, and was once more his charming and undeniably attractive self. "Let's just say it would be safer to leave it in our care until we have more information."

"'In our care' is a very loose term; just what is going to happen to it?"

He laughed. "You're very astute Darcy. Let me explain: I am a *theoretical* physicist, which means I analyse particle traces sent here from the world's major physics labs located in the States and Europe. We don't have an electron positron collider, accelerator or detector in Britain, and when I tell you that the super proton synchrotron at C.A.D.E. on the Swiss/French border has an underground diameter of 7km, I think you will understand why."

"C.A.D.E.?"

"The Colliders And Detectors in Europe H.Q."

"I see. And you intend sending samples of my meteorite there for testing?"

"With your permission of course. Particles will be passed through the accelerator at impossible speeds to charge them. When they have reached maximum energy, the beams so created will be put into head-on collision to encourage the particles to interact. The UA2 detector will then convert the flashes of light emitted by the charged particles into electronic signals. The data will come back to me for analysis. So?" he smiled disarmingly at her, "Do I have that permission?"

Darcy hesitated, reluctant to let this stranger in, but otherwise she would get to know nothing. And she certainly had no intention of running to Brant. If she withheld consent, he would take samples anyway, and be alienated. "Very well," she agreed at last.

"Excellent; thank you." Having obtained his objective, Jules Cain visibly relaxed. "Tell me, you've just moved to the Cumbrian property?"

Darcy nodded, wondering what was coming next.

"Have you noticed anything unusual about the place?"

She paused, afraid of making a fool of herself, but he nodded encouragement. "It sounds silly, but there is a sort of super-abundance. Everything seems to grow at several times the normal rate. The greenery, the flowers that are like hothouse blooms, and the scents and colours have a far greater intensity." She decided not to divulge her latest observation, that this 'abundance' now seemed to be dying back. She saw that he was nodding, as though he had heard what he expected.

"It may seem far-fetched," he was saying, "but that meteorite, despite being buried deep in the earth, may have played a significant part in producing that effect."

"*Effect?* Is there any danger?" she asked in alarm.

"All such matter emits a certain amount of radio-activity," he stated, confirming Mr. Ambrose's opinion, "but this thing is only dangerous if handled intensively. I doubt you or the boy have been exposed to any risk. However," and he smiled seductively, "One cannot be too careful – I should greatly enjoy keeping a personal eye on you from now on!"

The smile, and the look he gave her, made Darcy look away and rise to her feet. "Well thank you very much, Professor Cain," she said shaking his hand, "it's been very interesting. Goodbye."

"Goodbye – for now," he said pointedly. "Maybe next time we meet you'll feel able to call me 'Jules'," he said, his eyes sparkling with fun. The warmth of his smile teased a responding one from Darcy. Watch it girl, she admonished herself as she walked to the door, you're acting like a green undergraduate.

Which reminded her of the scheme she had cooked up. It was a gamble: on Frank agreeing to put her under cover at Hilldean, and on Caro keeping the reporter bit secret. "Please let me know immediately you have any results," she said, pausing with her hand on the door handle. "Did Caro mention that I was doing my 'Masters' this year? So I'll be around Hilldean from time to time," she rushed on without waiting for a reply. A Masters degree was loosely structured, not requiring daily attendance, but frequent trips to campus would not be remarked upon.

"Even better. I promise I'll root you out as soon as I have any news."

"Fine. Goodbye Professor."

She left the building and hurried over to say her farewells to Caro.

*

Caro was eyeing her now with distinct unease. "I don't like it, Darcy," she said, frowning with concern.

"But you'll cover for me?" Darcy insisted. She could see her prize moving out of reach before the project even got started.

"I'll back up your 'research degree' story if that's what you mean."

"So what's the problem?"

"I don't know," Caro said slowly, swirling the coffee dregs round in her cup. "But for all his charm, Jules Cain is not a good man to cross. He's a high-flyer in his field; he's not going to be happy when he reads about himself in the paper. Or," she said giving Darcy a direct look, "by you conning him into thinking you were just a student."

"I'll square it with him before then," Darcy said dismissively. *One thing at a time, Caro; let's get the story first.* "Look," she said standing up, "You've been great, but I'll have to go now before Alisdair gets home from school – otherwise, I'll have Brant accusing me of turning my orphaned nephew into a latch-key kid," she added acidly.

And now to face Mr. Ambrose, she thought, walking back to the car park.

Thirteen

~

"No, no, N-O!" Mr. Ambrose faced her, his anger vibrating around the lodge. The waves bounced back at her from the walls, in the way they sometimes did when Alisdair threw a tantrum. She looked round, half expecting one of the pictures to crash to the floor. He had spoken with emphasis, yet had not shouted, nor even raised his voice, so why did it *feel* like he did? "I'm sorry, Mr. Ambrose, but it's done," she said firmly, looking him in the eye. "And to be fair, I had little choice, did I?"

The dark brows beetled over eyes of electric blue. "It was not yours to decide."

"Nor yours either. If it does have some importance, then it belongs to the nation."

He faced her with such a strange expression that Darcy was momentarily afraid. "Little ants, tiny boxes."

"Pardon?" She thought his mind must be starting to wander.

"Nothing. You are the victim of your own limitations," he said absently and half to himself.

Darcy shrugged and decided to ignore his ramblings. "Apart from anything else," she persisted, "we don't know the dangers."

"That will come from putting this thing into the hands of men."

Darcy sighed with exasperation. "They are responsible and highly qualified scientists," she protested.

He glared at her, and his eyes blazed blue ice. "And you my dear, are an extremely naïve and foolish young woman," he said with asperity.

Darcy bridled. "There's no need to be abusive."

"There is every need. You do not know what you have done, Miss West."

"Well I'm sorry to disappoint you, but I have to live in the real world out there," she snapped, gesturing at the door.

Mr. Ambrose regarded her steadily, then appeared to sag as the anger that had supported his thin frame left it like gas from a hot air balloon. He looked old then, and world-weary. "Yes. Of course you do," he said, nodding his bird-like head. "It has to be. It was there to be found, and Man must make what he will of it – and pay the price."

Darcy looked at him without speaking, suddenly chilled by premonition. Once more she was assailed by the feeling that something inevitable had been set in motion. It was as though she and Alisdair, in releasing the meteorite to Jules Cain, had unwittingly opened some secret gate, and the dread Horsemen of the Apocalypse had come rushing out into the World, the beasts' nostrils snorting fire, the whites of their eyes rolling, and their mighty hooves flailing the fragile air.

To her dismay, she saw that the lodge had changed: the sunlight that had dappled the worn Aubusson carpet had died as swiftly as the flame of a snuffed candle. Beyond the leaded windows the light had dipped, as on a winter's afternoon, and the foliage pressing against the glass for entry added an eerie green glimmer to the room. She shivered involuntarily, aware of dampness and chill.

She shook her head as though to physically dispel the illusions and fears that clung to her mind like dusty cobwebs. "I'm sure it will be alright," she said, backing towards the door.

"Do you think so?"

Her legs refused to move. The blue-gimlet eyes transfixed her, caught her like a fly in a web. In the gloom Mr. Ambrose appeared to have acquired extra height and presence. For the first time since coming to Westwalls, Darcy realised her vulnerability and isolation. She knew very little about this elderly eccentric. Granted he was physically frail, but there was something about him that brought a *frisson* of fear.

"Well do you?" he demanded.

"No," she whispered.

"You are beginning then to realise the folly of your actions."

She said nothing; the silence was unnerving.

"Very well – you will have to learn," he said at last, and there was sorrow in the blue eyes.

Darcy turned, and by making a supreme effort, managed to walk rather than run from the lodge.

*

Mr. Ambrose stood at the window looking out into the night. Up there the stars burned bright: pin pricks in eternity. He shook his head in self-disapproval. In Alisdair's parlance, he had almost 'blown it'. How easy it was to be ruled by one's emotions. He had forgotten that things were occurring in their natural sequence. Once Alisdair had dug the thing up, these other developments were inevitable. In themselves, Mother Gaia's gifts were neutral: they could be used for good or evil ends. It wasn't the child's fault, she was only playing her part. Her part in helping the Earth fight back.

He must not become too involved, make the mistake of caring about the characters rather than the scene. He frowned and pushed wisps of white hair back from his forehead. But without compassion there seems little point in fighting on. Are we, he wondered, deluded in thinking that without us humans, there would be no Earth? Perhaps. Mother Gaia will certainly not consider us if it comes to the choice. She must save herself – at any cost.

He smiled to himself as a white form with heart-shaped face glided past the window. Old Hushwing was on the prowl; all's right with the world. But not for long, he thought sombrely, moving from the window. Unless Darcy could see it through, and Alisdair be her light. Outside in the wood, the white owl screeched.

Moving to the web, he touched the thread which held the smallest and brightest crystal.

Fourteen

~

Is it beginning already? Darcy mentally shook herself for being affected by an old man's predictions and dire warnings. But where was Alisdair? Why should he go missing just now? She moved to the window for the third time and peered out. On leaving the lodge she had stepped outside into a silent world of mist. The white stream had swirled around her feet, muffling her footsteps on the overgrown path. No birds had sung in the branches of trees that appeared to float on a white and shifting sea. Coincidence, she told herself firmly.

She leaned her head against the cold glass, closing her eyes to ease the ache behind them, then opened them again almost immediately to peer anxiously through the mist in the hope of catching a glimpse of Alisdair. But there was nothing to be seen, except the grey ghost of Jemima wandering past on her way to evening milking. The camel bell attached by a cord around her neck donged dolefully, the sound muffled by the vapour. Darcy had just decided to take the car and go searching for him when she saw a dishevelled figure, pushing a bicycle and looking incredibly lonely, walking slowly along the path towards the house.

*

"Alisdair! You look a sight! Come over here in the light so I can see."

"I'm alright." Reluctantly he stood by the window and Darcy turned him to face the last of the daylight. "Well, that's the best shiner I've seen since your Dad was in the fourth form," she pronounced, surveying the already brownish-blue skin around his eye. Immediately she realised from his expression that this was the very best thing to have said. He's identifying with his dad, bless him, she thought with a rush of compassion. "Your glasses are cracked," she exclaimed, then taking pity on him added,

"I suppose we've just got to be grateful it wasn't your new ones." She stood back with her hands on her hips. "Good God, Alisdair, you look like you've been pulled through a hedge backwards!" she added, taking in the rumpled and spiked hair above the grubby face, the buttonless shirt cuff, and the thing skewed round his neck that resembled a piece of chewed string rather than a school tie.

"Okay, what happened," she demanded.

"Some of the kids at school," he mumbled.

"And?"

"They found out where I live and started saying things about Mr. Ambrose."

"Such as?"

"They said he was mad," he admitted with reluctance.

"Well, you know, he is a bit eccentric."

Alisdair looked sulky. "He's not *really* mad."

"Perhaps not. But to kids who don't know him, and don't have your super-intelligence, maybe it seems that way," she soothed.

"Well they won't say it again," he said darkly.

He's obviously held his own then, Darcy thought with relief.

"And what do you think of Mr. Ambrose?" she asked, watching his face carefully for a response, but he remained impassive.

"I'm going upstairs to get washed and changed," was all he said.

"In a minute," she said sharply. "I asked you what you thought."

She frowned. He was staring at her in that strange way that Mr. Ambrose had; as though he was looking at her with something other than just his eyes.

He walked to the door then turned. "I think he is magic."

Darcy laughed nervously. There was something about the way he said it. "Not literally, of course."

Alisdair, battered but undefeated, regarded her with disdain. "Just because you've lost it, Darcy!"

"So does Mr. Ambrose think he is, too?" she pried, becoming more alarmed. This was unhealthy.

"Maybe. But it doesn't matter whether he does or not. There's lots of them, you know – all over the world. People who just *know* things, things the rest of us have forgotten."

Darcy folded her arms. "Okay, explain."

"Didn't you do Ancient Myths at school?" he demanded, peering at her over his glasses, then continued without waiting for her answer. "It's true what Mr. Ambrose told me: it's in the Four Ancient Books of Wales – the Black Book of Carmarthen, the Book of Taliesin, the Book of Aneurin and the Red book of Camarthen. There's a spirit, a force, the Protector of Earth Mother; a Keeper of the Planet and all its beasts. It's about the universal power to heal. And a way of talking about people like Mr. Ambrose, who haven't forgotten. 'Magic' is just a quick way of saying all this. Like when you do your shorthand, Darcy," he finished.

"How come you were able to accept all these *myths* as real?" she asked sceptically.

"I just always knew. The stories are a way of talking about the force which protects the Earth; the Universe and everything in it. A way of making it real for us."

"So why aren't we all like Mr. Ambrose?"

"We are," he said simply. "We've just forgotten. It's easier for the protective force to come through some people than others."

"People like Mr. Ambrose, I suppose," Darcy said dryly, still unconvinced.

"Yes," he replied, and his sincerity made her regret her sarcasm.

"Because," he continued, "they lead simple lives, in tune with Nature, and the Earth's rhythms and currents. And it's working. People are beginning to feel the changes. It's everywhere. There's books and films and T.V. programmes and videos – and people talk about 'psychic' things and 'healing' all the time."

"Yes, okay, I have noticed," Darcy admitted with reluctance. "But why is it happening? Why the sudden interest?"

"Because the Earth is in great danger. We're killing it Darcy! There's a Universal Will, and the Earth will try and heal itself by awakening our forgotten sense. It will come through people like Mr. Ambrose, but it will also come out in Science and the things we discover. But it gets misused, for wealth and power. People like Mr. Ambrose are here to show people like me the way, because there's lots of *us*, too," he said ingenuously.

"Who? What do you mean?"

"Children who know. The ones who – when we grow up – have to try and sort out the mess. Try and put things right first by learning, and then teaching what we've forgotten: that we are part of everything, and everything is part of us." He walked to the door and turned to face her, with extraordinary dignity for one so young. "That's why I said, 'he's not *really* mad'; not like those kids at school tried to say. He's half-mad, half-knowing. Whatever he is, he will help us."

He ran upstairs and Darcy stared reflectively at the closed door. Was there any truth in it? Was that where Alisdair's special gifts came from? She shook her head and decided it was too much for her to handle. Better to say no more about it. It just wasn't helpful to challenge Alisdair's concept of Mr. Ambrose.

*

When he came downstairs again she bathed the discolouration around his eye and dabbed it with witch-hazel. "We'll go and collect your new glasses straight after school tomorrow. Then we'll stop at that posh cafe we found for a slap-up cream tea," she promised.

His face flushed with pleasure. "Great! Thanks, Darcy."

She stood up and ruffled his hair. "You're okay, kid," she said in a mock 'John Wayne' voice. She carried the bowl to the sink and emptied it, tossing the used cotton wool into the bin. "Anyway," she said turning to face him, "did you give 'em what for?"

He shrugged. "They got the better of me at first. There were three of them; that's when they gave me this." He pointed to his swollen and discoloured eye. "But then I remembered things. Things Mr. Ambrose taught me – and they ran off, scared."

"What things?"

"How to hurt them with my mind."

"But thoughts aren't physical things." She broke two eggs into the poacher.

"But they have physical *effects*," he replied with the assurance of an adult.

"So tell me."

He looked at her for a moment. "Okay, I will."

He perched on the stool beside the Aga, swinging his legs as he thought. He nodded. "Okay, here we go. It's like when you think of something really sad – like Bambi when his mum died, or E.T. wanting to 'go home', yeah?"

Darcy suppressed a smile and nodded.

"And you picture it in your mind. It makes you cry, doesn't it, if you think about it hard enough? And if you picture somebody slipping on a banana skin, or doing something really silly, then that *thought* makes you smile, right?"

Darcy nodded. "Okay. But that only affects *me*, not the other guy."

"That's because you don't expect it too. Mr. Ambrose says the only thing holding us back is belief in our own limitations."

Darcy whipped two pieces of toast off the hot plate before they could burn. "Good fighting talk, but when it comes down to hey lads, hey," she said spreading each slice with butter, "Uri Geller apart, influencing events with mind-power takes some doing."

Alisdair's face took on the familiar look of stubbornness. "Okay. How many times have you thought about someone, or said *please come*, in your head, and they suddenly 'phone, or turn up on the doorstep?"

"Many times," Darcy admitted. "Are you *sure* you're going to be a physicist when you leave school?" she teased.

"'Course, why?"

"Well given your powers of argument, I reckon you'd make a pretty good philosopher," she said with a grin, placing poached eggs on toast before him. "Eat your heart out, Wittgenstein and all that."

"You can laugh, but it works."

"Okay, I believe you." She mussed his hair as she passed.

"What happened about my fossil?" he asked before going upstairs to bed.

"Oh, God, we forgot all about it didn't we in the excitement?" Darcy exclaimed. "Well it's all exciting stuff." She related what had happened at Hilldean, how she had met Jules Cain, an eminent physicist, and how he was sending samples to Europe for testing. He seemed content with this, and after discussing the whole thing animatedly and at length, went off happily to bed.

*

Her mind was still in turmoil as the hands of the clock reached eleven-thirty. No point in going upstairs to bed; sleep would not come. She had tried reading but had read the same line repeatedly. Even Paluccini had failed tonight, played low of course so as not to disturb Alisdair in the room above – though he was not always so considerate with his pop music. Getting up she went to the window and pulled aside the curtain.

The mist had thinned. Perhaps a stroll round the garden would bring calm and eventually, sleep. Slipping on a jacket she took a torch from the shelf of the spice cupboard set into the wall and opened the kitchen door.

The night was humid and clammy. Tendrils of mist still snaked around the trees, and the knees of the moss and lichen-encrusted cherub in the rockery. He had one arm missing, but she felt this bestowed him with an air of noble antiquity. Even by night the garden looked less healthy, she worried, noting the drooping flowers and shrivelled foliage. Finding her way by watery moonlight and the glimmer that rimmed the fells night-long, she put the torch in her pocket and crossed the grass to the bridge, shivering at the touch of the dew on her bare legs. On the far bank the rustling and twig-snapping betrayed the presence of badger, vole and other nocturnal creatures. The herb garden was ghostly, still and silent, but it was upon entering the woodland that she first sensed it.

It arose however, not from the undergrowth but within her own head; a sudden image of a wild beast: nothing distinct, just padding feet, slitted eyes, snarl and fangs. The fear was all the more disturbing for having no apparent source. The lines were smudged like a charcoal sketch; a form that fled beyond the reaches of recognition. Just 'beast'. Almost simultaneously the thought came of what she would do if a roaming rottweiler or other crazed dog attacked her here in the wood, as her mind supplied an acceptable definition for the image. It also supplied the probable outcome: more snarls, a slow-motion leap, and torn flesh; her mutilated corpse found the following day, soaked in dew and blood. She shook her head to dislodge fearful fantasy. Fear then trotted alongside, soft-padded and silent. Her steps slowed as she took out her torch. She swung the beam to left and right, then to the rear. Nothing. Except that terrifying sense of beast. Extinguishing the light she hurried on. One didn't hear of crazed dogs marauding in English country gardens.

The squat figure brought a stifled cry to her lips. Fumbling for the torch she directed the beam with trembling hand. The Mother-statue. She gave a nervous laugh as the effigy leapt to life. The smile died on her lips. The pitted and sightless face mocked her; the eroded nipple was a chilling reminder that flesh – even that most prized by men and sacred to women – must in the end rot and decay. The chill crept through Darcy's bones and from there to her very soul, numbing the instinct for Hope, and for Life itself. A deep depression and hopelessness ranged the wood and seeped into her being. A feeling as dark, damp and cold as the stagnant pool nearby, whose surface was covered by the over-bright green of a creeping algae that was slowly choking it to death.

It was here that the beast feeling was strongest. A rancid odour, not unlike that of the dog-fox she had chanced upon one evening, but stronger and more unpleasant. The hairs at the nape of her neck prickled, and centuries of civilisation peeled away like the skins of an onion. *Wolf!* The primitive age-old alarm sounded within.

Almost immediately the howl haunted the night. Sweat broke out on her forehead; her legs threatened to give way. Then the rational part of her brain whispered words of sanity, told her to recall that there were now no wolves in the wild in Britain, and hadn't been for a long time. But as always in the end, basic instinct defeated reason and her heart thumped in her chest as the dread sound faded away. And why had Mr. Ambrose also come to mind? For without doubt, he lurked there, in limbic dark recesses, where the light of logic never reached. And to think she had thought his revenge had come with Alisdair's black eye! How wrong could she have been? How much could she have under-estimated him? But stop thinking this way – because here lies madness. You are out for a stroll in the garden, and there is nothing more threatening here than a fox or badger. Turning her back on the statue she stumbled out of the glade.

But here where the wood was thickest, the odour became oppressive, the illusion, if that's what it was, more difficult to dispel. Here she was forced to use her torch: moon and star glow barely penetrated the foliage or the low-lying mist which beaded her hair with moisture. The beam however had changed from white to a dingy amber as the battery weakened. Progress was of necessity slow: hidden rabbit holes and concealed stones waited to trip heedlessly fleeing feet. But run she did, staggering and lurching through the wood to escape the sounds of lupine pursuit. A *pad-pant, pad-pant* sequence in slow motion, and barely audible till she stopped. Then it filled her ears and jolted her heart. So did the musky wolfish smell.

Then she saw it. A glimpse of grey-pelted form, long mean muzzle and ears flattened in intent. A second, no more, then it had glided out of sight. She screamed and ran faster, turning to throw wild looks over her shoulder, her gaze raking the shrubs and undergrowth for her merciless pursuer. *Pad-pant, pad-pant.* Louder now and closer. Sobbing with panic she fought a feeling of unreality and overwhelming nightmare. Another glance behind, and she stood transfixed with horror. Her pursuer also stood still. The yellow eyes glowed like two lamps in the fog. Stone-cold and slanted they watched her every movement. *Pad-pant, pad-pant.* It was on the move again, shortening the distance between them, inch by panting inch. Soon she must feel its foetid breath on her face; feel the fangs in that blood-red mouth tearing her flesh as it leapt. She screamed and ran for her life. Her foot caught in a burrow and she sprawled full-length on the ground.

Fifteen

~

Half-fainting, she waited for the weight of its body on her back, the heat of its breath and the mauling pain of its bite. Nothing happened. Somehow she struggled upright again and began to run, all the time waiting for the thud of impact, to be hurled once more to the forest floor. *Pad-pant, pad-pant.* Lungs bursting she ran out of the wood and into the garden. Her legs flew over grass and flower bed, not pausing in their pumping until the back door latch was cold beneath her fingers. Sobbing aloud, she fell into the kitchen and banged the door shut.

*

Half an hour and a stiff brandy later she was lying uneasily in her bed, working hard at convincing herself that the whole thing was some sort of crazy delusion; one furthermore that had been induced somehow by Mr. Ambrose. Ideas, images, flitted around in her head like moths around a candle flame. Had he hypnotised her? Implanted some delayed-action suggestion? His hand was in this somewhere. Twice had she got out of bed to pull the curtain back a few inches and peer down into the garden. No dark shape stained the white gauze that still lay over the garden. No long-ago howl haunted the twentieth-century night. She was just about to yield to the drifting sensation that promised sleep, when a warning prickle at the base of her neck made her sit up, alert, in bed. Through the half-open door came the sound of voices.

*

Candle in hand, she stood on the threshold of Alisdair's room. He was sitting up, talking in an animated under-tone. Even more disturbing was the way he was leaning forward, focusing, as though conversing with someone seated on the bed. She took a step forward, opened her mouth to say his name, then froze. The shadow of a woman had appeared on the wall by Alisdair, just as it would appear if she was sitting talking to him. Darcy almost dropped the candle. The flame leaped and danced, throwing the shadow into manic motion. By the time she had her hand, and the candle flame, under control, the shadow had vanished.

Alisdair turned as she advanced into the room. She saw with a shock that his one good eye was wide open and alert; not closed in sleep or glazed like a sleepwalker's as expected. In fact his face was alight with excitement, despite the discolouration and swelling around his right eye which was now all but shut.

"Are you alright?" she asked, looking surreptitiously about her, but there was no third person in the room.

"Mum was here," he blurted. "She was talking to me."

She stared at him for a moment, taken aback. The candlelight, the silence outside and the shadow she thought she saw on the wall made his statement bizarre yet almost credible. "You've been dreaming, Alisdair," she said, sitting on the bed and taking his hand.

"Yes, I did have a dream," he agreed, nodded his tousled head and peering myopically at her: his glasses were on the bedside table, cradled in their leather case for the night. Darcy felt a rush of relief until he continued, "and in it I was using my computer and Dad's face appeared on the screen. He said they had something important to tell me. Then I woke up and Mum appeared. She was sitting on my bed, just where you're sitting now, Darcy."

Darcy shivered, recalling the shadow on the wall. "No, you were still dreaming; you only thought you were awake," she said firmly.

"I wasn't, I wasn't," he shouted, becoming agitated. "I *know* I was awake."

"Alright, alright," she soothed. "Look, there's this thing called *hypnogogic imagery*, Alisdair: it happens when you are under stress and you are in the limbo-land between waking and sleeping. The things you see and hear seem very real," she explained, recalling one of her psychology lectures in her undergrad days at Hilldean.

Had that beastly old crank been getting at Alisdair's mind too? Anger surged through her at the thought, which was compounded as he went on to say, "No – it wasn't anything stupid like that. It was no different then than it is talking to you now. She *was* here, and she told me to follow Mr. Ambrose and do what he says. She said he would help me to find myself and become a man."

"Oh, Alisdair." Darcy stared helplessly at him, not knowing what to say.

"Don't be upset, Darcy; I'm not. Mum said she and Dad are still with me – even if I can't usually see them. She talked about my physics; told me to always remember that energy once created only changes, it never dies; and that human consciousness is energy, so we never die either, we only change. She touched my eye, and now it doesn't hurt anymore," he finished ingenuously.

Darcy felt a huge lump rise to her throat. "Dreams can be a great comfort to us when we lose someone we love." The words sounded hackneyed and banal even to her own ears. But it couldn't be right to encourage him in these delusions. "But that doesn't alter the truth of what you dreamed, you know, about energy never dying. I feel sure you will see your mum and dad again, but not here in this life – and hopefully not for a long time yet," she said with a smile. "Now lie down, and try to go back to sleep," she said, leaning forward to brush the hair back from his forehead. As she did so, she gave an involuntary exclamation and stared hard at his cheek.

"What is it Darcy?" he asked, his voice sleepy now.

"Nothing," she said, tucking him up in his quilt.

It was just from one of his felt tip pens, that faint smudge of red on his cheek. Ridiculous, that it brought to mind Gloria, and the fact that she had been a model. And that Alisdair's mother would never have been seen anywhere without her lipstick.

Sixteen

~

The letter from Brant was a curt three-liner. He proposed to collect Alisdair on Saturday – the following day – to take him to the observatory. He asked Darcy to have him ready and to send him out to the car on his arrival. The last time she had seen Brant they had made passionate love, now it seemed he couldn't even bear to see her face. If he didn't want her now, well fine, but did he have to humiliate her in this way? If a small voice asked if she *should* mind being left behind by a man she professed to no longer love, she resolutely ignored it. The misery of rejection washed over her; she felt truly alone for the first time since leaving Brant. Tears stung her eyes and she angrily blinked them back.

At least Alisdair would enjoy himself; he'd been a trifle odd since that night – the one she preferred to forget. For one thing, his self-assurance had burgeoned. Diplomatically of course, she had suggested it might be sensible to see a bit less of Mr. Ambrose and more of the kids at school. Alisdair had given her a look of scorn and stated that he was learning from Mr. Ambrose all the time, whereas the kids at school knew nothing about the things that really mattered. When she had asked what things, he had replied airily, "Oh, Life – and the nature of Reality, stuff like that," in a way that was old beyond his years.

Something had then come to mind. *He will help you find yourself and become a man.* The words Alisdair claimed to have heard from his mother that traumatic night, and relating of course to Mr. Ambrose. Which wasn't good. Despite her own resentment against Brant, he had to be good for Alisdair at the moment. A younger no-nonsense man would surely redress the balance. In the meantime, she thought, finishing her coffee and leaving the cup on the drainer, she had to go see Frank and whet his appetite sufficiently to get him to put her under cover as an M.Sc. student at Hilldean.

*

Frank Kelly was eyeing her from across his desk with something close to despair. "Not again, Darcy. No – I absolutely refuse," he added as she opened her mouth to protest.

"You have to Frank," she said unperturbed. "Just imagine – if I'm not crazy but *right*." She leaned forward, resting both hands on the edge of the desk. "Fancy reading *our* story in all the nationals, with some big-name snotty by-line?"

"Shit!" Frank Kelly chewed on his cigar. "You'll be the death of me, Darcy-girl," he muttered, shaking his shaggy head. "No – no can do," he added.

"Hey, come on Frank, give a girl a break," she said with a grin, knowing herself to be more than half way over the winning line.

Frank took the cigar out of his mouth and pointed it at her. "Now let's get this straight: you want me to authorise you, under cover at Hill-dean University, to snoop on one of our top research scientist's programmes – and without the consent of Max Dearden?"

"That's about it, boss." She permitted herself a grin. "Our dear Editor-in-Chief doesn't need to know anything about it, does he?"

"You mean you know he'd refuse," Frank growled, sticking the cigar back in his mouth and rolling it from side to side. "The last time I went out on a limb for you, it almost cost me my job."

"It did cost me mine," she reminded him.

"That's emotional blackmail."

"Sure is. In your own words: you owe me one, Frank."

He stared belligerently at her for a moment, then grinned. "And so I do. Okay Darcy – but if it goes wrong, don't expect me to bail you out with Max Dearden; I'll deny all knowledge of it."

"Fair enough." Darcy got up and went to the door.

"By the way," Frank said as she opened it to leave, "how's things with you and that man of yours?"

"The pits."

"Time you got sorted out."

"He tries to bully me."

"He has my sympathy."

"See you, Frank – and thanks a million."

Reckless with triumph, she saucily blew him a kiss as she went out.

*

On the way back she stopped off at Hilldean, and after giving Caro an update over coffee, set off for the Physics Department to pump Jules Cain about news from C.A.D.E.

She raised her hand to knock at his door when the sound of angry voices made her lower it again. A voice she didn't recognise filtered through. "You may be the darling of the media, Cain, and you may hold the professorial chair, but I am still head of this Department. And I tell you I will not allow it."

Darcy glanced down the corridor to ensure it was empty before pressing her ear to the door. Jules Cain was speaking now, and rather than respect there was insolence in his tone. "I don't know what's bothering you, Ashford. I've told you already: Caroline Stevens came to me personally. This is a major find, and I have every right to publish."

"On behalf of the Department, maybe; but only with my backing," the man called Ashford retorted.

"Are you jealous, Ashford? Is that why you're trying to stop me publishing as an individual?" Cain's voice now held contempt.

"Don't be ridiculous. You are basing your paper on my previous findings on matter and anti-matter in particle physics. That is plagiarism, Cain. I also have reason to believe you are selling to the highest bidder – and I don't just mean your paper – regardless of nationality. There's an ugly word for that."

"It's the world we live in, Ashford. Take my advice and wise up to it."

It was the man called Ashford's turn to speak with contempt. "Not my world, thank God."

"You're envious of my popularity and success."

"I'll treat that with the contempt it warrants. Whilst I am here – I have reason to suspect you are conducting unlawful experiments. I want to see your private lab."

It was Cain's turn to sound angry. "No. You have no right to police me in this way."

Darcy heard somebody moving about the room. "It's locked, Cain. Open this door if you please."

"I most certainly will not."

"Then I shall get formal authorisation to inspect. I warned you, Cain; I shall report you to the Chancellor, and the Institute of Physics."

Darcy leapt back from the door as footsteps sounded and it was yanked open.

Whipping a spiral-bound pad from her pocket she flicked over the leaves as though searching through her notes. The tall man with sandy hair who emerged however, strode past without a second glance. His white face, Darcy saw, was blotched with spots of anger. They *must* have been arguing about the meteorite, Darcy reasoned: *a major find* and *the lead came from Caroline Stevens*; it was too much of a coincidence. As soon as his footsteps had died away, she made for the stairs, judging it better not to court suspicion by walking in immediately on Cain.

*

About half an hour later, by dint of asking around in her role as post-grad student, she discovered he was on his lunch break and contrived to bump into him in the refectory queue at Langdale College. She greeted him with a smile and what she hoped was a convincing look of surprise.

"Hi Darcy. One of your lecture days?" he inquired, placing a fish cake and a side dish of salad on his tray.

"Yes," she lied, taking a roll and a portion of cheese. "Coffee, black, please."

"There you go, love – oops, watch you don't spill it now," the plump, white-overalled serving lady said as Darcy took the cup and saucer.

Jules Cain was waiting for her, tray in hand, beyond the check out. "Join me?" he asked with a quizzical smile.

Darcy responded to what, after Brant's rejection, was welcome warmth. "I was hoping for a word, actually."

"My pleasure." He held her gaze a little longer than necessary.

She made no comment when he chose a secluded table behind a large pillar.

"You don't eat then in splendid isolation?" she asked lightly, sitting down.

"God, no!"

"Professors used to when I was here – as an undergrad, I mean," she hastily added, forgetting her supposed present status as a post-grad student.

"Stupid snobbery." He tipped his salad onto his plate. "So what did you want to see me about?" he asked, munching on his fish cake. He watched her speculatively, head to one side, as he chewed. "Not that you need a reason – delighted any time."

"I wondered if there was any news yet from C.A.D.E."

His eyes narrowed, lending him a vulpine look. "As a matter of fact, I have. And," he continued, leaning across the table, "it has been confirmed that the object found by your nephew is a meteorite."

"So Alisdair can have it back, and Mr. Ambrose will stop giving me hassle," she said craftily, putting down her empty coffee cup.

"I'm afraid it's not as easy as that."

"Oh?"

"No, you see, during the tests we did here, it absorbed a certain amount of radio-activity," he said smoothly.

Darcy, watching his body language, knew he was lying.

"Just tell him it's in our care for the time being, and will be returned as soon as it is safe," he said, obviously noting her disquiet. "But look, he said wiping his mouth with a paper serviette, "we can't talk here. How about meeting me for a drink after your lecture?" Obviously he was aware, as was Darcy, of the curious stares they were attracting from students and lecturers alike.

"I'm sorry I can't. Alisdair will be home from school in just over an hour."

His disappointment showed. "Wouldn't your Mr. Ambrose keep an eye on him?"

"Yes, but there's no telephone so I can't ask."

"Okay, I'll be over at Westwalls anyway on Monday," he said, pushing aside his plate. "If you remember, I asked if it would be acceptable for a couple of field workers to take *in situ* samples."

Darcy frowned. "No, I don't recall – is it necessary?" she pressed, thinking of Mr. Ambrose and not relishing another scene.

"The site of any meteorite is worth investigating."

"I'll see you at Westwalls then," she agreed reluctantly.

"Fine. And as you have to make such elaborate arrangements, why not make it worthwhile and join me for dinner?" he asked with a persuasive smile.

Darcy hesitated. Then she thought of Brant's rejection, and the need to get Cain to talk. "You win," she said smiling back.

"Excellent." Jules Cain's pleasure was obvious.

"I'll meet you at the gates – seven thirty," she said, rising from her seat.

As she walked to the door, she felt Jules Cain's eyes scorching her back.

*

It was, she told herself, feeling forced to justify her decision, simply an opportunity to do her job and pump Jules Cain about C.A.D.E. It had nothing whatsoever to do with his suave charm and good looks. So preoccupied was she that she didn't see the young woman hurtle round the corner until they collided.

"Hey, Darcy! What are you doing here?" a familiar voice said.

"Jen! I might have known," Darcy laughed, then mindful of her student role added, "What are you doing this year?"

Jen's blonde curls bounced over her forehead as she made the extravagant gestures that for Darcy characterised her old friend. "I got my M.Sc., so now I'm doing a year of applied physics."

Physics? What a stroke of luck, Darcy thought. "Brainy bitch! What area?"

"It's an 'energy in the workplace module'. And you?"

"Media research," Darcy said shortly, hoping that Jen wouldn't push it. "Physics? That's Julian Cain's department isn't it?" she added casually.

"Yes." Jen's face held a strange expression. "He's quite a dish. Every female on campus is queuing up to show him a naked bottom in return for his charm," she said with what Darcy judged to be forced brightness.

"I've always wondered why they gave quarks silly names like *bottoms* and *charms*; now I know – it was so students could make corny jokes about them," Darcy said grinning.

Jen tossed her head in a camp gesture. "You never did appreciate my erudite brand of humour." She gave Darcy a speculative look. "How well do you know him?"

"Slightly." Darcy had a flash of the old intuition. "Why, got a crush on him?"

Jen laughed, but again it sounded forced. "Hell no: too smooth by half. He'll not charm the pants off me, thank you. So what about you? Not married then? Or are you playing away from home?"

Darcy hesitated. "Separated," she said in a flat voice, "and not playing anywhere."

"Didn't work out, huh?" Jen gave her a look of sympathy.

"No." Darcy busied herself with adjusting the strap of her shoulder bag.

"Then it's time you did start to play again; no guy is worth trashing your life for."

"How about you and Mark?" Darcy side-stepped.

"Oh we split ages ago. You know how it was. Same old rut. He put the car in the local garage, me in the bed, and we'd both get our twice yearly service – and that's if we were lucky!"

"Oh, Jen, you haven't changed."

They were so busy laughing they didn't see the lecturer hovering, trying to pass them to enter the building. A sociologist at a bet, Darcy thought as she suddenly espied him; given his earnest expression, longish hair, wire-framed glasses and essential sandals. "Have you two got no lectures to go to?"

Jen, who had her back to him, swung round. "Yes, why?"

"Then why not go there and stop blocking the doorway?"

The two women laughed afresh as he stuck his books under one arm and pushing between them, stalked through the doors.

"It's been great seeing you again, Jen." Darcy said warmly. "Got to go now, but I'll be seeing you around, okay?"

"Fine. We'll grab a coffee next time, or something stronger," Jen promised, running up the steps to the Physics entrance.

Good old Jen, Darcy thought as she made her way to the car park. She always did cheer me up; and who knows she may even be of some help with the investigation.

Seventeen

~

The sound of a car horn being impatiently pressed penetrated the kitchen. Darcy gave her wrists and neck a quick spray of perfume and pushed the bottle back into her bag. "Alright, I'm coming." She tossed aside her serviceable Barbour and grabbed a blouson jacket from the back of the chair. Fumbling in her haste, she put it on and paused to run her hands lightly over the surface. Silk was that little bit special, and today she needed to feel good about herself. Being in Brant's company wouldn't be easy. And was there ever such an impatient man? she thought irritably, as the horn sounded another staccato *pip pip pip*.

When Brant had come to the door asking her to accompany himself and Alisdair to the observatory, she hadn't known whether to be annoyed or pleased. She still didn't know. It was preferable, she supposed, to being forced to send Alisdair outside whilst she hid herself indoors like some kind of pariah.

It seemed Brant had to keep another appointment directly afterwards, and required her to drive Alisdair home. Her proposed call on Mr. Ambrose would have to wait until they returned. She paused at the front door, composed herself, then opened it and walked down the steps to Brant's Landrover.

*

The drive to St. Gildas Bay was a tense and unpleasant one for Darcy. Brant largely ignored her presence and talked instead to Alisdair who proudly perched next to him whilst Darcy sat alone in the back. She felt excluded from their masculine company and conversation and wished herself back home.

"It's not turned out a bad day, has it?" she tried again, "weatherwise, I mean?"

Brant grunted. "How's school going, Alisdair?" he said pointedly. Misery washed over Darcy, who lapsed once more into silence. The sight of his strong hands, the backs tanned and the hairs bleached gold, on the steering wheel filled her with pain and anger. Such a short time ago, those same hands had intimately caressed her, and now it was as though she didn't exist.

*

They had reached the sandy track that wound beyond the village of St. Gildas to climb the flank of the cliffs. Eventually it brought them to the long flat summit, and the farmhouse where they had spent the idyllic first months of their marriage. Alisdair chatted incessantly, and asked Brant numerous questions. So different to her last trip up here, Darcy couldn't help thinking. To divert her mind from painful memories she watched the crowds of gulls wheeling and dipping over the cliff-top, tossed like scraps of white paper in the breeze.

The raucous *yuk yuk yuk* of their quarrels filled the salt-spray air, and several feet below, the sea creamed around treacherous rocks. Then the Landrover was cresting the ridge of Sheep Howe and despite her down-beat mood, Darcy had to smile at Alisdair's gasp of excitement.

The metal dome of the observatory rose from the grassland like a giant metal blister. Alisdair's 'high' increased as the vehicle lurched down the fellside. Brant jumped out and unlocked the padlock on the gate in the chain link fence which guarded the perimeter. "In you go." He selected a key from his ring and opened the door of a square building attached to the dome.

"This is ace!" Alisdair had pushed through first. "Can I tell the kids at school, or is it top secret?"

"Classified, of course." Brant replied solemnly. As he held open the door for Darcy to enter, their eyes briefly met and the ghost of a smile passed between them.

Brant led the way through a sliding metal door into the dome of the observatory beyond. Here there was a complete absence of daylight. As Darcy breathed in the cool damp air, memories of previous visits came flooding back. Brant had already flicked the switch that activated the row of lamps that ringed the dome, and which now gleamed redly. Another set of switches brought monitors clicking and humming into life, and eventually filled their screens with configurations and inter-stellar maps.

But it was towards the gleaming telescope on its circular platform at the centre of the dome that Alisdair gravitated. "Wow! Just take a look at this!" he exclaimed, staring open-mouthed at the giant machine bristling with cables beneath the apex of the dome. "But how do you get at the stars, Brant?" he asked, looking puzzled.

"Watch." Brant tapped a few keys and pointed to the apex. A whirring sound first, then a crack appeared at the centre, gradually widening as the two halves split like an oyster, revealing the sky above. A few more taps, then the telescope whirred, tilted and rose clear of the dome. "I can view any section of the hemisphere from here at the touch of a button," Brant explained to an awed Alisdair. "The positions are all programmed in." He demonstrated as he talked. "Here, you have a go."

"Can I really?"

In response to Brant's nod of assent, Alisdair – eyes shining – placed his hands on the keyboard.

"What's this one? And this?" His thirst for knowledge was unquenchable. With a smile, Brant flicked another switch and the screens exploded into colours of electrifying intensity. Streamers of light rose and cascaded into the ever-changing and complex patterns of an electronic fireworks display. "What are they?" Alisdair breathed, mesmerised by the living spirographs.

"Particle traces," Brant answered, and turned as Darcy sucked in her breath.

She returned his look blandly. Of course he couldn't know she had talked to Jules Cain about particle physics; her guilt was making her see a chance remark as a sinister reference.

"Is there something the matter?" he asked politely, with the solicitude of a near-stranger for his guest.

She shook her head. "It's just breathtaking."

He seemed satisfied with this and turned back to Alisdair. "Atoms, that is electrons, protons and neutrons, are sent through a massive underground 'ring' plant – the synchatron accelerator – several miles long, which artificially charges the particles. They are then put in a bubble chamber, and when charged particles collide they give off these traces of electromagnetic radiation which are photographed so we can analyse them later. We now know that atoms are made up of even smaller particles called quarks, leptons and bosuns, and that these are irreducible."

"What does that mean?" Alisdair asked.

"That they are the basic building blocks of all matter."

"Even us?"

"Even us," Brant concurred gravely.

"So we are part of the stars."

"That's correct. We are part of everything in the Universe, and of the Universe itself."

"That's what Mr. Ambrose meant then when he said 'nothing is separate' and that we couldn't do anything – good or bad – without it 'affecting the web and everything in it'. I think by 'the web' he must have meant the Universe, don't you?"

Brant smiled. "You must ask him."

"Yes."

"I've tried to discourage –" Darcy started to say.

Brant frowned. "Well you shouldn't."

It was said in an under-voice and Alisdair was too busy pressing buttons to have attended, but Darcy still felt put down, and fell silent.

"And here's the truly amazing thing, Alisdair," Brant continued, turning away from Darcy, "each particle leaves its own distinct 'footprint'. Because of this, we can now recognise different kinds of quarks: this green shape here," he illustrated, freezing the frame to point it out, "is a charm quark, and this blue pattern is made by an upsilon quark, and this similar pattern here is made by a J/psi quark with its anti-quark."

Alisdair pulled a face. "What on earth is an *anti-quark?*"

"To put it simply, every particle has its 'opposite number'. When the two meet, they annihilate."

"Why?" Alisdair asked, in the manner of children since time immemorial.

"The mass of both is converted into energy." Brant explained.

"Mr. Ambrose says that's what happens when we die."

Alisdair turned his back on them and began tapping the keys of the main computer.

*

Darcy and Brant exchanged looks. The boy was obviously relating this to his parents.

"He could very well be right," Brant said, touching Alisdair on the shoulder.

The subject was obviously closed; Alisdair's eyes and attention seemed to be fixed on the huge telescope which whirred and moved in response to his hands on the keyboard. "It's great," he breathed. "I wish I could come at night and watch the stars."

There was a silence, during which Brant looked thoughtful. "Why," he said at last, "don't you ask Darcy to take you back to the farmhouse for the night? Then, when I get back from my meeting, I'll bring you up here."

"Oh *brill!* Can we Darcy?" His eyes behind the new glasses beseeched her.

Darcy glared at Brant. "I'm sorry, Alisdair, it's impossible."

"Don't worry, you'll have your own room," Brant said in an undervoice to Darcy.

"Sorry, out of the question." She had no intention of risking a further humiliation; better by far to avoid the situation.

"It's not fair!" Alisdair's voice echoed around the dome.

"Tough, Alisdair; life's like that sometimes." Darcy turned. "It's time we went."

"I won't go. I'm staying here with Brant."

"I guess it wasn't such a good idea after all." Brant's glance at Darcy held the germ of an apology. He turned back to Alisdair. "Come on now, don't make a fuss. Some other time – we'll fix it up soon."

"No! Now – I want to go now!"

Darcy saw that Alisdair's fists were tightly clenched at his sides, and even in the subdued light, she could see he was white with rage.

"That's enough, Alisdair." Darcy stepped forward to take his arm but he backed away. His eyes looked malevolent in the unnatural light, his slight body rigid with frustration. "Stay away from me. I hate you! I hate you!"

Darcy let out an involuntary scream as equipment exploded in sparks around them. Electronic panels crackled and flashed, and the monitors shuddered, flickered and finally died.

"Look out!"

The telescope, released from its programmed position, swung crazily out of control. Darcy gasped as Brant's body crashed against her, knocking her to the ground.

A huge metal cable swung across where, seconds before, she had been standing.

Brant's voice sounded from close by. "*Christ!* We've got shut-down here."

Darcy felt somebody groping and grasping her hand in the blackness. "Are you alright Darcy?"

For a second, she wondered at the frantic concern in Brant's voice, "Yes, I'm alright," but the sentiment died as she was yanked unceremoniously to her feet. "Where's Alisdair?" she said in sudden panic.

"I'm here," a small voice informed them.

"Just stand still both of you: I'll throw the emergency switch." Brant's calm voice was reassuring.

"I'm sorry. Really sorry – I didn't mean to lose my temper."

"It's okay, Alisdair."

But as Brant began to feel his way towards the switch that was situated, Darcy recalled, by the door – the lights and monitors flickered, whirred, and shuddered on and off then stabilised. The monitors displayed their stellar maps and particle traces as though the equipment had never blown.

*

Once outside, Darcy proceeded to tear a strip off a very subdued Alisdair. Brant drew her aside and said in her ear, "Ease up, Darcy. It wasn't his fault, you know."

She shook her head in disbelief. "Oh no? So what caused it?"

He shrugged. "Probably a faulty fuse or connection."

"Sorry – I'm not convinced. It had something to do with Alisdair's anger."

"Don't go filling his head with superstitious nonsense."

"You had to, didn't you?" she said bitterly, resenting the implied criticism. "Well for your information, it isn't the first time something like this has happened." She turned away from him and marched towards the Landrover. "In, Alisdair." She held open the door. "And if you want a lift back to the farmhouse, you'd better get in too," she added to Brant, climbing into the driving seat. She looked straight ahead through the windscreen as he settled in the passenger seat.

*

It was an even more miserable ride back to Westwalls. Alisdair said little and Darcy even less. Brant had taken the car from the farmhouse; that meant he would have to pick up the Landrover tomorrow or Monday. She wasn't sure whether to be dismayed or pleased at the prospect. She cast a sideways glance at Alisdair, who had an expression of utter misery on his face. "Cheer up, Alisdair, it's not the end of the world," she consoled. But she still wasn't convinced by Brant's explanation of what happened back there. And something else was disturbing: all that talk about matter, anti-matter and annihilation. Jules Cain was a particle physicist. Just what sort of experiments was he conducting on the meteorite? Darcy again found herself wondering if there was a connection between the decay of the garden, and the removal of the meteorite from Westwalls.

Eighteen

~

The bad taste left by the incident at the observatory gradually faded. Whilst Alisdair was somewhat subdued throughout Sunday, by the time he left for school Monday, he had recovered sufficiently to make bad jokes and rude comments about Paluccini as Darcy played one of his tapes. And now, she thought as she watched him wheel his bicycle down the path, to pay Mr. Ambrose a visit.

*

On the pretext of buying a pint of Jemima's milk, for which Mr. Ambrose made a nominal charge to be placed in the Animal Rescue box in the porch, she presented herself at the lodge. Whilst waiting at the door, she frowned and reached up to touch the shrivelled strands of clematis that straggled over the porch. The garden was still looking sick. But then the door was opened and she found herself wondering what sort of reception she could expect after their last fraught encounter. Mr. Ambrose however, smiled and greeted her as though nothing ill had passed between them. Even so, the prospect of broaching the subject of Jules Cain's imminent arrival at Westwalls to dig up samples, was daunting. First things first, she decided, following him inside.

*

"Can I speak frankly, Mr. Ambrose, without it leading to a quarrel?" she said, placing her chipped china cup back on its saucer. Better attack in bold capitals and save the small print for apologies, as Frank would say.

"I doubt I could stop you my dear!" Mr. Ambrose poured a second helping of cream into his coffee and licked his lips in anticipation. "So, what is troubling you?"

"Alisdair's having nightmares."

"Dear me." He stirred his coffee.

To hide her annoyance at his apparent lack of concern, Darcy rose and placed her cup and saucer on the table. "He believes his mother actually came and sat on his bed."

"Sit down girl, sit down," he said gesturing irritably at the chair. "Don't hover over me like that."

Darcy hesitated then sat on the edge of the chair.

"And was he distressed?" Mr. Ambrose asked, wiping the rim of cream from his upper lip with a grey-looking handkerchief taken from his pocket.

"Well, no – but that isn't the point."

"Is it not?"

Darcy sighed with impatience. She was getting nowhere; time to ditch the subtlety. "Look, I can scarcely believe it, but I do feel you are planting suggestions in his mind."

"Really?" Mr. Ambrose picked up his *pince-nez*, placed them on his hooked nose and regarded her from over them.

"He's at an impressionable age," she continued, refusing to be intimidated. "And he's emotionally unstable at present, so please leave him alone."

"You mean, you want me to reject him too?"

Darcy stared at him, frustration welling up inside. *He was right, he had her over the proverbial barrel.* She mentally shuddered at the prospect of forbidding Alisdair to see his one and only friend. "No," she conceded, "but keep it light and stop meddling with his mind."

"Have you now finished speaking frankly?"

She bridled at the spark in his eye that told her she had not won.

"No," she said rising from her seat, determined at least to discomfit him by 'hovering'. "I want you to know that I'm also aware of your tricks against myself."

"But my dear Miss West, what can you mean?"

"I thought I saw a wolf in the garden," she stated bluntly. "Of, course, it was a delusion," she added, recalling the strange sense of unreality she experienced at their last meeting. "I suspect, a result of post-hypnotic suggestion."

"Well, the last wolf was shot in Scotland in 1785," he admitted, wagging his head as though perplexed.

"You are playing games with me," she accused, lifting up her head.

"Am I?" He picked up a pipe and after tamping down the contents with the tip of one bony finger, lit it with an old-fashioned petrol lighter.

She clenched her fists so that her nails dug into her palms. "I know it was a delusion, and I know that you were somehow responsible."

He puffed at the pipe then exhaled a cloud of blue smoke. "My, we are doing well."

"What do you mean?" His gaze, the piercing eyes, were causing her discomfort. The room felt chilly, as though a ghost had just walked through it.

"Well I did say you would have to learn."

"Learn what?" she said angrily. "That you can mess about with our perceptions and play irresponsible tricks?"

"About wolves," he prevaricated with an infuriating little smile.

"Did you know they have been re-introduced at Yellowstone Park? That there is talk of reinstating them in the Scottish Highlands?" He allowed a thin trickle of smoke to escape through his pursed lips. "Are you absolutely sure you did not see one?"

His eyes were seducing her into believing. For a moment she wavered; could it possibly have been real? Common sense came to her rescue. "No, definitely not. I read about that, and a public debate is to be held in Elgin, but the Scottish farmers will never let it happen."

He rose to his feet and seemed taller than before. "The natural balance must be restored. He – Old Grey Pelt – will one day return."

Darcy shivered despite herself. Wolves were about superstition, about the supernatural. A fear and fascination that went back to the first *homo sapiens*. Her head felt swimmy, her thoughts muddled. "What *is* that stuff you're smoking?"

"Dried herbs from the garden; very beneficial for the nerves."

He was playing with her again, like a cat plays with a mouse. Were *poppy heads* amongst the ingredients in that pipe? With difficulty she pulled her attention away from the dancing web of smoke and light that swirled around the room.

"There is a lot of nonsense talked about wolves," he was saying as though from a distance. "They will take weak animals, leaving the strong, and not feast on human babies as believed; that is the stuff of fairy tales."

"Like this conversation!" Darcy said, making a determined move for the door. "Oh, just one thing more, Mr. Ambrose," she added, shaking off the delicious languor and leaden-limb intoxication, whilst opening the door in readiness for escape, "a Professor Cain – he's an eminent physicist – is coming here today to inspect the spot where the meteorite was found," she said quickly.

Suddenly fear put a cold hand round her heart. Mr. Ambrose's expression was one of malevolence, yet he spoke pleasantly, and only just loud enough for her to hear. "Time for another lesson; you have not done as well as I thought."

Darcy fled the lodge and hurried back to the house.

*

Silly child, silly child. Mr. Ambrose sighed and shook his grey head. People may change; the Land does not – that is something she must learn. She, the Goddess of the Land, still has to be appeased, still has to be rendered her dues.

Quarks or Magic, ether or electromagnetic force, it was all the same. They thought they knew everything, these youngsters. The Old Ways were nonsense because there was nothing there to be seen as *proof*; but who on earth has ever seen a quark? Or any of these particles they make much of? Nobody has, and that's the truth. All they saw was a trace of light – and made up the theory of particles to explain it. Very creative. Full marks for effort. But it had nothing to do with Absolute Truth as the men in white coats would have you believe. It was just another illustration, a different way of talking about Reality, about the web.

"What do *you* say, Old Grey Pelt?"

Yellow eyes looked up in worship as he stroked the grey shaggy head.

Nineteen

~

On her return to the house, Darcy was surprised to find Jules Cain sitting on the bench by the porch.

He rose to greet her. "Ah there you are. Good morning. This damned humidity – like walking around a Turkish bath," he complained, mopping his forehead with a handkerchief.

"You're early. I was over at the lodge."

"Thought you must be with the old man, but judged it best to stay out of the way."

Darcy grimaced. "You did right."

"I take it he's not happy to have us here."

"Something like that."

"Excuse the field gear," he said, indicating the khaki shirt and jacket and needlecord slacks. "I'll change for our dinner," he said with a smile.

Darcy, annoyed at the way he had staked his claim, said nothing.

"We've left the equipment vans down by the gate, and the team is at the site."

"Oh." Darcy looked taken aback.

"We knew roughly where on the fell from your description, and we found the new earthworks without any problem," he explained.

"I see." Darcy's eyebrows went up. "Well now that you've taken over Westwalls, I'll make coffee," she said, opening the door. "That's alright," she said swiftly, holding up her hand as he made to rise and follow her into the house, "I'll bring it out here."

＊

When they had drunk their coffee, Jules Cain expressed a desire to have a 'general poke round the place' and Darcy took him around the garden.

"Super-abundance?" he commented, touching the shrivelled leaves of an apple tree.

"I don't understand it. I first noticed this about a week or so ago." Darcy reached up to grasp a spike of lilac and it crumbled in her fingers to sepia dust.

"Actually, it's what I expected," Jules Cain commented, his gaze wandering over the sickening garden. "You see," he explained as Darcy looked puzzled, "the 'effect' I told you about can work both ways. But I'm reluctant to divulge any more here; we'll discuss it later when everyone else has gone."

"Why all the secrecy?" she protested.

He smiled and touched her arm. "You'll see; bear with me please."

She shrugged. "Very well," then raised her eyes to the watery sun and watched violet-grey nimbus clouds looming from the west. "I reckon we could be in for a storm."

He looked up. "Hope not, until we're through. I have to go and check on the team – coming?"

※

Darcy felt the first spots of rain on her face as she stood watching the team of field workers from Hilldean. The person who seemed to be in charge of the on-site experiments was a woman. "Who is that?" she asked.

"Andrea? Or rather Dr. Lascelles. She's been sent by C.A.D.E. and will report back to them."

"By the way, have you had anything back from them yet?" Darcy asked, taking in the woman's blonde hair cut in an elegant shoulder length bob that made her look nineteen, when given her status she must be twice that.

He gave her an enigmatic look. "I told you – later."

The large spots of rain were coming more frequently now, and the sky was ominously dark. He cupped his hands to his mouth and shouted across to his team, "Get down to the vans and wait there until it stops."

"There's a summer house." Darcy pointed; she had discovered it on one of her walks. An hexagonal building of wood and flaking paint, it had a bench that ran all the way round, a rickety cricket table at the centre of the tiled floor, and it was still water-tight.

"That'll be fine." Cupping his hands again he shouted, "Over there," and waved his arm in the general direction.

"Okay Jules," Dr. Lascelles replied in a voice that held a strong French accent. She gave him a thumbs up sign and turned her attention back to the dials of a machine that resembled a geiger counter.

"I'll take them some coffee if you like," Darcy offered.

"I'll give you a hand."

He had been unable to hide his eagerness. It's an excuse to be alone with me in the house, Darcy thought with mixed feelings. He was standing so close she became aware of the subtle scent of mossy after-shave with a hint of spice.

Something, a sense of being observed perhaps, made her suddenly turn round. "Mr. Ambrose!"

He stood before them with the air of an avenging angel. His lips were compressed in an angry line, his nostrils pinched and the knuckles of the hand that clutched the stout walking stick were white. And somehow he had approached without a sound.

"Good morning, Sir. Kind of you to allow us to come."

Mr. Ambrose ignored Jules Cain and watched in silence as electronic equipment was carried towards the summer house, and cases containing phials of samples were closed and covered by tarpaulins.

Darcy watched him, half-afraid of what he might do. "I'm sorry, Mr. Ambrose; but it has to be done."

But his attention was focused on Jules Cain, who shifted uncomfortably beneath the malignant gaze. "So you are to be the one?" Mr. Ambrose finally said, as though his scrutiny had told him all he needed to know. Thunder rumbled in the distance as though to underline his words.

"I beg your pardon, Sir? I'm Jules Cain, Professor of Physics at Hill-dean University. Pleased to meet you."

Mr. Ambrose ignored the outstretched hand and turned instead to Darcy.

"Despite my warnings, you have let him in. You have admitted the one who will bring chaos to the Land."

"I can assure you, Sir – we will leave everything –"

Mr. Ambrose cut him short with a gesture of contempt and turning, picked his way down the fellside.

"Old geysers like him should be put down," one of the technicians growled. "No use to anyone – sour old stick."

Mr. Ambrose paused and turned. "What did you say?"

"We're only doing our job here," the technician flung back. "We can't hold back progress for you, grandad."

"Okay, Anderson, that's enough," Jules Cain reprimanded him as Darcy sucked in her breath.

A few minutes later, as she followed Cain down the fell, Darcy couldn't help imagining that the 'chaos' Mr. Ambrose had referred to began with a capital – even biblical – letter 'C'.

*

From then on, it seemed, everything went wrong. By the time they reached the garden, raindrops the size of ten pence pieces splattered the parched earth. Noon had turned twilight and thunder grumbled and echoed around the mountains. The branches of pines, chestnuts and cedars lashed to and fro like the tails of big cats in anger. The odd flicker of blueish light warned of the storm to come.

"Will Dr. Lascelles and the crew be alright up there in the summer house?" Darcy worried.

"Don't worry, they're used to field conditions. By the time they got down here," he said grabbing her hand and racing with her towards the house, "they'd be like drowned rats. Come on, and when we get inside," he panted, rain streaming down his face, "I'll fix us a drink while you rustle up some lunch."

*

"The hell she will."

Darcy wrenched her hand out of Cain's grasp and slithered to a halt on the wet grass. "Brant!" Darcy's eyes widened beneath the rain-spattered curls that clung to her forehead. Trust Brant to come for the Landrover today; his timing was impeccable. He stepped from the porch, his hair whipped by the wind, his face and stance as angry as the threatening sky above. Jules Cain was also visibly taken aback, but quickly hid his dismay behind his usual urbane mask. "Kennedy – what brings you here?" he said conversationally, holding out a hand which Brant ignored.

"I might ask you that, Cain." Water streamed down Brant's face as the storm finally broke.

"Well actually, I was just about to help Darcy here make lunch."

Darcy groaned. Cain must be deliberately trying to scotch her with Brant.

"I don't think so." Thunder boomed like giant guns as Brant took a menacing step forward.

With alarm, Darcy saw that although his arms were by his sides, his fists were tightly clenched.

"Forgive me for asking, but what is it to you?" A flash of lightning revealed a viciousness lurking behind Cain's mask.

"You may not know it," and he paused to glare at Darcy, "but this is *my wife*."

"I told Jules about you at our first meeting," Darcy cut in, ramming her hands deep into her jacket pockets.

"So just how well acquainted are you?" he demanded.

"That's none of your goddammed business."

"Darcy *did* tell me," Cain cut in, "but as I understood it, you are no longer living together." His face and voice betrayed his malice.

Brant shook the rain from his dark hair like a bristling dog as water streamed down his face and into his eyes. "She is still my wife."

"A formality, surely?" Cain taunted. "As I understand it, 'conjugal rights' and all that are a thing of the past."

Darcy screamed as Brant lunged. In the strobe-like lightning, with his wild and windswept appearance, he resembled some modern day Heathcliffe intent on avenging his Cathy. His fist connected with Jules Cain's jawbone and Cain staggered and half-fell in a macabre dance in the twilight.

"You'll regret that, Kennedy," he snarled, one hand to his chin as he struggled upright.

"I doubt it. Now take a ride in that flash car of yours – and don't let me catch you sniffing around my wife again."

"I'm here with my team to do a job, Kennedy, and I'm going to finish it," Jules Cain said, brushing down his trousers with his hands. "I'm not going to stoop to your level and brawl in the mud. However," he said turning to Darcy, "I can see you have some talking to do, Darcy, so I'll see you later – as arranged."

"Don't push your luck, Cain," Brant said grimly before Darcy could speak. He grabbed her by the arm as Cain walked away in the direction of his car.

"Take your hands off me." Darcy automatically ducked as thunder clapped overhead.

"Inside, Mrs. Kennedy," he said pulling her after him. "I have one or two things to say to you."

*

Darcy, face streaming with water, and shivering uncontrollably with a combination of rage, chill and apprehension, rounded on Brant as he followed her inside and slammed the kitchen door shut.

"How *could* you?" Ripping off her wet jacket she flung it over the nearest chair.

As though to emphasise her fury, a cannonade of thunder sounded directly overhead.

"Quite easily. Cain's had that coming for some time."

As they faced one another, rain drummed the roof-tiles and a deluge cascaded past the windows: the overspill from burdened gutters.

"I was so ashamed – you behaved like some teenage lout out there," she raged.

"And you Mrs. Kennedy, are behaving like some stupid little tart," he flung back. "*Stupid* because Cain will disappear once he's got you to drop your knickers, and *tart* because judging by your behaviour you can't wait to oblige," he said, glaring at her from where he stood by the kitchen door.

"You bastard!" Darcy's face, in the flash of lightning, was deathly white. "It's no business of yours – whatever I choose to do."

He covered the distance between them in a couple of strides. "Take care what you say – you're an inch from that slapping I promised you, Darcy."

Never had she seen him so angry. Involuntarily she stepped backwards until the hard edge of the table pressed into her back. "You're jealous," she taunted.

His face took on an odd expression. "You'd like to think that, wouldn't you, Darcy? Sorry to disappoint you, but there's rather more to it than that." His eyes, grey as the huge nimbus clouds that darkened the windows, mocked her. "Now – what is Cain doing here?"

"I thought you'd already decided that," she said acidly.

He gave her a look of contempt. "I mean apart from trying to bed you. Must you always see yourself at the centre of every scenario?"

"Why the sudden interest?"

"He's known to the Department."

Her eyes widened. "He's been investigated?"

He shrugged. "Let's say we're 'keeping an open file' on him. He's a clever bastard – but we'll have him eventually."

Darcy recalled her own misgivings and made a decision. "Alisdair found this thing on the fell. We took it to Caro at Hilldean thinking it was a prehistoric skull, but it turns out –" she was halted by his look of amusement. "You *knew*," she accused.

He shrugged again. "Nobody can send samples to C.A.D.E. without it leaking to MI5."

"So that's why you're here today?"

"And to pick up the Landrover – Johnson, he farms at St. Gildas Bridge, you'll recall, was coming over this way and gave me a lift."

"Anyway – Caro then introduced to me to Jules Cain."

"Bravo, Caro."

"He sent the samples to C.A.D.E. for analysis," she added, ignoring his sarcasm. "And he came here today to test the land."

"I'll bet he did! And how much did he tell you about the thing Alisdair found?" he asked, watching her closely.

She hesitated, then decided there was nothing now to gain from holding back. "That it was a meteorite."

"Anything else?"

"Only that it could be having an effect on the environment, which he assures me is not dangerous."

"Is that all?"

"Yes."

It may have been her imagination, but she thought Brant looked relieved. At least his fury, like the storm, seemed to have abated.

"Good." He took a step towards her. "Now, I want you to promise you'll stay away from Jules Cain – he's dangerous."

Darcy shook her head. "I certainly won't promise, and you have no right to ask it of me."

"You can't intend getting involved with him after what I've just disclosed."

"That's for me to decide. But putting aside the personal, I'm on an investigation – and my nose tells me there's a story here."

Brant scowled. "It's too dangerous, I tell you."

"Do you know more about this than I do?" she asked shrewdly.

He turned away. "I'm going to see what Cain and his cronies are up to on the fell."

Before she could question him further, he opened the door and left.

*

The rain, Darcy noted as she watched him stride away down the path, had almost stopped. Disturbed about what may happen once Brant and Cain confronted one another again, she waited until Brant had disappeared, then left the house for the site on the fell.

*

The storm had passed, but spangled gorse bushes and a lemony sun were doing nothing to lift Darcy's mood. She watched Andrea Lascelles with growing indignation. Obviously, she was one of those females whose demeanour noticeably changed once an attractive man appeared on the scene. Gone was the professionalism and detached manner. For the past half hour she had been asking Brant's advice constantly – in that alluring accent, looking directly into his eyes, and touching his arm at every opportunity. And Brant was lapping it up, like a cat with an unexpected saucer of cream.

To make it worse, she thought miserably, the Frenchwoman had legs that went on forever, or at least, up to a small tight bottom accentuated by well-cut khaki pants. A fact that had not escaped Brant, judging by the looks he cast. That he was paying her back for Julian Cain went without saying, but that did nothing to assuage Darcy's anger. He was standing close to Dr. Lascelles as they talked. Too damned close; his dark head was all but touching her fair one as they examined a specimen. Every so often a whiff of expensive French perfume wafted Darcy's way.

She turned her attention back to Jules Cain who, despite the bruise on his chin, now seemed his usual self. On site at least, it seemed an uneasy truce had been declared. She tried to shut out the Frenchwoman's laughter as Brant amused her with some remark. "What's that?" Darcy asked, peering over Jules' shoulder at the machine he was using.

He looked up from testing a sample in a glass phial, handed to him earlier by the man called Anderson who had insulted Mr. Ambrose. "This," Cain said, indicating the complex machine he was using, "is a

G.E.M. detector: *Geological Exploration with Muons*," he supplied, anticipating her question. "Muons are unstable particles and their death can be very revealing. We're using them here to quantify the number of muons created by neutrinos – more particles – as they pass through the solid rock below the earth's surface."

With an effort of will, Darcy refrained from looking in Brant's direction as a woman's throaty laugh came to her ears. "So what will that tell you?" she asked, keeping her attention on Jules Cain's explanation.

"The high-energy muons are deeply penetrating and will travel out through the rock to the detector. Heavy material, such as uranium ore, will produce more muons than, say, granite and other types of surrounding rock."

Uranium ore. "So what you're really measuring is levels of radioactivity," she challenged.

He nodded. "You got it."

"And if they're at worrying levels?"

He removed the sample from the machine. "You'll be first to know."

"And this – what does this tell you?" She touched a dial on a machine with flashing green and amber indicator lights.

"The age of the organic matter in the surrounding soil from radio carbon dating. We can then estimate how long the meteor lay here." He seemed bored now with her questions, and grinning unpleasantly, looked over at Brant and the Lascelles woman. "A case of double standards, wouldn't you say?"

Darcy shrugged. "I couldn't care less."

"Are you sure you're not the tiniest bit jealous?"

"Not at all. Brant will get on with anyone who can talk astrophysics."

"Ah, that will be why she says he is taking her to dinner tonight – to talk shop."

His knowing smile enraged her. "It's none of your business," she snapped, pushing back a strand of hair that was teased across her face by the light wind.

But when Brant left with Andrea Lascelles in tow, she went white with anger and turned abruptly away.

*

She walked a little way along the ridge to be out of sight and get her act together. From here the lodge was visible below, and she frowned on seeing the man called Anderson moving along one wall to the porch. Then her face cleared; he must be going to apologise for his earlier rudeness. Perhaps Julian had ordered him to do so. He seemed to be moving furtively, she worried, but then decided he was probably nervous of approaching an irascible old man. She turned to walk back, and in doing so saw Mr. Ambrose watching Anderson. He was standing on a grassed knoll, silhouetted against a greenish sky, his frail figure belied by the strength of the image. There was something eerie about the scene. Suppressing a shiver, Darcy walked quickly away.

*

Eventually the equipment was packed into the Hilldean transit van and the team departed. "Seven thirty?" Jules Cain prompted as she turned to walk back to the house.

"Here at the gate," she confirmed, before walking on. She might as well; Brant would be dining that Gallic siren, and God knows what she had planned to follow the after-dinner mints.

*

On seeing the look of admiration on Jules Cain's face, part of Darcy regretted the clingy little black number she had chosen to wear. The part still smarting from Brant's rejection took pleasure in his obvious approval.

"You look stunning."

"So does your car," she side-stepped, settling into the brand new Porsche.

He turned to her and smiled. "I thought we'd motor over to Coniston – to the Waterside Restaurant. It's rather good."

"Fine."

And I hope you enjoy yourself Brant Kennedy, she thought with malice.

*

The Waterside stood alone on a premonitory over the lake and was surrounded by ancient yews. Darcy's immediate impression was of spacious rooms, wood panelling, tapestry hangings and the spit and crackle of a log fire, the glow reflecting from various silver and crystal containers: the typical country house hotel. As Cain escorted her to the bar, she caught the nostalgic scents of lavender and beeswax. Later, as they sat at their table, she enjoyed panoramic views over the lake and surrounding fells. The sun hung low over the water, a huge red lantern that sent long shafts of rose rippling along the surface. "It's beautiful," she breathed.

He touched her hand lightly. "So are you, Darcy."

She smiled and picked up the menu.

*

She paused in eating the delicious soufflé to reflect on how much she had missed a man's company of late. But this evening was about work too. "When do you expect to have the results of today's tests?" she asked, giving him a direct look.

"Oh, I should have a report on my desk by the end of the week; Andrea is very efficient and thorough."

"I can imagine," Darcy said dryly before she could check herself.

He grinned and placed his hand briefly over hers as it rested on the table. "Forget them Darcy – don't let Kennedy spoil our evening."

She ignored the barb. "If the meteorite isn't all that important, why have C.A.D.E. sent her here?"

Cain put down a claw from the lobster he had been eating and dabbed his lips with a napkin. "I didn't say it was unimportant," he said, refilling her glass with *pouilly fumée*. His dark brown eyes held an expression she could not fathom; he gave her a long, hard look as though appraising her and her intentions. He cast a glance around him before continuing, as if anxious to be absolutely sure the other diners could not overhear. "Look, Darcy, I like you – I like you a lot."

"I like you, too Jules," she responded, which was true after cocktails and several glasses of wine had dulled her basic misgivings. He was cultured and handsome and would, she decided returning his speculative look, make a good and considerate lover. And why not? Life with Brant was going exactly nowhere. But could she then shop Cain and print her story?

"No, I'm not being flippant, Darcy, delightful though it is to flirt with you," he said, leaning across the table and taking her hand again. "Look, forget Kennedy; throw yourself in with me. You'll have everything you've ever wanted."

All I ever wanted was to be happy with Brant, she reflected. However that bubble had burst. "It's too soon, Jules. We only met last week, and I haven't had time yet to pick up the pieces after Brant."

He made a gesture of impatience. "There isn't time to play by the book, Darcy." He stared at her, his eyes appearing almost black in their intensity.

She got the impression he was trying to judge how much to divulge. Suddenly he appeared to make up his mind.

"There's something I haven't told you. I *have* in fact received an initial report from C.A.D.E. From the first, I had suspicions about the meteorite, now they have been confirmed." His eyes glowed with suppressed excitement, and Darcy saw from the nervous movements of his hands, and the tiny muscle at the corner of his mouth, that he could scarcely contain it.

"Just *what* have they confirmed?" she asked, filled with a sense of dread.

Sometimes she wondered whether his genius verged on madness.

He pushed aside his plate with a gesture of impatience. "That it came from Mercury – and contains information about the birth of the planets."

Twenty

~

I was right! Darcy thought exhilarated. She had always known there was a story in there somewhere. "That makes it mega-important, yes?"

"You can't even begin to guess," he said in an excited undervoice. Most of his lobster was left uneaten; irritably he waited while the waiter descended and removed their plates. "Dessert?" he asked Darcy with ill-concealed impatience as the waiter returned and hovered.

She shook her head. "Just coffee, please."

"Coffee and cognac for two," Cain ordered. He didn't speak again until the waiter was out of earshot.

"Let me tell you something about Mercury," he continued.

"Very little was known," he began, "until in March 1974 the Mariner 10 space craft made a total of three close passes of Mercury. This revealed a surface pitted with craters – including the largest in the solar system, the *Caloris basin*. By measuring the planet's gravitational pull on Mariner and determining its diameter, it was possible to calculate that it is twice as dense as Earth, and that 70% of its mass is made up of iron."

"I remember you saying the meteorite contained a lot of iron," Darcy interrupted.

"That's right. I had my suspicions even then."

"Anyway, further research showed that this was the metallic core of a much older planet, whose surface is pitted with the scars of meteoric impacts that occurred at the birth of the solar system. These meteors contain material from the time the planets were formed, more than 4.5 billion years ago. Because of the strange properties of the thing Alisdair found, I believe it is not a fragment of Mercury itself, but one of these meteorites, catapulted into space by an explosion on the planet. We already know the surface of Mercury gets hot enough to melt metal. I'm sure you don't need me to tell you that this could revolutionise Big Bang and other start-of-the-Universe theories."

Darcy struggled to conceal her excitement. "Just what are the strange properties you refer to?"

"You saw a minor manifestation yourself," he said enigmatically. "The particles have a capacity to stimulate growth."

"The 'super-abundance' of the garden!" Darcy exclaimed, then fell silent as the waiter brought their coffee and brandy and Cain gave her a warning look.

He nodded as the waiter receded. "As I say, a minor effect. The particles are at present largely inert. They have to be activated by processing in the laboratory to obtain maximum effect." His eyes shone now with the zeal of a prophet, "But then we shall see miracles of growth. Cells will multiply millions of times over-night."

"*Christ!*" Darcy breathed as visions of lush deserts and crop-filled stony basins immediately took shape in her mind.

"I can see you are already grasping the possible applications."

"Yes, indeed," Darcy said slowly, a frown creasing her forehead.

"What is it?"

"It has just occurred to me: the growth in the garden was not sustained; it now appears to be dying back."

"As I said this morning: that is also to be expected. For every particle there is an *anti-particle* – and these have the opposite effect. If the two collide, they mutually annihilate."

"Wouldn't that make these particles useless in application?"

He shook his head. "In the laboratory, matter and anti-matter can be controlled. Increased growth or atrophy can be created on demand."

"Isn't it a bit like playing God?" Darcy asked, looking troubled as she sipped her brandy.

"Exactly!"

"I can see there is an enormous amount of money to be made from this," she admitted, thinking she had understood his secrecy and excitement.

But he was smiling and shaking his head. "Forget money – think *power.*"

New doors opened on concepts that were frightening.

Christ Frank, wait till you get a load of this!

"Darcy, I've told you all this against my better judgment. I don't suppose I have to tell you it's top secret, and that you are honour-bound to say nothing to anyone?" he said disconcertingly, as though reading her mind.

"Of course, Jules."

This, she told herself, was not the time to be over-burdened with conscience.

*

As they walked through the gardens to the hotel car park, he paused to pick an early rose and thread the stem through her curls. "There," he arranged the bloom so that it lay just over her left ear. "Now you look like Carmen!"

He pulled her close and Darcy allowed him to kiss her, but couldn't help thinking that Brant had a fiery temper – and that Carmen had come to a very sticky end.

*

The engine purred to a halt at the gates of Westwalls. "Are you going to invite me in for coffee?" Jules asked, swivelling round in his seat to give her a direct look.

"I'm afraid not."

He smiled. "I guessed as much, but it was worth a try."

"It's been quite an evening; let's not spoil it."

"Would it?" He leaned closer and touched one of her curls with his finger.

"Yes, if I wasn't ready – and I'm not."

"Not ready for what?" His arm had snaked across the back of the seat.

"Whatever you have in mind."

His eyes were slanted and heavy-lidded with passion; his lips were inches from her own. "Well now, let me show you." He lowered his head and placed his mouth over hers.

Instinctively her hands came up to his chest and she applied gentle pressure. The kiss in the restaurant garden had been innocent enough; this one was heavy with passion and desire. He paid no attention to her defensive gesture but crushed her to him. Then *why not?* she found herself asking. Jules found her desirable; Brant did not. So yes, why not? Since that awful day with Brant she'd been licking her wounds like a kicked dog. Jules' tongue flicked over her lips, teasing and tantalising. A hot little spurt of desire flared in her belly. It surprised her, and her lips returned the pressure.

Slowly, and with the confidence of a stoat that knows it has numbed the mind of the rabbit, he moved his torso so that her breasts were free of restriction. Her eyes were half-shut, her lips parted as his finger ran provocatively around the inside of her neckline. Slowly he widened the gap between fabric and flesh until he was palming her breast. It was pleasant to be touched, to be made to feel desirable again; but it wasn't like it had been with Brant. Then there had been a hunger and yearning the minute he touched her, and she had shuddered with desire. But if she closed her eyes, like this, and imagined herself not in a sordid situation in the car of a comparative stranger, but in the huge Victorian bed in the farmhouse, she could almost convince herself it was Brant. His eyes, she remembered, darkened from smoky-blue to dark slate in passion.

But it was contempt not passion she saw there. Because these weren't Brant's arms around her, and it wasn't Brant's hand caressing her breast. But it was his voice inside her head; *What are you doing?* Her eyes flew open. Her hand was still resting against Jules Cain's chest. The wedding ring of Welsh gold glowed with an almost supernatural light in the darkness. The ring with which he had offered his soul.

"No, don't!" She pushed hard against Cain's chest. "I *mean* it."

"Okay, okay." He held up his hands and leaned back on his seat.

Darcy adjusted her dress.

"It's still Kennedy, isn't it?"

She looked across at him in alarm; there was naked aggression and frustration in his voice and face.

"I did try to tell you." Carefully she stretched out her hand to un-fasten the door, fearful of provoking him further. But he seemed to sense her distress, and that he was on the edge of blowing it altogether.

"It's okay. Don't get upset. I'm sorry I tried to rush things. Forgive me, Darcy?"

He gave her a rueful smile and she relaxed. His teeth were very white in the twilight. "Maybe we should have that coffee on campus instead. Meet me in my department tomorrow?"

She hesitated only a fraction. After his earlier revelations about the meteor, there could be no backing down. "Around lunchtime then," she agreed, getting out of the car.

"Good night, Darcy – and I'm sorry."

"Let's forget it happened, Jules."

The sound of his wheels spinning on gravel, and the sight of his tail lights disappearing brought a profound sense of relief.

*

She stood for a moment by the gate listening to the silence and wondering how her life had got into such a mess. The walk to the house oppressed her mood further: there was a feeling of ineffable sadness permeating the garden; the bitter-sweet breath of Autumn in July.

Glancing at her watch she decided there was time to bathe and change before going to collect Alisdair from the lodge. They – he and Mr. Ambrose – always talked until late. Relief flooded her on reaching the door of the house. For a while at least she could shut out the melancholy of a garden that reproached her for failing to keep its secrets. She frowned as the outer door yielded to her touch, but assumed she must have forgotten to secure it on going out earlier that evening. She stepped into the porch and moved towards the inner door.

"What a touching scene."

She cried out and swung round at the sound of the masculine voice. "Brant! What are you doing in my house?"

He was lounging against the monks bench, his face in shadow. She stared at him in silence, guilt staining her cheeks – as surely as those dark brown tea-leaves on the white sink of childhood. He pulled himself upright and moved out of the shadows into the moonlight that silvered the floor. She winced at the coldness in his face. "You were spying on me," she accused.

"Snooping's my business, or so you constantly tell me."

"That's despicable." She pushed open the inner door, preparing to make her escape.

He smiled, but the smile failed to reach his eyes; they were cold as an iced winter tarn. "I can think of another, more colourful, adjective to describe your behaviour my dear."

"The same as I might apply to yours when you used me, then walked away."

She stepped into the hall. "Now please leave," she added, attempting to shut the door in his face. He was too quick, and followed her into the house.

Numbed by distress, she watched him strike a match and light the oil lamp above the table in the kitchen. "That's better," he said, "now I can see what a whore really looks like."

She recoiled as though he had physically hit her. Tears stung her eyes as his gaze raked her from head to toe. She became miserably aware of her tousled hair, swollen lips and dishevelled dress: evidence of her previous and illicit desire. She allowed anger to take over. "If I am – you made me into one, Brant Kennedy. Now get out and leave me in peace."

"You'll never have that, whether I go or not."

"And you'll never have me again."

"Then neither will anyone else."

He pulled her roughly to him and kissed her with anger rather than passion. The treacherous thought passed through her mind that Brant's anger was preferable to another man's love. She mustn't give in. Just in time he released her, a strange look on his face. A moment longer and she would have betrayed her feelings. He held her at arms length and looked intently into her eyes, as though failing to find what he sought, he pushed her from him, and so roughly that she stumbled against an arm-chair and fell. "Get out," she said in a low voice. Despite her efforts, tears ran down her cheeks.

"Don't worry, I'm going." He strode to the door and paused on the threshold. "Why him Darcy – why *him?*"

"Why not?" she was stung into replying.

"Because he is evil. Has he told you about the particles? About what happens when he converts them to anti-matter? And what he intends to create with them? That he intends going to the highest bidder? And what about the *observer effect?* Has he mentioned that?" His volley of questions hit her like machine gun bullets. He laughed derisively as she stared blankly at him. "I thought not; what a little fool you are."

He slammed the door so hard that his photograph – the one that had fallen from the wall the night of Alisdair's arrival – fell to the floor and smashed.

*

She must shower away the feeling of grubbiness and contamination. Going upstairs she stripped off her clothes and stepped into the cast iron bath with its primitive shower attachment. Antiquated, but tonight, a blessing. The jets of water, perfumed steam, and white lather sliding off her wet shiny limbs combined to calm and refresh. Jules' touch, Brant's insults, and her own sense of smuttiness all swirled and eddied and finally disappeared with the foam down the plug hole.

She leaned forward to turn off the taps, then paused like that, fascinated by the miniature gleaming whirlpool around the plug hole. She frowned and straightened up, her attention suddenly focused. There was something odd here; something she couldn't quite place. Then it struck. *The water was going round the wrong way.* She moved the oil lamp that stood on the shelf closer. There was no doubt about it; the flow was definitely reversed. What was it Brant had said about anti-matter? First the seasons, now the gravitational pull. Was everything at Westwalls being put into reverse?

It was then that she heard the laughter. Or thought she did. It was difficult to tell with the swishing of the water, but it somehow brought to mind Mr. Ambrose. Swiftly she turned off the flow. Heart pounding and ears straining, she listened. Nothing except the gurgle of water refilling the overhead tank. Terrified of what might confront her she pulled aside the shower curtain. The creak of old timbers and usually comforting noises of an elderly house settling on its haunches, now filled her with terror. Footsteps sounded from below. She stiffened, straining to hear, wondering if it was another delusion. No, it wasn't her imagination. There was somebody moving about downstairs.

Twenty-One

~

Brant? He must have returned and let himself in. *And neither will anyone else have you.* The words returned to chill her blood. Climbing out of the bath she wrapped herself in a towel to dry off the worst of the water and struggled into jeans and a sweater.

Taking a deep breath she carried the oil lamp onto the landing. Shadows leapt out at her from the stairwell, and a barn owl beyond the casement screeched at her folly at venturing out. She stood still and listened. No sound of human movement below; just the scrape of claws on wood as a mouse scurried across the ceiling above her head. She crept down the stairs and into the hallway. Moonlight streamed through the stained glass panels of red and blue that flanked the front door. The kitchen door at the end of the hall stood open. She clamped her hand over her mouth to hold back the scream. The shadow of a man had flitted across the threshold.

"Brant?" She called. It must be Brant. Her mind wouldn't admit the possibility of anyone else. Shadows leapt up the walls in a crazy dance as she ran along the hall, lamp in hand, flame flaring and spluttering and leaving a trail of acrid smoke. She halted in the doorway of the kitchen and stared in disbelief. "Jules!"

Cold anger flooded her. "What the hell are you doing in here?" she cried.

*

He moved away from the back door. "I was worried about you. I saw Kennedy's car parked under some trees at the end of the lane."

Darcy watched him in stony silence. The door, she saw now, was ajar.

"I thought he may have seen us," Cain added. He took a step towards her.

"Stay where you are," she ordered sharply.

He looked hurt. "I was concerned about you, that's all."

"So you broke into my home." She placed the oil lamp on the table; the dancing and flickering of the flame, she realised, was betraying the fact that her hand was far from steady. "And what if Brant was here? He is still my husband."

"I'm sorry, Darcy," he apologised moving closer. "But it was precisely that which made me come and check it out. I mean," he was moving closer with every word, "there's no saying what a jealous husband might do, is there? Especially one as mean as Kennedy."

He was looming over her now. Crazy to be afraid; this was Jules Cain, famous scientist, not some psychopathic stranger. Yet despite the look of concern on his face, the sense of threat remained.

"I mean," he continued, "he could have blown a fuse, and done something stupid. And if people had seen us together, they might say – *who could blame him?*"

Darcy felt as though icy water was trickling over her scalp and down her spine. Had Cain set her up? Taken her to a high profile place to dine so that he could be sure of being seen, and remembered? Then if anything should happen to her, Brant would be blamed. But would Cain go to those lengths to harm his old rival? *Not*, she told herself backing away, *unless he was mad*. Or the meteorite business was bigger than she had realised. Brant was in the same line of business, and could be seen by Cain as a threat. No, it was all too far-fetched. Defuse the situation; act normal. "Well as you can see, I'm perfectly alright – so *good night*," she said firmly.

He advanced slowly as she backed up. "Oh, but surely we could have that coffee now that I'm here?"

He was still smiling, but Darcy felt a *frisson* of alarm. "I have to collect Alisdair, so if you don't mind –"

In the flickering light of the lamp he resembled a satyr: darkly sensuous and predatory, with his white teeth, full lips and compelling eyes. He was standing so close she could smell the warm masculine odour of his skin, and the fresh 'laundry smell' of his shirt.

He stroked her cheek with one finger. "*Was* Brant here?"

"As a matter of fact, he was," she answered, but her tone implied it was none of his business. She attempted to back away, but his hands were now resting on her shoulders; their grip tightened.

"And what did he tell you, I wonder?"

"About what?"

"Me. My work. He doesn't approve of either, you know." His sudden bark of laughter made her jump and then try to pull away. His fingers dug into her flesh. His hands slid up and down, and suggestively close to her breasts. "Come now, don't be unfriendly." That was what the youth who accosted her at the railway station had said. Her lip curled in disdain.

"What is it?"

There was anger in his voice, and his eyes had turned almost black, but it was out before she could check it. "I was just reflecting that a man doesn't have to be working class and unemployed to be a yob."

She thought he would hit her. He took one hand from her shoulder, hesitated, then ran it through his hair as though in frustration. There was no disguising however the ugly expression on his face. His hands moved on her shoulders, massaging them, moving gradually inwards until his thumbs rested at the base of her throat. "You must take care, Darcy, dear," he said in a low seductive voice that chilled her to the bone. "It's Brant who is the threat, not I. He might do anything in a fit of jealous rage. My staff know how I got the bruise on my chin," he said slyly. His eyes were now almost black, so dilated were the pupils. Darcy looked into them, unable to move, like the deer transfixed by the headlamps of the on-rushing car.

She hadn't heard the door open, nor it seemed had Jules Cain; he didn't turn round until Mr. Ambrose spoke. "Alisdair is waiting for you."

Darcy heaved a sigh of relief as Cain dropped his hands to his sides and swung around. "I'm coming to collect him now, Mr. Ambrose." Never had she been so pleased to see him; she had the strangest sensation that he was here not by accident, but as her secret protector. He stood in the doorway, resplendent in smoking jacket of quilted silk, its wine-red colour enlivened by tufts of white stuffing where the fabric had worn threadbare.

Jules Cain swiftly recovered his composure. "I'll be off then, Darcy." It was said with such naturalness that she seriously wondered if she had been mistaken about his sinister intent. When she didn't answer, he spoke to Mr. Ambrose who stood between him and the door. "Just came to check on Darcy, here. I'd brought her home after taking her to dinner," he added, with a sly look at Darcy who flushed with guilt beneath

Mr. Ambrose's glare. "There's a car parked down the lane – I was a bit concerned. Well, good night then, sir." He stood waiting for Mr. Ambrose to step aside. Mr. Ambrose's eyes were blue chips of ice. Finally he moved, allowing Cain to pass. Without a word or a backward glance, Cain stepped out into the night.

She shifted uncomfortably in the ensuing silence, and beneath Mr. Ambrose's look of condemnation. "It's not what you are thinking," she said at last.

"I am thinking nothing. Except that Alisdair is sleepy. He may stay with me, if you like, until morning."

"No, I'll be right over."

"Very well." He turned to leave.

"Wait – I know Alisdair has talked about Brant – but he and I are separated, you know," she blurted, then was immediately annoyed with herself because it was none of his business.

He turned back to her, and taking her left hand in his, examined the wedding ring of Welsh gold. "I don't think so," he said with great politeness, and left.

*

It was later, once Alisdair was asleep and she was lying in her bed, that she heard it. The long drawn-out howl shivered on the night, rose and suddenly fell like a bird of prey, then died. She lay for a moment too petrified to move, then flung back the covers and went to the window. Nothing moved.

The dying garden was holding on to its secrets.

Twenty-Two

~

The Green Dragon: Lancaster

The man called Anderson lurched out of the Green Dragon Inn then steadied himself and walked towards his car. Okay, he'd had a wee drink or two, but no need to advertise the fact. Not with these bloody breathalyser jobs about. A chap had to be careful these days. Anyway, he'd earned himself a drink and a bit of relaxation. What a day! He'd been telling Harry and Ian about it. What with lugging equipment up and down the fell, and then being stuck in a rotting old summer house during that storm – who'd be a bloody lab technician? Glorified labourer more like. Oops, keep a low profile; it's okay, the police car has cruised past.

Where was he? Oh yes, then he'd told Harry and Ian about that tedious old fart mouthing off at him. Like he'd said at the time, should be put down when they got like that. No use to anyone. Couldn't stand old people. Canutes – every last one of 'em. Just like Dad, always grousing and putting down anyone younger, and trying to hold back the tide of progress. Well, he'd fixed him, hadn't he? Made him pay for his ill temper. His hand felt in the pocket of his jacket for the hard disc of onyx studded with gems. A paperweight, he supposed. Worth a mint anyway, whatever it was. Well he'd earned it, hadn't he? Lugging all that stuff about and putting up with abuse. Like hell he felt guilty. Why should he? Where's the bloody car?

Wait a minute, what the hell was that noise? He looked behind him, and then all around as he weaved across the car park. Nothing unusual; he must have had more to drink than he thought. No: there it was again. A sort of *pad-pant, pad-pant*, the sound a giant dog might make. He looked over his shoulder again, his heart beating a little faster. But no, there was nothing there; just a couple from the pub getting into their car, and a lad revving up his Thunderbird 500.

There, the car was just at the end if he remembered right, next to the shrubbery. God, what a row those things made. The motorbike roared off down the road, all flashy chrome, winking lights and growling exhausts. That was young fellas for you though, wasn't it? *Pad-pant, pad-pant.* There it went again. The couple in their car had driven past him now and out of the car park. He was alone. The lights in the Inn seemed a long way away. *Pad-pant, pad-pant.* He didn't like the sound; and there was a peculiar musky smell too. He'd smelled it before somewhere. Ah, now he remembered, at that old geyser's place. The fell had reeked of it.

Right, here we are: into the car, and soon be off home to bed. Good job Sue was staying over at her sister's. He grinned to himself as he put his key in the lock of the car door. She'd have had something to say about him coming back this late.

Bloody key was stuck. What was that? Fear trickled down the back of his neck. He swung round, heard the rustling in the shrubbery, saw leaves and branches falling back into place as though something large had just passed by. He screwed up his eyes, squinting into the shadows which seemed to move and threaten. Thank God he'd got the door open. Something strange about this place tonight. Or perhaps it was just that he'd had one too many. At least the engine fired first time. Anyway, he was safe now and about to turn out of the exit.

It loomed in front of him from nowhere. A fleeting impossible glimpse of grey fur, slanted yellow eyes and bared fangs. Then it sprang. The windscreen shattered into a shower of exploding stars. The fragments, flung wide by the force of impact, glinted in the light from the street lamps. The grey muzzle and head filled the space where it had been. The beast's mouth, red and gaping, was dripping saliva onto the dashboard. Automatically his foot stamped the brake. The car swerved, smashed into the gate post.

Then it was on him. Instinctively he flung up his arms to protect himself and screamed with pain as fangs sunk into his forearm. He screamed again, but nobody could hear. The snarling and growling was filling his ears, and *Oh my God*, the sound of crunching bone as a vice clamped onto his arm. Christ it was all flying limbs, spitting fury and sprayed blood. His blood. It was everywhere. Dripping from the car roof and running down the windows. *God, help me God!* He tried to scream again as he stared at the stump that had been his arm. But the fangs cut it short, locked onto his throat. Last thoughts struggling through the mists of inhuman pain and fear. What would they find? Would anything remain?

Or would this fiend from hell eat until there was nothing left?

*

"Stand back, stand back." The police officer gestured at the landlady, a handful of waiters and barmaids, and the last of the die-hard drinkers that came staggering out of the pub.

"What happened to him, d'you think?" he asked as the ambulance crew came in with the stretcher.

"Heart attack, more than likely. He hit the post, but that didn't do it. There's not a mark on him, see?"

"Poor beggar." The traffic officer replaced the driving licence back in the leather wallet. The man called Anderson had a look on his face like he'd never seen on anyone. Naked terror, that's what it was.

And to think he'd doubled back with the idea of breathalysing him; thought he was drunk. *Poor bastard.*

The officer shook his head as the ambulance doors were slammed shut.

Twenty-Three

~

Westwalls

Back at the lodge, Mr. Ambrose shook his head and made a clucking sound of regret. "A pity – but he did say I should be put down," he said, his expression malicious. "And a pity too, we couldn't remove the main offender," he added, gazing into the shining web. "But the girl, for good or ill, has jiggled the thread and brought him into play. We can't be stopping him now, my precious – he has to play out his hand for the sake of the Game."

He rose and moved to the window, and stood there for a time bathed in moonlight, watching the bats flitter around the eaves like fragments of charred paper. "Still, we can help things along a little; keep an eye on events and even out the odds," he said aloud, returning to his chair by the log fire. "I dare say tonight's move will give him cause for thought, eh precious?"

The firelight sparked green, blue and red fire from the jewels set in the paperweight that rested on the table.

Old Grey Pelt briefly looked up, then carried on licking the blood from his paws.

*

The item in the newspaper the following morning certainly gave Darcy something to think about. Was it coincidence, she found herself wondering, that the man called Anderson, who had been so callous about Mr. Ambrose, had died that night of a heart attack? Folding her paper, she sat looking out of the window at the mist-laden fells, trying to persuade herself that it was down to chance. A trifle difficult: given the man had appeared in perfect health and, according to the report, was only thirty-five years old.

*

If only Alisdair hadn't found that thing on the fell. The sight of the dying garden filled her with sadness and foreboding.

So far, it had brought only dissent, death and destruction to West-walls.

DEVELOPMENTS

One

~

Darcy glanced impatiently at the clock. Alisdair was taking his time this morning and she was waiting to set out for Hilldean. She gave him a speculative look as he stood with his back to her, shrugging his way into his blazer. He had eaten his breakfast as normal, but seemed rather subdued. *I hope he's not sickening for something,* she thought, watching him. That was all she needed: a sick kid to nurse in the middle of an investigation that was hotting up nicely. He slung his satchel onto his shoulder and as he was going through the kitchen door, paused and turned to face her. "Are you and Brant going to get back together again?" he demanded.

She put down her coffee cup and stared at him, taken aback. His spectacles had slipped slightly, revealing two ovoid marks like pink caterpillar suckers either side of his nose. For some reason these moved her to compassion. "I don't think so, Alisdair."

His bottom lip stuck out stubbornly. "I wish you would. But perhaps he doesn't want you now you have me."

Darcy got up and put an arm about his shoulder. "You mustn't think that, Alisdair. Brant really cares about you. It's *me* he doesn't want to live with, not you."

He turned to leave and appeared to be digesting this information. He turned again to confront her, and anger and bitterness were written across his face. "You went out with that Cain, didn't you?"

Darcy frowned. "That's not really your business. But yes, I did have dinner with him last week."

His face contorted with impotent rage. "Well why don't you stay away from him? Brant might want you again then," he cried, jerking open the door. Red-faced, he slammed it shut as he ran out.

Darcy shook her head and sighed. If only the lad knew: her main interest lay not in Casanova Cain, but in what she was becoming more and more convinced was Cain the unscrupulous scientist.

Which was why, she thought rinsing her cup and placing it on the drainer, it was time to set off for Hilldean in search of more evidence. Before Frank started hollering for her to 'get her ass back into the office' in his usual style.

*

On turning in at Hilldean, she frowned and glanced over her shoulder as she passed a police car going the opposite way along the winding drive. Even more startling was the sight of what appeared to be a police 'check point' around the next bend. Pulling up, she let down her window and waited for the approaching officer to speak.

"Good morning miss. Your business at the University?"

"Good Morning. What's wrong?"

"Just routine miss. Student or staff?"

"Student."

"And your name please?"

Shit. She needed this about as much as a missed deadline. When they ran her name through the computer, they would discover she wasn't a student and her cover would be blown. "Are you stopping everyone – or have I been singled out for the honour?" she asked, playing for time.

*

A W.P.C. left her post at the road barrier and strolled over to join her colleague, hands linked behind her back. "Something wrong, Sarge?"

"No problem. This lady wants to know why we are here."

"Just give the officer your details madam," the W.P.C. snapped.

Darcy however, in the course of her job, had survived too many brushes with the law to be intimidated by its officers. This W.P.C.'s eyes, just visible beneath the officious peak of her cap, were piggy and eager with the fervour of the newly initiated.

"New to the job, are you?" Darcy asked sweetly.

The policewoman's superior unsuccessfully tried to suppress a grin. He cleared his throat and leaned his forearm on the roof of Darcy's car. "Nothing personal, love. It applies to anyone going in today. So can I have your name please?" he repeated.

Darcy thought on her feet. *Professional name – or married name?* "Kennedy" she offered, deciding on the latter. If she used *Darcy West* she ran the risk of being identified as a reporter on the *Manchester News*. Her column was popular; her name a household one in the area. "Anne Kennedy," she added, using her middle name.

"Would that be 'miss' or 'mrs'?"

"I'm married."

"Lucky man," he said under his breath, then aloud, "And where have you come from this morning?"

"West Cumbria."

"Nice spot. May I see your Student I.D. card please."

So how to get out of this one? "Yes, sure." She rummaged through the glove compartment for the fictional card. "Damn, I seem to have left it at home."

"Your address then?"

This was going from bad to worse. "The Kennedy Farm, St. Gildas Bay, West Cumbria." *And God help her if Brant was there when they checked it out.*

"Have you any other form of I.D. on you?" the W.P.C. said waspishly.

"I'm afraid not. But Caroline Stevens, senior lecturer in Archaeology would vouch for me; so would Professor Julian Cain, in Physics." She wasn't happy about using his name, but he had the clout she needed. The officer however, was giving her an odd look. "Know him, do you – Professor Cain?"

"He's helping me with some research, but he's also a friend," she replied, thinking if she had to use it, she might as well make it work.

"Okay," he said exchanging a glance with his W.P.C. before straightening up. "You can go in now," he added, stuffing his notebook back into his pocket.

"But sarge?" The W.P.C. was craning her neck and standing on her well-polished toes to get his attention.

The sergeant straightened up and said, "Yes?" in a voice which Darcy thought with a grin, must freeze the buttons off her uniform.

"Nothing, Sarge."

He stood back and waved Darcy on.

Looking in her mirror, Darcy saw that he was standing in the middle of the road watching her drive away, and he was speaking into his radio.

*

She knew there was something wrong as she walked from the car park to the main campus area. There was a 'buzz' in the air which set her reporter's nose twitching. People were milling about, the car park was unusually full, and various official-looking vehicles zipped up and down the driveway, ignoring the 20 mph speed restriction. She rounded a corner to the tree-lined avenue that led to the Physics Department and stopped dead. The building was cordoned off. A crowd of on-lookers, mostly students judging by their appearance, were pressed up to the barrier and were being told to move back by a line of officers. Two police cars and a van were parked on the verge. Even more ominously, an ambulance waited, engine dead but blue light still eerily flashing in the silence. The rear doors gaped, awaiting its victim, and revealing the red blankets, black cylinders and clinical chrome of its stocks in trade.

Darcy carried on walking, aware that her progress was being observed. There was a crackling sound, and one of the officers watching her spoke into his radio. What the hell was going on here? She pushed through the crowd to the barrier.

"Mrs. Kennedy?"

She answered automatically. "Yes?"

"Come with me please." It was the officer who had just switched off his radio.

"But how did you know —" She stopped. Of course; the officer who had questioned her on the drive had relayed her name and description. But why?

Anxiety writhed like a worm in her stomach.

"If you don't mind, miss."

Two more officers had moved forward to join the first. Inexorably she was ushered through the barrier and into the building.

*

Along the corridor, up the stairs and onto the first floor. Is this anything to do with Jules Cain? she wondered, her mind reeling. The double doors at the end of the corridor were pushed wide and two ambulance men emerged, the lower portion of their faces covered by masks. The doors swung to behind them and shuddered to a standstill. They were carrying between them a laden stretcher. They hurried down the corridor towards Darcy and her police escort.

"Stand back please, Mrs. Kennedy," one of the officers said sharply.

She stood mesmerised, unable to move. *Who was on that stretcher?*

The other officer pushed her back against the corridor wall. But not quite quickly enough. The edge of the stretcher scraped her leg in passing, dragging the sheet covering its occupant partly off the face. She screamed.

"You alright, Mrs. Kennedy?" One of the officers said, taking her arm. She nodded, but turned away and retched uncontrollably.

Another officer covered what was left of the face and the stretcher was borne away to the lift.

"God in heaven – who was that? And what has happened to him?" Darcy whispered.

"Just come with me, Mrs. Kennedy."

She walked on in a daze. The man on the stretcher was unrecognisable. His face had been black, and both his eyeballs had burst.

*

They had reached double glass doors and Darcy turned to confront her escort. "God damn you, will you answer – is Professor Cain alright?"

"That's alright Barnes. Step this way, Mrs. Kennedy," a female voice brusquely instructed.

Darcy turned to face the woman who had appeared in the doorway.

*

Darcy found herself in what was obviously an improvised incident room. Police officers were manning a bank of telephones, feeding a fax machine and a W.P.C. sat before the flickering screen of a computer. A large map of the campus had been pinned to the blackboard. Two officers, one male and one female, were engaged in sticking pins with coloured flags attached, into its various sections. The woman who had spoken from the doorway was in her mid-thirties, Darcy guessed. She was wearing a white blouse tucked into a skirt which fell from her hips in soft folds, and a jacket cut along the same fluid lines. Waves of soft brown hair framed a face with a wide mouth and high cheekbones.

Her eyes were as cold and emotionally dead as a great white shark's.

"Sit down, Mrs. Kennedy." She was seated behind her desk now, and motioned to the chair opposite. "I'm Detective Inspector Gallagher," she added, as Darcy took the seat. She spoke in a clipped voice which suggested to Darcy a love of precision and efficiency and precious little patience with time-wasters. She also spoke with a Scottish accent, but with refinements, as though any rougher elements had been ironed-out, leaving only a soft burr. *Ambitious, and tough with it*, Darcy had her tagged.

"Are you alright? You look a little pale." She wore the slight look of contempt that seasoned officers have for squeamish and uninitiated members of the public.

Darcy pulled a face. "That man out there –"

"Yes. Unfortunate." The clipped tones dismissed the subject.

Darcy was left wondering whether the 'unfortunate' bit related to the man's death or the fact that she had seen his face. The memory of it made her feel nauseous. "But what on earth happened to him? An accident? A disease?"

Inspector Gallagher rested her elbows on the table and linked her fingers. "Why are you here today?"

Darcy met the cold eyes without flinching. "Why am I being interviewed?"

The other woman's eyelids briefly hooded them. "You're not – officially. I'm simply talking to anyone who is in any way connected with the Department."

Darcy rose. "In that case, I shall leave."

The only sound in the room was the rapid *click, clack, clackety clack* of the W.P.C.'s fingers on the computer keys.

"Benson – go check whether Davies has finished taking Professor Cain's statement yet."

At this, Darcy sucked in her breath noisily. *So the man on the stretcher wasn't Julian Cain.* She kept her thoughts to herself.

"Yes, Ma'am." The W.P.C. rose from her work station and crossed to a door at the rear of the room. Darcy became aware of the muted ringing of telephones, and the voices of police officers speaking into receivers.

Inspector Gallagher turned her attention back to Darcy. "Okay, now that you've heard what you wanted to hear – let's try again, shall we?"

Darcy hesitated. "Are you going to tell me why I'm here?"

"Sit down, don't get fresh and I might."

"Do you usually treat members of the public this way?"

"Only those who give me a hard time."

"So why are you trying to connect me with Jules Cain?"

"You told the officer at the road block that you knew him."

"And if I do?" Darcy's mind worked overtime: what did the police want with him? Why was he making a statement? What had he to do with that poor bastard on the stretcher?

"Do you also know Dr. Charles Ashford?"

Darcy shook her head. "I know he's head of department, but that's it. Why?"

Inspector Gallagher removed her elbows from the table and leaned back on her chair. "Because that was who you saw on the stretcher; and Jules Cain was the last person to see him alive."

Two

~

Darcy stared at Inspector Gallagher whilst her mind reeled. "What killed him?"

The inspector shrugged. "We don't know yet. But in the meantime, we are treating his death as suspicious."

"Murder? But why should–?" She thought of the sandy-haired man who had swept from Jules Cain's study that day and brushed past her in the corridor, but judged it wiser to keep quiet about what she had overheard. "Who would want to kill him?" she finished lamely.

Instead of answering, Gallagher looked over Darcy's shoulder and raised her eyebrows in query. Darcy looked round; the fresh-faced policewoman had returned.

"Sergeant Davies says it will be a while yet, ma'am. They've only just got under way," the W.P.C.'s face remained expressionless as she added, "the professor wouldn't start until his solicitor arrived."

Darcy strove to conceal her surprise. The W.P.C. and her superior conferred in muted tones, ignoring her for the present. *Solicitor?* Were they about to charge him? But perhaps it was commonplace for someone with such a high profile to refuse to say a word without their lawyer being present. The tabloids could twist the most innocent of statements and ruin reputations overnight.

Thoughts tumbled around in her head, spiralling and shifting shape like patterns in a kaleidoscope. Sinister thoughts: like how she had overheard Cain rowing with Charles Ashford only days ago; how he had stealthily entered her house, and scared her half to death; and the way he had loomed over her in that ominous manner. And perhaps most damning of all: the fact that Dr. Ashford had threatened to expose him for plagiarism and illicit experiments. The perfect motive. Suddenly she went rigid. *What experiments?* Could it be possible? She saw again the dead man's face – or what had remained of it, then as the W.P.C. went back to her work station and Inspector Gallagher addressed her once more, she dismissed the ludicrous connection.

"– so I don't require a statement from you at present," she was saying.

"Where was the body found?" Darcy asked, suddenly the reporter.

"In the corridor."

Inspector Gallagher was looking down, consulting some notes written on her pad. Darcy rushed heedlessly on. "Anywhere near Professor Cain's room?"

Gallagher's eyes narrowed as she looked up, and she stroked the grooved bit above her lip with her crooked finger, in thoughtful fashion. "I have you down here as a student – are you sure that is all you are?"

Darcy mentally cursed; she was close to blowing her cover. "I don't know what you mean."

Gallagher gave her a shrewd look. "Members of the public don't usually ask the questions."

Darcy made a dismissive gesture. "I'm hooked on 'who-dunnits'," she said facetiously.

She breathed more easily as the officer in charge of the telephones approached with a sheet of paper. The message was delivered and the officer, having received his instructions, went back to his bank of telephones. Inspector Gallagher turned her attention back to Darcy. "How well do you know Jules Cain?"

"I'm not sleeping with him if that's what you're implying."

"So?"

"I've been out to dinner with him – once."

"And where was your husband during this cosy dinner?"

"Out with a professional colleague – and it wasn't cosy." Better this female super-sleuth didn't know about the separation; it might not be too healthy at present to be linked romantically with Jules Cain.

"How did you meet?"

"My friend Caroline Stevens introduced us – she's a lecturer in Archaeology."

"Why?"

Darcy didn't hesitate; there was no way she was going to blab about the meteorite. Certainly not until she had done some investigating of her own. "She thought he might be able to help me with some research."

"Known her long?"

"We go back a long way. To when we were both undergraduates here at Hilldean."

Inspector Gallagher surveyed her through half closed lids whilst tapping the end of a pencil against her teeth. Darcy found the noise irritating.

"Thank you. You can go," she said at last, whilst writing on her pad.

"Thank *you*," Darcy responded, rising and stalking to the door.

"Don't go too far for a day or two: I may want to speak with you again," Gallagher added without looking up.

Darcy left without replying.

✻

Pushing her way through the crowd whilst doing her best to ignore the curious stares, she made her way to the refectory. She had intended looking up Jen this morning, before all hell had broken loose that is; perhaps she would find her in here. But first a 'phone call to make Frank's day, she thought grinning to herself. Stepping into a pay-phone she dialled his extension number at the *Manchester News*. "Hi, Frank? Yes, me – Darcy. Have I got one for you! Front page – this evening. No kidding. Listen …" Briefly she filled him in on the details. "Cause of death unknown yet – but I've got one of my hunches about that." Frank Kelly's groan was audible.

"You still there Frank?"

"Yes, Darcy – go on, slay me."

"Well, you know that –" she stopped abruptly. "No, never mind. Talk to you later on that one," she said instead. No point in saying anything about Cain's experiments until she had checked a few things out.

"Okay girl. Now get your ass back here."

"Hey come on, Frank. I've just given you a front-page first on a high profile murder!"

"Yeah, with yourself being interrogated as a suspect," he said dryly.

She laughed. "It's alright Frank. They're still calling me 'Mrs. Kennedy'."

"So?" he grunted.

"When the police start calling a suspect by their first name – it usually means they're about to arrest them!"

"You're crazy, girl. Okay – keep your nose clean though – or you're out on your own."

"No problem, Frank."

She was still grinning as she put down the receiver.

Almost immediately she lifted it again. Now for that other call. Dammit, what had she done with his car phone number? It was in here somewhere. She extracted a folded piece of paper from her handbag. Would he be in the car? Would it be switched on? She knew how he hated being interrupted when out on business. The ringing-out tone sounded. She was just about to replace the receiver when Brant's voice answered.

"Kennedy."

"It's Darcy. Are you still there?" she added as the silence lengthened.

"What is it?"

"I think we had better talk."

"Where are you?"

"Hilldean."

"That fits."

"Brant," she warned.

"I'll meet you at the Castle tea shop in an hour. Don't be late."

"I won't be."

She put the receiver down smartly.

Just one more call. It was probably too soon yet, but best to get her name in there for later. She dialled the number of the Lancashire and District General Hospital.

"Dr. Bartholomew, Path lab, please." She waited impatiently as the call was transferred. "Dr. Bartholomew? Hello there, it's Darcy, here – Darcy West. You had a body brought in this morning ..."

Brant's rudeness forgotten, Darcy felt pleased with herself as she left the kiosk.

Three

~

She was still feeling pleased with herself as she joined the queue for coffee in the refectory. Pity about having to forego the by-line, but she had to preserve her cover. She took her coffee over to a table near the window so that she could keep an eye open for Jen. To her disappointment, there was no sign of her by the time she had finished her coffee. She was about to get up and go, when she spied her coming through the door with a male companion. Judging by Jen's pallor and air of agitation, she had heard the news. She spoke briefly to her companion who joined the queue, then looked around for a table. Darcy waved and beckoned.

"I can't believe this has happened," Jen said sitting down at Darcy's invitation.

"It's terrible," Darcy agreed.

"I'll tell Chris to get you another coffee." Jen swung round on her chair to gesture to her companion.

"Thanks, but I have to go." She fiddled with the spoon in her saucer. "Actually, I'm meeting Brant."

Jen turned back to face her. "Brant? Your 'ex'?"

Darcy nodded. "There's still loose ends to tie up, you know the sort of thing."

"That sucks. Okay. But stay a few minutes, Darcy – for Chris'sakes, it's not everyday we lose our Head of Department." She leaned closer, across the table. "The rumour is, it's not down to natural causes."

"Heard something like that myself." Darcy pushed away her empty cup.

"Shit, I just can't believe it, Darcy. He was such a nice guy."

"A rotten bloody business." Using the tip of her index finger, Darcy drew a letter 'B' in the spilled sugar on the formica table top. "Surely they've got the Department wired up? Did nobody hear the alarm go off?" she asked craftily.

"There isn't one. They just lock up the building at night. Actually Professor Cain has been pushing for one lately. I think he's right. It's irresponsible – all that research equipment and experimental data. But that's cut-backs and bureaucracy for you, isn't it? Ten chits and three forms to fill in, to be told it will be considered next financial year."

No burglar alarm, Darcy thought as Jen prattled on. So why was Cain pushing just now for tighter security? What was he hiding? "Dead right; a few locked doors seems barely adequate, does it?" she prompted.

"Well, there's the security lighting outside of course; and security patrol – they check the building on the night round."

"Not sufficiently, it appears. The police seem to think –"

Jen looked up sharply. "The police? Why – did they interview you?"

Darcy brushed away the letter 'B' in the sugar and rose to her feet. "Sorry Jen, must dash. Here's your friend with the coffee. I'll be in touch."

She grabbed her bag and left as she spotted the man called Chris returning with a laden tray.

*

The aroma of roast coffee beans and toasted teacakes met Darcy as she opened the door and stepped inside the Castle Tea Rooms. Waitresses moved gracefully between tables as though running on clockwork, and china cups and saucers rested on white linen tablecloths. One reason why Brant used to bring her here in the past: he hated 'throw away plastic' syndrome. Another was that it was too expensive and conventional for the students of nearby Hilldean. It wasn't their flamboyance or scruffiness he objected to, she recalled declining the assistance of an approaching waitress, so much as the self-conscious way they paraded them, and according to Brant – without style.

His outdoor manliness, vigour and smart but definitely 'county' clothes set him apart from the other, mainly elderly, inhabitants of the tea shop: the magpie chattering women and faded masculinity by which he was now surrounded. Darcy watched for a moment, unobserved. He pushed up the sleeve of his jacket and glanced at his watch. His face was impassive, but she noted the way he twirled a teaspoon dexterously between his fingers and tapped first one end then the other on the table.

The action told her he was annoyed. But then she was a quarter of an hour late. Threading her way through the honeycomb of tables, she made her way to where Brant was sitting.

He replaced the spoon on his saucer and looked up as she reached the table. "I was just about to leave."

"Hello, Brant, nice to see you too." Her sarcasm was wasted: Brant ignored it and gestured to the hovering waitress.

"Tea and a teacake, please," Darcy said in response to Brant's raised eyebrow.

"Death doesn't affect your appetite then," he said as the waitress jotted down the order and departed.

Startled, Darcy gave him a direct look. "You know about Ashworth."

"It's my business to know."

"Don't be pompous."

"Would you rather I leave?" He made as though to rise.

"Oh, sit down Brant for heaven's sake, I've had one hell of a morning."

"Tell me."

But his expression, she noted, was no less unforgiving.

*

She waited whilst the waitress unloaded the contents of her tray on the table. "The bloody police grilled me," she admitted as the waitress left. Darcy poured herself some tea.

"So who was it interviewed you?"

"Some bolshy woman inspector. Gallagher, that was it."

"Take care, Darcy. Helen Gallagher is nobody's fool – and a real tough lady."

"Lady?" Darcy paused in lifting the cup to her lips. "You know her?" She looked at him with suspicion over her cup.

Brant shrugged. "Slightly. I certainly know of her: she has a reputation for being ambitious – and ruthless with it."

"Tell me," Darcy mocked. "She went on as though she thought I had something to do with Ashford's death. Ever heard anything so stupid?"

"Fly with the crows; get shot with the crows."

"What's that supposed to mean?" Darcy flared.

"The company you've been keeping."

Darcy wiped her buttery fingers on her napkin and gave him a stony glare. "I'm not here to discuss myself and Jules Cain."

"Okay, okay," he held up a hand.

Suddenly she relented. "Look Brant, what am I supposed to do?" She spread her hands in silent appeal but there was no softening of Brant's expression. "I'm lonely," she continued in a low voice, "We're separated, and I'm still in my twenties, for God's sake!"

"No Darcy, *we're* not separated," he said, leaning forward with his hands flat on the table and seemingly unaware of the curious stares he was attracting. "*You* walked away. *You* separated yourself from me. There is no 'we' about it."

"I had reason," she whispered, aware of the retired couple at the next table.

"You think so – *I* do not."

"You're *still* treating me badly."

"You're still behaving badly."

"And what about you and Andrea Lascelles?" Darcy threw at him.

And she had resolved not to quarrel with him today.

"I left Dr. Lascelles in the foyer of the Cross Keys Hotel," he replied coldly.

"You didn't dine with her?" She looked at him with open scepticism, but he met her gaze and held it.

"No. But it wouldn't do for me to ask *you* a similar question, would it?"

She took refuge in defiance. "Maybe there is nothing yet," she conceded, "But she's hot for you, and it won't take her long."

"The relationship is a professional one."

"Like all the others, when you couldn't get home nights." Darcy coloured: that was something he was never meant to hear.

Brant's eyes narrowed. "So that was it; you thought I was sleeping around."

"What would you think – stuck in the lonely farmhouse night after night?"

He raised his eyebrows in challenge.

"Okay, *most* nights. And in lonely hotel rooms when I was on a case."

He nodded. "Just like myself. But did I accuse you of infidelity?"

"No but you've made up for it since."

"*Touché.*"

He held up his hands and a hint of a smile softened his features at last. It caught at her chest, this glimpse of the old Brant, the man she used to know and love. "I've not been acting the tart Brant, despite all your accusations."

He frowned. "No, if you had, I could cope with all this so much the better."

"I don't understand."

"No, you wouldn't. You think only of yourself, and your own feelings," he said wearily. "Now, what did you want to speak to me about?"

The temptation to learn more about his personal feelings was strong, but she was afraid he might leave. "I overheard Jules Cain and Charles Ashford quarrelling."

The narrowing of his eyes and taughtening of facial muscles told her she had captured his attention.

"When, and about what?" he said, lowering his voice.

"One day last week – about the meteor and Jules' decision to publish."

"What was said?"

"He accused Jules of plagiarism."

"Cain got where he is by climbing on the backs of colleagues."

"You're biased; his work is renowned."

"Don't flatter yourself my girl; I never let private feelings interfere with professional judgement. I'm not referring to his competence – just his lack of integrity."

Darcy strove to keep her voice neutral. "Do you think he killed Ashford?"

Brant's expression became guarded. "It's not for me to say. But it's my guess he's done something worse."

"What could be worse than killing a man?"

"Killing thousands, maybe millions in the end, of men, women and children."

Darcy looked incredulous. "*What?*"

"If my guess is correct, he is after using the particles from your meteorite to tamper with D.N.A codes."

Four

~

Darcy held her breath for a couple of seconds in an effort to contain her excitement. "Is that possible?" Brant too, she noticed was buzzing, had that glazed look that said he was getting carried away with his first love – Science. Soon enough his training in secrecy would intervene and he would realise he was telling her too much.

"There are four basic units of D.N.A. – G, T, C, and A. These are arranged in strands – the famous double helix – to a coded 'recipe'. The simplest way to remove D.N.A. is by taking bone marrow from the subject. It can then be analysed, a legitimate practice in diagnostic medicine for example. Or if Cain has his way, be exposed to the meteorite particles, be processed and the code *tampered with* before being replaced."

Darcy gave an involuntary gasp. "Tampered with?"

"Remember that matter and *anti-matter* cannot co-exist – Dirac's theory, 1928," he said with obvious impatience.

"Of course, pardon me."

The irony in her voice served to remind him that he was not talking with a colleague. "Sorry." He fiddled with a teaspoon for a moment. "Okay," he said replacing it on the saucer, "I'll try and keep it simple."

"When a sub-atomic particle meets its opposite, or anti-particle, the two annihilate. The mass of both is converted to *energy*. This energy usually evaporates as photons, which are particles of light, or – and this is where Cain would be interested – they can be encouraged to *rematerialise* as particles and anti-particles that rush away from the point of creation. This could be used to dismantle and reassemble units of D.N.A."

"*Christ!*" Darcy looked at him with horror, then made a dismissive gesture with her hand. "He'd never get away with it. Even if he got past the scientific research bodies, volunteers taking part in trials would never consent."

"Absolutely. *If he informed them.*"

"He would do that – say nothing?"

Brant smiled cynically. "Jules Cain would sell his own mother for vivisection if he thought it would advance his career."

"But it's totally unethical to keep silent," Darcy protested.

Brant shrugged. "It goes on all the time, even in Establishment medicine. Many people are treated without ever being told they are part of a control group. In studies of cancer treatments for instance. And there are plenty of poorly-paid and out-of-work people, not to mention the homeless, who are willing to keep from asking questions in return for payment."

"Shades of Burke and Hare," Darcy said, her disgust evident in her face.

"Well, that's a bit strong. But unsavoury practise, yes."

"What do you think Cain is up to exactly then?" Darcy pressed, but immediately knew she had gone too far. His manner changed abruptly and he motioned to the waitress for the bill. "I don't know," he said rising to his feet, "But if you print one word of what I've just told you, I'll break your neck."

The waitress brought the bill; Brant placed it with the money on a plate and made for the door.

*

"Keep away from Cain, Darcy," he said, his expression inscrutable as they stood on the pavement. "I sometimes wonder if he's completely sane."

She thought of the way Jules Cain had crept back into her house that night. "I sometimes think none of you scientists are," she quipped to quell her own unease. She recoiled from the sudden venom in his face and voice.

"Don't ever class me with that bastard."

"I didn't mean –" she started to say, but he took her arm and propelled her into a ginnel that ran between the tea shop and the neighbouring book shop. "Does he know you overheard his quarrel with Ashford?" he asked urgently.

"No." She rubbed her arm as he released it.

"Then make sure he never does." He brushed back a curl that had strayed across her cheek and almost absent-mindedly, as though by force of past habit, tucked it behind her ear.

"Thanks for the coffee, Brant." She fidgeted with the clasp of her bag.

He took her chin in his hand. "Don't give me any more frights, okay?"

She shook her head, too overcome to speak.

His fingers touched her cheek in a whisper of a caress. "See you."

He gave her a long look, then walked away.

Ridiculous, to feel like crying as she watched his back recede. Nonetheless, loneliness engulfed her as his dark head and broad shoulders were swallowed up by the rush-hour crowd.

*

The garden at Westwalls did little to lift her mood. Parking by the gate she took a walk round. Leaves still hung limply from branches as though clinging to life itself. Passing beneath a giant horsechestnut she stretched and plucked a dessicated leaf which crumbled to amber dust in her fingers. On reaching the bridge she wrinkled her nose in disgust. The damp and fusty smell of decay pervaded the air. Various fungi of sinister shape and pallor clustered the base of gnarled tree trunks and the rotting posts of the bridge, beneath which the water lay dark and stagnant. The toe of one shoe poking experimentally at a large grey plate-like fungus brought forth a sickening odour and ooze of slime. Stepping back she cleaned her shoe on a tuft of grass. The action revealed a mass of white worms, writhing on the earth in fantastic convolutions. A hydra-headed brain pulsing with evil intent. Shuddering, she crossed the bridge and moved irresistibly to the woodland.

The Mother-statue leered from across the stagnant and stinking pond. Her face was even more pitted, her body swollen and grotesque. The spark of life had gone, leaving the glade empty and dead.

A slight movement caught Darcy's eye. She watched in horror as a small triangular head emerged from the statue's mouth. The body, marked with an ominous zig-zag down its length, slithered and writhed across the pitted cheeks and over the eroded breasts. She stifled a cry as it raised its head in classical striking pose and fixed her with its malevolent black eyes. The tongue flicked in and out of the scaly mouth, and the serpent of Eden came to mind. Was that what the slime and decay was about? The price of forbidden knowledge? If only Alisdair hadn't found that damned meteorite. With a last look at the viper, she turned to flee and cried aloud.

"Mr. Ambrose! You frightened me half to death."

He regarded her without speaking.

"*Why?*" she beseeched him, indicating the stricken garden with a sweep of her arm. "There has been a bizarre murder," she blurted as he still didn't speak. "At the University."

Mr. Ambrose surveyed her with his head to one side like some fierce and avenging bird of prey. "Why so surprised? I told you it would result in chaos."

"I've just about had it with your stupid games," Darcy snapped.

As she hurried towards the house, the sound of his laughter echoed eerily through the wood.

*

That night, just as she was preparing for bed, she heard a sound that chilled her blood. Moving to the window she twitched aside the curtain and peered out. Like an invalid, the garden had wrapped itself in summer dark and silence. Fear gripped her as a long howl rose and fell through the night. Heart pounding, Darcy peered out into the garden. The grey shape moved with loping stride to the edge of the copse, then was gone.

"You heard it this time, didn't you?"

Her hand let the curtain fall back. She spun round as though stung. "Alisdair!"

Clutching her chest she slumped against the window shutter.

"You scared me!"

"It was Old Grey Pelt."

"It was a dog," Darcy said firmly. "It must have run away from one of the farms. Gone bad at lambing. They do, sometimes." She recalled the collie bitch she had surprised once on holiday, padding down the lane, red of mouth and paw, the little black body limp in its mouth.

Alisdair shook his head. "No. It was Old Grey Pelt," he repeated. One leg of his pyjamas trailed the floor; he looked so young, yet spoke with such assurance. "He's a wolf."

"Don't be silly! There's been no wolves in Britain for centuries! Now come on – *bed!*" Crossing to his side she tried to propel him through the door but he resisted. "You don't believe anything, do you?" he sulked, holding onto the door jamb to prevent himself being hauled through.

"Oh, get real, Alisdair," Darcy said wearily. "And get yourself back to bed."

*

At last he was back beneath the covers. The candle flame danced and threw grotesque shadows up the walls. He squinted at her in the meagre light. "Mr. Ambrose said today that our shoulder blades are the remnants of wings."

"A nice idea," Darcy said from the doorway. "What were we then – pterodactyls?" she quipped.

"No – dragons," he said with a grave expression.

"Oh, really Alisdair, you don't believe –" she stopped as he dissolved in giggles. "Horrible kid," she said with a laugh.

His head emerged from the quilt like a tortoise from its shell. "I think he just meant we've lost something."

"Like what?"

He thought for a moment. "Our sense of wonder. Mr. Ambrose said 'vision' – but I guess that's what he meant."

"Maybe he's right at that. Now – off to sleep."

Darcy moved to the door.

"Do you think Mum and Dad have got their wings back?"

She turned, so moved she could hardly breathe. "Shouldn't be surprised," she managed.

Darcy snuffed the candle and pulled the door to.

*

Later that night, she was awakened by the sound of Alisdair singing. The ancient floor boards creaked beneath her feet as she trod a path of moonlight to the landing. The door to his room was partially open and Alisdair was kneeling by the window. He had his back to her, looking out at the stars. His pyjamas lay on the floor in a heap like a sloughed-off skin. A shudder passed through his white and immature body. Then it was Darcy's turn to shiver. The skin across his shoulder blades was moving, the surface rippling as though something was struggling to emerge.

Five

~

She gasped aloud. The flesh over Alisdair's scapulae was growing tighter and shinier, bulging to form two tiny protuberances: small rounded knobs like budding antlers. They were, she saw, white and downy, the tips flushed with innocence. She opened her mouth and shouted his name, but he gave no sign of having heard. Somehow, he had moved beyond her world, was in a different pocket of Space and Time.

She shuddered anew. The room had turned chill and clammy. The buds were growing, and painfully – judging by the arching of Alisdair's spine, and the spasms that curved his fingers like talons as they clawed at the air. The knobs were budding now, surging outwards, arcing into beauty but not yet unfurled. Twin embryos in the womb of flight, they glistened white and viscous, then unfolded in slow motion as she watched, and shed their shiny membrane. A first flush of feathers followed by down and quills, and then he was spreading his wings, drying them it seemed, like a butterfly emerging from the chrysalis into the sun. Then came the first wing-like movements: a timid quiver and flutter that rippled the currents of air like angel-breath.

"Alisdair?" Her whisper reverberated around the room. Slowly Alisdair turned, pinions poised for flight. She screamed. No angel this. The face was pockmarked and contorted, the nostrils flared and dripping mucus. She quailed before the baleful glare of eyes that glowed redly in the moonlight. The lips curled, turning what started as a smile into a ghastly grimace.

Then she knew. This was an *avenging* angel. This was the face of Vengeance. Alisdair's revenge for the loss of his parents; Mr. Ambrose's revenge for letting the Strangers in; the World's revenge for the rape of the planet, and for ruthless Progress, the eighth deadly sin.

What can I do? What can anyone do? she sobbed, sinking to her knees.

*

Instantly alert, Darcy shot upright in her bed. Some awful nightmare – or had it been real? Fearfully, she strained eyes and ears. No sound disturbed the old house; no incubus stirred in dark corners. She half-rose as memory flooded back, then sank back in a bed that was damp with perspiration. Alisdair, no doubt, lay asleep in bed, with nothing more sinister than his pyjama jacket on his back. But she wasn't about to check it out. She hugged herself for comfort. The only sound was that of the wind sighing through the eaves.

So why did she seem to hear Mr. Ambrose's mocking laughter?

Six

~

The idea had been growing ever since her talk with Jen. A crazy seed that dared send out a shoot from midnight scheming to the light of day. It was the only way to discover what Jules Cain was up to. Earlier, she had collected the post from the box at the end of the drive, and that had clinched the matter. One of the envelopes had been stamped *Lancaster and District Hospital*. It had contained a copy of Dr. Bartholomew's report on Charles Ashford's body. So tonight was the night. Her stomach muscles contracted at the thought.

But first she had to drive to Manchester. She had finished dictating her follow-up report on Charles Ashford's murder, and needed to deposit the tape on Frank's desk before the evening edition deadline. She put on her jacket and sifted through the mail brought up earlier and left lying unopened on the table. The squeal of tyres outside made her pause. Before she could reach the window to see who was arriving in such a hurry, the door was flung open and Brant stormed into the kitchen.

Recalling their amicable parting the previous evening, she smiled in greeting. "Coffee?"

He stood silhouetted against the light, the early sunshine contrasting with the darkness of face and mood. He slammed the door shut. "What in Christ's name are you up to now?" he demanded.

Her smile froze. "Actually I'm off to see Frank – but *do* come in," she said sarcastically.

He made a sound of disgust. "If you get that far, and aren't picked up first. Never mind," he went on, holding up his hands as she opened her mouth to speak, "My fault. I should have known you couldn't be trusted; wouldn't tell the truth where a lie would do!"

She frowned, stunned by this tirade. "What the hell's wrong with you? Last night we were friends, remember?"

"That was before the police arrived on my doorstep."

"Oh, shit."

"Precisely."

"They've been out to the farmhouse," she stated flatly.

"*And* crawling all over the observatory. What are you trying to do? Get me kicked out of the service?" He paced the room, then with his back to her, stood looking out of the window.

"Oh, for heaven's sake, it's not that bad."

He wheeled round to face her again. "What do they have on you?"

"Nothing. I told you already, the Gallagher woman knows I'm friendly with Jules Cain, and that's all."

"And how do you think it looked when I had to tell them you no longer live at the farmhouse? That we were separated – given you told them you live there with your husband," he shouted, moving from the window.

"You told me we weren't separated," she reminded him sweetly.

White around his mouth now, he raised a warning finger. "That's enough, Darcy. Now listen carefully: drop this thing now, or I blow your cover and have you picked up – for your own safety."

She looked shocked. "Of all the high-handed-, you may frighten the poor sods you hound out there, but it won't work with me."

With an angry gesture he pushed back a lock of hair that had fallen across his forehead. "O.K. Risk you're own fool neck if you must, but not my job."

"That's all you're bothered about really, isn't it?" she goaded. "You don't give a toss about me."

The slap caught her unawares. Light as it was, it stung her pride more than her cheek. She stalked to the door and yanked it open. "Get out."

He paused in passing her. "I could kill you, Darcy," he said between clenched teeth.

She slammed the door shut.

*

Frank had his tape. "Great stuff Darcy-girl, knew you could pull it off," he had growled in his usual manner. There was no surer bet for gaining Frank's favour than to throw egg in the face of the Nationals, Darcy had reflected as she ran down the steps to the car park. To do it with a high profile murder was to render him ecstatic. She had then driven to Hill-dean and gone straight to Caro's room. Over coffee they had discussed the death of Charles Ashford, and Darcy had subtly pumped Caro about aspects of security on campus. When she could ask nothing more without raising Caro's suspicion, she had confided Brant's latest iniquity.

Caro sipped her coffee serenely. "That's where it's at, of course," she said eying Darcy over her cup.

"You know something I don't?" Darcy said ironically.

"It's about you risking your neck. He's terrified something will happen to you."

Darcy looked at the ceiling. "Oh, yes, he is the protective sort, is Brant."

"He shouldn't have done it – but I can understand why. He loves you like crazy, and you accuse him of not giving a toss. I'm not surprised he got mad. Especially when it was *you* who walked out on him."

"Gee, thanks." Darcy folded her arms across her chest.

Caro brushed an imaginary speck of dust from her batik dyed skirt. "No problem. That's what friends are for."

Darcy laughed despite herself.

*

Five minutes or so later Darcy got to her feet. "Thanks for the coffee."

"Anytime. By the way," Caro said with a serious expression as she followed Darcy to the door. "Just how deep are you in this Ashford business? Are his death and the meteorite connected?"

"In answer to the first, I'm not – and to the second: not as far as I know."

"You were always a lousy liar!"

"See you, Caro."

"Take care, Darcy. And don't mess around with Cain. He may be brilliant, and a charmer, but he's a bad man to cross."

"I'll be fine."

"Yes, well I happen to think Brant's right: it's time to forget this 'under-cover student' bit. Look Darcy," she pushed the door to and lowered her voice. "There's something nasty involved in Charles Ashford's death. In my line of work it's sometimes necessary to get a path lab report on re-mains, so I have friends in the business," she added by way of explanation.

Darcy smiled and tapped her pocket. "So have I."

Stepping outside into the courtyard, Darcy glanced up at Caro's window. Satisfied that she was not being observed, she made her way to the Physics Department.

*

A half hour or so later she was skimming along the motorway on her way home. A seemingly casual stroll around the Physics building had told her what she needed to know. According to Dr. Bartholomew, parts of the department were still under restriction and subject to further tests, but outside at least, there was now no sign of official activity. All that remained was the orange and blue plastic 'police' tape that cordoned off the area, and which made an ominous whirring sound in the breeze. She had also noted the location of Jules Cain's office and laboratory, and the best point of entry: least-lit, shielded by trees and not overlooked by the windows of neighbouring departments. Hilldean being a traditional university, the doors and windows were original; no double glazed units here with impenetrable locks.

So, she had Dr. Bartholomew's disturbing report, Frank had his tape and the joint had been expertly cased. All in all, a satisfying day, she thought, swinging off the motorway to head for the western fells.

*

Thankfully, cloud cover obscured the moon. Nonetheless, Darcy peered anxiously through the windscreen at the northern light rimming the fells behind the university. This far north, it was never completely dark during the summer months. The dashboard clock showed ten minutes past midnight. She had made good time. The qualms that had disturbed her during the drive to Hilldean disappeared as she turned in at the driveway and the need for nerve and action took over. She grimaced and peered in her mirror. In the silence, the purr of the engine sounded like the cough and spit of a formula one racing car. And now for the tricky bit. Switching off the engine, she coasted off-road and onto the verge, gliding to a halt beneath the sprawl of a chestnut tree.

Leaving the car, she slung a rucksack containing tools and a torch onto her shoulder, and headed for the silhouettes of stone buildings and the copper-domed chapel that huddled on top of the hill.

*

Midnight-campus had a surrealist air. Empty walkways echoed with yesterday's bustle. Black windows winked with dull gleam, and rows of lamps with orangey eye – here and there a faulty bloodshot one – watched as she sped like a shadow beneath. She stopped, nerves tingling, as raised voices and laughter were carried on the breeze. A nearby doorway offered cover. She emerged when the last of the revellers, bottle in hand, had passed. A light flicked on in a residence block. No problem: a student was drawing the curtains. Okay to move on. More sounds of merriment made her look anxiously over her shoulder. Somewhere to the right a door banged shut and laughter was silenced. Not much further, thank God.

The approach of a slow-moving vehicle sent her darting into a second doorway. The security van prowled slowly past, yellow eyes searching the shadows for intruders. Through the cab windows, she could see the dark-visaged guards with their ominous peaked caps. She glanced at the luminous dial of her watch. If the info she had prised from Caro was correct, there was a gap of forty-five minutes before the next patrol was due.

A brisk run brought her to the darkened Physics block.

Precious minutes were wasted on the lock of the rear door, which refused to give to her pickings and probings. A ground floor window offered more hope. A sudden sound made her whip round. A can rolled on the concrete, knocked from an uncovered bin by a marauding cat. The fellow conspirator fixed her with an unblinking stare, dropped to the ground, and slinked off. Returning to the lock, Darcy found her hand was shaking.

What if Brant were to find out about this? His fury didn't bear thinking about. She turned her attention back to the window. It said a lot for her feelings, she supposed as the lock sprang with a *click*, that she feared his reaction more than Frank's. She held her breath. When no siren wailed, she breathed again. Yet Frank was her boss, and last time she had pulled a stunt like this, it had cost her a month's suspension and a 'Frank Kelly special': a reprimand that had blistered the paint on the walls. She eased up the sash. Damn, it was stuck. Brant could top him though – or was it simply that she cared more?

Pushing such thoughts aside, she crawled through the gap.

✻

Dropping to the floor she crouched low. No footsteps pounded, no door slammed and no light sliced the gloom. She crept to the door.

Opening it, she stuck her head out and peered along the shadowed corridor. The sole source of illumination came from the orangey-red lights in the square beyond the row of windows. One of the lamps had a faulty filament; it dipped and flickered, a strobe light playing on an empty and ghostly disco. Keeping to the wall, she made her way to the stairs.

Jules Cain's office. A sudden movement from below-stairs made her spin round. She stood for a moment, blood pounding in her ears. The sound of gnawing and scratching came from behind the wall panels. An instant image of thick body, long tail and eyes gleaming redly in the torchlight made her skin crawl. Every old building had its rats. Experimentally she turned the door handle. Locked. She took a skeleton key from her pocket. Minutes later she was inside.

*

The room gave her the creeps. Even in his absence, it seemed to resonate with Jules Cain's dynamic and sinister presence. Through the partially open slats of the window blind, the delinquent lamp in the square pulsed its eerie red strobes. A glance at her watch told her she was running five minutes late. A rifle through the papers on the desk yielded nothing of interest. Desk drawers next. A bunch of keys, an out-of-date American Express card, paper clips, pens – the usual office paraphernalia. Next drawer – and what was this? She moved the beam of the torch over the page as she skip read. Just a report for I.C.I. on polymer particles. She replaced it and moved on to the filing cabinet. No problem; a few minutes work on the lock and the drawer ran smoothly on its runners.

Her fingers closed on the file marked C.A.D.E.

Placing it on the desk she began to read through. First a copy of Jules Cain's initial letter about the meteorite and an incomprehensible list of required tests. The concluding paragraph halted her skip-reading. In it he voiced the opinion that this was a 'minor meteorite' of local significance, and of interest only to the team of Hilldean geologists in terms of the origins of the area. Darcy shook her head in disbelief. What was Cain's game? He had told her the meteorite held the secrets of the Universe.

A letter next from the institute acknowledging receipt of the particle samples. Then, and her hand shook now with excitement, the primary report from C.A.D.E. It consisted mostly of physics gobbledegook, with test results showing endless quotations and talk of 'quarks', 'leptons', 'bosuns' and other strange-sounding bodies. The accompanying letter however made her blood race. Signed by a Professor Aaron who apparently headed the institute, and who had so many letters after his name that they almost ran off the page, it confirmed Cain's own, but undeclared, hypothesis. The meteorite originated on Mercury at the time of the Big Bang. After a glut of jargon about *frozen stars, forbidden energy bands* and *red shift velocity*, there was an item that even she could understand: in this case, radio carbon dating was useless; it was only effective up to 70,000 years, and if the basic premise about its origins was correct – the meteorite was around *4.5 billion years old.*

The writer went on to warn that this was now classified and highly sensitive material, and must be treated as such: *with utmost discretion and secrecy,* and that an official investigation and report would follow. The letter further warned Cain that 'any attempts at publication of findings, or any leakage of information whatsoever', would not be sanctioned and indeed, would be 'instantly and heavily penalised'. In conclusion, Professor Aaron instructed Cain to 'submit the meteorite and all relevant data to the centre at C.A.D.E'.

There was no copy letter or cross reference in the file to suggest that Cain had done so.

Knowing Cain, he would in all probability have ignored Professor Aaron's instructions. How long before C.A.D.E. got nasty and piled on the pressure? Jules Cain, she surmised, must be in one hell of a hurry to publish. He must also be mad to think he could get away with it. And that was one hell of a motive for getting rid of Charles Ashford. After the quarrel, Cain must have seen disaster homing in like a heat-seeking missile to a furnace. Maybe, she thought as her infra-red camera clicked, it was time to tell Inspector Gallagher what she had heard. Returning the file, she closed the drawer.

She wondered if there was time to try and access the data base, and pulled back the cuff of her glove to consult her watch. Too risky. The next patrol was due in fifteen minutes, and there was still the laboratory to view. Besides, there was bound to be a password, and she would only get 'access denied'.

She switched off her torch. So where did Cain do his research? She moved to the work area at the rear of the study, finding her way by the light of the lamps filtering in from the square. Nothing much here. Monitors, centrifuges, rows of test tubes and slides: a system of basic laboratory equipment. A search of the shadowed area beyond revealed a door that fit flush to the wall so that at first glance it appeared to be part of it. It was cold to the touch; metal not wood lay beneath the paint, she decided, and it was probably reinforced. Most promising. Another glance at her watch made her curse under her breath. Time was running out and this bastard would be hard to crack. Buzzing now with a heady mixture of fear and excitement, she opened her rucksack and set to work.

Six minutes later the lock gave. Mentally patting herself on the back, she pushed open the door and slipped through.

A first impression of soft bleeping sounds, and darkness relieved only by the winking of various red and green indicator lights. The windows were presumably shuttered; no light from outside filtered through. She stood motionless, her senses testing the alien environment. A feeling of space, of a large area inhabited by bulky shadows. The pungent smell of formaldehyde stung her nostrils. Suddenly she was filled with foreboding. There was something not right here. Life pulsed in this place; as though unseen hearts beat rhythmically in the dark. Not a human presence exactly. More the difference between a room that holds plants and animals, and one that does not. The sort of distinction her family teased her about, because none of them could detect it. She fought down a mounting desire to turn and run and turned her attention to a different warning of danger. Something physical and immediate this time.

Instinctively she looked up. A solitary red eye mounted on a bracket, and its opposite number across the way, caused her to freeze. Slowly and with infinite care she eased back the zip on her bag and extracted a strip of shiny black polystyrene. Thank God, she thought flattening herself against the wall so as not to cross the invisible beam, for Frank's *unofficial* training programme. Checking with her finger for the adhesive side of the plastic, she reached up and 'blinded' the sensor. That, she thought grimly, had been a close run thing.

Whatever lurked in this room was secret enough to warrant an alarm.

She moved forward, then stopped again to listen. In addition to the monotonous *bleep, bleep, bleep* of the monitors she became aware of another sound: the soft, almost subliminal *lub-a-dub-dub* that resembled the beating of several hearts. An icy finger touched the length of her spine. There was an odd reluctance to switch on her torch, as though the beam may reveal things it would be better not to see.

*

The button clicked. The ray from the torch split the darkness and she let out an involuntary cry. The beam careered madly round the room as she almost dropped the torch. Steadying it with effort, she swept it along the row of bell jars and glass tanks that lined the benches. The *creatures*, and even that was a euphemism, floated in colourless liquid. Grey blobs of plasma undulated, stumps and distorted limbs waving, in a slow-motion *dance macabre*.

They watched her, if that was the word, through eyes blinded by opaque membranes, great bulges in misshapen head: a hideous hybrid of embryo and cataract-clouded ancient. Sick with horror, she retched and pressed her hand over her mouth. Here a stump, oozing pus where an arm should be; there, in place of genitalia, a viscous blue-veined bag that pulsed like a giant jellyfish. And over there – *oh, Christ*. She tried to steady the torch beam on target. A half-formed abdominal cavity trailed lengths of unhealthy greenish entrails. Some of these homunculi – were they male or female? (the thought instantly sickened her) lacked nostrils, limbs or ears. One over there had no mouth, just a spongy indentation. Some exhibited running sores and necrobiosis, the rotting tissues reminiscent of leprosy.

How could Jules Cain bear to witness the pathetic remains of his hellish creations? An incinerator was the only decent option. To play Dr. Frankenstein was evil enough, but to display these mock-human bodies was obscene. Mesmerised by horror she watched a bulbous head slowly turning to face her. It was tilted, like the head of an attentive bird, or rather a featherless nestling. The opaque bulges appeared to focus; one pathetic stump of an arm was raised. With a jolt that reverberated throughout her body, she realised that the light from her torch was acting as a stimulus.

Oh sweet Jesus, they are aware. These creatures were not only alive, but responsive. A terrible thought struck her: what if these things were not creations as such, but mutilations? Brant's words about the manipulation of D.N.A. returned to appal her. *That's where Cain's interest will lie*. That's what Brant had said. Had Cain been working on human embryos? The sad products of abortion and *ex vitro* fertilisation? It was possible. And this would fit in with the path lab report on Charles Ashford: the inexplicable breakdown and mutant regeneration of cells, as though his body had been subjected to a massive dose of radiation or a deviant virus. Is this what Jules Cain was doing with particles from the meteorite?

She felt the blood drain from her face and felt faint with shock. She had been about to take out her infra-red camera, but backed to the door instead. Slamming it on its dreadful secret, she fled Jules Cain's office and ran for the stairs.

*

A nightmare. That's what it is, she told herself, stifling a scream as rodent-gnawings and scratchings penetrated the walls. Any minute now she would awake, and discover that none of this had happened. The window was stuck. Her hands were trembling so much she couldn't cope with the catch. *Let me out of here; for God's sake let me out*. Nausea, threatening since her first glimpse of those monsters in there, rose to her throat. No time to be sick. A blessed stream of fresh air hit her as the window slid open. She gulped it greedily, then clambered through the window.

Instinctively she froze. The security patrol. In the horror back there, she had forgotten about those privatised-policemen with their batons and peaked caps. The sound of the engine told her it was only a block away. She dropped to the ground and began to run. Glancing over her shoulder she saw twin headlamps swing around the corner. They were going to catch her. The sudden revving, the squeal of tyres on acceleration, meant they had spotted her and were in pursuit.

Darting down the passageway between Physics and First Year Residence, she heard the squeal of brakes and slamming of doors, and knew they had not given up. Behind her, footsteps pounded the flags. A powerful beam caught her in its revealing light. A harsh male voice shouted for her to stop. She flung herself down a grassed embankment and half-rolled to the bottom. Chest heaving, she picked herself up and looked wildly about her. Impossible to reach the car. And there was no cover. They would be on her in seconds.

Then it came to her: *Jen*. No time to worry about whether Jen would back her up. As her pursuers emerged from the passage, she dived for the doorway of Post-grad Residence. The muffled shout told her she had been spotted.

Pushing open the inner door she raced for the lift and thumped the button. The whirring started up, but too late. On hearing the outer door open she took the stairs two at a time. First floor, and her lungs were bursting. The ground floor door banged against the wall. They were in the building. She raced up the next flight. With a bit of luck they would think she had gone through the door to the first floor corridor and begin searching there.

Second floor. Pain seared her side and groin. Jen's room was along here somewhere. A door opened a few yards along the darkened passage and Darcy bit back a scream. A man in his twenties wearing nothing but cropped and frayed jeans swayed towards her. He peered at her dreamily through metal rimmed spectacles. "Hi. Want some company?"

A strong smell of marijuana wafted through the half-open door. "No thanks." He tried to grab her hand as she passed. "Hey come on – what's the hurry?"

"Piss off!" Darcy hissed. No point in stringing it out, she thought pushing past, and agonising over each wasted second.

"Suit yourself. Stuck up bitch."

The door banged shut. That would bring those two bozos running.

Come on, Jen, where are you? She ran along the corridor, glancing at room numbers in passing. *This is it.* She rapped on the door bearing an anti-vivisection poster and a notice reading *Jen welcomes animal lovers* pinned underneath. A door banged at the end of the corridor. She rapped louder. *Come on Jen, for God's sake!*

At last Jen's sleepy face appeared.

*

Darcy pushed her way into the room and shut the door. She stood with her back against it, panting.

Jen rubbed her eyes as though to rid them of sleep. "Hey, what's going on here?"

Darcy put a warning finger to her lips. "Security," she whispered, jerking her head in the direction of the corridor.

"After *you?*"

"Explain later." She put her finger to her lips again then moved to the table and switched off the lamp. Too late. The light must surely have been visible beneath the door. Footsteps pounded the corridor; voices filtered into the room. Darcy and Jen looked at one another in silence. The footsteps stopped right outside. An imperative knock made them jump. Darcy felt her heart must be audible, so hard was it pounding. She held up a hand for a moment, then as a second knock sounded, nodded at Jen to open up. Jen simulated her earlier bleary-eyed look and opened the door a few inches. "Yes, what is it?"

Through the crack between the hinges, Darcy saw the ominous bulk and peaked caps of the security guards.

"Did someone come in here a few minutes ago?" a harsh voice asked.

Jen shook her head. "'Course not. It's the middle of night. You got me out of bed."

"Your light was on," a second voice accused.

"So I don't like the dark."

"No need to take that tone miss."

"Like I said, you got me out of bed. I fell asleep studying. Now if you guys don't mind –"

The first voice again. "Heard anything unusual? Someone running, coming in late maybe?"

"No. Nothing. Hey, what is this anyway?"

"Mind if we take a look?" the second voice said.

Darcy pressed her back even tighter against the wall behind the door.

Jen's voice was now indignant. "No way. I've got an early exam in the morning."

"Somebody was in 'Physics'. Whoever it was ran in here."

"I've already told you: I've seen nobody."

Darcy held her breath. The officers' frustration was palpable. Security men had no authority to enter rooms, but in this case, would they consider it justified? Evidently not worth the risk, she thought seconds later as the first man said with obvious reluctance, "Very well, miss. If you do hear anything –"

"You'll be first to know."

Jen shut the door. With relief, Darcy listened to the sound of their footsteps retreating down the corridor.

*

They looked at one another, still afraid to speak.

"Shift those and sit down, Darcy," Jen said at last as silence returned to the building.

Darcy removed a sweater and pair of jeans from the only chair in the room, tossed them on the end of the bed and sat down. Her own student's room at Hilldean seemed light years away. This one had a 'Save the Seals' poster showing a doe-eyed pup on one wall, and one of the Greenpeace ship *Rainbow Warrior* above the door. Jen picked up a bottle from a table littered with books and papers; more books teetered in piles on the floor. She held it up to the light whilst squinting at the contents. "Half empty," she declared with a grimace, dividing the cheap red wine between two mugs.

"Or half full. Depends on your outlook on life," Darcy commented, adding, "Thanks," as Jen handed her a mug.

Jen smiled. "I'll remember that."

"Here's to you Jen – and thanks," Darcy said, raising her mug before drinking.

"Anytime. Now tell me what's going on," Jen said giving her a shrewd look as she perched cross legged on the bed. "That guy said something about the Physics building – it wasn't *you* who broke in by any chance?"

Darcy grinned. "'Fraid so," then as those awful images flooded back in, her expression changed.

Jen was watching her with obvious concern. "Tell me."

"Can I trust you, Jen?"

"Haven't I just shown that?"

Darcy gave her a quick smile of apology. "Sure. But this is – well," she shrugged expressively. "I'm having my problems with Brant, right? But he tipped me off, hinted at Jules Cain being not quite Kosher. Brant's an astro-physicist," she explained, seeing Jen's puzzled look. "Anyway, I decided to check out his laboratory."

"Christ, Darcy!"

Darcy made a dismissive gesture with her hand. "I know, I know, but it was justified. Jen, you've no idea what Cain's up to; he's got to be evil."

Jen's face had drained of colour. "Leave well alone, Darcy; It's nothing to do with us."

"On the contrary, it concerns every last one of us," Darcy said sombrely.

Jen was looking at her shrewdly. "You've been seeing Julian, haven't you?" she said at last.

"I've been out to dinner with him, that's all," Darcy said casually, but the colour in her cheeks heightened at the memory of his grope in the car.

"And does this Brant guy know?" Jen demanded.

So that was her drift. "Yes but –"

Jen nodded sagely. "And Brant's your 'ex', right?"

"Not quite."

Jen wagged her head knowledgeably. "Even worse. He's jealous of Jules, and is bound to try and turn you against him."

"I admit Brant doesn't like Jules, but he's too professional to ever blacken another scientist's reputation. And what's more," Darcy added giving Jen a direct look, "you are carrying a torch for Cain – so *you* are bound to defend him."

The alarm clock by the bed ticked loudly in the silence.

Jen's defiance crumpled. "How did you guess?"

Darcy gave her a sympathetic smile. "Your reaction whenever his name is mentioned; the way you defended him just now. Dead giveaways. What happened?"

"He's not one to stick around. And why should he when he can choose any woman on campus?" Jen said gloomily.

"What about 'love', and 'commitment'?"

"Our Jules isn't too big on either of those, especially not 'commitment'. Jen's voice oozed bitterness and self-irony.

Darcy rose. "I'm sorry, Jen. You've nothing to fear from me." She picked up her rucksack and slung it over her shoulder. "But Brant is right. I've seen things – terrible things – in that laboratory of his."

Jen held up a hand to stem the flow of words. "I don't want to hear this."

"You have to know what he's like, Jen," Darcy argued. "It's awful in there. He's been messing about with genetics. They're kept in glass cases: sickening parodies of human beings."

"I don't want to know," Jen repeated.

"Look," Darcy persisted, "I'm not just talking here of professional rivalry and jealousy. This is definitely unethical, and probably illegal."

"And I've got a course to finish, and want to keep my nose clean. Jules Cain is real mean when he's crossed, and could screw up my degree without trying."

"And you're still hoping he'll come back to you."

Immediately on seeing the hurt in Jen's face, Darcy regretted this show of contempt. She put her arms around Jen and gave her a hug. "Oh, I'm sorry, Jen. I didn't mean that."

"But I'm scared you might be right," Jen said with a sigh. "Anyway, aren't you staying the night?" she added, as Darcy moved to the door.

"No. I don't want to put you at risk. Thanks for everything though, Jen. I owe you."

"Like I said – anytime."

Darcy opened the door a little and checked the corridor "Just one thing," she paused on the threshold.

"Yes?"

"When you and Jules were –" Darcy searched for the right words but found there were none. "Did he ever show, or threaten, violence?"

"No. Why?"

"No reason. Take care Jen. I'll be in touch."

She's lying, Darcy thought as she stepped outside the safety of Jen's room and closed the door.

Jen's heightened colour and the way she had looked away had been dead giveaways.

*

The dash to the car was a heart-stopper, but accomplished without discovery. As she drove down the motorway, Darcy's gaze constantly went to the mirror. No twin headlamps glared in pursuit. The immediate danger over, her journey home was haunted by nightmare visions of half-humans in glass prisons, silently begging for revenge. As she left the motorway and sped towards Westwalls, she felt an overwhelming urge to see Mr. Ambrose.

*

After checking that Alisdair was safe and sleeping, she wondered whether Mr. Ambrose would still be awake. According to Alisdair, his elderly friend often stayed up half the night reading. And sometimes, when she herself was unable to sleep and had stepped outside for a stroll, there had been a light at the lodge window. Of course an early-hours visit may be the last thing he would welcome; he may still be hostile. After pacing the floor in agitation, the need to confide in someone became overpowering. Putting her jacket back on, she went outside into the desolate garden and made her way to the lodge.

Seven

~

They sat opposite one another, glass of whisky in hand, before the fire. It wasn't a cold night by any means, but the glow went some way to thawing the chill from Darcy's mind. In the stillness and intimacy of night, she had dared to disclose her terrible secret. They sat now without speaking, the silence a heavy cloak about their shoulders.

At last Darcy brushed back the curls from her forehead in a gesture of despair. "*Why?* Why would anyone want to do that? To create those monsters – then take pride in them?" She broke off and chewed her lip. "Maybe even *kill* for them." *There, she had voiced the suspicion.*

Mr. Ambrose regarded her with serenity. "What makes you think he did?"

"The path lab report on Charles Ashford – and the evidence of my own eyes: I saw those things in the laboratory," she hesitated and briefly shut her eyes, "and also Dr. Ashford on the stretcher. The particles from the meteorite, when processed into anti-matter, have the power to corrupt and destroy. I believe Cain used them to create his creatures, and also against Charles Ashford."

"I told you they would bring Chaos," Mr. Ambrose reminded her without rancour.

"They should be shot, all of them," Darcy said suddenly and with extraordinary vehemence.

Mr. Ambrose looked amused. "Who? Who would you shoot?"

"Scientists. Every last one of them."

"And why is that?"

Darcy made a gesture of disgust. "Because they make out they are working for the good of Humankind – when really they are corrupt and motivated by greed," she said with passion. "And we, the ordinary people, are helpless against them." She held out her hands. "Can't you do something to stop them?"

He peered at her over his *pince-nez*. "I cannot intervene."

"But they are *evil*."

He held up a crooked finger in caution. "Not all of them."

"Perhaps not, but the rest are ego-maniacs," she retorted dryly, thinking of Brant.

Mr. Ambrose's dark brows met above the bridge of his hooked nose. "Have a care. They, the dedicated few, are the shamans of our Age. They step out into Space where most do not dare, and leave footprints on the edge of Infinity. They, Darcy, are the Magicians of Today."

"And *you*. What are you?"

"Just an old man out of his time."

Mr. Ambrose sipped his whisky as the silence lengthened.

"But you've been so scathing about modern Science. Take the research team that came here for instance," Darcy protested as he made no move to explain.

The blue eyes teased her over the *pince-nez*. "Someone must play devil's advocate."

"Only the advocate?" She smiled. "I wonder."

She swallowed the last of her whisky and caught her breath as the spirit burned.

She rolled the empty glass between her palms then held it out to the flames so that the light played in its depths. "Brant told me Cain was messing with D.N.A. – that's why I went to his laboratory tonight. But there's something puzzling me yet."

Mr. Ambrose drained his glass. "And what is that?"

"Well okay, there's not much of the shaman about Jules Cain – but he is a brilliant scientist. So how come his experiments went so disastrously wrong?"

Mr. Ambrose carefully placed his glass on the round table by his elbow.

"Unfortunately, the dark side of life also has its magicians." His voice dropped as though he was speaking to himself. "And as yet they are children playing in shadows. May Gaia help us when they know the source of their power."

With a sense of foreboding, Darcy leaned forward. "What do you mean?"

His shoulders sagged as though beneath the weight of a terrible burden. "I refer to the Observer Effect."

"Isn't that to do with the duality in the world of Quantum Physics?" Darcy offered, then added as Mr. Ambrose looked both surprised and edified by her knowledge. "Brant – my husband – is a physicist too, remember. He used to talk about these things: about how light can be shown as both wave and particle. I still don't understand how this can be though."

"Neither do the physicists," he replied dryly. "They still wonder at the fact that carefully controlled experiments can vary *according to who is doing them*. They discovered that particles like electrons don't exist until they make their trace on laboratory monitors. Do you understand the significance of what I am saying, Darcy?"

She frowned, concentrating. "I think so. Nothing exists unless we experience it."

"Roughly speaking, yes. Let me simplify: all things in the Universe are made up of these basic particles."

"Including ourselves," Darcy interrupted.

"That is so. And our particles interact with those which make up the Earth and everything on it, and the stars and all of our Universe. This opened philosophical doors. Hard-headed scientists began talking like mystics. They had no choice. Because they began to understand that nothing exists except through our consciousness and experience."

Fireworks exploded in Darcy's mind. "I've heard of the expanding universe, but an *interactive* one – that's incredible."

He nodded. "But they haven't yet followed it through. What they haven't realised yet is the role of *intent*. That Good begets Good, and Evil brings about Evil."

Darcy stared incredulous. "But surely, 'intention' is just an emotion?"

"So is 'fear' – but it has a physical reaction," he retorted, tossing a log from the basket onto the fire. "There is nothing abstract or 'purely emotional' about glands pumping adrenalin into the bloodstream. Those chemicals were released as a direct response to an emotional state; just as particles respond to the emotional state of the observer in an experiment."

Darcy stared at him with mingled horror and disbelief, but then recalled Alisdair's explanation of how he had hurt the school bullies 'with his mind'. Hadn't he said much the same as Mr. Ambrose had just done? "Are you telling me those monsters I saw tonight are a direct result of Jules Cain's corruption and greed?"

Mr. Ambrose sighed but did not speak. Once more, silence wrapped its folds around them.

*

Darcy spread her hands in a gesture of helplessness. "What are we to do?"

"You must work to expose him."

"Why me?"

"Because you were brought here."

"Who will listen to a small-time reporter on a local rag?"

"Argue for your limitations and you'll surely have them!"

Darcy sighed. "So I heard from Alisdair." So much was at stake; why was she listening to this old fool's mystical ramblings? "Very quotable and suitably obscure for the in-garden guru, but hardly of help to us lesser mortals," she mocked, starting up from her chair.

"Wait."

She sat down again at the curt command, and watched intrigued as Mr. Ambrose wheeled a small trolley closer to the fire. As he placed it between them, Darcy saw that it held a marble chess board, and the most exquisite pieces she had ever seen.

"How beautiful." She fingered a queen in medieval gown and head-dress, before replacing it on the board. The pawns were represented as pages, the knights in traditional armour.

Mr. Ambrose was back on his chair. "Think of life as a game played out on a chessboard of Space and Time." He picked up a pawn. "Most, like this pawn here, can move only forward, and then only one square at a time. The King and Queen may move in any direction, but their game – and often their fate – is determined by the moves of pawns. Don't ever forget that," he said, replacing the piece on the board.

"And I am a pawn," Darcy confirmed. "And my moves may influence those in power to act. But what about *you*, Mr. Ambrose?" she asked, holding his gaze. "What moves can *you* make?"

He smiled enigmatically. "Perhaps I can best be likened to the 'bishop' – though only in relation to his possible moves, I hasten to add!" He picked up a bearded mystic with tangled tresses and snake-coiled staff and held it aloft. "He may cut across Space and Time." He illustrated by sweeping the piece diagonally from one corner of the board to the other. "This one is white, but remember, he may also be black. Now, let us see what happens." He dangled the piece before her eyes saying, "Watch him as he moves."

His voice took on a low and hypnotic tone. As it swung to and fro in his grasp, Darcy found her lids growing heavy.

"Watch him closely."

The chiselled features and alabaster hair became confused with Mr. Ambrose's image. Mr. Ambrose's appearance was undergoing a change.

Her head began to swim, her limbs felt leaden. She tried to speak but the words refused to form on her tongue. In a flash of panic, she realised she could not move as nerves and muscles succumbed to the thrall.

"Don't worry, it is only like when we sleep." Mr. Ambrose's voice reached her through a fog, and from a long way off. "Our bodies become paralysed then, too," the voice continued, "to stop us acting out our dreams and causing injury to ourselves. Did you know that?"

Darcy tried to answer but was struck dumb. She also tried to rise, but the greater her struggles, the more she seemed rooted to the chair. Her will to resist faded as a curious languor muffled her mind and wrapped her body in luxurious warmth. Her eyelids were now unbearably heavy. Her eyes closed.

*

The scene unfolded as though in a waking dream. A desert. The Sahara? So vivid was the image, that she could smell the dust, feel the pitiless heat on her face and arms. But then as if from nowhere, clouds appeared overhead. Now she could feel dampness like a cool compress pressing against her skin. Miraculously, foliage was springing up, unfurling and growing before her eyes, like one of those speeded-up nature films they were always showing on television. Or a model for a seven day Creation. Only this was real. So real and three dimensional that she could step inside the frame and into the picture.

She wandered at will, mesmerised by the huge and waxy blooms that unfolded ever more petals in her path. Pushing aside the fleshy spikes of a giant aloe, she penetrated the newly-formed jungle. Steam rose in thin spirals and the air was filled not with dust but exotic perfume. It was like a Turkish bath in here: moist but hot. Sweat beaded her forehead and her armpits felt sticky. She swung round at the sound of an eerie cry. A bird rose in the air, its plumage jewel-bright in the sun. Suddenly she stopped. There was somebody up ahead. Or maybe it was just one of those peculiar squat trees – what do they call them now, oh yes – baobabs, that was it.

No, it was definitely a man. A figure darting through the undergrowth. He was running, trying to escape. From what? Her befogged mind struggled to focus on the scenario. He turned as he ran, and there was terror in his eyes. Blue eyes, with a mesh of lines around them from working in the sun. A face she knew.

"Carl?"

She tried to run; her legs moved in slow motion. He looked to be struggling, was staggering about and tugging at his shirt neck. For the first time, she noticed the change of air. It was difficult to breathe. Gasping now she stumbled after him. Must reach Carl and save him. He turned to face her in mute appeal. She opened her mouth to scream but no sound came forth. His eyeballs were filled with blood. Blood dripped from his nostrils and gushed from his ears. "Carl! Carl!" Her mind screamed his name but her lips were still.

She watched him sink to the ground, writhe in agony, then lie motionless.

It was then that she heard the music. An ethereal sound like pan pipes, or the wind chimes of a Japanese garden. Something she knew had never been heard before. And its beauty filled her with dread.

*

The sound of Mr. Ambrose's palms being clapped smartly together brought her instantly back to alertness.

"*Carl?*" She started forward on her seat. "What happened?" She stared at Mr. Ambrose in distress. Her lungs still laboured for breath and she slumped back on her chair.

He spoke with great calmness. "You are safe."

"I must have dreamed it. Must have." She ran her hand through her curls in a distracted manner. "But how could I be dreaming when I wasn't even asleep?" she appealed.

"Ask yourself how light a sleep is needed to dream; heavy sleep is dreamless sleep."

She watched him, unconvinced, then abruptly rose. "Thank you for listening, now I have to go." She clutched the back of the chair as dizziness assailed her, then walked unsteadily to the door.

He nodded and made no effort to rise. Nor did he persuade her to stay. "You are too late to save your friend, but there will be many more whom you can save."

She paused on the threshold, opened her mouth to speak but did not. *Carl?* Carl was alright; it had been a waking-dream, the hypnogogic images she had explained to Alisdair. So why couldn't she believe it? Fear propelled her out of the lodge and into the moonless garden.

*

Back inside the house, she tiptoed upstairs then halted on the landing. From Alisdair's room came the soft sound of singing. Moving closer, she listened outside the door. The words chilled her to the bone:

> *The bright star of the East brings dawn's first breath*
> *The watery star of the West brings Life's emotional quest*
> *The summer-star of the South fires poet and bard*
> *But the dark star of the North brings to Earth*
> *Retribution, Silence and Death.*

She shuddered and went to her room.

Eight

~

The following morning Darcy watched Alisdair as he dashed off his breakfast and got ready for school. At least he was accompanying Radio One with the latest chart topper instead of singing that doom-laden nocturnal lament. "You'll need your kagoul; it's started to drizzle," she warned as he put on his blazer.

"Where did you go last night?" he asked, taking his waterproof down from the hook.

"Oh just out." She evaded.

"I thought you'd gone to meet that crumby Professor Cain."

"Well I hadn't. And Alisdair, will you stop speculating about my private life!" She tossed the frying pan into the sink with a clatter. "Did you sleep alright?" she asked casually, handing him his lunch box.

"Not bad." He reached for the half sausage left on his plate and crammed it into his mouth. He gave her a sideways look. "I heard Brant though."

Her hand froze as she moved to clear the dishes from the table. She flicked a switch on the radio and the *thump thump thump* of pop music ceased. "*What?*"

Alisdair wiped grease from his chin with the back of his hand. He shrugged his way into his kagoul and looked ready for a hasty exit. "I was awake when Brant came," he repeated. He pushed his glasses further up his nose and left smears of grease on the lens. Opening the door he dashed out to the shed. Darcy followed. "Wait! What did he want?"

"You."

Recalling his previous and artlessly casual questions, Darcy felt the chill of doom. "What did you tell him?" she demanded, advancing down the path.

Obviously aware he was on a sticky wicket, Alisdair had already wheeled his bicycle out of the shed and mounted it with alacrity. "That you were probably with Professor Cain."

"Oh shit!" she groaned, her worst fears confirmed. "Thanks, Alisdair. Thanks a million."

Alisdair was already through the gate. "Sorry," he called over his shoulder. "Thought you were."

She cupped her hands to her mouth and shouted, "Get back here Alisdair, like NOW!" But Alisdair, hood flying and legs plunging like pistons, had disappeared into the mizzle.

*

Could things get any worse? she asked herself, grabbing her car keys from the shelf. Now Brant would be out for her blood again. No time to mope about it now; she had to get to Frank Kelly and warn him about Carl Bayliss.

She and Carl had a thing going in the days before Brant. She recalled him now with affection as she walked towards the car. Nothing too heavy or serious, but they'd had fun. As senior correspondent he had helped her career along too, and would always be a bit special. She started the car up and drove out of Westwalls.

There was probably nothing in it. Last night she had been stressed out, exhausted and had drunk whisky before a blazing fire. Sleep must have caught her unawares and the whole damned thing had been just a dream. But she would sound Frank out on Carl's whereabouts – just in case. Thank God for civilised radio after Alisdair's Radio One, she thought with a grin, tuning in to her favourite station. Good timing: only ten minutes to the News.

She was now approaching the main road to the motorway. First the World Trade Agreement talks; then the search for a missing mother. Then the news reader went on to announce the final item. Darcy overshot a white line on the road. Luckily there was no vehicle in her path. Stamping on the brakes, she regained control and turned up the volume.

The report concerned an area of rapid and unexplained plant growth in the Sahara.

*

They had known where to pick her up. She was still trying to make sense of that enigmatic report as the vehicle pulled out of the lay-by. Within minutes of leaving the motorway the police car, sign lit and blue lights flashing, had pulled her in. Now she knew what lay behind Brant's enigmatic remark of 'if you get that far'. He had probably withheld her new address, or they would have visited Westwalls by now, but it was a simple thing to circulate the description and registration number of her car. After confirming her identity, the officer at her window 'requested' she follow him in for questioning. For a moment she knew a *frisson* of fear. Did the authorities know she was responsible for the Hilldean break-in? Almost immediately, she dismissed the suspicion that Jen had talked. Jen was too afraid of upsetting Jules Cain to risk being implicated, she decided, ignominiously following the police escort car into Manchester Police Headquarters.

*

Inspector Helen Gallagher leaned back on her chair and gave Darcy a look that said: *Mess with me at your peril, lady.* "You're not exactly helping that husband of yours, are you?"

Darcy shrugged, whilst secretly worrying: did she know about Brant's status with the Secret Services? Perhaps not. "I don't know what you mean," she fenced.

"You don't live at the farmhouse with your husband. Nor are you a student as you claimed."

Irritated, Darcy dislodged a hair that had stuck to her lipstick. "I didn't lie. I *am* still Mrs. Kennedy, and I *am* doing research at Hilldean. As for the farmhouse, it is still in my name as well as Mr. Kennedy's."

"You didn't give us the full circumstances."

"You didn't ask for a C.V."

Helen Gallagher tapped the desk smartly with her pencil. "Quite the Miss Smarty-Pants aren't we?"

Darcy looked her in the eye. "Where's the tape recorder?"

Helen Gallagher's gaze wavered. "This still isn't a formal interview."

"Then what do you want with me?"

Inspector Gallagher supported her chin on her hand and surveyed Darcy through narrowed eyes. "I don't know. I just have this vague feeling you fit somewhere into this jigsaw."

Brilliant deduction, Darcy thought.

Swiftly, she made up her mind. "There's something I think you should know."

Helen Gallagher almost managed to look bored. "Oh?"

"I overheard a quarrel between Charles Ashford and Jules Cain."

The bored expression was replaced by guarded interest. "When?"

"A few days before Dr. Ashford's death."

"What were they quarrelling about?"

"Cain wanted to publish – certain material," Darcy improvised, "Dr. Ashford accused him of plagiarism and threatened to expose him."

Helen Gallagher's cool had plummeted to sub-zero. "You should have told me this before."

"I didn't think of it at the time," Darcy lied.

The inspector shuffled the papers on her desk. "We'll look into it. I may need to contact you again. Your present address?"

Reluctantly Darcy provided it.

"Thank you. You may go now."

"That's not all. Ashford also accused Cain of conducting illegal experiments. I have, shall we say 'inside information' and know this accusation to be true."

"What sort of experiments?"

"He is using particles from a meteorite to corrupt D.N.A. and create mutant beings."

Helen Gallagher's expression was now inscrutable. "And where does he keep these – creatures?"

Darcy felt uneasy, as though she were being led by the nose. "In his laboratory at Hilldean University."

"Who gave you this 'inside information'?"

"I can't say."

Helen Gallagher suddenly leaned forward. "Security reported a break-in at the laboratory last night. Isn't that more to the point?"

"I don't understand."

"I think you do. I can't prove it – yet. But watch out, because I'm watching *you*. And I must also warn you about making false accusations against Professor Cain – it could get you into a lot of bother."

"It's all true, I tell you," Darcy protested.

Helen Gallagher stood up. "I think you should know we searched every inch of those laboratories this morning, and found nothing suspicious."

Darcy had also risen to her feet. "Then he moved them first! You have to believe me," Darcy persisted, as Helen Gallagher nodded at a police-woman standing at the back of the room, and the W.P.C stepped forward.

"A lover's tiff, Miss West? Is that why you have it in for Cain? Or is it the story-at-any-price syndrome, for that trendy column of yours?" Inspector Gallagher sneered. "Just don't try manufacturing news on my patch. Pushy reporters are my pet hate."

Darcy pulled her arm away as the policewoman tried to usher her to the door. "But you've got to do something! He's making money out of this thing. Selling it to unscrupulous people. Didn't you hear on the news this morning – the strange happenings in the Sahara? Somebody is testing the particles! What if it's Iraq? What if they are used –"

"I knew it – anything for a story! Get her out of here, Jones."

"Come on, miss."

The W.P.C. hustled Darcy out of the Inspector's office.

*

She had gone straight to the offices of the *Manchester News*, where she was faring little better with Frank. Uneasily, she wondered what lay behind his hostility.

"You heard it on the radio this morning; and probably saw the early edition," he accused. He rammed his cigar into one corner of his mouth and spoke out of the other. "I know you don't enjoy the luxury of tele-vision in the wilderness, but I assume you do have radio and newspapers," he added sarcastically.

Darcy tried to hide her impatience. "Yes, but I 'dreamed' this thing *last night*," she repeated. "You have to pull Carl out, Frank. He's in terrible danger."

"You've flipped," he said rudely, taking a cigar from the box on his desk. "Pull out my best reporter when he's first on the scene with a lead story? You have to be mad."

Darcy looked at him in horror. "You mean Carl's out there *alone?*" She had envisaged scores of reporters all vying for the best explanation and angle.

Frank smirked and threw the morning edition of the 'News' down on the desk before her. The front page headlines, Darcy saw, proclaimed a 'world exclusive' on the strange rumours in the Sahara. So how did Carl know what no-one else did?

"He heard the rumours first hand from the Bedouin. He was out there recently researching 'safety on safari holidays'," Frank supplied, obviously reading her thoughts from her expression. He puffed at his cigar until the end glowed red. "And anytime now, he's going to contact me with one helluva story."

"Great stuff, Frank," she said changing tack. "But it's so much bigger than that. Look, you know I'm researching these meteorite particles at Hilldean?" She repeated her theory about Jules Cain and his unlawful experiments. "And I believe he's behind this Sahara thing too. He's selling to the highest bidder, and given the location that could be Iraq. Think what that could mean! Those particles can also *destroy*. First we have to pull Carl out. Then we have to go to print like yesterday, and let the authorities know what Cain is up to before it's too late."

Frank chewed the end of his cigar, always a bad sign. "The authorities have already come to *us*," he said acidly.

Darcy cursed under her breath. So that was it. Helen Gallagher and her crew had got to Frank before her. Now she was in *deep* shit. That much became apparent as soon as Frank opened his mouth to continue.

"Now let me get this right. You gave false information to the police in what could turn out to be a murder investigation. Eventually they traced you to the 'News'. So tell me, what are you trying to do to me here? And to my paper?" His voice had been rising with each fresh word. Now it reached a crescendo. "They also tell me the Physics block was broken into last night. It was *you*, wasn't it?" he yelled, pointing at her with his cigar.

"Yes, but –"

Darcy didn't get the chance to finish.

"*Shit!* I knew it!" The muscles of his face worked spasmodically as he shifted the cigar from one side of his mouth to the other. "Just what the hell did you think you were doing? Well that's it – forget the whole thing! No more cover at Hilldean. And you're suspended for a month!" he added.

"Frank, no – you've got to listen," she tried to explain, "It's happened, and you'd better believe it! I *saw* those things in there."

"Like you 'saw' Carl in a vision? Come on Darcy, you've finally cracked. I told you to get your personal life together. Get to the doctors and get some rest. You're losing your touch, girl," he said cruelly.

Suddenly Darcy stiffened. *If I have to, I'll have you picked up for your own safety.* "Brant!" she exclaimed aloud. His hand was in here somewhere.

"Je'ez, that guy has my bloody sympathy," Frank groaned.

"Frank – I *saw* those things in Cain's laboratory, and I am *not* having a nervous breakdown! Now *trust me*, please!"

But Frank was shaking his head. "No way. Even if you did, you have no proof whatsoever that Cain has illicitly used the particles from that thing you found, nor do you know that his experiments haven't been sanctioned."

"So why had the creatures gone this morning?" she argued.

"The police have searched – and found nothing?" he said, sounding incredulous. He looked up at the ceiling. "And you want me to accuse this guy – one of the country's top-flight scientists – on the front page of the 'News'? Now I *know* you've really flipped."

Darcy rose, knowing herself defeated. "You'll think back to this day, Frank," she said moving to the door. "Because there'll be more rumours like the one on the Sahara today. Only there will be growth or devastation to order. And all for the price of a fat cheque from some foreign power. And another one, and another. Christ – I wouldn't like your conscience Frank, when Carl fails to come back – and the Western world is under threat!"

"Crazy dame."

She slammed the door so hard that Frank's girlie calender swung drunkenly on its hook.

*

As the route home led her past Hilldean, she decided to call in, maybe grab a coffee and pick up the latest gossip. Later, as she walked by the physics building on the way to the car park, she saw Jules Cain in conversation with Jen. Jen, she saw, looked distraught, and Darcy was debating whether to intrude when her friend hurried away. Cain's expression was black, but the mask of urbane charm dropped into place as she tried to slip past unseen. "Darcy! How about that coffee you promised?" he called.

Reluctantly she crossed to where he stood waiting. "Sorry. Just leaving," she said shortly. It seemed in the light of what she now knew, that this man emanated evil.

"Haven't seen you since poor Ashford died. Terrible business."

The scene in the laboratory came vividly into mind. It was probably a mixture of guilt and paranoia, but it seemed his dark eyes had penetrated her secret, and that he knew her to be the culprit. "Yes, awful." She studied his face, but he was giving nothing away.

"Have the police talked to you?" he inquired casually.

He knows they have, she guessed. "I told them I couldn't help them," she hedged. "I guess they're talking to anyone who used the department."

"We could have had that coffee, instead of standing here," he pressed.

"I really must go now. I'll see you around Jules, then we'll have that drink," she added, attempting to convince him that all was normal.

After all, she thought getting into the car, if her suspicions were correct, Jules Cain was a dangerous man.

Nine

~

Almost a week later, an insistent knocking brought her to the front door. She fumbled with the little-used lock, wondering if it was Brant. He had stayed away since the night of her midnight raid on Hilldean, when Alisdair had obligingly told him she was out with Jules Cain. Frank had proved equally unforgiving, she reflected, and had not answered her letter requesting reprieve from her suspension. As the door opened, she saw that it was not Brant who stood on the doorstep but a young man whom she could not place, yet who seemed vaguely familiar. There were thread lines of anxiety round his eyes, and he looked as if he could use a good night's sleep.

"Hi. Darcy West, isn't it? I'm Chris Forster. Hope you don't mind me dropping in on you like this. I left the bike down by the gate, if that's okay?" he said in a rush.

"Er, yes, sure." She had been down there minutes earlier to collect her mail from the box. Whilst there she had heard what had sounded at first like the throb of an approaching engine, but had dismissed it as some-body passing in the distance.

The piece clicked into place in the jigsaw: *the refectory on the day of Ashford's death.* This man, she realised now, was Jen's boyfriend. "What on earth brings you out here?" she demanded, then added as she could see no reason for him to visit her alone, "Where's Jen?"

His shoulders visibly drooped. "I was hoping you could tell me that. She isn't with you then?"

Darcy frowned. "No. Should she be?"

He seemed nervous, and wiped the palms of his hands on his faded jeans as though they were sweating. "I've tried everyone else."

"You'd better come in and I'll make some coffee."

Darcy placed the envelope she had been holding on the hall table and led the way into the kitchen.

*

Chris stood looking about him as she poured water from the kettle into two mugs.

"Your husband?" he asked, stopping before a photograph of Brant on the shelf by the door.

"Ex." Darcy replied shortly. Not strictly true, but it dispensed with the need for explanations.

"Sorry," he said, looking uncomfortable.

"That's okay." She frowned. "What is it?"

He shrugged and moved away. "Oh, nothing. Thought I knew his face from somewhere. Must be mistaken."

He sat down as she indicated a chair.

"When did you last see Jen?" Darcy asked, placing a mug of coffee before him on the sun-drenched table top.

"Thanks. About five days ago."

"Has she not been seen around campus?"

He pushed his fingers through his sandy hair. "No."

"Did she seem okay when you last saw her?"

"Kinda moody. It was probably down to Dr. Ashford dying. She liked him and was really upset. But when it still carried on I thought maybe she was pining again for that bastard Cain." He stopped, and his embarrassment showed.

"It's okay. Jen told me," Darcy said swiftly. "She's still hooked on him then?"

He shrugged. "I'm not sure. It's more like she despises herself for getting involved and putting up with his crap." His face darkened. "He treated her pretty rough," he added, confirming Darcy's earlier suspicions about Cain.

"Look, I may be talking out of turn here, but the last time I saw Jen she was talking to Cain on campus and looked pretty upset," Darcy confided.

He sighed and shook his head. "Christ! When was that?"

"Last Wednesday."

"Someone should do something about that guy; trouble is, he's protected by his status." Chris's voice was filled with bitterness.

"Has she ever gone off before?" Darcy asked, tracing with her finger a leafy pattern of light and shade that latticed the table top. Strange, despite the warmth of the day, no flies buzzed in the kitchen. With sadness she recalled the dying garden. No flowers, no insect life.

He finished his coffee and put down the mug. "Once, after a row, she went to her brother in Lincoln. I've already tried him," he added, pre-empting her next question.

Darcy frowned, struggling with a growing sense of unease. Telling herself that Jen had gone off to make her point after a tiff with Chris over Cain, simply wasn't working. "Look, I don't want to alarm you, but shouldn't you mention this to the police?"

"I'd already decided on that if she wasn't with you," he assured her, rising.

"Anyway, thanks for listening. I'll let you know if she turns up."

"Yes, do. Likewise," she said, leading the way from the kitchen.

As they were passing the shelf by the door, Chris stopped before the photograph of Brant, and clicked his fingers. "Got it! I've seen him a couple of lunch times lately in the Boot and Shoe by Hilldean. Has he remarried then?"

Darcy froze. "Not that I know of! Why?"

"Oh, he was with a woman. I remembered because of her French accent." He stopped. "Sorry, have I put my foot in something here?"

She forced brightness into her voice. "Of course not. Brant and I are history."

Chris left. She closed the door and leant against it. *Andrea Lascelles!* It had to be. *The bastard!* And after all he'd had to say about herself and Julian Cain.

The thought brought to mind the letter she had left on the hall table. Picking it up, she read it through again. It was from Cain. Her face set in an expression of resolve. She would do as he requested and meet him at the Black Bull Inn at Coniston, two nights hence. It was risky; but it was also the only way of continuing her investigation, now that she was no longer officially under cover at Hilldean. And it seemed she had nothing more to lose as far as Brant was concerned. But first, she would check out the Boot and Shoe for herself. She was due to have lunch with Caro the following day.

Ten

~

Don't let them be here, Darcy prayed, yet part of her had to know. She pushed open the door of the Boot and Shoe Inn, and squaring her shoulders walked inside. Caro, following behind, kept up a stream of chatter about a three day course she had just been on. Darcy threw the odd question over her shoulder and made 'interested noises' as they made their way to the bar, but her eyes and attention were elsewhere. In fact her stomach was in knots as she scanned the tables. Most students and tutors ate and drank at the on-campus bars, despite the proximity of the Boot and Shoe to the University, so there were no faces she recognised.

"What are you going to have?" Caro was asking, indicating the menu chalked up on the miniature blackboard. "Say, are you alright? You seem to be somewhere else today," she added, giving Darcy a penetrating look.

"Sure. I'm fine." Darcy was just beginning to think this was true when she spotted them. They were seated next to one another in a secluded alcove beside the period fireplace. Her fair head was very close to his dark one, and they were deep in conversation. So much so that they seemed oblivious to the world, let alone Darcy's presence.

"I think I'll have the lasagne. What about you? Hey, wake up Darcy! Have you decided yet what –" Caro stopped in mid sentence. "For God's sake what is it? You look like you've seen a ghost." She fell silent as her gaze followed her friend's. "That's Andrea Lascelles," she whispered at last. "From C.A.D.E. – on sabbatical attached to Julian Cain's department."

"We've already met," Darcy shot back, "And it's Brant she's attached herself to!"

Caro looked distressed and when she spoke, her optimism was forced. "It could be innocent. They are in the same line of work."

Darcy turned and gave her a look of pure scepticism. "With their heads that close? Do they look like they're engrossed in some boring theorem?"

Caro sighed. "Suppose not. Are you going to let him know you're here?"

Darcy shook her head. "What's the point?"

Caro was eyeing her shrewdly. "You knew he would be here, didn't you?" she said sharply.

"I hoped not. Sorry, Caro; I didn't mean to embarrass you."

Caro sighed with annoyance. "Look, if you two are playing silly games off one another – don't involve me."

Darcy felt close to tears. "No games. Somebody told me; I had to know."

"Okay, don't be upset; I understand." Caro's eyes narrowed. "Is this about Jules?"

"Partly."

"Are you seeing him?"

Darcy hesitated, agonising over whether to confide what she knew about Cain, then recalling Jen, decided she couldn't put Caro at risk. "I'm meeting him tomorrow evening for a drink," she admitted, and cringed as Caro looked over at Brant and his companion, then back at herself. *She's thinking it's my own fault* Darcy told herself miserably.

"Okay. That's your business. I just hope both you and Brant know what you are doing," Caro said, scanning the menu again to indicate the subject was closed.

"Are you ready to order, ladies?" The barman polished the copper-topped bar with a cloth and looked enquiringly at them.

"Sorry Caro. I couldn't eat anything."

"Okay, no problem." Caro raised her voice, "Not hungry thanks," she said dismissing the barman, then squeezed Darcy's arm. "Come on," she said taking over, "We'll grab a drink and a sandwich on campus and take it to my room."

Darcy allowed herself to be ushered towards the door. As they reached it, she could not resist a backward glance. Brant chose that moment to look up. He met her gaze, but gave no sign of recognition.

Darcy hurried out as the Lascelles woman touched his arm, and once more claimed his attention.

*

It was a relief to be back at Westwalls, to fasten the gate and shut out the rest of the world. At least here she could lick her wounds in peace. Alisdair however, didn't allow her to wallow for long. He came home from school and put his head cautiously round the kitchen door. "Am I in trouble?" he asked disarmingly.

She tried to look stern and failed. "No, of course not. It wasn't your fault I screwed-up all round."

He grinned at the school yard parlance. "Will it come right?"

"Oh, I guess. Want some tea?" She rose from her seat by the Aga as he nodded, and poured him a cup.

"Good. Because I've got more bother here," he said cheerfully, holding out a buff-coloured envelope.

"School?"

He nodded and looked resigned.

"Okay, let me see."

"You had a bad day too, Darcy?" he asked as she let out a huge sigh and ripped open the envelope.

"Life's a bitch, Alisdair."

He grinned and spooned extra sugar into his tea.

*

Darcy put the letter down on the table and said nothing for a moment or two. Alisdair, she saw on raising her head, was regarding her with an anxious look. "This teacher, Mrs. Grey – she says there are problems. That you're far ahead of the others and aren't being stretched enough. They're at a loss about how to keep you interested."

He looked indignant. "It's not my fault."

"No. But you can't mess about, be disruptive in class, because you find it easy and get bored."

"But I don't! I try to help the other kids, teach them about *real* things, but the teachers think I'm weird." His eyes loomed huge behind his glasses as he gave her an injured look.

She stood up, and laughing gave him a hug. "I'm not surprised! But don't worry, we'll be social outcasts together." But then she was suddenly serious. "But she says there's something else. It concerns the boys that set on you and gave you that black eye."

"Yes?" he said with an air of innocence.

"Apparently two of them are having recurrent nightmares, and are becoming withdrawn."

Alisdair nodded vigorously. "Jones – he held me. And Baker – he hit me. And she means they don't bully anyone any more."

Darcy hid her amusement at this deft summing up and alternative interpretation.

"So do you want to tell me about it?"

"I already told you. I hurt them with my mind, like Mr. Ambrose taught me."

"Pull the other one, Alisdair! You've been telling them ghost stories haven't –"

She stopped on seeing Alisdair's expression. His eyes, magnified by the glasses, were fixed and staring, their expression malignant. For one crazy second she was reminded of the Angel of Retribution in that awful dream.

"Stop it, Alisdair," she ordered sharply. Though what it was he was supposed to stop, she wasn't at all sure. Suddenly pain seared her head. She let out a cry and held her hands to her temples. Immediately the pain ceased.

"Sorry, Darcy." Alisdair appeared normal now, and was looking apologetic. "It was easier to show you what I could do."

"Mr. Ambrose taught you to do *that?*"

He ignored the question and taking her empty cup from the table, refilled it with tea from the pot. "Don't fret. I'll start sending them some good vibes. There'll be no more trouble at school," he announced, then walked over to the door. "I'm going to see Mr. Ambrose. I'm a bit worried about him; he seems thinner. Soon he'll be transparent."

Leaving Darcy speechless, he left the kitchen.

*

Mr. Ambrose stood on top of the fell, watching the eagle soar overhead. It had already begun. Deserts would bloom; rain forests would die, then cities too. Unless the rot could be stopped. But the deadly seeds were already being sown; the grim reaper waited in the wings. What fools they are, what fools!

It was almost time. Lifting a wizened hand he touched his cheek. The skin felt paper-thin and fragile; he was becoming more transparent. His attention returned to the eagle. The slight shift of wing-feathers seemed to beckon as they fingered the air-current. He could help for a while longer, then it would be up to Alisdair and all the other youngsters like him. They must carry on.

Because he was not alone. There were many out there; gifted youngsters who would grow into men and women of integrity and vision. They would penetrate the mysteries of the New Physics; they alone would sense the Truth behind the white coats and clinical trappings. They would use their knowledge of the Universe, but for the Good not the destruction of the Earth, of Mother Gaia.

He sighed. Was it too late? Had the Cains of this world got too deep a hold? Had rank evil and greed sapped the will and motivation of even the Alisdair's of this world? Only Time would tell.

But now it was time for the Darcy-girl's trials to begin. He turned and the wind lifted his hair so that it flowed behind him like eagle-feathers. And here was the boy coming up the fell for his next lesson.

Alisdair would be a strength during those trials.

Eleven

~

It was mid-week and 'walking weather', so despite the autumnal nip in the air ramblers were making use of the seating and tables provided outside the Black Bull. The bars and restaurant however, were almost deserted. Several 'locals' propped up the bar discussing hound trailing and sheep, and a retired couple fussed over a tray of coffee at one of the tables. According to the guide books, out-of-season Coniston was still comparatively unspoilt, Darcy recalled as she sipped a gin and tonic, but for a week or two yet shops would be vying to sell kagouls and boots to novice walkers, and cafes to tempt the less energetic tourist with 'Lakeland' teas and ice-cream.

She sighed and wished herself back at Westwalls. Seeing Brant with that Lascelles bitch the day before had left her raw and less inclined to tangle with Jules Cain. Perhaps he wouldn't turn up. She took out a pen and began the *Telegraph* crossword, and so didn't see him approach.

"Darcy – so glad you could make it."

She looked up into his smiling and handsome face, but saw only the creatures of his laboratory.

✽

Ten minutes or so later, she began to wonder what she could possibly learn from this encounter. Her thoughts had gone no further than to grasp the opportunity offered by his letter. So far, the conversation had been superficial and innocuous, ranging from the weather to the latest gossip on campus. He had skilfully sidestepped her every attempt to get him round to the subject of the meteorite, or his work.

"Would you like to eat?" he asked now, indicating the menu.

"I ate earlier, thanks. But please, don't let me stop you."

He made a dismissive gesture with one hand. "Another drink then?"

"Just one."

"G and T?"

"Please."

He rose and stood for a moment, looking down at her. The expression in his eyes left her with no illusions about his feelings.

She watched him at the bar. He stood with his back to her, his shoulders broad beneath the full-length and caped Barbour coat. Its long line accentuated his above-average height, and, she had to admit, he possessed an air of distinction. It was difficult to equate this man with Charles Ashford's murder. Doubts began to erode her confidence. Could she possibly be wrong? No. There still remained those horrendous and pitiable creatures. There had been no mistake about those. Could questionable experiments be placed on a moral par with murder? Somehow she doubted it, and was left even more confused. She watched him walk back towards her, a glass in either hand, his hair gleaming blue-black even in this subdued lighting. She saw him smile and bid the elderly couple 'good evening' as he passed their table, and the whole thing seemed even more incredible.

"So," Darcy started deliberately once he had sat down again. "Why did you ask me to meet you, Jules?"

He gave her one of his most disarming smiles. "Isn't wanting your company reason enough?"

Darcy sipped her drink. "Very flattering, but no," she said, replacing her glass on the table.

"You know how I feel about you, Darcy. I can't watch you throw yourself away on that fool Kennedy."

"That's my affair."

He raised one of his startlingly black eyebrows. "I'm afraid *affair* is a loaded word."

"If you brought me here to tell me Brant is seeing Andrea Lascelles, then you are wasting your time. I already know," Darcy said brusquely.

"That would hardly endear me to you, now would it? I don't fancy playing Boudicca's messenger."

Darcy looked blank. "Oh?"

"She had the bearer of bad news done to death."

"I see." She couldn't help smiling. "Now – what did you *really* want to see me about?"

He sighed and twisted his glass to and fro on the table. "You're very astute. And quite right of course. I do have a slight problem. A rather delicate one in fact. I hardly know how to begin. May I speak to you in confidence?" He gave her a look of silent appeal.

"Of course." Darcy's mind was a ferment of speculation.

"One of my students. I was stupid enough to get briefly involved. Is anything the matter?" he asked, breaking off his narrative.

With an effort, Darcy pulled herself together. "No, nothing. Do go on," she urged, whilst thinking: *he's going to tell me about Jen.*

"Well anyway, I tried to end it; told her it couldn't go on, but she wouldn't accept it. The upshot is, she had a row with her current boy-friend and ran away. The day I wrote to you she turned up at my house, distraught and hysterical. I couldn't just turn her away. I tried reasoning with her, being supportive without encouraging false hope – after all, by dint of my position, I am partly to blame." He looked suitably concerned, whilst Darcy thought: *clever bastard; playing for sympathy.*

"Anyway," he continued, "She quietened down, but I wasn't really getting through. So I left her under the care of my housekeeper. She's a discreet soul and didn't ask questions. But I needn't tell you," he said lowering his voice, "what a stink there would be at Hilldean should all this come out."

"So why are you telling me?" Darcy said guardedly.

He leaned across the table in a conspiratorial manner. "Because you know her. Her name is Jennifer Simpson. She talks about you. Says you are her only real friend."

"You mean Jen is still at your home?"

"Yes. And that's why I asked you to meet me tonight. Will you come and see her? I believe she would listen to you."

"What now? Come home with you?" Darcy exclaimed.

The dark eyes pleaded with her. "I know it's a lot to ask. A real big one, in fact. I wouldn't ask you for my own sake, but I can't keep Jen there after tonight. I'm divorced, and it's my weekend to have the boys." He took her hand. "Will you come?"

Darcy only hesitated a moment. It was Jen, for God's sake, and she was in a corner. She wasn't keen on accompanying Cain, but his story did check out with what Chris had told her. Except he had glossed over his own part, she thought with disgust. "You want me to try and per-suade her to return to Hilldean?"

"Yes, and then perhaps enlist the help of her boyfriend. I can hardly approach him."

"Perhaps for the time being, she would come back to Westwalls with me," Darcy suggested.

"Then you'll come?"

Darcy rose. "I have no choice."

Relief flooded his face as she stood up. "Thank you. I knew you wouldn't let me down."

As they left, the elderly couple smiled and bid them good night.

*

"Whereabouts is your house?" she asked as they reached the car park.

He stopped by his B.M.W. "Oh, you wouldn't know it. It's about twenty miles from here. Very secluded: my moorland retreat. Just follow me."

As she followed the red tail lights out of Coniston and on to Yewdale, it did occur to Darcy that *Jen* had presumably found this inaccessible house. She dismissed the thought; at some time in the past, Cain must have taken her there.

*

That journey seemed endless. She trailed Cain's car round convoluted lanes, over mountain passes and was soon completely lost. *How much further?* Nobody knows where I am, she worried, and Alisdair was waiting at home. The suspicion that Cain was deliberately taking a circuitous route flashed through her mind. The deepening twilight added to the confusion: nothing clear-cut, all shifting shadows, purplish haze and blurred edges; neither light nor dark, and a time, Mr. Ambrose might say, when the Other-World moved closer and mortals were at risk.

There followed a long climb with one-in-four gradients and a couple of hairpin bends. Then a single-track road that writhed over a desolate moor with a backdrop of glowering fells. And darkness was falling. A lonely sprinkling of stars punctured the night-sky, and a fat moon struggled to free itself from marauding cloud. She was just about to flash Cain to stop, when a roof and chimneys came into view and his indicator flashed.

Jen had come all the way out here to confront Cain?

She must have been desperate, Darcy thought, following Cain down the rutted track to the rambling house.

*

To Darcy, the slamming of Cain's car door was an ominous sound. It echoed in the empty silence, stressing her isolation.

He strolled over as she got out of the car. "Did you think you were never getting here?"

In the darkness, his teeth seemed very white as he smiled. His tone was light, he seemed relaxed and Darcy was reassured. "You said it was secluded," she quipped, gazing at the Victorian hunting lodge with its bristling chimneys, wrought iron roof finials and bedroom balconies. The windows stared blankly out, inky-black with secrets. A dark hedge of yew added a further sinister touch. "You have a *housekeeper*?" she said incredulously, looking about her.

"Of sorts," he said easily, leading the way. "The wife of one of the local farmers. She drives over each morning, cleans and keeps the place aired when I'm at Hilldean."

"Is Jen in there alone then?" she demanded.

He didn't answer, but beckoned for her to follow.

She stumbled on the flagged path that led to the door.

"Careful." He reached out and steadied her, then put a protective arm about her shoulders. Instinctively she moved aside and gave him a wary look. At that moment the moon broke free, and something in his expression made her involuntarily shiver. But then he was smiling again, and she thought it must have been her imagination. A trick of the moonlight perhaps, that had blackened his eyes and made them appear to glitter with malice.

"Come on in."

He was holding the front door open for her to pass inside.

*

The interior contrasted sharply with the austerity outside. Once in the hall, Cain had taken a cigarette lighter from his pocket and lit the Victorian glass wall lights. Darcy noticed a slight hissing sound, then the mantels glowed from dull amber to incandescent white.

"Calor gas," he commented, also lighting an oil-lamp with a tall glass funnel.

She nodded, noting the ancient tapestry drapes and the monk's settle, the date *1675* carved into the blackened wood. A slight mustiness rose to her nostrils, the smell of ancient furnishings and decay. Carrying the lamp, he led the way down the passage to an inner door. Their footsteps were muffled by the Persian and Aubusson rugs which partially covered the stone-flagged floor.

*

The room into which he now ushered her had an intimate air with its rich coral walls, deep winged chairs and gilt-framed oil paintings. The crystal lamps flared at the touch of Cain's lighter, adding to the ambience of warmth and comfort. "Do sit down," he invited, turning to her with a smile and indicating a leather chesterfield sheltered from draughts by a tapestry screen. "Drink?" he asked, moving to a side table on which bottles and a decanter were arranged. As though we had just returned from a concert or the opera, Darcy thought in amazement. Taking out his lighter again, he stooped and held the flame to the newspaper and kindling laid ready in the hearth.

Darcy, prey to a growing sense of unreality, shook her head and remained standing. "Thanks, but I can't stay long. Where's Jen?" she added.

The room, she noted, gave no sign that there was a female occupant in the house.

Cain poured himself a brandy, and despite her refusal, a liqueur for herself. "Patience, Darcy. All in good time."

That's the second time he's evaded a question about Jen, she thought with a sense of rising panic. What's more, she was sensitive to atmosphere, and this house felt empty apart from themselves. "May I use the bathroom, please?" she asked.

"Of course. Let me show you."

He handed her the glass of liqueur which she placed on a carved octagonal table as they passed.

Returning to the hall he pointed to the stairs. "Up there, second door on the right."

"Thank you."

She mounted the stairs, every sense straining for clues. With a sigh of relief she heard Cain walk back to the sitting room.

*

In addition to the bathroom, three other doors flanked the landing. Opening the first, she quickly scanned the interior: a bedroom, bed unmade and furniture covered with dust sheets. The room next to it was in a similar state. In the final one, the bed was made up and items of male clothing were draped on the chair. Cain's room at a guess. If Jen was here, she certainly wasn't upstairs. Slipping into the bathroom she waited a minute then flushed the toilet and washed her hands. No sign of a female presence here, either. The room had a definite masculine look with its mahogany panelled bath, dark colour scheme and its lack of clutter. Any feminine article would stick out like a sore thumb. So how to play it? Could she steal downstairs and be through the front door without Cain knowing?

Opening the bathroom door she crept out onto the landing.

Jules Cain was smiling up at her from the bottom of the stairs.

He was blocking her path to the front door; there was no choice but to walk into the sitting room. She rounded on him at once. "Jen's not here, is she?"

"Relax, Darcy, relax."

"Answer my question, damn you," she shouted, momentarily losing control.

"Forget her, she won't bother us any more."

Darcy stared at him, her eyes widening in horror. "What have you done?" she whispered.

"Look how the fire is getting up. Come and sit over here by the blaze – oh, and bring your drink," he added pleasantly, picking it up himself. She shook her head in disbelief; this whole thing had become a nightmare. He took her arm with his other hand and tried to usher her to a sofa by the fire. She tore her arm away. "You've brought me here under false pretences, haven't you?" she accused, playing for time as her mind worked.

"I prefer to call it a lover's ploy. You wouldn't have come here otherwise, would you?"

Darcy looked wildly around her. Once more he was blocking the way to the door. "Where's Jen?" she pleaded. "Is she alright?" There was no doubt in her mind that he knew her whereabouts.

The benign mask slipped for a second or two: his eyes were dead and black like a shark's. "I've told you, forget the silly bitch." He quickly recovered himself as Darcy recoiled. "Would you like coffee with your liqueur?"

She backed away. "You're mad of course. Quite mad."

His face contorted with rage. A twitch appeared at the corner of his mouth.

The blow sent her spinning across the room.

Twelve

~

The place in which she came to was vastly different from the luxury she had encountered upstairs. The sound of water incessantly dripping penetrated her consciousness first. Then the flickering of a light. A solitary flame that seemed like sixty thousand candle power as it burst and hammered behind her eyelids. Painfully she opened her eyes. The lone candle stood on an up-ended barrel. She touched her chin then opened and shut her mouth experimentally. Her jaw felt broken but wasn't. As memory returned, she began to shake. Cain was mad. A psychotic. The worse part was his periods of seeming sanity. That was when she began to wonder if it wasn't herself that was certifiable.

Which was how he had managed to hold down his job without anyone suspecting. He had probably killed Jen, and the odds were, she would end up the same way. Why else should he hold her here? The prospect of death was bad enough, but worse still was the thought of what might happen in between.

Pain, exhaustion and fear allowed weakness to come flooding in. *Brant. Oh Brant, why didn't I listen to you?* Now she would end up dead in this awful cellar – at least, it had the feel of a cellar, or was it an attic? No, because the mattress on which she was lying rested on a stone floor, that much she knew from the coldness and hardness beneath her hand as her arm lolled over the edge. And the constant sound of water suggested an underground stream. This basic exercise in deduction did much to squash the panic. It imposed a sense of order on nightmare and chaos. Besides, no use thinking of Brant. He was probably in Andrea Lascelles' arms and bed. Okay then, she would survive without him.

She struggled to hold panic at bay as footsteps approached, and a key turned in the lock.

*

He paced the stone floor then dropped on his hunkers before her. "I don't want to hurt you. Be nice to me, Darcy," he pleaded, reaching out for her hand. The instant she drew back in revulsion, his hand shot out and grabbed her hair. "You wouldn't do that if I was Kennedy, would you?" He wrenched back her head until she screamed. "Kennedy, always Brant Kennedy. That's how it's been all along," he released her so that she sank forward on the mattress. "He gets the goodies; he gets *you*. I get the fame and prizes, yet he gets the respect. But not for long. From now on, the world will have to respect *me*."

"For destroying it?"

The blow caught her on the side of the head.

Immediately he picked her up again, cradled her in his arms and seemed distraught. "I'm so sorry Darcy. But you mustn't say those things, then I won't get angry," he said soothingly whilst tenderly stroking her hair. She remained silent. The safest course it seemed. Her head was buzzing; fear and pain were turning her sick.

"We belong together Darcy. I knew it from when we first met. But *you* have to feel it too. You have to want me, in the way you want Brant Kennedy. I can't let you go till you do. You understand that, don't you?"

She nodded, striving to hide her revulsion, having learned it would earn her more pain.

He stroked her cheek, and then her hair and she forced herself not to cringe.

"In the end, you'll come to me Darcy, beg me to make love to you."

A shudder ran through her at this thinly veiled threat.

She sensed rather than saw his change of mood.

Standing up, he recommenced the pacing. "It was *you*, Darcy, wasn't it?" he said suddenly, stopping before her. Darcy's stomach lurched as she had a presentiment of what was to come.

"*You* broke into the laboratory, didn't you?"

"No," she lied desperately, "I swear!"

"Liar! What did you see? Who did you tell?"

"Nothing, I saw nothing. Please Jules, we're friends, you shouldn't be treating me like this," she sobbed.

He stood looking down on her, shaking his head. "You shouldn't lie to me, Darcy. He towered over her, his fist clenched and raised. She closed her eyes and prayed. The blow didn't come. Instead he took a torch from his pocket and switched it on. Walking across to the candle he blew it out. "Sweet dreams, Darcy," he said, "you'll tell me everything in time. *Then* we can be friends."

She heard the door open and shut, the key turn in the lock, then the sound of his footsteps receding.

It was then that she understood, and the knowledge brought paralysing fear. Because now she knew where he was at. The man was a sadist, and a clever and subtle one at that.

The reason she was allowed a candle in the first place, was so she could feel its loss.

*

It was the worst and longest night of Darcy's life. Caught as she was between the fear of being left alone with the squeaking and scratching that issued from corners, and the terror of hearing Jules Cain's key turn in the lock. Cain didn't come. The rats did.

She reminded herself that the 'rat's go for the throat' tale was nothing but myth and a case of mistaken intent, the truth being that a cornered rat would leap for the only available route of escape: over the person's shoulder. It was still hard to keep from screaming when eyes glowed redly in the gloom. After the candle had been extinguished, it became apparent from a greyish glow above her head that there was a small window set into the wall, admitting intermittent moonlight through the bars. It was hard to decide which was worse: being alone in suffocating darkness as cloud covered the moon, or having sufficient light to make out the heavy sloping bodies and serpentine tails of her rodent companions.

She did pluck up courage enough to make one trip to the door, but in the darkness could glean nothing, except that it was locked. Her handbag: what about the skeleton key in her handbag? Feverishly then she had felt the floor immediately around the mattress, heart in mouth lest her hands encounter bristly fur or sharp teeth. They didn't. But neither did they touch on her handbag. Not surprising; Cain would scarcely have brought it for her. There was nothing to do now but try and conserve her energy till it was light. She resigned herself to endless hours of darkness.

*

Yet pass the night did, and somehow she got through it. Largely by praying as she had not since leaving school, and by saying Brant's name over and over again. Yet strangely, as she fitfully dozed it was Alisdair, not Brant whom she saw. Alisdair, with N.H.S. spectacles and angel wings. Alisdair waiting for her return, and avenging her when she did not come.

Thirteen

~

As the first grey light seeped in through the small window, she crawled painfully from the mattress and explored her prison. The immediate space proved to be a cellar with shelves and wine racks holding dusty bottles, jars of preserves which looked as though they had been there since World War II, and various casks and wooden boxes festooned with cobwebs. The air was dank and the sound of running water ever-present. Apart from the door through which Cain had come – and she shivered at the memory – the only opening on the outside world was the small window high on the wall above the mattress.

This, she discovered by dragging one of the crates and standing upon it, represented ground level, and was firmly sealed, with no give whatsoever in the stout iron bars. A daylight examination of the door showed it to be of thick timber which though old was still sound, and with large gothic-style hinges. There was a gap between the edge of the door and the jamb, due to the bulbous hinge and the fact that the door had dropped slightly over the years, but this was of little help, she mourned, pushing her fingers through.

Beyond this main area she found a smaller chamber, empty except for a primitive chemical toilet and a chipped enamelled bowl with a jug containing water. *How long before they are removed?* she thought grimly.

It was patently obvious that this whole thing had been planned.

The knowledge brought a chill of fear.

*

She felt marginally better after making use of the improvised bathroom and swilling her aching and swollen face with ice-cold water. Her plight, she assessed, was desperate but not hopeless. And she had one or two advantages. As a reporter she was not a total stranger to life-threatening situations. In addition, her knowledge of psychological intimidation was above average, due to a piece of research on 'Amnesty'; so in theory at least, she should be better equipped than most to survive it. Whilst she was still alive, retained her wits, and was physically able to function, there was always the chance of escape. If a small voice within warned that this situation was not guaranteed to continue, she ruthlessly shut it out.

The question was how to play it. Cain obviously had periods of lucidity and apparent normality, and during these was maybe open to reason. During his episodes of irrationality, it was vital to go along with him and not provoke one of those sudden and terrifying bouts of violence. Having worked out this basic survival plan, she settled down to wait.

*

It was with mixed feelings that she heard approaching footsteps and then the key turn in the lock. Several hours had passed, or so it seemed: her watch must have been damaged during her fall and had stopped. Whilst the approach of Cain brought terror, it also offered a chance to negotiate.

As Cain entered, she was relieved to see that he seemed calm and that his eyes, whilst dark, were not black. He was carrying a tray containing a steaming mug and a couple of slices of toast. Play it by ear. She waited for him to speak.

"Good morning, Darcy." He set down the tray on an upturned barrel.

She rose to confront him: bad tack to allow him the advantage of looking down on her. "Look, Jules. We're friends you and I, let's talk about this sensibly," she said in a calm and firm voice.

He pushed her back down on the mattress. "Friends don't break into premises and threaten to ruin a life's work."

"I wouldn't do that," she ventured, avoiding an outright denial which might only inflame him. "Why are you keeping me here? What do you want from me?" she pleaded.

"I want *you*, Darcy." He smiled benignly as though it was the most natural thing in the world. "But on my terms. Not still whinging and pining over that bastard Kennedy."

"But there's no need for this," she tried next. "Just give me a little time. My marriage has not long broken up."

"I haven't got time. Neither have you, my dear," he added chillingly. "You see I'm supposed to kill you. There's a contract out on you, and I was instructed to carry it out. Only," he stooped and grabbed her chin in a vice-like grip, "I want you *alive*, not dead. Whether that can be achieved, is largely up to yourself." He kissed her full on the mouth. His tongue flicked over her lips, then pushed for entry. But it was not a brutal kiss; rather a tentative, thoughtful one as though to explore her deeper feelings. Try as she might, knowing her life may depend upon it, she could not refrain from cringing. Retribution was instant. She sprawled on the mattress, her face stinging and with the taste of blood in her mouth.

"Bitch! You wouldn't cringe from Kennedy, would you?" he snarled.

She wiped her lip on the back of her hand and struggled into a sitting position, determined he would not see her subdued. "But who would put a contract out on *me*?" she asked, attempting to wean him from the dangerous subject of Brant.

"C.A.D.E. of course."

"What? I don't believe you!"

Too late she realised her mistake.

He took the tray with him when he left.

Oh God, please help me. She curled up on the mattress in foetal position. Battered and humiliated, her previous strength and optimism were running away like water down the drain. *Water.* Not a drop had passed her lips for over twelve hours. There was an old saying, and it penetrated the fog of her despair: *God helps those that help themselves.* She had no right to give up. Alisdair was waiting for her at home. Was he to be left bereaved yet again? She struggled upright and staggered through to where she had seen the water jug. Thankfully it was still there. After bathing her face, then washing out her mouth and swallowing a little of the water, she went back to the wine shelves and found an enamel jug beneath a shroud of cobwebs. Once it was reasonably clean, she filled it and hid it behind the bottles on the shelf. Now at least, if that madman removed the jug and bowl, she would not be without water. This gesture of defiance, and the small sense of victory that accompanied it, went some way to restoring her morale.

*

Until he came in again. This time he said nothing. Just stood there by the door, running his finger along the wicked-looking blade of a knife. He caressed it, paced the floor still without speaking, then ran it lightly over his own cheek. A masterly move that filled her with terror, implanting the seed of anticipation, the idea it would be used on her own face next. He took a step towards her, then as though unable to make up his mind, he turned and abruptly left.

This psychological torture continued at intervals throughout the day. On one occasion he spoke to her, knelt down and caressed her cheek. She forced herself to endure it, and when he kissed her, didn't pull away. He said no more, but left and returned five minutes later with a tray holding fresh tea, toast and a piece of cheese.

The stick and carrot method was still in force.

She drank the tea greedily and then ate the toast and cheese, telling herself she had to keep up her strength, and that a show of pride would only earn her another beating. Some hours later he returned. Her stomach leapt with fear as she saw he was holding a small machine. Was it to be electric shocks? She held her breath. He pressed a button and Paluccini's voice filled the cellar. She breathed again; it was only a portable cassette player.

"You appreciate that, do you Darcy?" was all he said.

Let him think I'm giving in, becoming submissive; then he'll relax his guard. "Yes. Thank you Jules; it's very kind of you," she forced herself to say, whilst wondering what lay behind this bizarre behaviour. As though guessing her thoughts, he patted the cassette player and laughed. It was a demonic laugh; a laugh of triumph. He left without another word.

*

He returned when sunlight was slanting across the floor from the window, so she knew it was afternoon and that the window faced west. He removed the tape recorder, and left her another tray. This one held a bowl of soup and a bread roll.

I must be playing it right, she consoled herself.

*

It was growing dark when he entered again. This time he placed a radio on the upturned barrel and turned it on. He gave her a strange knowing smile and left. His timing was accurate. The ten o'clock news was just beginning. She listened with growing horror to the announcer's voice reporting an ecological disaster of major proportions in the Sargasso. Thousands of baby eels had perished in the spawning grounds off Bermuda, and all plant and marine life in the area had been similarly devastated. The cause of the catastrophe was as yet unverified, but experts were hinting at a connection between this and the recent bizarre events in the Sahara. Oliver Bryce, a British newspaper correspondent, the announcer concluded, had failed to return from the disaster area. Not Oliver too, she mourned, recalling the tall man with the quiet ways and sense of fair dealing. First Carl, and now Oliver. And terrible though that was, she knew it was nothing compared to the losses that might yet come.

The door opened again within minutes of the report ending. Cain switched off the radio, picked it up and turned to leave.

Darcy exploded in voice and action. "You bastard! You evil bastard!" she yelled, leaping upright. "You caused that, didn't you? And the Sahara thing – with the particles," she screamed, her anger now righteous and ranging beyond cares for her personal safety. "Who did you sell them to? Which of our enemies now has the power to destroy the western world? You *fool* Cain! Do you really think you will be spared when it comes?"

She waited for the attack, bracing herself to endure it. This time, when she thought him likely to kill her, he did nothing. His ego, for the time being, was intact; it seemed he was content to gloat and laugh at her helplessness and frustration. His laughter still reached her through the locked door.

There was no candle that night.

※

Two, three or more days and nights passed in this way. There was no way of being sure. Disoriented and sick with trauma, cut off from all human contact except for the visits of her tormentor, she lost track of time and place. The only reality was the tread of Cain's approaching feet: the measure of her fear. Little by little her spirit was being broken. Already she had considered offering Cain her body, of doing anything his depraved taste demanded, in exchange for freedom.

Except that it wouldn't work. That wasn't how he wanted her; such was not the nature of his fixation. He was demanding the impossible, that she love him as she had loved Brant. In fact if she threw herself at him, it would probably make things worse; the idealised image he had constructed would crumble, and in his eyes she would be worse than a common prostitute. That might be the point at which he would kill. Besides if that was all he wanted, he could take her at any time. Sick with self-disgust, she retched in a corner. Such was the force for survival, over-riding dignity and decency. All that mattered was to survive.

*

Alisdair? She moaned and reached out a hand. He was trying to tell her something. "Alisdair?" This time she said it aloud, her cracked and split lips forming the word with difficulty. Confused, she wondered if she were asleep or awake. It was night-time, that was the only thing of which she could be sure. Moonlight paled the walls and bar-shadows patterned the floor. Then there was the usual nocturnal scurrying as claws rattled and scratched minutely over stone. This, she had discovered, was an effect of sensory deprivation: everything sounded 'mega-loud', as Alisdair would say. That was it. Alisdair was trying to tell her something. He was asking her to remember. Something about a tree.

She could see his face clearly in the darkness, his eyes huge and earnest behind those glasses. Next came the image of a pine tree. One that had almost fallen down in the gale. Now she remembered. *But why, Alisdair?* What was the point? It had nothing to do with her being here.

But then she began seeing him clearly, moving purposefully about the land at Westwalls.

"*Come on Darcy,*" he called, turning to beckon her on, his glasses filling his face as he loomed close, like an actor in some weird drama giving an aside. Now she understood. He was showing her the young pine that had caught the blast of a March gale. It was leaning at a drunken angle, part of its root system exposed. She felt distress. Ten or twelve years growth wasted and lost. Bereft of its roots, like Alisdair. And also like Alisdair, it had to be saved. He was turning to her now, his face alight with calm certainty. "*Don't worry, Darcy; I'll soon have it up again.*"

"How can you – a boy – do that?"

"*Leverages. Mr. Ambrose taught me a woodman's trick.*" His voice echoed inside her head, as though he were speaking down a tunnel.

Sceptically she watched him secure one end of the rope around the stricken tree. The other end he tied to a strong healthy beech, leaving plenty of slack in the middle. Then a second rope tied at the middle of the slack, and passed around the bole of a third healthy tree. He spit on his palms, then catching hold of the rope, strained against it with all his weight. Miraculously the tree was moving, raised by the action of opposing forces. Several barrows of top soil and some heavy rocks on the roots later, and the pine was upright again and secure.

"*Remember, Darcy,*" Alisdair was pushing his face right up to hers, "*leverage is the answer.*"

His face was filling her dream, or was it reality? She moaned and tossed on the mattress.

"*Darcy!*"

She awoke with a start, having slept from sheer exhaustion. But that voice calling her name had sounded in her ear, not her dream. She lay in the darkness, straining for any sound. That incident with the pine tree had really happened; but when? Some time ago or just now? She touched her feverish and aching head. Her mind began to clear. Maybe it was more than a dream. Alisdair was able to do some pretty strange things of late. But what did he mean? Why tell her this now? She wasn't interested in saving trees tonight, only her own life. *Trees.* Timber came from trees. Timber was used to make – doors. But wait. Her heart nearly stopped, then she pictured Cain coming in to the cellar and knew it was alright. This particular door opened *inwards.* She was on her feet in seconds, despite the pain of her injuries.

*

In the half-light she stood before the door, weighing the possibilities. The gap between door and jamb didn't now seem so useless. At a pinch, there was room enough to secure something round the hinges. "You could just be right, Alisdair lad!" she said aloud, kicking out at a rat that had ventured too close. Only she had no rope. Returning to her bed she ripped off the sheet that covered the mattress and began tearing it into strips. Then the cotton bedspread provided for cover. Each strip on its own, useless – plaited together, she would have her 'rope'. Useful activity, coupled with a real prospect of escape, helped her slough off weakness and confusion. Now she knew exactly what she was doing. And the timing was right too, as close as she could guess. There was as yet no light filtering through the window, so even if it was morning, she had at least a couple of hours before Cain put in his usual appearance. Her teeth tore at the cotton, getting it started so it would rip; her fingers moved swiftly, plaiting the strips into a sturdy length.

An hour had passed and one 'rope' lay beside her on the mattress, the second was under way. Soon that too was finished. She crossed to the door carrying her precious burden, finding her way easily in the moonlight. She stood there a while, listening. Too close to escape now to blow it. Nothing. No sound except the dripping of water and scraping of claws. Then she heard Alisdair's voice in her head saying 'Remember – leverage'. Carefully she threaded the end of the first rope through the gap between door and jamb, passing it over the top hinge. That would give her the greater leverage. Retrieving the end was more difficult. At last it was threaded through and secured.

Next she took the other end of the plaited material over to the window. Laying it down, she dragged a box over, stopping heart in mouth to listen, then it was finally in place. When no lights showed through the chink, and the door didn't burst open, she breathed again and standing on the box, threaded the rope through the bars and secured it. Now for the final part. Getting down from the box she took the second rope and tied it as Alisdair had done, in the middle of the first one at the slack. Then, looking around her, she tested the bracket of the wine shelves and found it was set into concrete. That would do nicely. She looked first at the hinge, then at the stout window bars and knew that something would have to give, and odds on it would be the hinge. Looping the end over the bracket, she tested it for 'run'. It ran smooth as butter, and as soon as she put any weight to it, Darcy knew she had won.

*

It was ridiculously easy. At the first few pulls she felt the hinge give. At the next attempt the screws shifted and bent and the door hung drunkenly on its hinges. A few more heaves and the screws sprung clear of the wood and the door gaped, hanging only by the bottom hinge. A few choice pulls and the gap was wide enough to clamber through. Propping the door up with a box which she had positioned nearby, she squeezed through and stood in the darkness listening. A short stone passage led her to a flight of steps. Her heart lurched. Would it be locked? Her fears proved groundless. The latch was unsecured and the door opened. *Free!* Now all that remained was to get out of this God-forsaken house.

Fourteen

~

This door opened onto the hall from under the stairs. Terrified now of walking into recapture, she listened intently, then slipped through. After the dimness of her prison, the brightness of the calor lamps hurt her eyes and she had to squint at the long case clock that ticked sonorously in the corner. She stared at the ornate hands in disbelief. *Only eleven thirty-five?* Not morning then at all. A shiver ran through her: the sound of the hissing lamps brought back that first night so vividly.

She held her breath and stood absolutely still. The sound of someone moving about came from behind one of the closed doors that led off the hall. Agonisingly, she stared at the front door. Only fifteen yards or so away, yet it seemed more like five hundred. The urge to make one mad dash was almost overwhelming. Only the knowledge that she would be caught and overpowered before getting the car started, prevented it. And that was another consideration.

Given the isolation of this house, and because on her arrival she had not intended staying long, she had left the car unlocked and the key in the ignition. Had Cain removed it? She decided there was no reason for him to do so, and prayed she was right. The muffled noises continued, encouraging her to chance a couple of steps towards her goal. Thank God for stone floors with no floorboards to creak.

Nearly there. The front door was almost within her reach. Two bolts: one at the top, one at the bottom. She stretched out to draw back the first, then froze, her hand suspended in mid-air. She must be mistaken. She listened, every nerve straining. No mistake. The sound of an approaching car, and it was drawing ever closer. As though to emphasise this, twin beams hit the stained glass door surround in a blaze of blue, green and blood red. As swiftly as she dare, Darcy turned and went back along the hall, knowing that Cain too must be aware of the car's approach. He was: she barely had time to pull to the below-stairs door before he emerged. The very sight of him filled her with terror and repugnance. Her limbs began to tremble as she watched him through the gap. The engine-sound died and a car door slammed. Cain drew back the bolts and the door swung open.

"Good evening, Jules. Is it done?"

Darcy stiffened. The caller had a strong French accent.

Jules Cain's visitor was none other than Andrea Lascelles.

*

"I hope so," the Frenchwoman was saying as she stepped into the hall. Darcy muffled a gasp. Maybe Cain had been telling the truth and it really was C.A.D.E. who had put out the contract. It seemed she was hearing about her own proposed death. It had to be true: Lascelles was one of C.A.D.E.'s agents. "You haven't done it, have you?" Lascelles' voice now had a sharp edge.

"You're over-wrought, my dear. Was the journey awful?"

This evasion, the ignoring of reality, was familiar to Darcy, who shuddered and pressed her eye closer to the crack. Andrea Lascelle's angelic face beneath the blonde bob was at odds with the toughness of her words and manner. "Your obsession was useful in the beginning, Jules – but now it's getting in the way."

"Andrea darling, do come through and have a drink," Cain was saying. "There's plenty of time yet for business." Now he was moving along the hall to the sitting room door past the stairs. As he drew closer, Darcy watched his face in horrid fascination.

"Your time just ran out, Cain."

Andrea Lascelles raised her arm. There was a report, and Cain fell to the ground.

Darcy stared at his upturned face, and the neat bullet hole between his eyes.

*

Her first feeling was of disbelief, followed by intense relief. Now escape was assured. Andrea Lascelles would hardly hang around after having murdered Cain. Just as quickly her hopes were dashed. Lascelles would be bound to go to the cellar with the intention of murder, and the only way down there was through this door. And Lascelles had a gun. Her best chance lay in a surprise attack. She was about to leap out when she saw Lascelles disappear into the room from which Cain had emerged earlier. There followed the sound of breaking glass and much banging and thudding, as though heavy objects were being flung to the floor. Then more breaking glass. Darcy opened the door a fraction wider. Another thought struck, one that devastated: *Brant was involved with a woman out to kill his own wife.* It was possible but unlikely that he was innocent of Lascelles' conspiracy with Cain. His involvement could well extend to her dealings in death and destruction. It was beyond credibility that a man who spent his working life tracking down crime and criminals, could remain in ignorance of her activities. *I could kill you, Darcy.* Those words uttered in anger now took on sinister connotations. She could accept that they were all washed up – *but that he wanted her dead?* The possibility stabbed at the very centre of her being.

Minutes later Andrea Lascelles emerged and moved swiftly to the front door. Almost immediately an engine coughed into life and head-lamps illuminated the stained glass window. Tyres squealed and a car was driven away at furious speed.

Weak with relief, Darcy listened to the sound of its engine fading into the night.

*

Stepping over Cain's body she moved towards the room from which all the noise had issued, and wondered what it was that Lascelles had been so anxious to destroy. And something else was bothering her: it didn't make sense – why had she left without finishing off the 'captive' she believed to be still in the cellar? She jumped and spun round as the clock on the wall made a *clunking* sound but failed to chime. Cain's eyes were still open. They seemed to be following her movements. His expression appeared to mock her, as though he knew something she did not. She shook off the morbid fantasy and turned her back.

The clock had receded from her consciousness. Advancing, she became aware of noises coming from within that room. A sort of slithering, and a slapping sound, such as a fish might make when flapping about on a wet deck. The door had been left ajar.

Darcy pushed it wider and entered the room.

She screamed in terror and revulsion. It was a scene from hell. Broken tanks and jars littered the floor, which was swimming in colourless fluid. Bottles of methylated spirit had been thrown about also, and the smell was overpowering. "Oh, my God, oh, my God," she moaned over and over, leaning against the door frame for support. Now the sounds heard from outside made horrible sense.

Writhing and flopping amidst this debris were Cain's pitiable creatures.

*

She forced herself to step inside his improvised laboratory. *So this is where he had brought them!* Nausea rose at the revolting scene. It was like something out of a Bosch painting: pot-bellied monsters caught up in their own entrails; swollen heads and undersized bodies, twisted bones and putrefied flesh, and swellings that oozed green pus. One of the hybrids flapped its malformed limbs and lurched across the stone flags towards her feet. She screamed as it made a jack-knife movement, and landed with it's under-belly across her foot. Retching uncontrollably, she kicked it off and convulsively rubbed her shoe against the table leg to remove the smear of mucus. Whilst filled with repugnance, she was also moved to pity. It had landed on its back. The blueish membrane-covered eyes sought hers, seemed to plead with her for release.

She gazed about her, unable to comprehend. Something else was tugging at her awareness, a sound maybe or an acrid smell. Nothing registered except the nightmare reality of these creatures. What should she do? What *could* she do? Thirty or so masses of protoplasm, each a parody of a human being, writhed across the floor, leaving trails of slime like so many giant slugs. The sound of their fleshy stumps slapping stone slabs, and splashing in the liquid from broken tanks, was something she knew would haunt her for ever. And they all seemed to be moving in her direction. Either they were sentient beings fully aware of her and their surroundings, or like amoebae, were merely attracted to the stimuli of sound and movement. She prayed the latter was the truth.

The smell that had been lurking behind the meths now penetrated awareness. She sniffed. *Burning!* Something was burning. And an instant later a subliminal sound crackled into terrifying life. A tongue of flame shot from a pile of papers and books in the far corner. It had been smouldering all the time, Darcy realised now. And the place was awash with spirit. Dark splashes stained the drapes at the window, and the upholstery of a well-stuffed armchair. The creatures squirming on the floor also seemed to sense danger. Their movements became more erratic, the threshing of limbs more frenzied.

Tongues of flame lapped greedily at the chair and ran roaring and hissing up the curtains. With one last desperate look at the twitching hybrids, Darcy turned and fled the room. In a desperate bid for time, she paused and closed the door behind her in the hope of briefly containing the flames.

*

The sound of the windows exploding followed her down the hall.

Even in full flight, the sight of the wall lamps brought back Cain's voice: *Calor gas*, he had said as he lit them. Any moment now this place would erupt into the night like a volcano. Sobbing with fear and trauma she tugged open the door and stumbled out into the dark. Her flight was checked by what she could have sworn were headlamps dying as they were switched off. Her heart missed a beat. Lascelles may have returned for some reason. The sound of the engine would not have been audible over the fire. She strained to make sense of the shadows. That bulky shadow could be a rocky outcrop – or a car. She could be running full tilt into danger and recapture.

A glance over her shoulder showed her that flames were spurting from all the windows. Any time now they must reach the gas canisters. At a guess she had only seconds to get clear. She coughed and caught her breath as the building belched smoke. More windows exploded with terrifying noise, and flames shot out of the gaps. The sound of timbers collapsing thundered in her ears. The peril behind proved greater than the unknown out front. Blindly she began to run. Her feet stumbled over ruts and stones. She risked another glance over her shoulder. The night sky was stained orange and blood-red.

The blast came first and almost deafened her. Almost simultaneously, a geyser of flames and golden sparks shot up to the sky. Strangely at that second her thoughts were not for her safety but the creatures within. A fitting funeral pyre, and the only possible end. Glowing debris rained down.

The force that hit her between the shoulder blades, carried her several feet and sent her sprawling on the ground.

The red beyond her eyelids turned black and she lay still.

Fifteen

~

There was a weight on top of her. Movement was impossible. Darcy struggled to understand, then memory flooded back. Maybe blazing roof timbers pinned her down. Perhaps she was paralysed. Terror gripped her as she struggled in vain to rise. Suddenly the weight lifted from her back. Wincing with pain, she rolled over, and screamed.

A dark figure was looming over her. Still half dazed, she thought for an instant that it was Cain, then saw in her mind the body sprawled in the hallway, the hole in his head, and the spreading pool of blood. Not Cain. Frantically she tried to sit up, to push the man off. Her shoulders felt like they had been the target of a battering ram. Hands gripped her arms like a vice. "Let me go! Let me go, you bastard!" she screamed.

"Be still!"

The voice of authority brought her bucking and threshing to an abrupt stop.

"Brant?" Relief flooded her, and the memory of the explosion returned; Brant must have pushed her out of the way. Then she remembered. *Brant and that Lascelles bitch.* "You murdering bastard! You would have let them kill me."

"Do as I say and be still, damn you!"

"Get away from me. You want me dead."

"Stupid woman," he sighed. "If you won't do as I say, I'll have to knock you out," he added matter of factly, his hands busy over her limbs.

Judging him capable of carrying out his threat, she endured his ministrations.

"Nothing broken. *Now* you can get up."

She struggled to her feet, pulling away as he attempted to help. The house was now an inferno. There would be nothing left, she thought with satisfaction, except a pile of ash. What an awful thought: if she hadn't escaped, she would have roasted to death in that cellar. Thoughts of escape made her dart forward. Brant's arm shot out and restrained her. "Where do you think you are going?"

"My car!" she exclaimed, straining against his hold.

"I moved it whilst you were still unconscious."

"Thank you," she allowed begrudgingly as he let go.

But gratitude went against the grain. This man had conspired in her death.

She rounded on him. "Did you come to finish me off?" she goaded. "Didn't you trust your French bitch to do the job properly?"

In the red glow of the blaze, she saw his face set. "That's enough. I'm making allowances for how things must seem; and for your state of mind after your ordeal –"

"Just what do you know about *my ordeal*, as you euphemistically call it?" she interrupted.

"Only that you arrived shortly before me, and obviously tangled with Andrea Lascelles."

She stared at him in shock. "Do you really expect me to believe that?"

He frowned. "Why shouldn't you?"

She confronted him with loathing in her eyes. "Are you trying to say you were ignorant of what went on here? Of Cain locking me in the cellar for," she paused and rubbed a hand over her eyes, "– for, I don't know, three or four days."

"*What?*" She was taken aback by his shocked expression.

"Tell me," he stopped as though unable to continue. "What did Cain –?"

"Enough." Weariness and disillusionment washed over her; suddenly all she wanted was to blot everything out in sleep. But he had hold of her arm, was pulling her round so that her features were illuminated by the blaze. He was staring into her face, and his expression was terrible. "He did this to you?" His voice conveyed calmness and control, yet it made her shiver. He touched the bruising and swelling around her eyes and mouth. Dumbly she nodded.

"Did he–?"

"No," she confirmed swiftly, reading the question in his eyes.

"Tell me," he demanded grimly.

She did, omitting unnecessary detail. She sensed he wanted to hold her and offer comfort, but was still unsure of him, and so by her manner kept him at a distance. He raised his arm at one point as though to put it around her shoulders, but she stepped back out of reach. She could trust no-one, especially not Brant. Her account finished, she fell silent.

His eyes blazed hatred. "I'll kill him for this."

"What's the matter – wasn't that part of the plan? Did he 'exceed orders' as they say?" Darcy said bitterly.

He gave her a long hard look then turned and walked away.

"You're too late!" she yelled, half-demented. "He's in *there*. Your charming girlfriend murdered him." Fear took over as she watched his back receding into the night. "Brant?"

She shouted again, but louder, in order to be heard above the crackle and roar, the crash of falling timber and roof tiles. Surely he wouldn't leave her here alone? She brushed a smut from her face – the air was full of charred and floating fragments – and stared anxiously after him.

He stopped and turned. "Can you manage to drive?"

"Yes." She stumbled over the uneven ground towards him, and saw two vehicles at the roadside.

He waited until she had caught him up. "Get in your car and follow me," he ordered. Darcy waited for him to say something more, but he climbed into his Landrover without another word.

*

She had been right about one thing: Cain had deliberately brought her to his detestable house by a round-about route in order to confuse. In no time at all, it seemed, she was pulling in behind Brant at the junction with the main road that linked Westwalls to the motorway. She watched him get out, and wound down her window as he approached.

"You'll be alright from here?"

Darcy stared at him in disbelief. "You're not escorting me home?"

"There's no need. You'll be safe enough now."

Shock and exhaustion for once rendered her inarticulate. There were no words to adequately describe her present need so she merely said, "But there are things to discuss."

She felt like crying because it sounded so prosaic and unemotional, and nothing like what she was feeling.

"There are," he said shortly. "But I have something to attend to first."

She stared at him with ice-cold fury as the truth hit. "You're going to Andrea Lascelles, aren't you?"

He gave her a long look, then sighed. "Whatever you say, Darcy."

He turned his back, climbed into the Landrover and roared away.

Darcy watched the tail lights disappear round a bend and mentally shook herself. *She was free.* Looking back over the horror, that had to make up for the lump of lead that had replaced her heart. And at least one of her tormentors was dead. Throttling up, she set off for Westwalls, and home.

Sixteen

~

It was gone two in the morning before she parked up and wearily let herself into the house. Alisdair was waiting in the kitchen. "Alisdair! What are you doing still up?"

"Waiting for you."

"How did you know I'd be home tonight?"

"I just knew."

"God, am I glad to see you," she held him briefly, ignoring his patent embarrassment.

"Darcy! You'll be kissing me next – like, *like an aunt*," he complained.

"But I *am* your aunt." Her laughter, she knew, verged on hysteria.

"No you're not; you're my – *friend*," he muttered, banging the kettle down on the hotplate.

Over-emotional and traumatised as she was, Darcy felt a lump rise in her throat, but knew she mustn't blow it. "Thanks, Alisdair," she managed to say with admirable cool. "And you're most definitely mine!"

She was rewarded by the faint flush that rose to his cheeks, followed by a huge wink and a grin.

*

"Look Alisdair, I'm sorry I've been," she started to explain as he placed a cup of anaemic-looking tea, with most of it floating on the surface, before her.

"It's alright. I know," he interrupted.

"But how could you?" She spiked the weak tea with a generous swoosh of brandy from the bottle kept in the pantry.

He answered her with another question, "How did you get out?"

She stared at him. "You tell me."

"Leverages?"

She stared at him, feeling again that she moved through some improbable dream. "But how was it possible?"

"It worked for the tree."

"Not funny Alisdair. You're scaring the pants off me."

"I just concentrated. Sent you my thoughts."

"Most people can't do that, Alisdair."

"Most people don't have Mr. Ambrose."

"Fair comment. I guess he took care of you whilst I was gone?"

"You could say that."

She grinned at him and thought how good it felt to be home.

✻

An hour later they were still talking. Darcy had made a fresh pot of tea, and they sat eating their way through a packet of digestives. He seemed older, more assured. She had not intended telling him the full story, but then changed her mind. "It's serious stuff, Alisdair," she said concluding her account.

Alisdair nodded solemnly. "I know. There was another report on the radio today. A rain forest this time in South America – totally wiped out, but the Sahara continues to bloom. And there's been another raid on Kuwait. Too much of a coincidence. The Americans are making ugly noises, Darcy. They're hinting at 'chemical weapons', and there's talk of a second Gulf War."

Darcy looked stricken. "But if they are right – it will be *nations* next. These are just warnings. If their cage is rattled, the arabs will use the particles in warfare." She shuddered. "If you'd seen those things on the floor, Alisdair. And Charles Ashford's body. The effect those particles can have on D.N.A. is horrendous."

"They're after holding the western world to ransom. But it's under control," he said enigmatically.

Almost as though he had inside information. Which was ridiculous of course. But better to let him think that way, Darcy decided with compassion.

✻

They talked for another half hour. "I have to get some sleep." She stifled a third yawn and stood up. "Come on, friend – time for bed." Her own bed, with a light if she wanted it, and no rats to speak of. *No lying in terror waiting for footfalls approaching the door.* At least, not Jules Cain's. She was shaking again. Reaching for the brandy she poured some into a cup and swallowed it in one, grimacing as the spirit burned. If it wasn't for Brant, she would rest secure tonight. But had he gone back to Andrea Lascelles? And was he involved in the kidnap? If he was, he would tell her that she, Darcy, was still alive, and the danger would be far from over. Lascelles would be out to silence her, may even dare come here. Alisdair and Mr. Ambrose may also be exposed to danger, she worried. She might also fire this house.

"Brant may be involved in this, Alisdair," she thought it only fair to prepare him.

He shook his head. "No."

She shrugged. "I'd like to have confidence in your judgment, but everything points to it. His profession doesn't make him incorruptible, you know. Andrea Lascelles is with C.A.D.E., and if an organisation like that, involving God knows how many western governments, will cheat and murder to keep its secrets, then there isn't much hope. Brant's probably with Andrea Lascelles right now."

Alisdair consulted the kitchen clock. "No, he's on a flight to the Middle East. And Andrea Lascelles isn't with C.A.D.E. – she was, but sold out."

Darcy paused at the open door with her hand on the latch. "Not more clairvoyance Alisdair," she said wearily. "Because I'm not buying."

"No problem. Brant told me."

She started. "When?"

"The day after you went missing. He'd just got back from Kuwait. He's under cover out there, advising the top brass of the military and medical units on this thing. He was to fly back tonight to settle some business."

"That's top secret stuff, Alisdair!" she said, scandalised. "Brant shouldn't have told you – and you certainly shouldn't repeat it."

"So who are you going to tell?" he said, giving her a cheeky grin. "Good to have you back home, Darcy," he said, rushing past her and up the stairs.

Darcy, giving up on a situation that was proving too much for her exhausted brain, shook her head and followed. Sighing she went into the bathroom and turned on the taps. No matter how late it was, there had to be time for a bath, to sluice away the vileness of the past few days and watch it drain away.

*

Once bathed and in bed, she relaxed for the first time since it all began. Alisdair, she felt sure was telling the truth. Which meant that Andrea Lascelles still thought she had burned her alive, along with the house and Cain's body. So there was no immediate danger. And it seemed Brant wasn't with that French bitch after all, so perhaps he hadn't wanted her dead. But there was still Jen. The mystery of her disappearance. She would have to check that Chris really had gone to the police. That was as far as she got. So deep was her sleep that she didn't even hear Alisdair's song as he kept his lonely vigil.

Seventeen

~

It was growing dark, but inside the lodge the candles were lit. Mr. Ambrose stood by the shining web. One by one he touched the three crystals so that they shivered and shimmered bravely in the candlelight. "Are they ready, do you think?" he asked of the spider which had come out to investigate. "I think so too," he concurred with a nod. The girl Darcy had gone through her ordeal and come out the other side. There had been the odd wobble and loss of tension, but no tremors of earthquake proportions had disrupted the web. All things considered, she had coped well. Not that it was over yet, not by a long way.

That man of hers – though she would object to the possessive pronoun – was taking care of the practicalities, and in him they had the best man for the job. He was there to nurture the seeds already sown by the boy's father. How surprised Alisdair had been by all that! He had long since grasped the basic idea behind the web, but had failed to relate the interconnectedness of threads and events to his own life. He chuckled and scratched his chin with his forefinger. His skin had become so thin and yellowed that the light from the lamp shone through it, giving the appearance of an X-ray picture. But Alisdair had grasped it now, and it had helped him to come to terms with the loss of his parents.

As for the lad's progress: well, it never failed to delight.

Old Grey Pelt was out there already waiting. So was Hush-wing, her heart-shaped face inscrutable as she stood by. They all knew, these old friends. The deer on the fell were nervously lifting their heads as they browsed. He sighed, snuffed the candles, and took his staff from the umbrella stand in the porch. Mother moon was at the full; heavy round and cheesy yellow, birthing conclusions and new beginnings.

One last look round, and no regrets.

Stepping outside, he smiled to himself as a ghostly white shape sailed overhead. The wail of the screech owl ululated eerily through the wood.

Eighteen

~

The following day was a Saturday, so there was no school for Alisdair. They rose late and met up in the kitchen. "Fancy a lovely unhealthy fry-up?" Darcy called from the depths of the pantry. She felt ravenous after eight hours deep and undisturbed sleep.

"Super. With fried bread?"

Darcy laughed. "Why not?" She emerged with eggs, beans, a dish of tomatoes and some mushrooms gathered the day before by Alisdair. He would never, she thought with a grin, starve in her absence.

They had spoken little during the serious business of eating. They did however listen to the radio, and the latest bulletin on the mounting Gulf crisis. Now replete, they sat in the sunlit kitchen with mugs of tea.

She stirred hers slowly and with deliberation. "Is Brant really in Kuwait?"

Alisdair nodded. "I told you, didn't I?"

"You did." Alisdair, she reflected with humility, didn't tell lies.

*

He gave her a challenging look. "It's something to do with Dad – and the Internet."

Darcy frowned. "Timothy? What on earth can he have to do with all this?" Of course, she recalled, big brother Timothy had been out there for several years before the accident, and was a highly respected computer analyst and systems programmer, but he had been dead a full year.

"He wasn't just an analyst," Alisdair said, as though reading her thoughts.

"What do you mean, Alisdair?"

"I mean in the way that Brant isn't just an astro-physicist."

"He was an *agent?*"

"Not officially. But he sniffed a rat and decided to investigate. He got in deep.

"He found they already had the technology and the formulae. Dad hacked into their systems and analysed the data. So, Brant says, we've been prepared for something like this all along."

Darcy was mystified. "But technology and formulae for *what?*"

"Using Particle Physics as a means of destruction. Don't forget what Brant told us that day at the observatory," he reminded her, his eyes huge and earnest behind his glasses. "*Everything* in our Universe is made up of these same basic particles – *including us.* They had no physical evidence, but there's none for black holes come to that! In *theory* they could infect quarks and leptons with anti-quarks and anti-leptons – remember, matter and anti-matter can't get along together; they annihilate one another. Imagine what that could do to plant cells and human D.N.A."

"The blossoming Sahara and the dying Sargasso," Darcy said grimly. "Not to mention Carl's terrible death, and Dr. Ashford's – and Cain's mutants. I wonder why Andrea Lascelles destroyed them?"

"Too much of a risk," Alisdair answered promptly. "Beings created in the laboratory from elementary sub-atomic particles? That sort of thing wouldn't stay under wraps for long. Establishment Science, Bio-Medical units – the whole caboodle, would take it over. Then there would be laws, and controls, and *penalties* for breaking them. That was no good to her. She would know from her time at C.A.D.E. that someone had already sold the hypothesis to the Arabs, and that they already had the technology to apply it, once the right particles were available. Then suddenly they *were.*

"And to think they came from that meteorite I found on the fell," he said ingenuously, so that Darcy caught a glimpse of the boy he once was, and such a short time ago. "All of it comes from there," he continued. "And I think Mr. Ambrose knew what would happen before I even found it. Anyway, the simplest way for her to make a fortune was to sell them samples of the meteorite particles. They obviously carried out experimental tests, and bingo! – we get the reports about the Sargasso and Sahara," he finished.

"Are you saying they got the formulae from C.A.D.E.?" Darcy asked shaking her head in disbelief.

"Indirectly. And before the Gulf War flared up."

"What do you mean by *indirectly?*"

Alisdair shrugged and raised his eyebrows. "C.A.D.E. is financed mainly by the Pentagon and the British Government."

Darcy recalled Professor Aaron, head of C.A.D.E., and the long line of U.S. honours after his name. "You're saying *they* sanctioned it?"

"There would be lots of money involved – *millions*. Remember the 'Arms for Iraq' scandal?" Alisdair said with an irony beyond his years. "They didn't mind selling them rockets."

Darcy lapsed into silence.

"I was just thinking about your Mum and Dad," she said after several minutes had passed. "Was Timothy – your Dad, over here to make his report when the accident happened?"

"It wasn't an accident," Alisdair said flatly.

"I thought as much. But if all you've said is true, I just wonder who was responsible. I don't suppose we'll ever really know. Timothy must have been a threat to the Iraqis, but also an embarrassment to the U.S. and British Governments."

"Dad never did things by halves."

"Sorry, Alisdair – what can I say?"

"It's alright. At least their dying means something now. It's not just senseless."

She ran a hand through her curls and looked perplexed. "But how did you learn all this?"

"From Brant. And Mr. Ambrose."

"Brant, yes, okay – it's his job. But what could Mr. Ambrose know about it?"

He regarded her gravely. "Mr. Ambrose knows everything."

"Would he know what happened to Jen?" she said half to herself.

"I think Jen is dead," he said soberly.

Darcy sighed. "I'm afraid I do too, Alisdair."

They sat for several minutes, then Darcy broke the silence. "How can it be stopped, this thing with Iraq?"

Alisdair beamed. "Easy. Brant has gone over to pick up where Dad left off. He'll hack into their system and make subtle changes to their formulae. It will be undetectable to anyone outside of C.A.D.E., but enough to sabotage their experiments. It will cause the particles to mutually annihilate, thus making them useless."

"Brilliant!"

Darcy rose from the table and said brusquely, "Right, let's clear away this mess. You wash, I'll dry."

*

There was a small oasis of peace inside Darcy. It was to do with knowing that Brant had not turned bad. That was all there could be now, she thought, recalling some of the awful things she had believed and said of late. He must despise her. At least Alisdair was coming to, she thought watching him go down the path to the lodge. It was as though he had grown up overnight. For some reason, the phrase he claimed to have heard from his mother that strange night came into her mind: "*Follow Mr. Ambrose ... and he will help you become a man.*"

*

He didn't come flying in, distraught. He walked in calmly, pale of face but dry-eyed and with dignity.

"What is it Alisdair?" Darcy asked, looking up from a glossy magazine that seemed to have very little to do with real country life, despite the title.

"I found Mr. Ambrose at the woodland pool."

Looking at him, she went cold with premonition. "Is he hurt?"

"No," he said quietly. "He's dead."

Nineteen

~

Darcy stared at him open-mouthed, then jumped up as his words sunk in. "Tell me," she said tersely, moving to the door.

"He wasn't at the lodge. His bed hadn't been slept in," Alisdair explained as they ran through the garden to the woodland.

*

"Oh, my God." Darcy stared, and felt the colour drain from her face. Mr. Ambrose was lying at the feet of the Mother-statue, with his face partly submerged in the pool. She saw that his head was resting on a large stone. He must have slipped on the bank, fallen and hit his head on the rock. Autumn leaves of red, russet and gold were strewn over his body.

"Stay there, Alisdair." She climbed down the bank and stooped over the inert form. Reaching out, she rested two fingers on his neck. There was no pulse. He had, she surmised, been there some hours; his body was stiff and his flesh waxen. "He's dead," she confirmed, looking up at Alisdair, who was remarkably composed.

She was just about to straighten up and climb back up the bank, when a gleam caught her eye. Beside him in the mud lay the gold *pince-nez*. One of the eye-pieces was cracked. Seeing them lying there brought home the vulnerability and pathos, released her grief and tears. They were not for the eyes of strangers. She slipped the *pince-nez* into her pocket.

*

An hour later, they were back in the kitchen and Darcy was making a pot of strong tea. She had telephoned the emergency services from the village. The local doctor and police officer had been, and an ambulance had taken the body. That in itself had been trauma enough: Alisdair had protested that they shouldn't remove Mr. Ambrose from Westwalls.

"There may have to be a post-mortem, son," one of the ambulance crew, a kindly if rather gruff man, had said. "It being a bit sudden like." He had stuck out his lower lip, looked pointedly at the body and then at his female partner.

"Well, can he come back and be buried here?" he had asked Darcy in an undervoice.

Darcy had shook her head. "I don't think so, Alisdair. But if you agree to cremation – I promise we'll bring his ashes back here. Okay?" She was sticking her neck out, but Mr. Ambrose had no family or friends she was aware of, so who was to know or say any different?

Alisdair had capitulated without further fuss.

*

"Why? Why such a horrible end?" she said now, pouring tea into two mugs.

"It wasn't," Alisdair said calmly.

"Alisdair, you saw what had happened," she protested. It was all very healthy this laid back attitude of his, but bordering on the insensitive.

"He just knew it was his time."

"I know, but if he had to die, well – kinder surely in his own bed?" she protested.

"The earth *was* his bed," Alisdair said with that strange serenity. "And he didn't die – he just went through another door to a different part of the web."

He was sounding more and more like Mr. Ambrose, Darcy marvelled. In fact, he spoke as though the wisdom of the man had passed into the boy.

*

That night as they walked upstairs one behind the other, a chilling howl stopped them in their tracks.

"Old Grey Pelt," Alisdair whispered.

Silence enfolded them once more. Not having the heart to argue with him, she followed Alisdair into his room. Side by side they peered out of the window into the autumnal dark. A grey shape slunk into the woodland where Mr. Ambrose's body had lain. Once again the howl haunted the night.

Above the tree tops a white-owl hovered, its heart-shaped face turned towards the window.

Twenty

~

The next few days were filled with pain and hectic activity. As Mr. Ambrose had no relatives that she knew of, Darcy felt obliged to make the necessary arrangements; a task aggravated by the need to make any telephone calls from the village. Notices were placed in several national newspapers ranging from the *The Times* to the *The Sun*, though she could not imagine any relation of Mr. Ambrose's reading the latter, but you never could tell. Regardless, except for herself and Alisdair, nobody turned up at the funeral, sent floral tributes, or contacted the solicitor she had engaged. The simple service over, they collected the ashes at the gate house – a bit too slick for Darcy's taste this; but as Alisdair sensibly pointed out, there was less chance of getting someone else's by mistake, or worse still, a cross-section of the recently-deceased public!

Shaking her head, Darcy smothered a smile and ushered him back to the car. In silence they travelled the thirty-odd miles back to Westwalls. Alisdair sat clutching the urn the whole way, content to be 'bringing Mr. Ambrose back home'.

*

On the solicitor's advice, she had searched the lodge and found a will. The lodge and everything in it was left to Alisdair, as in Mr. Ambrose's own words he 'had no living relatives'. So too was the walled garden and any other land not included in the original purchase of house and land by Darcy, prior to her taking it over. Alisdair's most precious possession was now the painting of Merlin and Nimue. The urn he deposited in the lodge, placing it on a table in the window embrasure, next to Mr. Ambrose's telescope.

All very sad, but at least tidied up as Mr. Ambrose would have desired, and no loose ends. Talking of loose ends, it was time she did something about Jen. As far as Cain was concerned, Brant knew the fact and manner of his death and could deal with it in his official capacity. But Jen was something else. Offering to take Alisdair with her, but respecting his wish to remain at home, she set off for Hilldean.

Leaving a note in Chris Forster's pigeon hole requesting he meet her in an hour's time at the Study Room – less public than the refectory – she made her way to the Department of Archaeology. Caro took one look at her friend's strained and still slightly discoloured face, and pulled her inside. She then sat her down, fetched two coffees from the machine, and stuck a 'not to be disturbed' notice on the door. "Now tell me," she demanded.

Darcy gave her an expurgated version of events, omitting the link with the Gulf crisis, and also Brant's whereabouts.

*

"I can't believe it!" Caro breathed some fifteen minutes or so later. "Who would have thought it of him? He was always so charming, though come to think of it –"

"Yes?" Darcy prompted.

Caro frowned. "I don't know – there was something lurking beneath the surface. A bomb waiting to explode. And now he's dead?"

Darcy nodded. "But say nothing yet, Caro. I've not told anyone else, not even the police. It's in the hands of Brant's department now. All top secret stuff."

"Don't worry; I know nothing. Talking of Brant – where is he now? And what's the script?" Caro asked, finishing her coffee and tossing the cardboard cup into the waste paper bin.

"You know Brant when he's on a case – he tells me sweet eff-all," Darcy said smoothly. "As for the personal situation, I accused him of plotting my murder!"

"That's pretty bad," Caro said nodding, and Darcy had to smile.

"Seriously, Darcy, are you alright?" Caro asked as, having related the death of Mr. Ambrose, Darcy got up to go. "You and Alisdair would be more than welcome at our house."

"Thanks Caro, that's really kind – but I have things to sort out." For starters, just a little thing like saving the World, Darcy thought dryly. "I'll be in touch."

"Make sure you are. Don't have me worrying to death!"

"I promise." Darcy paused as she was about to open the door. "Has Andrea Lascelles been seen on campus?"

"Well I haven't had sight of her for over a week. I don't think she is around."

"Good. I'd rather she didn't see me, either."

Caro shivered. "Yes, of course. You're supposed to be dead. Burned to a crisp in that fire." Her face crumpled in concern. "Darcy, I really think you should come home with me."

"Nonsense. I'll be fine. You can't kill a corpse!" Darcy said with a laugh, squeezing Caro's arm.

She left before Caro could protest further.

*

Frank next, she thought making her way to the car park. She cast surreptitious glances over her shoulder, but there was no sign of Lascelles.

Chris had not met her in the refectory as requested, but had left a scribbled note in her pigeon hole. In it he made his excuses, claiming an exam later that morning, but that yes, he had reported Jen's disappearance but that the police didn't really want to know. Stuffing the note in her pocket, and resolving to do what she could later, she set off for Manchester and the offices of *The News*.

*

"So how do you think I got these Frank?" Darcy demanded, pointing to the fading bruises on her face. "And no, I've not come to beg about the suspension – just to let you know you were wrong to impose it in the first place!" she added, before he could argue.

"Okay, okay I believe you! It all sounds bloody fantastic mind, but I believe you. Will that do?"

"No – I want you to do something about it!" she shouted.

Frank rammed a cigar between his teeth and wandered over to the map on the wall. "I've lost two bloody good men out there," he said stabbing at the relevant points on the map with his cigar.

He turned back to her, and she saw the pain in his eyes. "I know. And I'm sorry Frank. They were special to me too – particularly Carl. I won't say 'maybe you should have listened to me when there was still time'."

"I know, I know." He wagged his great bear's head and spread his hands in a characteristic gesture. "But I couldn't do anything now, even if I wanted – there's a complete press ban, a news blackout. We received notice of it yesterday morning."

Brant and his Department didn't waste time, she thought, shot down in flames.

"Okay, Frank. I'll see you."

"I'm sorry kid – I was wrong," he said gruffly. "Forget the suspension."

But she sensed his reluctance. "Thanks Frank. But I have things to do."

"Watch your ass, for Christ's sake."

She could also see his relief: she was literally 'bad news', safer not to have her around for the present. "I will."

She helped herself to an early edition and left.

*

She should have felt relieved that everything was under control, but something, she worried on getting into her car, was still bothering her. It came to her as she joined the motorway. Selecting some music to while away this dreary stage of the journey, she pushed a cassette into the player. Paluccini's voice jolted her memory. Cain had been gloating over something. She had sensed it at the time, she recalled now. Something secret, that made him smirk whilst making her listen to the Paluccini tape. She saw him patting the cassette player before taking it away. That pat had said: *just wait, this is it.* But what? What had he planned?

One thing was sure, it wouldn't do anyone any good.

She ejected the cassette and turned the radio on instead. It was too soon: Paluccini's voice disturbed her, evoking as it did feelings and memories associated with her captivity; feelings she could not yet handle.

*

She was almost home when the news came on. She turned up the volume as an item caught her attention: *Security measures for the Mercury Space Convention due to open next week, were today under review, and causing a 'major headache' for the Metropolitan Police Special Branch. A Cabinet spokesman said earlier today that it was a high-profile event requiring maximum security. The conference will be attended by the Prime Minister and selected cabinet members; the U.S. President, the Russian and all E.E.C. Premiers, and leading physicists from the Einstein and C.A.D.E. Institutes.*

Darcy sucked in her breath noisily. She knew about the convention of course; Brant had told her about it, but she had not realised it was imminent. Nor had she seen previously the significance of the title: the *Mercury* Space Convention. Alisdair's meteorite had come originally from Mercury, and if the two events weren't connected, then it was one hell of a coincidence. She recalled Brant telling her that pressure was now on for the governments of the main space-contender nations to provide cash for a Mercury Mission. He had also explained that the photographs taken by Mariner 10 had shown its ancient origins. Craters on the side of the planet permanently hidden from the sun's rays contained ice that had never melted since it was formed – at the Birth of the Planets some four and a half billion years ago. It must, Brant had disclosed, contain debris from the primaeval explosion. Even before C.A.D.E. had its hands on the meteorite samples, it must have been desperate for that data. Now that it was supported by the meteorite particles, the race to get it must be on.

Mr. Ambrose had been right, she decided. It was all interconnected: Alisdair finding the meteorite; Cain using samples of it to work on D.N.A. and produce his mutants; and Lascelles selling the particles to the highest bidder, because that, Darcy was convinced, was the explanation behind the Sargasso tragedy and the Sahara affair. And the chances were that the 'highest bidder' was the Iraqi regime, preparing once more to raise its tyrannical head. If she was right, they could be well on the way to a second Gulf Crisis. Only this time, she reflected sombrely, the result would be catastrophic for the Western World. Something evil was at work here; the thing that Mr. Ambrose, and youngsters like Alisdair, had been working to counteract. Still preoccupied with her problems, she swung off the motorway and headed for Westwalls.

*

It was late evening before she sat down to read her edition of 'The News'. Alisdair was engrossed in a book of Mr. Ambrose's from the lodge. There was a nip in the air outside, now that the nights were drawing in, and he had kindled a fire in the inglenook before starting to read. The tang of pine and sweetness of apple wood from the crackling logs took Darcy back to Mr. Ambrose's fireside, filling her with sadness. *I actually miss the old tyrant* she thought with surprise. She turned the page of her paper and found a colour supplement had been inserted. "They're going to town on this Mercury Convention thing," she commented.

Alisdair looked up. He had been deeply engrossed in his book, and stared through her for a moment like an absent-minded owl. "Oh, I forgot to tell you: I heard it on the radio whilst you were out. There's to be a grand opening or something. A private concert for the heads of state and top physicists. They've booked your favourite for them."

"Pardon?" Darcy gave up trying to read on and lowered her paper. "What was that?"

"Your favourite. They've booked Paluccini for the concert."

"Lucky sods," she commented. "I'd give a month's salary and more to be there."

One day, she vowed, it would be her turn to hear the great tenor in person.

*

"Darcy," Alisdair said tentatively, putting down his book.

"Yes?" She looked up from her paper.

"Oh, it doesn't matter."

"No, go on, Alisdair," she urged, folding her newspaper. He had that look about him that usually preceded some major revelation.

"I had a dream last night."

"About?"

"Jen."

Darcy looked at him in silence, recalling his words at the breakfast table: *I think Jen is dead.*

"Tell me about it," she said quietly, taking care not to dramatise and therefore cause him embarrassment.

Alisdair, for all his new-found maturity, looked troubled. "I know where she is."

"Why didn't you tell me sooner?"

He frowned. "I was scared I was wrong. That it was just a dream; but it wasn't.

"It was like a black and white film. I saw her body. It was lying in a wood, partly covered by leaves. She'd been stabbed."

Darcy swallowed, then took a long slow breath. "Okay, Alisdair. Do you know where this wood is?"

He nodded, his eyes huge. "Before I 'went into' the wood, I saw a lonely moor. There was a house with tall chimneys and wrought iron points on the roof." He closed his eyes and screwed up his face as though striving to picture the scene. "Oh, and there were iron balconies at the windows. And a yew hedge. I remember that particularly because it was dark and sinister looking. The wood was about half a mile away. Just a copse, really."

Darcy stood up, paced the kitchen then returned to her chair. "Alisdair, you've just described the house Cain took me to."

"What should we do?"

"In the morning, we're going straight to Inspector Gallagher."

"Will she believe me?" Alisdair said looking apprehensive.

"We'll make her," Darcy replied grimly.

Alisdair was telling the truth about his dream, there was no doubt about that, she thought, pouring the milk in the pan for their supper-drink. But was this a case of genuine clairvoyance, or was it merely the contents of Alisdair's subconscious? Well, Mr. Ambrose had long hinted at Alisdair's 'gift', and in some extraordinary way he had helped to free her from her prison. Which had to be good enough. Somebody had to believe in the kid.

*

That night Darcy slept little. She kept thinking of Jen, alone in that desolate place without a decent burial. When she did finally sleep it was to dream of Paluccini singing to an auditorium of Einstein look-alikes. In the middle of the performance, in walked Jen, autumn leaves clinging to clothes and hair, her face ghastly white and beginning to decompose. With a cry Darcy awoke. She sat up in her bed, trembling. It was then that she made the connection. Made sense of the thing that had been bothering her all along. Cain, the Paluccuni tape, his smugness and air of secrecy, the Mercury Convention, and the key to them all – the Paluccini concert!

But how, what and why? Something dreadful had been planned by Cain, of that she was sure. But how to stop it when she didn't even know what it was?

The third question at least she could answer. *Power.* There would be heads of state and the world's greatest scientists present at that concert. Cain had been a megalomaniac. He had expected to be alive at the time of the concert. He would also have had advance information about the event, or even an invitation. Her train of thought juddered to a halt. *And that could be it.* The invitation. He may have been passed over, not received one. His ego could never accept such a blow. She rose and paced the moonlit bedroom. That could be it. Something as breathtakingly simple and trivial as that could have triggered his plan of destruction. Had he planted a bomb, a device of some sort? *Oh God, the irony of it: post humous revenge.*

Cain would appreciate that, even though it wasn't intended that way. And if he had done something of the kind, the question now had to be: was it already pre-set, primed to go off in Cain's absence? It had to be, she realised with a sickening jolt; if she was right, and Cain hadn't had an invitation.

Another thought struck her: what about Andrea Lascelles? Was she an accomplice in this too? Or as a former member of C.A.D.E. working in England, had she been automatically invited? *And that was the answer.* Cain had planned to double-cross her, only she had got to him first. If she had been included but not Cain, then that would add to his fury and sense of being slighted. He would have been content to let her perish with the rest.

Giving up on sleep, she went downstairs, made a hot milk drink and took it back with her to bed.

Like Alisdair earlier, she found herself wondering if anyone would believe her suspicions.

Tomorrow, she thought, would be the time to find out.

Twenty-One

~

Helen Gallagher gave Darcy a look that said: *Just what do you take me for lady?* "Let me get this straight, Miss West," she said pointing at Darcy with her pen, "you claim you were kidnapped and taken to a house in the middle of a moor but it is now a burned out shell. Your nephew here," she paused to give Alisdair a sceptical glance, "knows the girl Jen has been murdered, and that her body is lying in some wood near this house where you say you were kept; and that he knows this because he saw the girl – and the house as it was before it burned down – in a dream."

"I know how it must sound –"

"It sounds like another crazy pitch for a story," Inspector Gallagher snapped, tossing the pen down on the desk.

Darcy turned white. "How dare you! Jen was my friend."

Helen Gallagher shrugged. "Chill out, Darcy. You can't blame me – it *is* bloody incredible. And where's the motive? The affair between Cain and your friend was done and dusted."

"I believe initially he thought it was Jen who broke into the laboratory. And that she would talk about what she had seen. Only it wasn't her, it was me," Darcy added, looking Inspector Gallagher in the eye. "But by the time he knew that, Jen was already dead."

"Yes, well," she said dryly. "We'll gloss over that one for now. But I still don't buy your story."

"Have you found Jen? Have you got any leads at all?" Darcy threw back.

Helen Gallagher picked up a pencil and tapped the desk. "Tell me again," she said with a heavy sigh, "what exactly did he 'see'?"

"Ask him yourself; he's not a moron you know."

"Yes, please don't talk as though I'm not here," Alisdair piped up, evidently as little over-awed as Darcy by Helen Gallagher's rank.

Darcy waited for them to be shown the door, but to her surprise, the inspector laughed. "Sorry, Alisdair; you're quite right. So tell me, what did you see?"

Alisdair went through his story again.

"What was Jen wearing in the dream?" Helen Gallagher asked as he finished.

Alisdair sat quietly for a moment, thinking. "A white sweater – you know, one of those with the raised patterns like twisted rope. I think they're called 'Arran' or something like that. I know it was white because the blood showed up so clearly in a big dark patch. Black leggings and black boots, oh, and she had a patterned scarf but it came off in the struggle. It was lying on the ground. I don't know the colours because it was all in black and white."

Helen Gallagher looked down at some writing on her desk and nodded.

"Okay. That checks with the description we have of what she was last seen wearing. But," she raised a warning hand as Darcy sighed with relief, "you could have seen that description on television, Alisdair."

"We haven't got television; we have no electric," he said promptly.

"The newspapers then."

"Don't read them."

"What, and your aunt's a reporter?"

Helen Gallagher was smiling though. She gave him a long hard look. "Okay, we'll take a look, Alisdair." She turned to Darcy who was just starting to offer her thanks. "But if I find this is just a bit of sensational journalism, I'll put you on a charge of wasting police time!"

Darcy shrugged and gave Alisdair a look that said; *Gee, I hope you've got this right.*

*

The return to the locality of Cain's house proved more traumatic than Darcy had expected. The weather seemed to be in sympathy with the tone of their mission. She rode with Alisdair in the second of the two police vehicles, and the journey over the wind and rain swept moor filled her with a mounting sense of dread. As the shell of the house came into view, the remaining rafters jutting up to the sky like blackened bones, she relived in her mind the horror of that night and wished herself a hundred miles away. Beside her, Alisdair stiffened. "That must have been the house I saw; look, there's the yew hedge." He pointed out of the window at the singed and sombre trees.

The policeman sitting next to him asked, "Where to from here, son?"

"Not far. Those trees over there, I think."

He pointed to a wedge-shaped wood silhouetted against the horizon.

*

Helen Gallagher's face was as grim as the weather. Led by Alisdair, they had tramped along a slippery, mud-caked path to a small clearing.

Several police officers, one of them a handler with his dog, had combed the area, but found nothing. They now stood beneath the dripping trees, rain streaking their faces and running down their clothes in rivulets.

"Just as I thought, there's nothing here." Inspector Gallagher turned up her collar and threw an accusing look at Darcy.

"It was here. I *know* it was," Alisdair protested, looking pale and stressed. He pointed to the drifts of leaves at their feet. "Just there. That's where I saw her."

"It's alright, Alisdair. Not your fault." Gallagher turned and looked at her team. "Let's call it a day, shall we."

"No wait. She *is* here, I can *feel* it." Alisdair was now decidedly agitated. He was pacing the area with erratic movements. Suddenly he stopped, and nodded as though having suddenly realised something. He turned to Inspector Gallagher. "Dig! You have to dig," he said emphatically, pointing to the spot where he claimed to have seen Jen's body.

"I think this has gone far enough, don't you?" Helen Gallagher said coldly.

"No, you must *dig*."

"Do it for heaven's sake!" Darcy cried.

The dog, as though picking up on Alisdair's mood, began to whimper and strain at the leash. "Seek, girl, seek," her handler urged. The dog moved swiftly, nose to ground, around the perimeter of the clearing. The whimpering grew louder, and the dog's front paws scrabbled frantically in the bramble-infested undergrowth.

"She's found something, ma'am."

The handler stooped and removed the torn and sodden scarf from the dog's mouth.

Darcy confronted Helen Gallagher. "*Now* will you dig?"

The inspector turned and gave her men a brief nod.

*

A woman police officer took Alisdair back to the car. Darcy stayed only long enough to be sure. When an arm appeared, with the silver bangle Jen always wore at the wrist, she turned and retraced her steps to the edge of the wood, where she stood alone and wept for her friend.

A half hour or so later, she formally identified Jen's stabbed and battered body.

*

"At least Jen's family can now give her a proper burial – thanks to you," she comforted Alisdair on the grim journey back to the Manchester Police Headquarters where she had left her car.

Before leaving Helen Gallagher, Darcy tried to explain her fears about the Mercury Space Convention and the Paluccini concert. She had to admit as she drove away that her story had sounded crazy and insubstantial even in her own ears. Helen Gallagher would no more 'look into it' as she had promised, than poor Jen would get up and walk. "You're very upset, and understandably so," she had said, patting her on the arm. "We'll talk about this again."

Like hell! Darcy thought. Nobody wanted to know.

Well she was damned if she was going to sit back and wait for Cain to wreak his revenge from the grave.

*

That night Darcy awoke, unsure of what had disturbed her. In her dream, a barn owl had circled over the fell on which she was standing. Lower and lower it had swooped, stark white against the night, a ghostly shape in the moonlight. In the dream she had idly wondered what, if anything, it was trying to tell her. As though despairing of subtlety, it rent the air with its weird screech.

She lay for a moment, eyes half-closed, senses still drowsing. Gradually she became aware of something different, a presence in the room – but a benign one, as though a friend sat watching over her as she rested.

She sat up, and thought herself still in the dream. The clock on the bedside table ticked in a very normal way; the hands showed ten past three. Moonlight streamed through the window onto the quilt, illuminating the small brown stain where the other morning she had spilt a little tea. *I am awake.*

"Mr Ambrose?"

The figure seated at the foot of her bed smiled.

*

Darcy rubbed her eyes and when she opened them again expected he would be gone, as this was obviously some sort of delusion. He was still there.

"My, Old Hushwing had to work hard there; you were deeply asleep."

"But – *you're dead.*"

"Am I?" he commented mildly.

Darcy sat watching him in silence. Was he real? Or a product of her frayed nerves and imagination? There was no sense of weight around her feet, where he was sitting; but on the other hand, he *looked* real and substantial. His old self in fact. She opened her mouth to scream for Alisdair, but he raised a bony finger and put it to his lips whilst shaking his head. A part of her trembled with fear, whilst the other – a calm knowing self – seemed to hover just above her body, looking down with curiosity and interest.

"Why have you come?" she whispered.

"You called me."

"I never mentioned your name."

"You summoned me with your need."

Darcy fell silent; there was no denying her desperation.

"Can you help me?"

He scratched the side of his nose, then shrugged with a characteristic gesture. "A hint here, a nudge there."

"Is that all?"

"The conflict must be resolved by your own selflessness and courage."

"Conflict?"

"Between Good and Evil."

"That sounds rather too biblical for me."

"If that's how you want to see it. It simply means that opposing forces are at war in your World."

"But it's all so huge," she said in despair.

"Concentrate on your own aspect. The rest is being taken care of."

"The concert. The opening of the Mercury Convention."

He nodded. "Remember the chessboard. Ask yourself 'why the Maestro Paluccini'. What part can he, and only he, play in the game? What 'move' is exclusive to him? Sleep now – and remember. Just a hint, a symbol," he said gravely. "But first," he added, his gaze moving to the bedside table. "You have something belonging to me, I think."

"No, I don't –" then she remembered. Opening the drawer she took out the gold *pince-nez* and handed the glasses to him. "Do you still need them?" she asked puzzled.

He looked amused. "No." The touch of his fingers on her palm was no more than a breath of cool air. "But it may be useful to *you*, to know that I have them."

She didn't understand. But as he lapsed into silence and watched her with an unblinking stare, her eyelids grew heavy once more. She leaned back against the pillows, and as she did so, heard him whisper, "Sleep now, and remember."

Her eyelids drooped and she was back in her dream.

The white owl was leading her up a mountain, over the rocks and on to a waterfall that tumbled into a rocky basin. Night, she saw, was giving way to Dawn and a frieze of rose rimmed the fells. The owl circled three times, gave a last shriek and chased what was left of Night. The sun rose above the horizon, touching the land with long, low fingers of light. At the centre of the pool, she saw now, stood the meteorite on a slab of marble. As she watched, it turned to a goblet of gold. Streams of blue and silver cascaded into this fabulous chalice and overflowed, sparkling, onto the land. From there the streams of light danced downhill to the valleys, making them green and fertile, and made wonderful music as they leapt and darted over the bones of the Earth.

A beam of sunlight struck the chalice. Darcy, watching, was blinded by glancing shafts of golden light, and an aura that pulsed with power. The vessel of Courage and Plenty. Darcy knelt and was bathed in the light of the grail.

*

Sun was streaming through the window and onto the bed when she awoke. She lay for a time, still bathed in light, reluctant to relinquish the

251

vision. It wasn't lost, as many dreams are on reaching full awareness. The image stayed with her, warming her throughout the day. Despite this she was no closer to understanding its message. Mr. Ambrose had said: *a hint, a symbol*, but it was hard to see what relevance the grail could have today. And what had he meant about Paluccini? Maybe she had also dreamed Mr. Ambrose.

A flash of recollection sent her running upstairs and into her bedroom. Half wanting, half dreading, she opened the drawer of her bedside cabinet.

The gold *pince-nez* were no longer inside. Now she understood.

Mr. Ambrose had given her proof of his coming.

*

It was Darcy's turn to confide in Alisdair, just as he had come to her earlier. "Alisdair," she said hesitantly.

"Yes?" He looked up; he was cleaning with 'Brasso' the metal bands on Mr. Ambrose's telescope.

"Remember how you felt about your dream – the one about Jen?"

"Pretty weird. Why?"

"Something even more bizarre happened to me."

"Like what?"

"Last night I saw Mr. Ambrose – only I wasn't dreaming."

A look of excitement rather than fear spread across his face. "Wow! That really *is* something."

"Absolutely."

"What did he say? Tell me what happened," he clamoured.

Briefly, Darcy related the experience. Alisdair carried on rubbing the brass, but from his expression she knew he was deep in thought. "So, come on Master Einstein, how could that happen?"

"Easy," he replied promptly. "The Everett-Wheeler-Graham Theory."

"Pardon?"

"It's to do with wave functions, and the Many Worlds Theory of Quantum Physics."

"Alisdair – I need 'Physics for Idiots' not Nobel Prize stuff!"

He grinned and put down his polishing cloth. "Okay – let's take Schrodinger's Cat."

"Yes, but where?" Darcy quipped.

"It's a *hypothetical* cat. A famous experiment," he said severely.

"Imagine a cat being put in a box. Inside the box is a device which can release a gas, instantly killing the cat. It's only a make-believe cat," he added with a sigh, seeing Darcy's outraged expression. "Nobody wants to *really* kill one! Anyway, the radio-active decay of an atom, something which happens at random and nobody can predict it, is the trigger, the thing which decides whether the gas goes off or not. The box is closed and the experiment is activated. A moment later, the gas has either gone off, or it hasn't. The only way of knowing is by opening the box to look. Ordinary physics says the cat is dead, or it is not. Quantum Physics however, says it's not that simple.

"To make things even harder," he continued, "there are two ways of looking at it within Quantum Physics itself. The Copenhagen Interpretation says the cat is in a kind of limbo represented by a wave function, which has within it the possibility of both outcomes: that the cat is alive, and the cat is dead. Obviously only one of these states materialises."

"You've just lost me, Alisdair."

"Stick with it, Darcy. It's simple really. The important thing for you to know is they are saying that when we look into the box, and not before, one of these possibilities actually happens, and the other disappears. This is known as the collapse of the wave function."

"Mr. Ambrose said something about this 'Observer Effect'," Darcy contributed. "He said *nothing is there*, until we observe it."

"That's it; you've got it," Alisdair said with an air of satisfaction. "That's why the fate of the cat is not decided *until we look into the box!*"

"Fascinating. But what has all this got to do with my seeing Mr. Ambrose?" Darcy protested.

"I'm getting there – just stick with it a bit longer! Now then, the Copenhagen Interpretation says: once we look the cat is either dead or alive. But the Many Worlds Interpretation of Quantum Physics says, no – it is dead or alive *in this world*, but not in another. The instant the atom decays, (or doesn't) the world splits into two branches, each with a different version of the cat. The wave function isn't collapsed, only *split*. If the cat is dead in this world, it is alive in the other, and vice versa. Do you think you can handle that?" Alisdair asked solicitously.

"Just about," Darcy said, holding her head. "Mr. Ambrose is 'dead' in *this* dimension, but not in the *other*. Or in his jargon: he is dead in this section of the web, but not in another."

"Brill! You got it," he continued, looking pleased. "And as the wave, and the world split, our consciousness – as the observer – also divides. Normally, one self is not aware of the other, or of any other reality except the one it is in. In other words, you see this world as complete, and you don't imagine there being another you in another world somewhere.

"Right, now this is what I think must have happened: Somehow one of your many other selves, living in other worlds, was allowed to meet one of Mr. Ambrose's other selves. Remember, if he is 'dead' in this reality, he has to be alive in any other because all the possibilities have to be played out."

"I see." It wasn't Darcy thought, as crazy as it at first seemed. She recalled the sense of 'another self' looking down on her body in the bed. "There's one thing still puzzling me though."

Alisdair grinned. "Only one?"

"Cheeky monkey! Why was it 'allowed' to happen?"

Alisdair shrugged. "Now that I don't know. Maybe it was something to do with *need*. Perhaps strong emotions like fear, or desperately wanting something, have a sort of physical backlash."

Darcy looked startled. "Mr. Ambrose said that too: about how the intentions and feelings of the observer, or the scientist in the laboratory doing experiments, can influence the outcome of events."

"That's right; and the planet is in danger from the Julian Cain's of this world, who misuse knowledge to gain power. But there's also a universal force which works to counter the evil they do, and it comes through people like Mr. Ambrose."

"A sort of in-system power for Good, you might say," Darcy chipped in, bemused.

"Simple isn't it?" Alisdair beamed.

Picking up his rag, he resumed his task of polishing Mr. Ambrose's telescope.

*

Later that afternoon he came rushing into the kitchen from the lodge. "There's a car stopped at the gate!" he cried breathlessly.

Darcy grabbed his arm. "Who?"

"I don't know. A woman."

Darcy thought on her feet. Lascelles? Had she dared come here? If so, they were in trouble; she had a gun. And there were only two days to the concert. Lascelles must have discovered she was not dead after all. "Run up to the old summerhouse Alisdair – and stay there," she said brusquely. "Don't come down until you hear the car leave."

Alisdair had turned pale. "What about you?"

"I'll be alright." She gave him a push towards the door. "If it does go wrong, run to the village when she's gone and phone Brant and the police. Wait there for them to come. Now – *Go!*" She gave him another shove, and reluctantly he left.

A couple of minutes later there was an imperative knocking at the door.

She stared at her visitor for a moment, dazed. It wasn't Andrea Lascelles who was standing on her doorstep.

"Are you going to ask me in?" Helen Gallagher asked brusquely.

*

Relief had turned Darcy's legs to water. *Not the French bitch after all.* The chances were Lascelles didn't know she was still alive; she would have been here before now. She pulled herself together and led Helen Gallagher into the kitchen. "Coffee?" she asked, her mind working furiously. What on earth had brought her here?

"Thanks – but no. I haven't time."

"So what can I do for you?"

Helen Gallagher opened her briefcase and took something out. "It's what *I'm* about to do for *you*," she said dryly. "I've been thinking about everything you've told me. What with Alisdair being right about that girl's body – well, it saved me getting egg on my face. Anyway, I got to thinking I owed you one. Not only that, if there's any truth in what you suspect, and that place is booby-trapped, I don't want it on my conscience. I don't know what you can do, but at least you'll have half a chance. Here, take this." She thrust a plastic-covered card into Darcy's hand. "I've had a word or two in certain ears. Just show that at the door and they'll admit you."

"Door?" Darcy looked mystified.

"The Opera House. You are 'official correspondent' – there to cover the Opening. Once inside, it's up to you to persuade the right people to listen."

Darcy shook her head in disbelief. "Thank you. I never expected –"

"Don't get carried away." Helen Gallagher snapped her briefcase shut. "It's all unofficial. You're on your own. Got that?"

Darcy nodded. "Of course."

"Good." Helen Gallagher reached the front door and turned. "Because if you ever refer to me, or apply to me for back-up, I'll deny this conversation. I'll also do you for unlawful possession of a security card."

"Fair enough. I'll have a go."

"Good luck Darcy." She opened the door and looked back at her. "You've got balls."

I reckon I'm going to need them, Darcy thought, shutting the door.

＊

Alisdair returned within minutes of Helen Gallagher leaving. He burst into the kitchen, his face white and drawn with anxiety.

"It's Okay," she swiftly reassured him. "It was Inspector Gallagher."

Relief flooded his features, bringing back the colour. "What did she want?"

"I have to go to London the day after tomorrow. Will you be alright here on your own?"

"Can't I come?" he entreated.

"Not this time. Besides I need you here sending out the Good Vibes."

"Okay." He sighed. "It's the concert, isn't it?"

"Yes, Alisdair. But I'll be back – and in one piece, I promise!"

And let's hope that's one promise I can keep, she thought anxiously.

＊

Whatever, it made sense to sort something out for Alisdair in case of emergency. *In case I don't come back.* "Alisdair – walk down to the village with me?" she said casually a little later.

She sent him to buy some chocolate whilst she went into the telephone booth and dialled Brant's number. No reply. She tried his car 'phone next. Nothing. He must still be in Kuwait. The only alternative was to write him a letter tonight and post it the following day. She would ring Caro now; Caro would provide immediate help for Alisdair if necessary, and until the family could be contacted.

Her mind was quieter as she left the kiosk. She had merely asked permission to give Alisdair Caro's number to ring, should her return from a trip to London be delayed. Even so, Caro had been anxious, rightly suspecting Darcy of being involved in something dangerous, but had agreed to her request. Such had been the level of Caro's concern that Darcy felt consumed by guilt. I'll just have to make sure I come back, she thought, walking down the lane to meet Alisdair as he came out of the shop.

CONCLUSIONS
– OF A KIND

One

~

September – London

And that's how it was. And now here *she* was: on a one way ticket to save the World, she thought in self-mockery. And she was still no nearer to solving the riddle. In fact Mr. Ambrose's 'hint' was about as useful as a Christmas card in July. Her stomach lurched every time she thought of the ordeal ahead. Perhaps nobody would listen. They may even throw her out.

Then the western world would be in one hell of a mess.

The image arose of Charles Ashford's body, and she was scared. Really scared. Because tonight that could happen to her. And those miss-hapen creatures in Cain's laboratory; they could be the prototype of the next generation. For now more than ever before, she was sure the bomb or whatever it was that Cain had placed, would contain those deadly particles. Particles that would contaminate not only London but be spread via wind currents and water systems to infect the whole of Britain. And not just for one generation. Anger welled up. It wasn't right that she had to shoulder this burden alone. The authorities should be doing something. Brant for a start, and his precious Department. And worse still, she couldn't detect Mr. Ambrose's influence in this conflict of Good and Evil. But it was no use whining, she decided as the train drew into Euston station.

*

She alighted and looked around for suspicious-looking individuals. Cain was beyond stopping her now, but her chief fear was of running into Andrea Lascelles. If the French physicist had been invited to the concert, and the odds were she had given her previous connection with C.A.D.E, then a chance meeting was a distinct possibility. Darcy knew she was safe only as long as Lascelles thought her dead. At least the yuppy who had been seated opposite turned out to be no more than that, and he melted into the crowd. The Buffet was packed and she had to queue for her coffee and sandwich, but there would be neither time nor opportunity later. She glanced at the clock. Time to be moving. Aware of a mounting tension within, she headed for the Underground and Covent Garden.

*

The crowds, the noise, the traffic and extra police on duty all testified to the importance of the occasion. Consulting her watch, Darcy decided her timing was about right. Doubts and worries, her own sense of power-lessness, had briefly subsided in the excitement. The air was filled not only with petrol fumes and clamour, but with expectancy and anticipation for the next arrival. From snatches of overheard conversation, she gathered the U.S. President and First Lady had arrived ten minutes or so before.

The crowd pressed forward. Police officers formed a cordon and strove to hold back the tidal wave of people as a cavalcade of limousines drew up. The British prime minister emerged; his normally dowdy wife was resplendent in peacock silk and diamante. Darcy waited until the obliga-tory pause and smiles and firework-display of camera flashes had sub-sided, then thrust through the crowd. Camera on shoulder, heart in mouth and I.D. press card firmly in hand, she boldly approached the police blockading the entrance.

*

She had done it; she was inside and had been shown to the special press box. It provided a vantage point from which to select her target and plot her offensive. Except that she hadn't got one. She still had no idea how to proceed. The scene in all its glitz and glitter lay before her. She looked across at the premiers' boxes – the heavy-jowled Russian premier had also arrived – noting the members and numbers in their retinues, and the burly bodyguards standing discreetly at the rear. Little chance there. She wouldn't get within twenty yards. Her eyes scanned the packed audi-torium; her mind skimmed the possibilities. The French, German and Italian premiers were also present, she realised, picking them out one by one; but they too were heavily guarded. She studied the complimentary programme. *Why Paluccini?* Mr. Ambrose had asked. *What was his special move on the board of Life?* But she was no closer to an answer.

Her gaze ran constantly over audience and theatre, searching for any anomaly. Nothing leapt to her attention.

Except the unashamed luxury. Spurts of blue, green and red fire danced through crystal pyramids, was refracted back again by the diamonds of necklace, brooch and tiara. The auditorium buzzed with muted conversation, the rustling of gowns, and now and again, a flurry of polite laughter. And running beneath it all, the intellectual buzz. The world's most eminent scientists were gathered here tonight, the entire senior staff of the Einstein and C.A.D.E. Institutes; men and women who spent their lives searching deep Space for answers, albeit via computers, unseen particles and giant radio telescopes.

And there was Professor David Aaron. She recognised the stocky grey-haired man from her research. He was larger and more imposing than his photographs in the scientific journals. He should be her first target. Disparate and discordant notes issued from the pit; the orchestra was tuning up. The clock was ticking and time was running out. If only she knew when Cain's device was due to go off. Darcy's palms were damp with sweat. Excusing herself as she pushed past fellow reporters, she left the box and advanced on David Aaron.

*

"But you *must* listen to me, sir," she entreated, aware that eyes were now looking their way, and that tongues were already wagging as she confronted the head of C.A.D.E. in his box. Her attempts to get him to take her seriously had so far met with little success. "Jules Cain sent you those particles to analyse," she said lowering her voice, "but he didn't surrender the meteorite as you ordered, did he?"

David Aaron removed his horn-rimmed glasses and pointed them at her. "Young woman, how did you come by such information?"

"Never mind that now," she said impatiently and close to despair. "Believe me, I've seen the results of his experiments. You must get everyone out of here. I tell you we're all in grave danger, so is the rest of London. God knows how far those particles will spread. You must stand up and make an announcement – they'll listen to you."

Two security men moved forward from where they had been standing at the rear of the box. "The lady bothering you, Professor?" one of them asked.

David Aaron checked them with a half-raised hand and replaced his glasses. "So where is this imputed device?" he said turning back to Darcy.

She sighed with despair. "I don't know," she confessed.

"And when is it set to explode?"

"I don't know that either – but I know it's *here*."

"I think you should leave now," he said politely.

Throughout the exchange, the strains of the orchestra had provided an incongruous note. The main auditorium lights now began to dip.

A woman whom Darcy took to be Aaron's wife leaned across from the adjacent seat. "What is it dear? Some problem?" she asked her husband.

"No, nothing. This young woman is just leaving," he said smoothly. He lifted his hand and the two men stepped forward. "She's a reporter," he said dismissively, as though this was explanation enough. "I think she's lost her way; escort her back to her seat."

Darcy found her arms firmly grasped.

*

She had not argued or resisted, knowing she was within a centimetre of being thrown out, or worse, being handed over to the police as a suspicious character. As it was, just before the house lights were completely extinguished, she saw her 'escort' talking to a couple of officers, whilst pointing in her direction. Obviously she would now be under discreet surveillance. In this threatening climate, it was hard to keep doubts at bay. She could be wrong, be making a mega-fool of herself.

The music swelled, the spotlight beam split the darkness and the curtain rose.

*

The orchestra's rendition of the *Intermezzo* from *Cavalleria Rusticana* had drawn to a close. The opening speeches had been made, and a tension and hushed expectancy had descended. The curtain rose, the spotlight hit the back of the stage, and Paluccini emerged. The audience erupted into ecstatic applause. Despite the urgency and desperation of her mission, a thrill ran along Darcy's spine as the great tenor stood centre stage. The fact that he was a big man could not detract from a natural sensuality, enhanced by a full sensitive mouth, an engaging smile and expressive eyes.

He held up his hands. The shuffling and whispers of excitement were stilled. The music began, and the great voice soared. First, *Non Ti Scordar Di Me*, the drama of it filling the auditorium and holding his listeners spellbound. Then *Che Gelida Manina* from *La Boheme*. The purity of each note, the passion and tenderness in turn, so enthralled Darcy that she almost forgot why she was there. Arias from *Aida*, *Turandot*, and *Tosca* followed, each one ending in tumultuous applause.

*

The curtain came down for the intermission and nothing untoward had yet occurred. The house lights went up. Darcy, growing more desperate by the minute, left the press area and moved around, wondering whom she might approach next. The prime minister might listen. The cliché 'man of the people' seemed to apply to him more than his predecessors. But listen to what? Hope plummeted again. All she had was a crazy hunch: a premonition, with nothing more sound than a gut-feeling for evidence. Something in that train of thought was tugging at the corner of her mind. In some way it seemed to have some connection with Mr. Ambrose's clue. *She almost had it.* No, it had gone again.

*

She had been heading for the exit which she guessed led to the stairs by which the P.M.'s box could be reached, but found herself under scrutiny. The two policemen who had been alerted to her earlier began slowly walking her way. She swerved and made her way instead to the ladies' toilets, sure at least of not being followed there. She pushed open the door and seeing the queue, was about to turn and leave. It was then that she saw her. The fair hair and French chic were unmistakable. Andrea Lascelles had her back to her, but Darcy could see her profile in the mirror. Lascelles half turned, glanced in the mirror, and raised a hand to pat her hair into place. Their eyes briefly met. Darcy turned and pushed her way past the women thronging the doorway.

*

Now she was in double trouble. She glanced over her shoulder as she hurried back to the press enclosure. Andrea Lascelles now knew she was still alive, but couldn't afford to leave it that way. If Cain's particles don't get me, Darcy thought wryly, Lascelles probably will.

Damn her, and damn Helen Gallagher! *I should never have come.* She could hope to accomplish nothing alone. The futility, the stupidity of her actions made her want to weep. It was no use. One way or another, she stood to die – and Alisdair would be left alone yet again. She hadn't seen Lascelles return yet. Not a good feeling, to be watched by an unseen adversary, especially one as ruthless as she.

The only hope left, she decided, was to forget Lascelles for the moment and try to crack Mr. Ambrose's clues. She scanned the night's programme, but found nothing of sinister significance. *Nothing more sound than a gut feeling* ... The lights began to dim in warning; the orchestra settled itself in readiness. The lighting sunk lower; the orchestra struck up the first notes. The house lights faded completely, giving way to stage lights of blue and violet and green. *Nothing more sound* ... Why did that chance thought keep going around in her head? She froze. *Sound.* Was that it? Ask yourself, Mr. Ambrose had said, '*Why Paluccini? What particular move in the game could he make?*'

Her heart almost stopped. What move indeed, if not connected with *sound?* That was the business he was in, for God's sake. Her mind spun into orbit. At home she had a pocket recorder, useful for storing ideas for her column. And it was *voice-activated.* But that would be no use: the device whatever it was, would have been detonated by the first person to enter the theatre and speak! Unless ... It was almost as though the shock of seeing Lascelles had cleared her brain. Swiftly, before the lights went down altogether, she scanned the second half of the programme. And there it was! *O soave fanciulla,* the duet from *La Boheme.* The final scheduled item – and famous for that final top 'C'!

If she was right, tonight there would be no obligatory encores.

*

The second half of the performance passed in a blur of mental anguish. Aria followed aria, and Paluccini was joined by Sylvia Mastrianni, the foremost soprano. Could there be any justification for disrupting this gala performance on such a flimsy assumption? 'You've got balls Darcy,'

Helen Gallagher had said: well, she'd certainly need them for this. It was impossible. She couldn't do it.

But then the pendulum would swing the other way. There was no mistake. This had to be it. The perfect revenge which would suit Cain's ego and love of drama. What better way to annihilate his rivals as he had seen them, than on a final note, sung by the world's greatest tenor? When Paluccini hit that top 'C' the canister would explode – and they would all die a horrible death. Such a voice-activated device would be child's play to a brilliant scientist like Cain. So was she going to sit here calmly and wait for it to happen? But then she pictured herself standing up, making a spectacle of herself, and in would flood the doubts. *It's crazy; they'll lock you up and lose the key.* And so the pendulum swung the other way yet again.

*

The penultimate song. Make up your mind time. The audience were with him all the way; women dabbed at their eyes, overcome by emotion. The atmosphere was charged, and the minutes were ticking away. More applause. He was holding up his arms now, appealing for silence. Little by little the waves of applause were subsiding. Sylvia Mastrianni joined him, standing at his side. The orchestra struck up, and the beautiful duet began. Darcy felt faint with heat and the stress of conflict. She had just decided to take her chance and do nothing, when Mr. Ambrose's voice sounded inside her head: *a hint, that is all you are allowed. The conflict between Good and Evil must be resolved by your selflessness and courage.*

She couldn't sit by and let Cain's evil win.

It was in that split second that the proverbial scales were lifted from her eyes. It was as though, in making that decision of personal sacrifice, she was granted the power of vision. She saw the chalice of her dream, filled with the light of salvation. She saw the letters formed in light, and they lit the touch-paper of inspiration. She almost laughed aloud. *Trust Mr. Ambrose.* A trickster to the end. Forget holiness and sanctity – this was perfectly mundane.

Not 'Grail' – but *G-rail*. That was the meaning of the symbol. How she knew it with such certainty lay beyond her; but know it she did. There *was* a bomb – and that was where it would be found. Right now there was no way of determining where 'G' row was located, whether in stalls, circle or gods. It didn't matter; it was irrelevant. A detailed search would sort that out later. All that mattered now was preventing the explosion.

Paluccini and Mastrianni were reaching the final phrase. They were both visibly gathering themselves, psyching themselves up for that final and deadly top 'C'. Paluccini took Sylvia Mastrianni's hand in his own. The music soared, the couple on the stage drew gigantic breath. Not a second to waste: It had to be now. Darcy leapt to her feet. Heads turned, people tutted and voices hissed. "Sit down!" and she ignored them all. "Stop!" she yelled at the top of her voice. "For God's sake **stop**! There's a **bomb!**"

The sudden silence was deafening.

Then pandemonium broke loose.

*

"Oh, no!"

As the shot rang out, her first thought was for Paluccini. Why should he have to die? A simultaneous impression of the tenor, and Andrea Lascelles' face, filled her consciousness.

So it was with a sense of surprise that she felt the impact of the bullet.

Two

~

She was lying on the floor. The crystal lights of the auditorium dazzled her, deepening her confusion and disorientation. She was surrounded by screams and shouts and stampeding feet, a sense of panic. This must be another dream; either that or she was dead, because Brant's face was above her own. His eyes were looking intently into hers. "Darcy? Speak to me!"

There he went, ordering her about again. She tried to move, but it hurt.

Then she remembered. The shot. "Am I going to die?" she whispered.

She saw Brant's expression change. "Certainly not. You've too much explaining to do!"

But he took hold of her hand.

"This is getting to be rather a habit," he commented, placing a folded blanket beneath her head.

"Ditto. But you still need practice; your timing was lousy."

"I'll see she pays, Darcy," he said grimly.

"More important: look for –" she struggled against the pain, "a device or something. Fastened to the rail, 'G' row."

Brant turned and said something, nodded at his men. "You can stop worrying now, Darcy."

She winced with pain and let out a long sigh. "At last." Something else was troubling her, then she remembered. "What are you doing here Brant?"

"Like you – a half-cocked idea that something would come off."

"Mr. Ambrose?"

He nodded and said no more.

"Paluccini?" she asked weakly.

"Is deeply indebted to you. As of course, are we all. Now shut up and save your strength. The ambulance will be here any minute."

"I can't – Alisdair," she protested.

"I'll see to him."

"Lascelles?"

Brant's face set into granite. "Don't worry; we have her."

Darcy nodded and her eyes closed.

*

Darcy sighed. After a couple of days spent recuperating in hospital, the luxury and novelty was beginning to pale, despite a bouquet and hand-written message from Paluccini, and a personal visit from an apologetic David Aaron. The ward sister swished past, and gave Brant a look of mock severity. "Only another ten minutes, Mr. Kennedy."

"You're a martinet, Sister!"

"And none of your cheek, please."

"She adores you," Darcy observed.

"All women do – except you."

She chose to ignore the remark. "How's Alisdair?"

"Enjoying being spoiled rotten. You'll have a job to prise him back from Caro!"

"So much for the loyalty of youth," she said with a laugh.

"How's the shoulder?"

She grimaced and shifted her arm in the sling. "Sore – but I'll live."

"Have you had the analysis yet?" she asked, changing the subject. On his first visit to the hospital, he had told her that they had in fact found a small gadget, taped to the inside of the hand rail on 'G' row.

"We received the analysis and report this morning. An explosive device containing activated particles."

"Hell!"

"It would have been. Clever girl."

She blushed. That was extravagant praise, coming from Brant.

"Frank's been," she volunteered, as the silence lengthened.

"Good. What did he have to say?"

"Abject apologies. Well," Darcy amended, "he actually said to hurry and get my ass back there – it was too peaceful without me!"

"That's Frank."

"I suppose. Oh, I almost forgot: there's something I've been meaning to ask."

"Go ahead."

"Andrea Lascelles: was she playing kamikaze – or did she not know about the bomb?"

"She didn't know," he said shortly.

"So her pot-shot at me was purely to keep my mouth shut about her own activities."

His face darkened. "Yes."

He picked one of the grapes from the bunch he had brought from Alisdair, then put it back in the dish.

Darcy frowned. "What's the matter, Brant?"

"Nothing, why?"

"Because this conversation is hard work," she said candidly. "So come on, what's wrong?"

He sighed and shook his head. "I've let you down."

"What on earth do you mean?"

"I promised Andrea Lascelles would pay for what she did," he began.

Darcy nodded. "So?"

"She's appealed to C.A.D.E. and they've taken up her case."

"They would, wouldn't they?" Darcy said bitterly. "I mean, there would be too much come out about *their* unsavoury deals with Iraq, should they refuse."

Brant's face was like thunder. "Precisely. The upshot is, they've applied for extradition. They'll get it, of course."

"And?" Darcy prompted, suspecting there was more.

"She has denied arson and anything to do with Cain's death."

"That's ridiculous," Darcy protested, raising herself up then wincing at the movement.

She sighed with frustration as Sister passed again and motioned her to lean back on the pillows. "I saw her kill him. I'll stand witness."

But Brant was shaking his head and looking grave. "Won't do, I'm afraid. You would be a prejudiced witness. You see, she's claiming *you* killed Cain in a fit of jealous rage. Because he ended his affair with you to be with her."

"That's absolute bullshit."

"I agree. And she wouldn't stand a chance over here. But once in France, she will admit to shooting at you, but claim *crime passionnel*, and probably get away with it, or a nominal sentence."

Darcy stared at him in horror. "That means I can never feel really safe. And worse still, she may try to get even with me through Alisdair."

The blue-grey of Brant's eyes deepened in intensity. "Don't worry Darcy. I'll see to her – one way or another."

Darcy looked alarmed. "Brant, you mustn't take this into your own hands. I couldn't bear it if –" She stopped in confusion. "That is, don't do it."

"It's not your problem, Darcy," he said quietly.

"Just tell me, you and she, were you-?"

He stood up, a look of disgust on his face. "How can you even ask?"

"Same way you did, I guess, about myself and Cain."

Sister sailed past again pushing the drugs trolley. "Not upsetting my patient, I hope? After all," she called over her shoulder as she bustled away down the ward, "She's quite the heroine."

"See, you mustn't upset me," Darcy said smugly.

"Bullshit," he replied.

"Anyway, there was never anything between myself and that bitch."

"You could have fooled me," Darcy muttered.

"That's just what I *had* to do. I had to fool her too; convince her I'd cut you out completely, or she wouldn't have dealt me in. If she had suspected for one minute I wasn't bent and out for a 'kill' – I'd never have got the crack on the Iraqi situation."

"What did happen there?" Darcy asked curiously.

Brant grinned. "By now they will have followed the 'modified' formulae and destroyed every single particle they possessed! The second they turned on the Collider, the particles would mutually annihilate."

"Clever. Well done."

"Thanks."

He looked down at her with a strange expression in his eyes. "So – where to from here?"

"Home to Westwalls, of course."

"I see."

That's all I can cope with right now, she thought minutes later, watching him walk away down the ward.

Three

~

The bark of the dogwood glowed red as blood against the first hard frost. Darcy looked up as a clamour of rooks cawed and circled the skeletal trees. There was something not right here; something missing. She emptied a bag of scraps, seeds and nuts onto the bird table. Maybe it was Mr. Ambrose. She still couldn't get used to the idea of never seeing him again. Daily she expected him to walk around some corner, or find him strolling through the garden. Would the place ever feel whole again without him? Yet despite its air of despondency and impoverished garden, it drew her still. Values were different here at Westwalls. Here it was who you were, not what you looked like, how much money you had, or who you knew. And Alisdair was thriving. He loved the place with a quiet and taken-for-granted passion. And here there were no thugs, no drugs and no amusement arcades with addictive slot machines.

But he was maturing fast.

She watched him jogging towards her across the rimed grass, his breath rising like puffs of white candy floss. He had celebrated his twelfth birthday a couple of weeks ago. She had bought him a new computer; Brant had bought the generator. Even she, a complete novice at physics, could see that the formulae displayed on Alisdair's screen were way beyond most men, never mind a youth of his age. "Hi. What have you been doing?" she asked as he reached her side.

"Lagging a couple of pipes at the lodge."

He took his inheritance seriously, she reflected. "Ready for coffee?"

"You bet. And scones?"

"You smelled them baking!"

*

"Will it ever be right here again, Alisdair?" she asked suddenly as they walked back to the house together, their footprints a dark trail on the frosted grass.

He nodded with a surety she envied. "Yes. Soon now." He paused and looked up at a buzzard mewing and circling overhead. "Brant will come; then we can bury Mr. Ambrose's ashes."

Darcy walked on to the house, saying nothing. She had thought he was hanging on out of sentimentality; it seemed he was waiting for something else.

*

They sat in the inglenook, looking into the fire whilst drinking their coffee. "Do you still want to be a physicist?" she asked.

He nodded. "I've never wanted to be anything else."

"Was there anything in what Mr. Ambrose said, do you think: you know, that young people like yourself can alter things for the good?"

He gave her a quizzical look. "We can't do much worse."

"That's true."

"I think we're more sensitive to the things Science can't measure. More receptive to them – and therefore they can work through us."

"And back full circle to Mr. Ambrose," Darcy commented ironically.

Alisdair grinned. "There's no getting away from him."

Darcy finished her coffee and in silence, sat looking into the fire.

"What's wrong?" Alisdair asked, immediately picking up on her mood.

"I was just thinking of Andrea Lascelles – and how wrong it is she should get around the law."

There was a strange look on Alisdair's face; his eyes behind the lenses of his glasses were like deep unfathomable pools. "I've been thinking that, too," he said slowly.

"I'm so scared Brant will do something outside the law. And beyond the protection of the Department." She sighed and picking up the poker, raked the ashes in the basket so that the smallest cinders fell with a clinking sound into the ash can beneath.

Alisdair stared thoughtfully into the flames. When he turned to her, she was startled by the way the fire glowed and burned in his eyes. Obviously a reflection, but an uncanny effect.

"Don't worry, Darcy. Nothing bad will happen to Brant. I promise."

She was touched by his faith, and wished she could share his optimism.

*

Later that day, Brant called. He brought with him a sealed metal box which he placed carefully on the table. Alisdair's expression changed, but he said nothing. Darcy noted the look of intensity and understanding which passed between him and Brant. "What is it?" she asked, pointing to the box.

"It's the meteorite."

It was Alisdair who had answered, not Brant.

Darcy looked startled. She looked quickly at Brant. "Is it?"

For answer he took a key from his pocket and inserted it in the lock. He lifted the lid, and Darcy saw that the box was lead-lined. A smaller container nestled within. "Just routine precautions," he said as Darcy began to look anxious. He opened the second box. The greenish-amber glow brought a gasp from Darcy.

"It's safe enough in its natural state," Brant reassured her. "It's Men that render it harmful with their processes and greed."

"How did you manage –?"

Brant lowered the lid of both boxes. "I'm not in the Service for nothing! Just let's say *it was arranged.*" He winked at Alisdair then turned back to Darcy.

"Basically, because it was expedient," he explained more soberly. "After the furore at the Opera House, and given the timing of the Mercury Mission Convention, it wouldn't be too convenient for this to be officially 'found' right now. Nobody wants to accept responsibility for knowing about it. There'd be lots of awkward questions asked – in Parliament."

"About non-existent security – and 'Formulas for Iraq'," Alisdair chipped in. "Not to mention unrecorded millions!"

"Why have you brought it here?" Darcy whispered.

Brant looked at her as though it was a ridiculous question to ask. "We must put it back. Mr. Ambrose wishes it."

Darcy frowned and looked thoughtful. *What an odd expression; he speaks as though Mr. Ambrose is still here.* "You knew about him?" Darcy asked, scrutinising his face.

He nodded. "But my scientist's mind just couldn't get around it at first.

"Then gradually it began to make sense. It's just a matter of perspective: different people explaining the same thing in differing ways. For Alisdair Mr. Ambrose was a sort of 'myth-come-true': a channel for the protective force that guards the planet. I guess that was how Mr. Ambrose made sense of his powers too. I must confess, it took me some time to accept the idea."

Darcy nodded. "Me too. How did you work your way around it?"

"By talking with Mr. Ambrose. And Alisdair here, too. And in the end, by drawing on one of my 'heroes', if you like."

"Who was that?"

"Carl Gustav Jung."

Darcy frowned. "I can't quite see the connection here."

Brant pushed the hair back from his forehead. "Let me explain. You see for *me*, it was the Earth's protective mechanism coming into play: a natural energy or power that has nothing to do with humans. A means by which the Earth somehow has a long-term chance of regeneration.

"Anyway, I recalled what Jung had to say about the importance of myth in his *Psychology and Religion*. He says 'myth is not fiction, it consists of facts that are continually repeated ...' He goes on to explain that myths and the archetypes they embody are real. They are things that happen to us, and that we have 'mythical fates' just as the Greek heroes did. Who knows, maybe we were all 'suitable' subjects once, but the facility has become overlaid with 'progress' and push-button lifestyles. Most importantly, Jung says that eventually the archetype fulfills itself not only psychically in the individual, but *objectively* outside that person.

"So although as a scientist I was happier with my notion of a natural energy like gravity, say – I began to see that the truth of the matter may be much more complex. It's my bet there are many of them – men and women like Mr. Ambrose. Spread through the world, they work in silence and secrecy, helping to bring the next generation to awareness.

"Hopefully when they – the youngsters – inherit this planet, they will halt the rot. But the task is phenomenal. Not content with trashing the Earth, we are now hell-bent on using Space as a dustbin. Not just the Earth, but the Universe itself is fighting back, and these special people are a personification of its will to survive. I have to believe it is strong enough."

"Will it end here, Brant? This particular evil I mean," Darcy asked anxiously.

He sighed and shrugged his broad shoulders. "Tell her Alisdair."

Alisdair looked up from his scrutiny of the box. "I keep telling you: energy once released doesn't fade away, it only undergoes change."

"The scientific community still has some particles?" Darcy asked, making a conceptual leap.

Brant nodded again. "It's inevitable. Subject to the Official Secrets Act of course, and locked away in a secret vault in some hidden laboratory, but there nonetheless."

Darcy walked over to the window and looked out, then turned back to face Brant. "Do you know about the Observer Effect? I mean Mr. Ambrose-style – that the intent of the experimenter can influence the result?"

"Yes, but it's no use giving in to despair, Darcy. We'll just have to do as Mr. Ambrose says and put our faith in Alisdair and his generation. Believe in their basic goodness and integrity. We have no choice."

He picked up the box and moved to the door. "Now, let's go and set this to rest."

Darcy and Alisdair followed him outside and onto the fell.

*

The frost had long ago melted and sunlight warmed their faces as they watched Brant digging, re-opening Alisdair's earlier excavations.

Eventually the meteorite and Mr. Ambrose's remains were laid to rest.

"He will guard it for us," Alisdair said.

In silence they trooped back down the fell.

*

A couple of night's later, Darcy awoke and lay in the darkness listening. Her flesh crawled as she heard the familiar words. She must be mistaken, or dreaming. Surely all that was now at an end? Slipping out of bed, she crept to Alisdair's room and pushed open the door. The sheets lay smooth and white in the darkness; his bed was empty.

As she stood on the landing, the words drifted up the stairs:

The bright star of the East brings dawn's first breath
The watery star of the West brings Life's emotional quest

The summer-star of the South fires poet and bard
But the dark star of the North brings to Earth
Retribution, Silence and Death.

He was seated in the inglenook, staring into the embers of the fire. He turned as she stood behind him, and Darcy was shocked by his expression. His face was set; his eyes glowed with fire. "What are you doing here, Alisdair?" she asked, afraid.

"Just concentrating."

"On what?"

"I was thinking about Andrea Lascelles."

Although he spoke quietly, there was something terrible in his voice. Despite the heat from the embers, Darcy shivered and drew her dressing gown tighter around her. "You're scaring me, Alisdair."

"Go back to bed, Darcy."

She stared at him. He had spoken not as a boy, but as a man.

She turned and went back upstairs.

Four

~

Holloway Prison

The wardress eyed the prisoner with a mixture of hostility and envy. Drab and shapeless prison clothes couldn't truly disguise the French-woman's underlying style and elegance. It went beyond top show, she thought, her hands automatically smoothing her own faultlessly neat uniform. You either had it, or not, she thought glumly; and this cool bitch certainly had. But she couldn't take to her. Not in a month of Sundays. "So you'll be leaving us in the morning, Lascelles," she said coldly, moving to the door. As well she was going. There was something about this one; she disturbed the others. Having her here as a lifer would be a nightmare.

Well, she had to be pretty weird and callous to do a thing like that, didn't she? Because she killed that professor guy alright; the one they found traces of in the burned out house. And now she was trying to blame it on that woman reporter she took a pot shot at. Yet she was as guilty as hell. The wardress's eyes narrowed. Twelve years in the job gave you a sort of feel for it. "Don't suppose you'll be sorry to see the back of us," she added grimly.

Andrea Lascelles shrugged her shoulders with a dismissive flair that was truly Gallic. Picking up some cigarettes from the small table by her bunk she took one from the packet. "May I have a light?"

"It's five minutes to lights-out."

"Oh, come on; you will be rid of me tomorrow."

The wardress hesitated. "You'll be costing me my job," but she put her hand in her pocket and drew out a silver lighter.

*

278

The door clanged shut behind the wardress. Andrea Lascelles drew on her cigarette and exhaled contempt along with the smoke. Tomorrow was the first step towards her freedom. "No problem," Pierre DuPont had said today. And he should know; his name was a legend on the international circuit. C.A.D.E. had been more than generous in their choice of lawyers. But they would be, wouldn't they? Their skin was as much at risk here as her own. They couldn't afford to have awkward questions asked in Parliament. About the sale in the past of formulae for potentially lethal weapons, for instance.

No, there would be no problem. Her touching portrayal of a young woman in love, betrayed by her English lover and his scheming bitch, would have the jurors eating out of her hand. In love with that psychopath Cain? What a laugh! Her mouth twisted into a leer, transforming her angelic features into an expression of consummate evil. Her own red-blooded countrymen would have no problem deciding on *crime passionnel*. Not like these British jurors, with their coldness and lack of passion. And then *freedom*. No more slopping out, no more pig-swill for food and no more humiliation. Just a fortune awaiting her in a Swiss bank account.

And there were no regrets. Except that the reporter bitch had not after all perished in the fire. It would have been pleasant to lie here now, imagining the bitch's knuckles bloody from hammering at the door, and her screams as the smoke and flames reached the cellar. Ideally her body should have burned to a cinder along with Cain's. But *no problem*, as DuPont was fond of saying: C.A.D.E. was prepared to pay well to keep her mouth shut. A hit would be arranged. A double pleasure. Because that double-crossing Kennedy would also suffer. She could see him now at the graveside. He would look well in black.

"*Lights out!*"

The call echoed along the corridor. As it did every night.

Viciously, Andrea Lascelles reached for the ashtray and stubbed out her cigarette.

*

The pain brought her to instant awareness. A red hot agony in her stomach that spread to her abdomen. Her hands clutched helplessly at her body as it convulsed. The heat was unbearable. She was burning up, as though a flame had ignited inside her. This was how it must be to be

279

struck by lightning. An acrid smell stung her nostrils. She stared, not understanding, as a wisp of smoke rose from the coarse cloth over her belly. Her brain gave signals, urged her to leap from the bed. But her limbs refused to react. It was as though something, someone, controlled her mind.

The cell reeked of charred flesh. *Move! Move!* No time. Her body was twitching and beyond her control. *Mon Dieu*, what agony! She watched, her eyes starting from her head as the material flared then curled and blackened.

Like the skin over her belly. She watched mesmerised as it browned and crisped like barbecued meat. Her mouth gaped to scream but no sound came.

The particles? Had she somehow infected herself with the particles?

Her last thought before her body imploded.

Five

~

Westwalls

The following noon they heard it on the radio. Darcy had been making coffee and almost dropped the kettle as shock waves ran through her body. She turned up the volume.

"*... when the wardress entered the cell early this morning. And now a special report: Kate Saunders speaks to us live from Holloway prison:*"

"*Andrea Lascelles,*" the fresh voice intoned with suppressed drama, "*was awaiting extradition to France where she would have stood trial for attempted murder. In fact she should have left Holloway today. When the wardress came to supervise Lascelles for the move, she found only the charred remains of the Frenchwoman's body. The grisly finds included a burnt and shrivelled liver, a spleen and a fragment of backbone. Baffled forensic police and scientists say it is too soon to make an official state-ment, but that the fire was confined to the woman's body. Books and papers on an adjacent table were intact, and showed no signs of being burnt or scorched. It appears that the woman was smoking last night in her cell, but this, even if it were the cause of the fire, does not explain the localised nature of the burning, nor the intense temperatures involved.*

"*Dr. James Clarke, head of the Department for Forensic Science at London University claims the case bears a strong resemblance to that of Mrs. Mary Reeser – who was found in similar circumstances in her apartment in St. Petersburg, Florida on 1 July, 1951. Nothing but frag-ments of her burned body were found, and her skull had shrunk to the size of a clenched fist. It appears the same was true of Lascelles, pointing to an intense heat in excess of 2,500 degrees. Dr. Clarke concluded that incredible though it may seem, the evidence suggests that they cannot completely rule out the bizarre phenomenon of spontaneous human com-bustion.*"

"Alisdair?" Darcy looked at him with eyes that were wide with horror.

"Just a nudge, a hint," he said with an enigmatic little smile. "We are allowed that much."

"But you have to do only *good*; otherwise, what hope have we got?"

"Brant won't get himself banged up for life now will he?" he asked, his eyes huge with innocence.

She switched off the radio. The letter from the head teacher leapt into mind; the accusation that Alisdair was somehow causing the bullies to have nightmares. And his own words: *I hurt them with my mind.* "Oh, Alisdair, Alisdair." She sank down on the nearest chair. "What have you done?"

"Nothing." He picked up the kettle and placed it on the hotplate, then turned to face her again. His expression was stern but untroubled. "She was consumed by her own evil."

Looking at him, Darcy felt life could never be the same again.

Six

~

Darcy shielded her eyes from the brilliance. The garden slumbered beneath a white blanket, yet the sun shone from a cloudless blue sky. "It's wonderful – magic," she enthused, her breath rising in clouds as she talked. The air crackled with cold and the water beneath the bridge was frozen. Yet there was a subtle difference: the garden was no longer dying but a coiled spring, waiting to burst into life. She reached up and touched a spray of blackthorn blossom, then quickly lowered her arm. Her shoulder was now healed, but the spot where the bullet had lodged and from where it was later extracted, ached in the intense cold.

Elsewhere hazel catkins were just appearing; here at Westwalls sticky brown buds were ready to burst on every tree and shrub, and embryo flower spikes had already formed on the lilac. And the birds were back. Blue tits, coal tits and yellow waist-coated great tits, previously absent, now swung on nets of peanuts strung from hook and branch, and the robin hopped around their feet hoping for a titbit.

"You love this place, don't you?" Brant said, watching the robin take a biscuit crumb from her outstretched hand.

"I suppose I do."

"More than the farmhouse?"

She thought back to the house on the cliffs at St. Gildas; an ideal spot but somehow never her own. She was walking slightly ahead and turned to answer.

"Don't bother, I can see it in your face."

"I'm sorry."

"It needn't be a problem."

He dug his hands deep in his jacket pockets. "Alisdair can't stay here for ever."

"I know." She turned for a moment to watch Alisdair in the distance:

he was clearing a path through the snow from the house to the lodge. The scraping of spade on stone rang through the cold metallic air. As though sensing her scrutiny, he looked up and waved. "He'll have to go away to school," she added, waving back.

"College – or even University," Brant corrected. "He's beyond school already."

Darcy kicked up the snow with the toe of her wellington boot. "I accept there has to be changes. But he can use the lodge during vacs and things. It does belong to him, remember. And I would want to be here for him."

Brant reached out and put a hand on her arm, forcing her to stop. He turned her round to face him. "And what other changes do you accept?"

"Not now." She looked away, embarrassed.

"I've been patient. Time's up."

She shrugged as though it was of no consequence, but in actual fact was saving face; she knew from his expression that it was useless to argue. "I suppose I'll have to make some sort of decision about my career, once Alisdair is away during term-time."

He caught hold of her chin, forcing her to look into his face. "And what about your marriage? Isn't it time that came under review?"

Her eyes were troubled. "What are the options?"

"There are none."

She had to smile. "That's unfair."

"In Love and War, remember …?"

"Which is it?"

"Both."

She fought a strong desire to be held close.

"You made love to me then walked out," she accused.

"I had to. Don't you understand Darcy? I was terrified you would hurt me again." He looked down, kicked the snow into a wedge at his feet, then flattened it with the sole of his boot. "But I was wrong, and I'm sorry."

"I'm sorry I hurt you too."

"Yes, well, least said I think, on that score," he said brusquely. "Being crazed with jealousy isn't very edifying."

The heat of the sun was melting the snow on the branches, and from all around came a soft *plop, plop, plopping* sound as snow thudded to earth. When he pulled her close, and his cold lips pressed against hers, she felt a resurgence of the old passion.

"Shall I stay?" he said, his lips against her hair.

She nodded and leaned against him.

*

They walked hand in hand through the frozen water garden to the woodland. Beneath a thin skin of ice the lifeblood of the garden raced like a millstream. It was, Darcy thought looking at it all, as though the garden were being cleansed, purged by a white fire of all the impurities of the past year. *Fire.* She thought of Alisdair and a chill wind swept over her happiness. He had acted quite normal since. As normal as could be expected, given his highly developed intelligence and senses. Could life ever be ordinary again? she worried.

She looked to the man at her side for reassurance. "Is it really all over, Brant?"

For answer he put an arm around her shoulders and pointed. They had just reached the edge of the glade. At the foot of the Mother-Statue, clusters of primroses, croci and daffodils opened petals of gold to the sun.

"Daffodils in January!" Darcy exclaimed in delight.

He nodded. "A New Year, A New Beginning, and New Hope. Come on, let's go and tell Alisdair our news."

Darcy smiled to herself as they walked back through the wood to the house. The meteorite was back at Westwalls so all should be right with the world.

EPILOGUE

~

The Sahara

The sun beat down mercilessly on the burnished sand hills. A heat haze shimmered as far as the horizon, distorting the earth's undulations and giving the impression of wave-like movement. The sand in the sliver of shade beneath a rock stirred slightly. Then again: a tremor like a minuscule earthquake. A dip appeared, an indentation as at the centre of a whirlpool. The surface broke, and the tip of a small green shoot poked through.

It rose, straight as a bush-man's spear, exploring its new environment, thrusting for light and air. The top swelled and formed a fat bulbous bud. The sepals of the calyx unfolded one by one, peeling back like the skin of a ripe banana. The petals unfurled next, banners of crimson expanding at incredible speed, like a multi-exposure nature film. In no time at all it was displaying its orchid-like finery. A leaf dipped, then another, then another. A raindrop settled at the centre of the bloom; a diamond in the desert.

The seed had yielded a deadly harvest.

Night fell; the petals folded. Stars and planets crystalised the midnight sky, and of them all, Mercury blazed the brightest. The desert waited, hushed and tense. Then the silence trembled, like the thread of a giant spider web stirred by the breeze. It came stealing over the sand dunes: a sound like the tinkling of wind chimes. The folded flower head, now many times its original size, inclined slightly as though it listened.

Listened that is, to the Music of the Spheres.